WOLF MATE

THE FORBIDDEN MATE TRILOGY
BOOK 1

JEN L. GREY

Copyright © 2024 by Grey Valor Publishing, LLC

All rights reserved.

No part of this book may be reproduced in any form or by any electronic or mechanical means, including information storage and retrieval systems, without written permission from the author, except for the use of brief quotations in a book review.

CHAPTER ONE

My blood jolted in my veins.

Hands tightening on the steering wheel, I drove under the black iron sign with the words *Evergreen Elite University* molded into the center. Even on this cloudy day, the words, thick with large gaping holes between each letter, were easy to see. Add in the two gigantic brick pillars on either side of the road that held up the sign in all its glory, and it was an old-world version of a neon light. Already, this school screamed prestige and wealth, and I couldn't believe I was here.

I hadn't even applied.

The thought had never crossed my mind.

My blood gave an extra jolt, informing me that coming here had been a bad idea—as if I didn't know.

Only the top five percent of applicants were admitted to this exclusive Portland, Oregon university, and one semester here cost more than what my parents made in a year combined.

I couldn't even dream of affording it, despite having

sity was so prestigious that even most class valedictorians didn't believe they had a chance of getting in. Believe me. I knew. I was one of them.

This place was known for producing some of the greatest minds in America, along with shaping the future of students from the country's wealthiest and most influential families. Some people dared to say it was even more elite than the Ivy Leagues out East.

Mysteriously, *I* had received a full scholarship, including room and board. The advisor assigned to me still hadn't given me a clear answer as to why. All he'd said was that an anonymous donor had sponsored me and believed I had the makings of greatness, which this place supported and celebrated.

Anyone saying something that nice about me was a first, and my parents had practically pushed me out the door to attend. Mom couldn't believe I'd seriously considered not coming here, and Dad had piped in, proclaiming it as an opportunity of a lifetime.

Maybe it was, but I suspected my parents were also eager to get me out of the house. I tended to hole up in my room whenever I wasn't out hiking, and they worried about my lack of social life.

As I coasted onto campus, my heart sank. Two parts of me were at war, one part telling me to turn around and drive the two hours back home and the other part bursting with butterflies of excitement because this was a fresh start.

I had to calm down. How was I supposed to meet my roommate like this? We'd texted one another after getting our room assignments, and Lucy seemed like a fun person. I'd let her know when I planned on arriving, and she'd said she'd be there to meet me. But whenever I got anxious, weird shit happened, and "weird" wasn't the first impression I wanted to make.

No one I knew went to school here, so there would be no preconceived notions about me. I had a chance to make my first real friend and, maybe—just maybe—fit in.

The latter was the scariest hope of all because I doubted it would happen. My emotions were running rampant. The last thing I needed was to put pressure on myself, hoping to find a place that might feel like an actual home.

With my track record, that wouldn't happen.

I was setting myself up for an inevitable disappointment.

A huge brick stadium that housed the college's renowned football team towered to my right, and the student center loomed straight ahead. The pictures I'd seen online didn't do justice to my view of the towering cherry trees framing the lawn in front of the student center where myriad students gathered and lounged lazily on this Sunday afternoon.

The administrator had told me to take a left here for the quickest route to the apartment I'd been assigned, and I followed his instructions, driving past soccer fields and tennis courts.

Hope expanded in my chest even as cold tendrils of fear knotted in my stomach. The two opposing emotions contrasted with each other like repelling magnets. My breathing quickened, and my blood jolted higher, informing me everything was about to crash and burn.

Whenever my blood jolted and worked up to a hum, strange incidents occurred around me—things that didn't make sense and proved that something was seriously wrong with me: Dishes rattled on the table, lights flickered, and a sense of how people were feeling sometimes swamped me. The jolt was the first sign of an episode, making me feel as if I'd gotten a dose of some drug and could go full-on humming at any time.

I took deep breaths to calm myself. Soon, I passed the

administration building, and the parking lot the advisor had instructed me to use appeared on the left. I was *here*. As in, going inside and unpacking my stuff in my room imminently.

As I pulled into the lot, my breathing technique was *not* working, especially as my janky old Honda Civic passed by Lexuses, Mercedes, BMWs, and a Rolls-Royce.

My vehicle screamed *outcast*, and I hated to see what would happen when I did something so strange it defied the laws of physics.

By the time I pulled into the last spot in the back corner farthest from the apartment buildings, my blood had an extra fizzle to it. The fizzle came between the jolt and the hum.

If I didn't squelch this now, there would be no reining in the weirdness.

My eyes homed in on the woods behind the apartment buildings.

Woods.

Comfort.

Freedom to be myself.

A place I could escape to get my anxiety under control.

I got out and slammed the car door shut, locking it with the fob. It was the only bougie thing my car could do.

Five students were loitering between the two five-story brick buildings, talking to each other like they didn't have a care in the world. The two women had an air of confidence, and three men towered over them, their muscular bodies emphasized by their tight shirts. Even as I told myself not to look, my eyes betrayed me, locking on the tallest one with dark hair and a chiseled jaw, who seemed to tug at my very essence. The fizzing in my blood kicked up higher, teetering near a hum.

When his head turned my way, I forced my attention to the woods, not wanting to be caught staring at them. I needed to get out there and be alone so I could get myself under control.

Refusing to look at anything but the Douglas firs along the perimeter, I put one foot in front of the other. If I could get into the woods and immerse myself in nature, it should ground me.

It usually did.

Accepting the random scholarship hadn't been smart. I should've done the online college program at another university this fall. That had been the plan since I'd graduated with an Associate of Science from Columbia Gorge Community College last spring, but an online school would make it harder for me to get into vet school. Not like graduating from *here*. That was the only reason I hadn't fought Mom more.

Moments before I reached the tree line, my blood hummed. The needles on the fir I'd been focused on started to shake.

Shit. My heart squeezed uncomfortably, and I almost wished it would stop beating. I didn't understand why things like this kept happening to me.

The sounds of a sapsucker drilling into a tree filled my ears. No one was anywhere near me. Between the comforting sound of the bird and the lack of witnesses to my meltdown, I slipped into the woods, ready to surround myself with nature and calm down.

A few steps into the trees, I was sure no one could see me from the EEU campus. I rubbed my chest to relieve the tension. I hated how my emotions took over at times. It was as if something inside me amped them up, and the anxiety-controlling coping mechanisms countless counselors had taught me didn't do shit to help, though I still tried them.

I walked a mile into the woods, not slowing until I'd taken the edge off the hysteria. When I spotted a sizable fallen tree trunk, I sat on the wood, ignoring the faint dampness from the rain the night before that was soaking into my jeans.

A cool breeze contrasted with the warmth of the air, and I leaned my head back and looked skyward, hoping I'd see a bird fly overhead.

As I breathed in the forest pine scent, the wolf I'd helped right before I graduated from community college flitted into my mind. He'd been caught in a hunter's trap, a hunting practice that was illegal in that part of the mountains. When I'd stumbled upon him, he'd growled, but those bright-yellow eyes had seemed so intelligent ... so real. I'd told him I was there to help him, and it was as if he'd understood me. It was the type of moment that made me want to be a vet.

A sense of calm embraced me. My lungs filled with fresh air, and the sounds of animals scurrying in the woods brought me serenity.

Home. The word echoed in my head, and a vision of the tall guy popped into my brain. My stomach bubbled, not out of discomfort but from excitement and expectation.

This had to stop. I had to clear my head.

The fizzle subsided to a jolt as I allowed the tranquility of the moment to wash over me. I dug my shoes into the mulch, slowing the momentum of the thoughts that kept invading my mind.

I was sitting there in silence, lost in the moment, when curiosity brushed against my mind. A branch snapped, and I wasn't surprised to find a deer twenty feet away. Its head tilted as it took me in and slowly inched forward.

This was why I visited the woods: to be one with nature and see its miraculous creatures alone and up close. The deer continued toward me, curiosity brimming in its dark eyes. I held out both hands, wanting her to see I meant her no harm.

A chill ran down my spine, and the hair on the nape of my neck rose.

I tensed as an all-too-familiar sensation washed over me, and the deer paused. She averted her eyes to my right, confirming my fear.

Someone was watching us.

Huffing, the deer spun and ran in the opposite direction, and the lump in my throat tripled in size.

I tried to swallow and failed.

Perhaps someone was merely hiking in the woods, but my skin was crawling. I'd seen the evil mankind could do when they encountered something they didn't understand—like a deer walking straight up to me without concern. Not that the deer had gotten that close, but it had been approaching.

I wouldn't stay here to see if the person meant me harm. After all, I needed to move my stuff into my apartment and didn't want to worry Lucy by how late I was.

I stretched as if I didn't have a care in the world. Showing my fear was the worst thing I could do; if this was a bullying tactic, it would make whoever was spying on me feel more powerful. I pretended to yawn, hoping it would help my act, though my blood was already fizzing again.

I stood slowly, attempting to come off like nothing was wrong, but every cell in my body wanted to run. The last time this had happened was in high school. A group of students had cornered me in the back of the school and shoved me around. Worse, the ringleader had been Lizzy, a girl who'd been my best friend in preschool.

Acid inched up my throat as I started to hike back toward the campus. I had an inkling where the person was, thanks to my deer friend, so I made sure to move to the left of that area.

The woods were supposed to be my salvation, not a place

where I didn't feel safe. This was the one place I could go to find a little sanity and feel as if I belonged.

Gritting my teeth, I listened hard for sounds that the person was following me or trying to cut me off. All I could hear was my rapid heartbeat.

Adrenaline shot through me, and the jolt turned into the fizzing sensation *again*. Something like sinister curiosity rolled over me, and sweat pooled under my arms. Something was *definitely* out here with me.

The trees thinned, and I was almost free.

My skin tingled as my blood hummed within me. I glanced over my shoulder, searching for the cause. Any pretense of calmness was gone, and I sensed that someone was nearly on top of me. I began to jog, often glancing over my shoulder for anyone behind me. Then I crashed into something that felt a damn lot like a brick wall.

CHAPTER TWO

My body bounced off the wall, and my feet slipped from underneath me. I winced and was preparing for the inevitable crash landing when strong hands gripped my shoulders.

Heart dropping into my stomach, I forced my eyes to look straight ahead and found myself staring at a chest.

The gray polo shirt was molded to muscle, and I shook my head to clear it. It didn't help. I couldn't get over the way the muscles curved and tensed, and something inside me *yanked*.

Between the hard chest and the run-in, my blood calmed to a jolt.

I knew people could be strong, but I hadn't realized running into someone this fit would feel like hitting a wall. Like, what the hell? I ran my fingertips over the muscles, reveling in the heat and smoothness, then froze. Two snickers sounded from Muscular Chest's side.

Oh my God.

My face burned, and I dropped my hand like I'd touched something hot.

In fairness, I had. This chest alone had jumbled my thoughts. I needed space and air.

Fast.

I took a step back and stumbled all over again, but the hands were still on my shoulders, keeping me upright.

"Uh ... thanks." I jerked my head up, hoping to pull myself together, but when I locked eyes with the brick wall and his scent invaded my senses, my thoughts vanished entirely, and my mouth dropped open.

He was more than handsome but gorgeous didn't sound manly enough—because this guy was *all man*. He had at least six inches on me, and his black hair hung into his crystal-blue eyes, emphasizing their color. I wanted to get lost in them, and his amber-sandalwood scent made me want to rub myself all over him.

Which would make this situation even more embarrassing; otherwise, I wouldn't have restrained myself.

His eyes warmed as he looked me over, but then he sniffed. His jaw clenched, and his full lips mashed together in a grimace. "Do you think you can stand without falling now?"

I was used to getting that look from almost everyone I met, but it cut deeper coming from *him*. Seeing the warmth vanish from his eyes hurt, which was preposterous. I didn't even *know* him.

"Man, I think you broke her." The guy on my right chuckled. "I swear she's got drool puddling in the corner of her mouth."

That snapped me out of my stupor. I looked at his friend, who was *almost* as hot as Sexy Chest. His friend's milk-chocolate-brown eyes danced with mirth as he ran a hand over brown scruff that was a shade darker than his short hair. His dark skin crinkled around his eyes—further proof that he was trying to hide a smile.

"Leave her alone, Keith." The man with lighter-brown skin on the other side of Sexy Chest scoffed. "She's scared." He stepped toward me, his shaggy, curly hair ruffling in the breeze. "She was running." His honey-brown eyes seemed warmer than the others, but his body was stiff, giving off clear stay-back vibes. He lifted his head to scan the area behind me. "It looked like something was chasing her."

These three were the sexiest guys I'd ever seen, and I'd proven that neither my mouth nor my balance was stable, but I despised being talked about as if I weren't standing right here. I had to say *something*. "I saw a deer."

Keith laughed, not hiding his amusement anymore. "And you thought it was chasing you?"

"What? No!" Deer weren't aggressive toward humans. Even nonanimal people knew that, so I was still speaking nonsense. "I meant, I ..." How did I salvage this? At least I wasn't exposing myself as a freak ... *sorta*. "I wanted to take a picture, but I forgot my phone."

As if there were a higher being that hated me, my phone dinged in my pocket.

"I believe we all found it." Sexy Chest's deep, husky voice rumbled.

My damn traitorous eyes glanced back at him, and my breath caught at the suspicion etched into every line of his face. He dropped his hands from my shoulders, and I noticed a detailed wolf tattoo peeking from under the sleeve of his shirt. The olive tone of his skin gave it more definition, making it appear almost lifelike.

I looked over my shoulder, wondering if I could catch a glimpse of whatever had been following me.

The nicer guy followed my gaze. "Judging by your expression, I'm assuming you aren't searching for a deer."

"Adam, come on." Keith snorted. "She can't walk, she was

gawking at Raffe, and she can barely put together a coherent sentence. She probably bumped into a tree and thought it was someone grabbing her."

And here was when the teasing began. My blood jolted, and my mouth went dry. I needed to get away from them before I had an epic meltdown ... again. "It felt like I was being watched." I shrugged, staring at the mulchy ground. "I'm sure it was nothing ... just me being paranoid."

"Why don't you go to your room, and the three of us can check out the area?" Raffe said, a little bit of the warmth springing back into his eyes.

Part of me snapped to attention, ready to follow his suggestion, which irritated me. Why in the world would I want to obey someone I'd just met? But there was something about *him* that I couldn't explain.

I lifted my chin. "I appreciate the sentiment, but I'm sure it was nothing. And if something was chasing me, I'd hate for you to go out there and have something happen. I couldn't live with you all getting hurt because of me."

Raffe scowled, and his eyes narrowed as he stepped back into my space. For a moment, I swore his blue eyes glowed, but Adam punched him in the shoulder.

"We'll be fine, pigeon." Keith shoved his hands into his khaki pants pockets and smirked. "Besides, Raffe eats birds in his sleep."

Pigeon. Sigh. It was the equivalent of being called chicken, though most people didn't realize that. Unfortunately, Keith might be smarter than he seemed.

I hated what these people stood for. They were the type who bullied and berated people for being different. Hell, Keith was already doing that with me even when it was clear I'd been scared.

I could either stand here and let them ridicule me or get

my shit together and meet my roommate like I should have done already. The latter would let me hold on to a smidge of dignity. At least they were willing to search the woods in case something *was* off. That had to count for something.

I settled on saying, "Don't hurt the deer if you see her."

"Her?" Keith arched his brow. "Did you name her too? Let me guess, Bambi? Thumper? Flower?"

Raffe cut his eyes to his friend, and after a few seconds, Keith huffed and lowered his head slightly.

Here I'd thought weird things only happened around me. Something strange was going on between them.

Well, the last thing I needed was to learn more about it. I had enough freak inside me to last a lifetime without adding glowing eyes and people talking through expressions without looking at each other.

"No, but if you meet up with her, ask her what it is and let me know." The words had popped out before I processed my response. I couldn't stand smart-asses. "Unlike people here, I don't limit names to Disney movies."

"Hey." Keith sneered. "I can come up with more—"

Pinching the bridge of his nose, Raffe took a giant step back and cut off Keith. He stared at me and frowned. "Please, head somewhere safe. If someone is out here, we want to catch them. And I don't want to leave you alone when you were clearly scared."

Even though he'd dismissed me, he'd done it kindly, and I didn't want to make a further fool of myself.

My phone dinged again, no doubt my parents wondering why I hadn't checked in. Without another word, I marched past the three of them and went toward my car.

I waited for the snickers and snide comments to begin, but nothing happened. The three of them remained silent as if they'd disappeared.

I glanced behind me.

Only Raffe was there. The other two had vanished.

Our eyes locked, and my heart started to race. Something strange surged between us. He sighed, shoulders slumping, and his face twisted as if he were warring with whether to say something. Then he said tenderly, "Be careful, okay? Things aren't as safe as they seem around here, and I don't want anything to happen to you."

Butterflies took flight in my stomach as our gazes remained locked. We both took a step closer to one another, something drawing us together.

Then his eyes glowed again, and he huffed. "I need to check on them, but I can't until you're away from the woods."

Great. I was lingering, his effect on me obvious. How stupid. It wasn't like something would ever happen between us.

Snapping my head forward once more, I hurried to my car, determined to forget Raffe and the eerie sensation of the woods.

"Everything is fine," I told my parents for the hundredth time, trying to keep the annoyance out of my voice. My poor lilac comforter was taking the brunt of my frustration. I yanked on the edges, smoothing out the wrinkles as I finished setting up my room. I moved away from my new queen-size bed and took in the room, which was far nicer than I'd expected.

I heard some shuffling on their end, likely a hand covering the speaker while they whispered to one another. They always thought I didn't know what they were doing, but it wasn't hard to figure out, especially since it happened every time they were worried about me.

Waiting for them to say whatever else was on their minds, I snatched the string of butterflies I'd cut out of craft paper to hang up and add some purple to my room. All shades of purple were my favorite colors. I hadn't expected the room to have a small chandelier, but it was perfect for what I had in mind. I removed my lilac sneakers and climbed onto the bed then threaded the butterflies through the curved arms of the light fixture so that the butterflies hung down like a cascading chandelier of their own.

"We know you try, honey, but ... try not to do those ... things." Mom sighed then laughed as if to lighten the mood.

Sometimes, I believed they regretted adopting me, and honestly, I couldn't blame them. I was weird, I freaked out teachers, and I'd been expelled from a few schools because parents refused to let their kids attend class with someone who petrified them. I did believe they cared about me, but I didn't fit in with them. Hell, my own biological parents had given me up, and I'd never once wondered why. I *was* a freak. "I'm going to try really hard, Mom. I don't like it when those *things* happen either."

"Of course, none of that matters to us. We love you," Dad interjected. "But if you want to make friends—"

It was the same speech they'd given me millions of times over my twenty-one years. You'd think they'd have realized it didn't help. "I know. I know. I love you too."

The door to the apartment opened, and I stiffened. "Hey, my roommate just got back. I need to go."

"Oh. Okay," Mom said excitedly. "Just remember—"

"Noted, Mom." I didn't let her finish. She'd already said it five times in the past five minutes. "I'll call or text you two later. Love you. Bye." I hung up and jumped down from my bed onto the fake wood floor.

"Skylar?" a warm female voice called out, and my blood went straight to fizzing.

Ugh. My hands grew clammy as footsteps walked down the small hallway between our rooms, and a girl stuck her head in my open doorway.

I swallowed and immediately felt inadequate. Her long caramel-brown hair hung over her shoulders, highlighting her light olive skin and delicate features.

"Hey, I'm Lucy. Sorry I wasn't here when you arrived." She stepped through the doorway, her hauntingly luminous gray eyes scanning my room and stopping on me. She sniffed, and her brows furrowed. "Something came up, and I had to leave."

"No worries," I squeaked then cleared my throat. With her looks, she fit right in with Keith, Raffe, and Adam, which meant the two of us probably wouldn't get along. "I'm Skylar. I got delayed too, and I don't blame you for not waiting." I rubbed my hands along my jeans, discreetly wiping the sweat from my palms.

"I figured something came up," she said as her gaze landed on the painting I'd hung on the cream wall over the bed. "Nice artwork."

"Thanks." It was a picture of a purple sky on a cloudy day with messy purple, pink, and white flowers that appeared to be wet with rain. It brought me calm when I needed it, and I'd pulled it out first thing after I'd moved everything into the room.

An awkward silence descended, and the fizz damn near increased to a hum. Fear clawed into my chest, and I felt naked. I shouldn't have come here. I couldn't even escape to my room because I had to share this small apartment with her, including the one bathroom.

Lucy glanced at her watch. "The bookstore closes in an hour. They stayed open for students who arrived last minute. You could still go if you need to."

In other words, she wasn't willing to take me there. That wasn't surprising. "Yeah, I should do that." I needed my books for tomorrow, and that was an amazing excuse to get away from here and explore the campus. "Thanks for the information."

"Sure." She ran a hand down her gray EEU shirt, which showed the outline of a black wolf and a silver full moon. "Anytime." She tucked a piece of hair behind her ear and yawned. "I gotta get some things ready for class tomorrow, or I'd offer to go with you."

"No worries." I sensed she was lying, but I wouldn't call her out on it. At least she was being nice.

"Yeah. Okay. Text me if you get lost or need anything." She lifted her phone then spun and left just as quickly as she'd arrived.

That had gone well. And what was it with all these people sniffing me?

When Lucy's bedroom door closed, I hurried past the sterile gray dresser and headed through the den and kitchen out the door. The hallway was surprisingly empty. In all the shows I watched, students were always hanging outside their rooms in the hallways. Maybe that happened in the residence dorms and not here.

Lucy and I lived in an end unit. Apartment doors lined the light-gray hallway walls, and my sneakers padded over the dark-gray carpet to the elevator.

On the ground floor, I marched through the double glass doors and headed across the road toward the student center.

The damp wind filled my lungs, making things feel not quite so bad as I walked between two massive brick buildings that were damn near identical, except the one to my left was taller.

Some guys were playing frisbee in the open area between the buildings and the student center. I watched as they laughed and joked with several girls who lay on blankets, all of them comfortable in their own skin and with friends ... two things I'd never experienced.

A pang of jealousy surged through me, and I inhaled, keeping my gaze focused straight ahead on the student center. I needed to hurry before the bookstore closed.

I marched on, but the laughter and shrieks of fun behind me had tears burning in my eyes. I'd been foolish to come here. I wanted to go home, but if I did, my parents would never let me live it down.

Worse, I'd disappoint them again.

Something I'd done far too many times.

When I reached the back of the student center, I blinked to clear my eyes. I found a back door and stepped inside.

The bookstore was to my right, and luckily, the lights were still on. Near the front, by four open glass doors, an employee stood at the cash register. I scanned the area and saw that each section was marked with subjects. On the left, by the history section, was one person I never wanted to see again.

Raffe.

That strange *tug* urged me to close the distance between us, but I wasn't an idiot. Someone like him would never want to be with a person like me.

He was handsome, strong, and confident.

I was *not*.

Forcing myself to ignore him, I went to the section labeled

Science. A sizzle ran down my spine, and I somehow knew Raffe had seen me. But that was crazy. It wasn't possible.

Shaking my head, I focused on locating my microbiology and chemistry books. This educational opportunity was important to me, and I needed to excel in those two classes to get into veterinary school.

My microbiology textbook was shelved at the bottom, and I dug around for a decent used copy.

Something rattled over my head, and metal groaned. When I glanced up, I couldn't believe what I saw.

CHAPTER THREE

My lungs seized, and I stared in horror as three textbooks tumbled off the bookcase toward me.

I'd pushed myself back to get out of the way when strong arms wrapped around my waist, yanking me against a human brick wall I already knew so well.

The tugging in my chest stirred again, confirming my suspicion, as three ginormous chemistry books landed, kicking up a bit of dust where I'd been squatting mere seconds ago.

Silence surrounded us as I froze in Raffe's arms.

When his chest expanded, the moment was over.

"I swear, you have a fucking death wish," he gritted out and dropped his arms from my waist, taking a huge step back. "Are you okay?"

My blood was pumping, but it wasn't only from the jolt running through me from whatever strange phenomena I lived with. Pure, unadulterated fear had mixed with attraction to make my pulse race, which *never* happened.

I spun around, coming way too close to slipping on one of the fallen textbooks. I caught myself and hoped like hell he hadn't noticed my clumsiness. "Yeah, but I don't understand what happened! The bookcase wasn't shaking. Then suddenly, I heard a noise. It was as if something other than me pushed the books." As soon as the words left my mouth, I regretted saying them. That was definitely weirdo level.

I blamed his rugged good looks and sculpted body.

The corner of his mouth tipped upward, and he shook his head. "You say that after almost tripping and falling over books that barely missed your head. You're a magnet for trouble, and that's a huge problem for me."

Of course he'd noticed. I was beginning to think he noticed everything about me, and the thought had my body thrumming with feelings I didn't understand. Feelings that risked me doing something incredibly stupid. I studied the top of the bookcase. "Did you see what made the books fall?" The shelf hadn't moved, and while I'd been scanning the course names for the books I needed, I hadn't seen any books near the edge. "It sounded like something scooted above me, but the entire shelf was sturdy where I was."

"Are you sure?" He stepped beside me, our arms brushing. "Because it'd be strange that something like that would happen to you."

Ugh, I sounded paranoid, but he was right. It wasn't like books could move on their own. I hadn't felt my blood humming, so maybe I was remembering wrong? "You're right." I exhaled noisily. The one time I hadn't caused the weirdness, I still sounded like I was imagining things. Maybe I would never fit in. "Sorry. I don't know what happened. I must have knocked into the bookcase while digging for a biochemistry book."

I kept my attention forward, not wanting to see the inevitable look of disgust on his face. He'd witnessed two of my "special" incidents in the span of mere hours. A new record for me.

"Hey, everything will be okay. It's been a long day, and I won't let anything happen to you," he said softly and turned to me.

Unable to stop myself, I mirrored his motion, the two of us a couple of feet apart. His focus flicked to my lips as he continued, "Maybe you should go back to your room like I suggested earlier."

My head jerked back. "Did you three find anything?"

His face creased. "No, unfortunately. But don't worry. We've alerted the school board that students aren't feeling safe in the woods."

He seemed like he genuinely cared. "Thanks for everything," I forced out, physically restraining myself from moving closer to him.

A worker strolled from the far side of the store through the door that led to the counter.

He rang a bell that was probably meant to alert customer service. "Bookstore is closing in ten minutes."

Of course. The worker must have done something to cause the books to fall. I was being stupid and paranoid. This was what happened when weird shit always followed you around. You considered unexplainable things instead of thinking through the actual cause.

I bit my bottom lip, and Raffe's gaze moved there again. His eyes glowed faintly, and the intensity of his stare had me finding the thin gray carpet underneath me *very* interesting. "Thanks for saving me twice today." He hadn't hesitated when he'd thought I might be in danger. "I'll try not to cause any more scenes. I swear it's not intentional."

"Look, let me give you my number in case you get into another situation where you don't feel safe."

My head snapped up. Okay, I hadn't expected that. He stepped closer to me, leaving only a sliver of space between us.

"Or you can give me your number since you aren't taking out your phone." He pulled his phone from his back pocket and arched an eyebrow.

If I hadn't been in a complete trance, I would've laughed. He was so sure of himself. As if I wouldn't even consider not giving him my phone number. Worse, he was right. I rattled off my number, *pretty* confident he couldn't hear me since I was damn near breathless, but he typed it in with confidence.

Like he did everything.

My phone dinged.

"There. If you ever find yourself in trouble, call or text me. Don't hesitate." He tilted his head and winced. "Even if you think I'm a jerk, please know that your safety is important to me."

With everything he'd done for me today, I couldn't imagine why I'd think he was a jerk. "Okay." The *tug* was becoming too damn strong to resist, and I leaned forward, about to close the distance between us.

"Raffe!" A voice echoed down the hallway of the student center. Keith. "I thought you were going to be quick."

Raffe tensed and took four large steps away from me, moving into the political science section.

The abrupt change left me reeling.

He turned and snatched a book from the shelf just as Keith and Adam walked into the store. Their attention landed on me.

Keith snorted and elbowed Adam as they strolled to their friend.

"Looks like the lost pup from the woods is nipping at your

heels." Keith waggled his brows at me, still looking attractive despite his over-the-top antics.

I spun away, not wanting to engage with him. When Raffe didn't tell him to back off, my heart ached with disappointment.

Adam sighed. "All the new girls think they have a chance with you or any of us. She'll learn like the rest of them."

That stung, even though I knew it was true when Raffe remained silent. My blood jolted, and I snatched a microbiology book from the bottom shelf, not caring anymore if it wasn't used. The school had said they'd cover the cost of my books, and my effort to be frugal was going out the window, thanks to their snide remarks.

"This is my last book." Raffe yawned as if he was bored and wanted to be anywhere but here. "The rest of them are at the counter."

It was as if he'd taken on a different personality. Though he wasn't being cruel, he wasn't stopping his friends from making fun of me either. In my world, not speaking up for someone was just as bad, if not worse, than doing the actual bullying.

Wanting to gain distance, I moved down to the chemistry section and grabbed my advanced chemistry book and accompanying lab notebook.

"Hurry up, man," Keith said. "Josie is getting tired of holding the table and said your ass better hurry up or she won't be wearing your jersey at the game on Saturday."

Pain exploded in my heart, catching me off guard. My blood fizzed to damn near a hum. The thought of Raffe with someone else bothered me more than should have been possible. I didn't even know him, and developing a super unhealthy obsession with him wouldn't bode well for anyone, especially not *me*.

"She'll wear it." Raffe chuckled. "She always gives in to me."

Jealousy clutched my chest, and I eagerly moved across the bookstore, searching for my last two books—Statistics II and Economics I. Luckily, they were close together on the other side of the store where Raffe had been before the untimely fall.

The three guys laughed and headed to the register, and I loitered with my last two books. I would wait until they were gone before I made my way there. I didn't need any more comments thrown my way about following Raffe around.

When the three of them headed to the bookstore's exit into the student center, I marched to the cashier, ready to buy my books and hide in my room for the rest of the night. But when Raffe reached the door, he turned and nodded at me. "Remember, calm down, and go back to your residence hall."

He must have thought I was a freshman, but I didn't care to correct him. What bothered me was that he thought he could boss me around as if I were worthless.

Before I could retort, the three of them were gone.

"You ready to check out?" the guy at the counter asked. "It's closing time."

"Right. Sorry." I shook my head, putting all five textbooks on the counter. "I'm a little out of sorts."

"They're assholes." The guy rolled his hazel eyes as he scanned the books. "Don't take it personally. They treat everyone who isn't in their little clique like they're beneath them."

My brows lifted. For some reason, the fact they treated me like everyone else bothered me. "And everyone lets them get away with it?"

The guy shrugged and flipped his auburn bangs out of his

eyes. "What can you do when Raffe is the star quarterback, EEU's football team captain, and the son of a billionaire who owns a majority of all the commercial real estate in Oregon? Add in the fact that Mr. Wright donates five million dollars to this school annually, and they don't get into much trouble."

I snorted. That didn't surprise me. The way the three of them acted screamed of arrogance. The kind you got from having money. "And the other two?"

"Their dads are Mr. Wright's right-hand men." He pushed some buttons on the register. "They all grew up together, and from what I hear, they live in the same ritzy neighborhood in Seattle. Everyone in that group does. It's sort of strange if you ask me, but the girls here don't seem to care one bit. Any of them would love to be with one of those three."

No wonder the guys had made so many snide comments. They were used to girls doing things to get their attention. Part of me was disgusted that they would lump me in with other women, but it wasn't as if they knew me. Just because I felt something weird around Raffe didn't mean it was reciprocated. "Well, thanks for the info. I'll make sure to stay clear of them."

The guy grinned and leaned back against the counter. He chuckled. "Is that so? You won't try to lure one into your grasp? Raffe talked to you more than he does most other people outside their group."

My heart kick-started, and my blood jolted. *Down, girl.* "It wasn't out of the kindness of his heart. Besides, I'm here to concentrate on my studies." And make friends, but I left out that last part. It sounded a little too pathetic.

"That's smart."

That was the one thing I had going for me. Intelligence.

Not beauty or a good personality. But hand me a test, and I could ace it with minimal effort. Besides, with my blood heightened, I could read he had sincere intentions, so I added, "I have a scholarship, grant, or something that covers my books." Hell, I wasn't sure what to call what they'd given me since I hadn't applied or turned in my financials. All I'd had to do was send my transcripts over two weeks ago. "They said it'd be under my name, Skylar Greene."

"Oh. Okay." He tapped on the computer and nodded. "I found it, and you're covered." He put my books into an evergreen plastic bag with the school emblem and letters. "Here you go."

"Thanks." I took the bag. "And sorry if I held you up. I know you must want to get out of here."

"Don't worry about it." He winked. "I'm just meeting with my band to practice. No big deal. But I'm sure I'll see you around."

I smiled so wide my cheeks hurt. "Yeah. Maybe."

Instead of heading to the cafeteria to get dinner, I made my way back to the apartment. I'd had my first normal interaction with someone, and I wasn't about to risk something else happening in front of Raffe and his friends to ruin the progress I'd made.

Part of me wanted to go find Raffe, but I pushed the instinct aside. He was with *Josie*.

The thought nagged at me, so I focused on the small win I'd just had. Maybe coming here would wind up being okay after all.

THAT NIGHT, I didn't sleep well. I dreamed of Raffe with some woman with no face. I woke up in a foul mood and with red eyes, feeling as if I'd been run over by a truck.

I kicked off my comforter and walked to the closet at the foot of my bed then snatched up a thin lilac sweater and jeans and headed into the bathroom to take a quick shower, hoping I could soothe my swollen eyes.

The bathroom was between my room and Lucy's, and I wasn't sure when her first class was. I slipped inside, turned on the water in the marble-tiled shower, and placed my clothes on the sink while snatching a towel from under the counter so I could grab both easily when I was done.

Not wanting to be late for my first class, microbiology, I rushed to get clean then stepped out, the cool tile floor sending a chill down my spine. Within ten minutes, I had my hair dried, and I was dressed with makeup on. I checked my appearance for signs that some random guy I'd known for all of five minutes had kept me up all night.

Luckily, my amber eyes were back to their normal brightness and no longer swollen, and I'd gotten all the knots out of my long, dark-brown hair. My olive complexion was a hint lighter than usual, but at least I didn't look as pale as the cashier from last night.

I blew out a breath, opened the door ... and heard a whisper from Lucy's room.

"This isn't funny, Lafayette. Something needs to be done. This is unacceptable." Her tone held a tinge of anger.

Knowing I shouldn't listen, I froze because that was what normal people who wanted to fit in did: stayed and eavesdropped. *Dammit, Skylar. Move. Nothing good can come of you being curious, and if she finds out—*

"I can't be stuck with *her* as a roommate." She scoffed. "Do you think she'll be willing to go outside and run with me under the moon? Or understand when I need to disappear and take care of my own needs? This can't happen. You know the rules—you're on the housing board. She should've never been assigned to me in the first place."

My blood jolted and my chest constricted. I hadn't done a thing to Lucy, and she was making me sound like the judgmental one. I didn't care if she liked running under the moon or sleeping around. None of that mattered to me, but instead of talking to me, she was talking to the housing office, trying to get me moved.

Now I was thankful that I'd eavesdropped so I wouldn't be blindsided later today.

No longer worried about being quiet, I stomped to my room and grabbed my bag. It was eight-forty in the morning, and my first class began in twenty minutes. I didn't want to rush trying to find it.

I slung on my lilac backpack and was heading into the living room when Lucy's bedroom door opened.

"Skylar, wait," she said as she hurried after me. "Please, let me explain."

I stopped between the round wooden kitchen table and the TV stand and turned around as she stopped near the brown cloth couch across the room.

I swallowed the words I wanted to say and tried to act like the type of person people didn't mind hanging around. "No need." I forced a smile, but from her wince, I could tell I'd missed the mark for looking casual.

Okay, I needed to try harder, so I smiled even wider.

When her entire body cringed, I gave up. I didn't know how to people.

"Look, I heard you in the hall, and I'm assuming you heard my conversation. I just want to say—"

"Can we not?" I most definitely did not want to have this

conversation. My blood was already escalating from a jolt to a fizz. The one thing I could control at the moment was getting out of this room and away from Lucy.

I adjusted my bag, needing to expend the energy before the walls started shaking or the kitchen table rattled. "I don't know where my class is, and I need to find it."

Her expression crumpled. "Yeah, okay." She placed her hands behind her head, her white shirt inching up to reveal a small section of her stomach. "Just ... can we talk later?"

"Sure." I had no plan to follow through. I could sleep in my car and come in here only to shower until Lucy got the room situation worked out. The idea of living in a residence hall surrounded by lowerclassmen worried me due to the lack of privacy, but I'd do whatever I had to. I'd learned that forcing people to be around you accomplished only one thing —becoming the butt of every joke.

With that, I marched out of the apartment.

The charge through me was now fizzing to the point that a hum would happen at any second, so I walked faster than necessary to the elevator and counted the seconds until I was outside.

I didn't understand why Lucy had such a problem with me. We'd said only a few words to each other, and she hadn't been in the apartment when I returned from the bookstore last night. I'd gotten ready for bed and eaten some crackers then hung out in my room, hoping that the nice conversation I'd had with the pale clerk at the bookstore was a sign that things would start to go right.

Clearly, I'd been wrong.

Even as I walked into the partially sunny day, I couldn't keep the pressure from building. I needed to squelch my anxiousness, but between the encounters with Raffe yesterday and Lucy's actions this morning, I felt out of control.

Students were milling around outside, several in groups, heading in the same direction I was.

And, as always, I was alone.

That was when the hum happened.

Shit.

I was going to implode.

CHAPTER FOUR

I clutched my chest and stopped walking, staring at the ground in hopes of containing whatever was inside me. The intensity was worse than ever, and I wished I'd never come to this university. At home, I'd had a true haven where I could be alone for hours and not worry about someone living next door.

The hum vibrated under my skin, and the ground began trembling underneath me.

Holy shit. Was I causing an earthquake? Surely not.

"Hey, are you okay?" someone asked, startling me.

My emotions flared higher, and the ground moved under my feet, toppling me over.

"Whoa," the guy said, and a hand grasped my arm.

Instead of hitting the ground, I was tugged into the side of some random guy. That was enough to take my focus away from my internal turmoil. This guy wasn't nearly as muscular as Raffe, and when I looked at his face, my thoughts didn't scatter.

Bright-emerald eyes stared back at me from under spiky, dark-blond hair. The guy dropped his hand and bit his thin bottom lip. "Sorry, I didn't mean to manhandle you. It looked like you were going to fall."

Fall? He hadn't felt the ground shake or move? Thank fuck. My anxiety lessened, reducing the energy in my blood to a fizzle. "No, it's fine. I was dizzy. Thanks for helping me."

He was the second handsome guy to offer me assistance in less than twenty-four hours. What was it with all the men here resembling models? This guy had the whole Ken doll vibe going on but with a mysterious edge that made him damn alluring.

He continued to examine me, which made me feel as if I were under a microscope. My skin crawled, and my heart skipped a beat.

I needed to be on my way to class. Unsure what else to say, I took a step forward, but the guy stepped in front of me, blocking my path.

Something weird washed over me, like curiosity and determination—emotions that were definitely not mine, which meant they were his, and my blood was dangerously close to humming again. Though I never understood how, I could sometimes read other people's emotions. "I'm going to be late." I tried to pivot around him, but he blocked me again.

He went for my hand then paused. "I'm not trying to make you late, but I want to make sure you're okay. You looked upset before you stumbled."

I blew out a breath, and the tension in my shoulders eased. "My roommate isn't thrilled about rooming with me." I shrugged, playing it off like it was no big deal.

"Ah." He frowned. "Well, it hasn't been long. I'm sure she'll change her mind."

Mom had told me similar things over the years, but the more time a person spent around me, the less they wanted to do with me.

"Not likely. She was on the phone with the housing administrator." Why was I spilling my guts to him? I rubbed the spot in my chest that felt like a gaping void.

"That's her loss, then."

I snorted and tilted my head, expecting to see a condescending expression, but Nice Guy's face was lined with concern.

His eyebrows rose. "What? You don't agree?"

"No." Wait. I wasn't sure how to answer that. "Yes?"

"You're not sure?" He smiled, and a dimple appeared in his right cheek, adding to his good looks. "Well, I do. I can already tell you're good people." He tapped his head.

Could he be strange like me? My stomach fluttered. "Like a buzzing or something?"

He laughed. "Or something. But someone selfish or who didn't care wouldn't be upset about their roommate not liking them."

Oh. Right. That made more sense, but my body sagged. "Maybe I'm upset for purely selfish reasons. You don't know." People assuming things about others caused a lot of problems in this world. "Anyway, thanks for the assist, but I need to head to class."

This time, when I turned and marched away, Nice Guy didn't stop me. For some reason, a knot of disappointment twisted hard within me—which was ridiculous. I would've been annoyed if he'd delayed me again.

I took my phone from my jeans pocket and pulled up the campus map. Science classes were held in the Howling Building, across the road from the apartments.

I strode in that direction, noticing a ton of students loitering around. Back at my old school, the classes got fuller as the day went on, but this was a totally different sort of place.

When I opened the thick wooden back door to the building, someone behind me bumped into me. My sneakers squeaked on the shiny vinyl floor as I caught my balance. The person didn't bother apologizing as he hurried to the second set of doors ten feet in front of us.

Jerk.

I took the staircase on the right to the third floor. My classroom was the first one on the right.

I entered the room, relieved to find that it looked like a normal college classroom. I wasn't sure what I'd expected. Something similar to Hogwarts, old and fancy, like I'd seen on television? The lackluster tan walls and desk seats seemed typical and not intimidating.

There were open seats in the front and the middle of the classroom. The early risers had gotten their choice of the back-row seating, but that was fine with me. I picked a front-row seat to ensure I maintained focus. I needed to be engaged, take notes, and ace this class if I wanted a chance of getting accepted into vet school the first time I applied.

A few students nodded at me, but I kept my mouth shut, not wanting to scare them away with my pointless rambling.

As I slid into the seat, I heard a familiar chuckle and glanced up.

Nice Guy.

He grinned as he strolled toward me, and I blinked as he sat in the seat next to mine. I hadn't expected to see him again so soon.

"If this doesn't prove we're meant to get to know each other, I don't know what would."

I wasn't sure what to say, but one thing was certain, I didn't want anyone to think I was weird. "You don't have to sit next to me." I flinched. I hadn't meant to be rude, but he was a talker and observant. I didn't want to ramble or, worse, have my blood do its funny stuff and make him think I was weird.

His lips mashed together. "Is that your way of asking me to move?"

Great. Now, I was the asshole. "No, sorry." I lifted my hands. "I meant don't feel obligated to sit next to me. You know I'm having a bad day and ..." How the hell did I even finish that sentence? I sounded like a fucking loser.

He unzipped his navy backpack and pulled out a binder. "The chance to sit next to a gorgeous woman will make microbiology easier to bear, even if she's playing hard to get."

My face flamed. "Oh, I'm not playing." The last thing I wanted him to think was that I was manipulating him. After being the target of so many kids, I deplored games like that.

"You're not interested." He leaned his head back and groaned. "You have a boyfriend, don't you?"

My eyes widened. I'd never had a boyfriend. No one had ever talked to me more than they had to, let alone tried to kiss me. "No boyfriend, but ... I'm here for the education." I snatched a purple pen from my bag, needing a moment to collect myself.

I straightened, and then Nice Guy beamed.

He winked. "So I *do* have a chance. It might just take some effort. I can handle that."

I remained silent, my brain scrambling for something to say. A handsome guy was flirting with me, and I had no idea how to respond. Even though I wanted to make friends, dating someone was more than I was ready for. That would cause strong emotions, and I couldn't risk it. "How about being friends?"

"Fine." He held out his hand. "Since we're friends, we should know each other's name. I'm Slade."

Names. That wasn't too personal. "Skylar." I shook his hand.

That was when the professor decided to glide in.

He began class, jumping right into microbes and cell structure, and I finally felt normal as I listened and took notes, the crazy past twenty-four hours slipping from my mind.

I STUFFED my notebook and pen into my bag, ready to search for my next class.

"Where are you off to now?" Slade asked as he packed up his stuff.

"Economics." I zipped up my backpack and tossed it over my shoulder. "It's in the Evergreen Building."

He stood and bowed slightly. "Well then, follow me."

I tilted my head. "I can find it on my own, but thanks. You don't need to be late for your next class."

"Okay. See you soon, Skylar." His words sounded like a promise.

I bit the inside of my cheek, creating just enough pain to prevent a stupid grin from spreading across my face. Slade was nice, and something about him was comforting. He didn't look at me strangely, despite how we'd met ... unlike Raffe, Keith, and Adam from yesterday.

Glancing at my phone map, I located the Evergreen Building and headed down the stairs. Luckily, the building was next door, so I didn't have a long walk.

My class was on the first floor. Even more students were out, and I got stuck behind a group as I made my way to the room at the far end of the hall.

As soon as I walked through the door, awareness prickled at the base of my neck. My traitorous gaze landed on Raffe, who sat lazily in the back row of the class. His attention was already on me, and when our eyes met, his softened. A few guys sat next to him, and a girl sat in front of him with her body turned toward him, but he wasn't talking to any of them.

I hurriedly took the open seat in the front of the middle row, feeling the intensity of his gaze on me the entire way. If I didn't have my back to him, I'd gawk at him during class. I was thankful he'd sat in the back; it would've been way too obvious if I turned around to stare at him. This would prevent me from doing something embarrassing … I hoped.

"Raffe, did you hear what I said?" the girl asked.

The image of her was burned into my mind, her long blonde hair waving down her back and her tight black shirt highlighting her slim frame. Thankfully, I'd seen her only from behind. I bet if I'd seen her face, I'd be even more jealous.

"No," he replied curtly, the same tone he'd used with me.

"Oh, I said—"

"I'm not interested," he replied. "I already have plans with my friends after the game."

I placed my hands on the cool desk to keep facing forward. For whatever reason, the tugging had started up again, bringing with it the urge to change seats to get closer to him. This was fucking ridiculous, but at least his jerk comment made sense now. It had to be some kind of act. But why?

"The whole football team is invited." The girl laughed a little too loudly. "It's the cheerleaders and the football players. Your friends can come."

"Yeah, man," a guy near him said. "The rest of the football team are your friends too. You should come hang out with us."

I stared at the whiteboard in the front of the room, a slight smile forming on my lips. I already knew how he'd react to that pressure.

"We already made plans," Raffe replied.

A friendly face entered the classroom, and my chest relaxed marginally.

"Fancy meeting you here." Slade strolled to the open seat next to me and paused. Mirth danced in his eyes. "May I sit here, or will you tell me to move like last time?"

Laughter bubbled in my throat. "In fairness, I didn't tell you that you couldn't last class."

He pretended to wipe sweat from his forehead as he settled into the seat next to me. "You kinda did, but at least I came prepared, even though you did snub me *again* about walking together."

I leaned my head back and giggled ... and froze. I hadn't done that since ... hell, I couldn't remember ever feeling this lighthearted, not even with my parents.

"Hey, I'm just giving you a hard time. I thought you were having fun." He touched my arm. "I didn't mean—"

A growling noise came from behind us, and the tugging in my chest yanked. I glanced over my shoulder. Raffe's nostrils were flared, and his eyes were glowing. His glare was on Slade, who had followed my gaze.

Slade's demeanor changed as he dropped his hand, the easy go-with-the-flow attitude slipping into a hardened sneer.

Clearly, they had some history between the two of them, and I hated that I wanted to know every single detail. I'd bet the problem was Raffe, but something inside me didn't want to listen to rationale.

I had to stop dwelling on him.

"You two don't like each other?" I couldn't help but ask. I forced my eyes to look away from Raffe and focus on Slade. Even then, they wanted to go back to him.

"That's a nice way of putting it." Slade turned back to me, and his friendly expression returned, though his eyes weren't as bright. "Let's just say the Wrights and their ... followers don't necessarily get along with the rest of the university students."

"Someone said the same thing at the bookstore." I clutched my pen, not as eager for economics class as I had been for microbiology.

Slade groaned and covered his face with his hands. "Of course you've already had a run-in with them."

"Yeah, but they also helped me, so I can't criticize them too much." I bit my bottom lip, wondering why I was defending them. They'd done more for me than anyone at my previous school would've done if I'd been scared and in danger.

His brows furrowed, and I swore he was about to ask a question, but class started.

I tried to pay attention, but my spine tingled the entire time. I sensed Raffe staring at me. The notion was foolish, especially since I was in front of him and directly in line with the whiteboard. Besides that, he'd made it clear he had no interest in talking to me, so the last thing he'd be doing was watching me. But that didn't keep me from being keenly aware of his proximity, and I had to fight the urge to steal glances at him over my shoulder.

At one point, I pressed my purple pen down too hard and broke the tip out of mere frustration.

When the professor wrapped up the class, I tossed my things into my bag and hurried out the door.

"Skylar!" Slade called after me, but I was already marching down the hallway.

Outside, I had no idea where I was heading. I didn't want

to go back to the apartment in case Lucy was there, and I didn't have another class today.

I marched to my car, needing to get away from here, even for just a few hours.

I was nearly at my car when a large, rough hand grabbed my arm and turned me around. A scream strangled me as I came face to face with a clearly annoyed Raffe.

His chest heaved, and he rasped, "What the fuck is it with you attracting danger?"

CHAPTER FIVE

I snorted and tried to ignore my body's demand to close the small distance between us. "I was in class, and now I'm walking to my car. I'm not sure what danger you're alluding to, other than your hand gripping my arm." I hated people who thought they could manhandle others, and my blood jolted as my emotions rose. Worse, I wanted the Raffe I'd met before we exchanged numbers. Not *this* version.

He snarled almost animalistically and released his hold on me. His face twisted as if letting go were painful. "I need you to be *safe*. And you're making it hard by hanging out with people like Slade."

My head snapped back. He was being domineering, implying I should avoid Slade when he'd been nothing but welcoming to me. "Are you serious? Slade's been nice to me, even around other people." I wouldn't let him think I'd take this split personality thing in stride. Lifting my head defiantly, I stared straight into his eyes while keeping my emotions in check. "I have my own mind and will say no to something if I believe it's dangerous." My blood fizzed as anger replaced the shock of him being here with me.

Leaning forward, he inhaled and searched for something on my face.

The intensity of his stare caught me off guard, and his unique sandalwood-and-amber scent made me dizzy. My mind went blank, and something in the air between us pulled me toward him like a magnet. It calmed everything inside me.

What the hell?

"Is everything okay here?" Slade asked from behind Raffe.

Raffe stiffened, becoming as still as a statue.

Whatever had been brewing between us vanished as he turned away and stood between me and Slade.

The fizz returned in one huge burst.

"What do *you* want?" Raffe snapped, disgust and contempt dripping from each word.

"Skylar rushed out of class, and I was worried, especially when you followed her." Slade stepped to the side where he could see me. "And it seems she's very uncomfortable in your presence."

Uncomfortable wasn't the word I'd use, but I wouldn't correct him.

"Seeing as none of this is your business, maybe you should head back to your own kind." Raffe's hands clenched at his sides.

"Interesting." Slade crossed his arms and rocked back on his heels. "Are you saying she's one of yours? Because—"

"I'm not *saying* that." Raffe relaxed his hands. "You should know better than to insinuate such a thing. There's something I need to talk with her about." His demeanor relaxed though his tone hadn't changed. It was as if he'd changed personalities a third time in the span of a minute.

They were talking about me as if I wasn't here, so this was an excellent time to leave. I wasn't comfortable around Raffe, nor did I want to be caught up in whatever was brewing between them. I had enough issues without adding theirs to my own.

I spun to leave, but Raffe somehow moved quickly enough to block me. How the hell was he that fast? No wonder he was the quarterback of the football team.

"We aren't done with our conversation." Raffe lifted a brow, his attention back on me.

"Uh ... when you two started pretending that I wasn't around, that was the end of ..." I trailed off, unsure what to say. We hadn't been having a conversation to begin with. More like accusations and glares. "Whatever it was we were having." I couldn't come up with a better alternative. "So, please, carry on with your posturing. Pretend I'm still standing here. It'll be better for all of us." My blood was so damn close to humming I couldn't breathe.

Slade laughed. "Yeah, she's definitely not one of yours."

Why did they keep saying that like they owned people? I glared at Slade and said, "I'm no one's." My heart ached at that sentiment, which was ridiculous. But it would've been nice to fit in somewhere.

Slade had the decency to wince, but Raffe's expression slid into a mask of indifference.

"Listen, as fun as this is, I've got somewhere to go." This time, I meant it. I had to get out of here before the ground started shaking again or something equally bad. The best way to relax was to remove myself from the situation. I needed to leave all this bullshit with Raffe and Lucy behind for a few hours.

When I walked past Raffe, he didn't stop me, but he strolled next to me to my beat-up, black Honda Civic. He looked the car over, and his nose wrinkled.

Elitist jackass.

I had nothing to be ashamed of just because I hadn't been

born into money. I made a show out of unlocking my car with the fob because that was the one perk it had—beyond the electric windows—and opened the car door.

When he sidled up beside me, my breath caught.

"Things here aren't what they seem," he murmured softly. "Be careful. You're a magnet for danger, and I don't want anything bad to happen to you. Remember to call or text me if you get into trouble, and that includes getting stranded."

The concern in his voice made me pause, and when I looked at him, I realized I'd gotten myself into more trouble. Instead of the standoffish expression and fuck-off attitude he so often projected, he looked like a different person.

One who truly cared.

My heart stuttered, and words wouldn't form, so I nodded. My blood warmed, but it wasn't from the usual strangeness inside me.

"Good." He sighed, and his expression hardened as he took a step back and laughed coldly. "And if your car acts up, let me know." His eyes flicked to Slade.

And now he was insulting my car. The sexy jackass was back. That was good. I understood how to deal with jerks. It was when he seemed to care that I became tongue-tied.

When I didn't respond, he arched a brow. "You will, right?" He sounded uncertain.

"My car runs fine." I slid into the driver's seat, slammed my door, and then started the car. I shifted into reverse. I needed to get out of here and fast. Fortunately, Raffe moved out of the way quickly, and I was able to step on the gas and back out.

My window rattled, and my stomach clenched. It was like being at EEU had increased the volatility of my abilities more than ever before.

When I braked and put the car into drive, I couldn't stop myself from glancing in his direction.

The corners of his mouth tipped upward, and dammit, he somehow looked even sexier. It was enough of a shock that my blood cooled marginally to a high fizz.

A sense of mischief overtook me, and I saluted him with my middle finger as I drove away.

I forgot that Slade was there until I pulled out of the university and headed toward Portland, wanting to lose myself in the city and get my blood back under control before I ran into one of them again.

After a few hours of driving around and visiting bookstores and an animal shelter, I finally pulled back into the school parking lot.

I'd managed to calm down and find a way around one stupid stipulation the university had set on me for attending—I couldn't get a job. My entire focus had to be on my studies to ensure I maintained good grades.

But I'd thought of a loophole.

The administration hadn't said anything about volunteering, and obtaining hours at an animal shelter would increase my chances of getting into a top vet school. I'd filled out the application, and they'd informed me that I'd have to take a required class before I could begin, but I was more than happy with that. They'd even said they would work around my schedule, so EEU shouldn't have an issue with my hours there if they did find out.

As I returned to the school, my blood jolted again. I grimaced. Just pulling onto the campus had me all amped up.

I parked back in the far-end spot that no one wanted,

likely because it was the farthest from the apartment buildings and residence halls. In a way, it symbolized what I warred with inside myself—being in the back and invisible while wanting to fit in.

It was around five o'clock, and students were milling around everywhere. I hoped that meant Lucy was out and I could slip into the apartment and grab some clothes. I suspected she had a ton of friends, so if I wanted to avoid her, I could pack several days' worth of clothes and shower in the gym locker room or *something*. I hoped the housing admin would figure out where to reassign me soon.

Slipping from the car, I surveyed the area. With my luck, something would attack or chase me.

Things here aren't what they seem. Raffe's words replayed in my mind.

I'd pushed that weird situation from my mind while I was gone, but now that I was back, the conversation and strange interactions sprang back up. He'd been trying to convey a convoluted message to me, but I had no clue what it was.

I gritted my teeth. If he wanted to tell me something, why didn't he come right out with it?

Whatever.

If he cared, he'd be direct. I didn't need to waste any more time thinking about him.

I hurried through the front doors and up the elevator. Soon, I was at the apartment door. I paused and listened for any noise from within.

Nothing greeted me, so I punched in the code and opened the door quietly.

I stepped inside.

Then I heard a noise coming from Lucy's bedroom.

Shit.

I spun around to leave, but I heard her step into the hallway.

What was it with people moving so fast here?

Before I could go, Lucy said hurriedly, "Skylar, wait. Please. I've been upset over how things went down this morning."

For a moment, I considered marching out the door, but she sounded sorry. I didn't want to be the asshole. I understood what it was like to be on her end, wanting a chance to explain things. I'd wished so many times that people would hear me out, so what type of hypocrite would I be to deny her?

My blood jolted as I shut the door and faced her.

I lifted a hand. "You don't have to explain anything. I get it. You weren't expecting someone like *me* to be your roommate." It was clear I wasn't on the same level as her. She was gorgeous, dressed nicely, and screamed *money*. "I just came to grab a few things so I can get out of your hair until you sort this out with Lafayette." I forced a smile, wanting her to believe there were no hard feelings. At this point, I'd do anything to end this conversation.

"*You* aren't the problem." She wrung her hands. "Well, not you as a person."

I was trying to be nice, but I hated when people skirted around the truth. The bullies who'd tormented me all my life had gotten away with most of their shit because they chose their words carefully. Whether it was the wide-eyed, innocent stare and the proclamation that they hadn't *meant* it that way, or that I must have slipped and they'd only been trying to help, every time, the teachers and principals had believed them because they were the favored students or because it was just easier than dealing with the problem. I was *so* tired of people getting away with things. "Actually, that was exactly what you meant. But just so you know, running under the moon sounds amazing, and if I had guys hitting on me like I'm sure you do, I'd sleep with the ones I wanted to as well."

She blinked then laughed.

Great. This was when her nice facade vanished and her claws came out.

"You're blunt." She pressed her lips together. "I've never met anyone like you."

"Most people don't like me, so there's no point in playing nice. All it does is make the rejection hurt more." I hadn't meant to say that, but it was the truth. "I'll get out of your way until it's handled."

"You have a person willing to let you room with them?" She dropped her hands to her sides.

"No, but don't worry about it." Since we were having this conversation, I might as well get my things now instead of having to come back later. "I'm just going to pack some stuff."

"There's no need." She blew out a breath. "Lafayette told me there's no way to change the assignment. All the apartments are full, so we're stuck together."

Ugh. I couldn't sleep in my car forever. It would eventually get cold. The fizzing sensation swirled within me, and I deadpanned, "That's great."

She snorted and placed a hand on her chest. "This might actually be a good thing."

I tensed, waiting for the punch line.

But she didn't continue. Instead, she smirked.

"Why? So I can wash your clothes? Clean the bathroom?" Cinderella status made sense to me. I doubted she wanted to ruin her long, burnt-orange nails. I glanced in the kitchen at the black stove. "I hate to tell you, but my cooking skills are subpar at best."

"What?" She flipped a hand, looking genuinely perplexed. "Why would you do any of that? We have a cleaner who comes in weekly, and I wouldn't be surprised if the stove is just for looks. Besides, I mainly eat meat, rare, so I doubt I'd want you to fix me anything even if you were a great cook."

I wrinkled my nose. "Rare?"

"And you said you weren't judgy." She arched a brow.

She had me there. I shrugged. "Food is a whole different thing. If it can moo or cluck, you might need to rethink your stance on things. Maybe even possibly life."

"I could say the same thing about you." She plopped onto the couch, making no move to slink back into her room.

Strange.

My chest expanded, and I tried to rein it in. I didn't need to get my hopes up that we could get along. She'd tried to get a new roommate earlier. If someone left university housing, I had no doubt she'd try again. "You'd be wrong."

"You know what? I'm glad he wasn't able to change our arrangement." Her eyes twinkled. "Because you are *so* refreshing."

Sweat pooled in my armpits. She was acting nice and sounded sincere. But I didn't know how to respond. This was new territory, and what if she changed her mind later? I needed to keep my distance. I twirled my key ring on my finger. "Was there anything else you wanted to talk about?"

She shook her head. "I'm just sorry for not talking to you first. When I realized you might have overheard the conversation, I felt like a huge bitch. I'm sorry."

"It's not a big deal." I caught the key in my hand and sighed. "On that note, I'm going to head into my room and rest. It was kind of a big day."

"Sounds good." She stood and rubbed her hands on her

arms. "I'm going to meet my cousin and friends for dinner, so I'll see you later."

She was leaving, and I'd have the place to myself for a while. That sounded amazing.

When the front door shut, I let out a shaky breath and went to my room. I tossed my keys onto my dresser and sat on my bed, taking deep, calming breaths. That conversation had gone better than I'd expected, and as icing on the cake, I no longer felt compelled to sleep in my car.

Now that the weight of that had lifted, I was restless, and my body began to fizz again.

Shit. I had to move.

After spending so much on gas today, I could think of only one option.

The woods.

But I wouldn't go in deep. I'd stay near the tree line. Just deep enough to breathe with no one watching.

I grabbed my phone and headed back outside.

The cool evening air brushed my face, refreshing me.

Only a few people were around now, and they were in deep conversation, not noticing me as I stepped out.

I hung a right, going in the opposite direction, and walked toward the woods. Knowing that I'd soon be immersed in nature had me quickening my pace.

When I stepped past two towering Douglas firs, I inhaled the crisp, clean air, the kind that only nature could provide, away from pollution and smog.

I walked in about a quarter of a mile, deep enough that no one could see me from the university lawn.

The fizzing floated through me, but I wasn't petrified. No one was here to witness anything weird. I stopped and listened, ready to completely relax.

A whimper sounded close by, and a knot formed deep in my stomach.

Then I heard a suckling noise that sounded like a rabid animal feasting on a fresh carcass.

"Please," a shaky female voice murmured.

Acid burned my throat.

Someone was in trouble.

CHAPTER SIX

I followed the whimpers, the noise growing louder with each step. The closer I got, the more human the animalistic sounds became, like someone slurping and gulping.

My stomach roiled, and everything within me shouted to *run*. But with the way my blood hummed, I didn't have a choice. My legs propelled me forward. I didn't have a weapon, but I couldn't abandon someone who needed help.

I snatched my phone and shot Raffe a text: *Something weird is going on in the woods. I'm going to check it out.*

There. I'd done what I'd promised—texted him. At least I wasn't heading into danger without making someone else aware.

Stepping between two firs, I froze. I blinked, trying to understand what the fuck I was seeing. A woman leaned with her head tilted back against a tree and a man's head at her neck. But he wasn't giving her loving kisses; the sounds he was making reminded me of the noises newborn babies made when they ate.

Crimson dripped down her neck, and I gasped. I had to be seeing things because the image before me couldn't be real

The guy was drinking this woman's blood, and her eyes bulged in terror.

His eyes locked on mine. He winked as he lazily retracted his teeth and licked a trickle of blood from her neck. I could feel pleasure and power wafting from him, but the girl was scared and confused.

This had to be a horrible dream. My entire time at EEU had been one strange thing after another, but *this* was the icing on the cake.

The man appeared to be near my age, so early to midtwenties, with shaggy, dark-blond hair hanging in his eyes. He might have looked like a nice guy who was into sports if he hadn't had blood dripping down his mouth.

I wanted to run, but I suspected he would chase after me. Worse, if he didn't, he'd go back to drinking this woman's blood.

His victim opened her mouth as if she were going to scream, but no sound came out.

He chuckled and grabbed her head, staring into her eyes. He said, "I told you that you weren't allowed to scream, and now you'll wait here until I take care of our little interruption."

Her bottom lip quivered, and her auburn hair fell into her face, her fear hitching up a notch.

Shit, I had to get out of here but in a way he couldn't come back to her. I spun and ran back the way I'd come from.

He laughed darkly. "I love it when they act like prey."

The trees flew past me, and my heart pounded. The weight of my limbs receded as my flight response replaced my shock. My hearing seemed to enhance as I ran past trees, running faster than I ever had before. My blood hummed, and I welcomed it.

A shiver ran down my spine a moment before something

wrapped around my waist. I lunged forward, trying to break free, only to be tossed into the closest tree. My back slammed into the trunk, knocking the breath out of me.

In a blur, the guy appeared in front of me. His light-brown eyes were ringed with crimson and twinkling with excitement as he lowered his face to mine. His breath smelled of copper.

Acid burned my throat as I averted my gaze to the tree behind him. I didn't want to stare into his freaky-ass eyes.

"You're going to wish you hadn't come searching," he cooed as he restrained my head like the girl he'd left behind. His annoyance and pleasure slammed into me, and my lungs stopped working. But that compared to nothing when he sniffed me and moaned, "You smell incredible."

The humming spilled out of me into the tree behind us, and when he maneuvered for his head to block my view, a sharp, piercing hum sprang up around us. The sound was loud, and the guy stumbled back, covering his ears with his hands.

I didn't know what was going on, but the sound echoed the vibration I felt within my body.

When the guy hunched over and groaned, I pushed off the tree and ran toward the university. The humming continued to pierce the air as I took off. But after a few steps, I got light-headed, and I tripped and dropped to my hands and knees.

A piece of bark or branch cut into one knee, causing it to sting, but I gritted my teeth and got my feet back underneath me. A scrape I could heal from—a person drinking my blood had no such guarantee.

My chest constricted, and I wheezed. Fatigue hit me, weighing my body down, which was so much worse than fear. Fear you could run through, but not exhaustion.

The humming continued, but I wasn't sure how long it

would last. My blood pulsed as if it might also give out, and I had to move until I couldn't anymore. I'd been a quarter mile into the woods, so I should be close to campus.

My body gave out, and I crumpled onto the ground. The humming in my veins slowed, and so did the noise that had taken the guy down.

This was it. I couldn't help myself or the girl. We'd both die, and I could only wonder what the news around campus would be.

"You bitch," the guy snarled, and hands gripped my right shoulder and flipped me onto my back.

The guy straddled me, his fangs extending over his bottom lip. The faint humming was still there, but with the way his nostrils flared, it seemed to piss him off more than hurt him.

"You're going to pay for that." He opened his mouth and lowered his head to my neck.

A bloodcurdling scream escaped me, but even that was cut short. I didn't have the energy to spur it on further.

"Don't scream again," he commanded, the crimson in his eyes spiraling hypnotically. "And you won't remember finding me drinking from that woman or me chasing after you and feeding. All you'll remember is that you had a good evening stroll."

My brain hazed, and part of me wanted to concede to his demand, but another part fought back. He lowered his head to my neck, and I winced, bracing for the pain. Instead, he rubbed his nose against where my pulse pounded.

"You smell delectable." His tongue darted out, leaving a trail of saliva behind. "What *are* you?"

I had no clue what he meant, but his dragging this encounter out was deepening my fear. Maybe that was what he was going for.

"Mix that with the scent of your fear, and you may be my best meal yet." He snickered, and the tips of his teeth grazed my skin but didn't pierce it. I turned my head in the opposite direction, not wanting to see his face as he drank from me.

Something caught my eye.

Three sets of eyes glowed at me from past the tree I'd been tossed into moments ago.

The pair of eyes closest to me was a familiar crystal blue.

A sharp pain pierced my neck as the guy bit me, and those glowing blue eyes leaped around the tree, revealing a big fucking black wolf.

For a minute, the pain ebbed as awe and more fear warred inside me. The wolf lunged onto the guy's back, and the fangs left my neck.

When the other two glowing-eyed beings moved out, I wasn't shocked to see they were wolves as well.

The black wolf clawed at my attacker's back, and the guy rolled off me and knocked the wolf into a tree across from us in a blur.

No wonder the biter had been able to attack me so fast.

The other two wolves were here, and I tensed, but their focus stayed on my attacker.

I clasped my neck, warm blood slipping through my fingers, and tried to sit up. The world spun around me, and I couldn't tell up from down. Nausea churned in my stomach, and I deplored my luck. The one time my blood had sort of helped me, I couldn't get away, and three random wolves had come to my rescue. Clearly, I was meant to die tonight whether from being drained of blood or as a meal for the wolves.

Wolves were very intelligent—smarter than most humans thought—and they understood cause and effect. So maybe they wanted to be the ones to kill me instead of this guy?

The thought caused me to shiver, but all I could do was sink back onto the forest floor. Fortunately, I landed on the dried needles and leaves the trees had shed.

My eyes closed, despite the sounds of skin tearing and a loud scream of agony. Everything inside me tensed, but sleep still overcame me.

At least, when it was my turn to die, I'd be unconscious and unable to feel the pain.

"Skylar." A sexy and familiar rasp filtered into my consciousness.

I wanted the voice to keep talking ... to say more. The sound sent all sorts of strong emotions surging through me, but I noticed one overlying emotion I'd never felt before, and I never wanted it to end.

It knotted my stomach and both scared and thrilled me.

Intrigue.

My shoulders moved as someone nudged me, and that deep voice spoke again. "We need you to wake up."

Raffe.

Then the word *we* had my eyes bolting open.

Raffe was kneeling at my side with Adam, Keith, and some other man I didn't know standing at my feet. The nameless guy stood between Adam and Keith, rubbing his hands together.

All four of them stared at me, and I sat up, needing to get away from prying eyes.

Realization warmed my chest. I'd texted him, and he'd come. I hadn't expected that.

"Hey, are you okay?" Raffe asked way more gently than

any other time he'd talked to me. "You seem like you've been through a lot."

"*A lot?*" My mind fuzzed, sort of like the sensation you had when you knew something had happened but you couldn't quite put your finger on what. I rubbed my hands together and felt hints of stickiness. I stilled and glanced at my hand to find a few dots of dried blood on my fingertips, my skin wet as if someone had washed it.

Raffe nodded and mashed his lips together. "Did you fall and hit your head?"

I bit my lip, trying to recall, and my head pounded. Something was there. I remembered feeling terror, but the reason was just out of reach. "Uh ..." I shook my head to clear it and rubbed my neck. Blurry memories sprang into my head.

The people involved were out of focus, but I remembered what had happened. I wrapped an arm around my middle and scanned the area for a faceless attacker and wolves.

The chill in my bones didn't budge. A smart person would have kept her mouth shut. In fact, under normal circumstances, I would have, not wanting to be targeted as a freak, and the guy who'd bitten me had wanted me to forget about the attack, but when I touched my neck, I remembered how his bite had felt.

I frantically looked for the attacker, my chest clenching so tightly I feared a heart attack was imminent. "This guy was drinking blood from a woman not far from here. They both looked like students, and when I stumbled upon them, he attacked me. Then three wolves came and fought him off, but —" They were nowhere to be seen, nor was my attacker.

Had I dreamed it? The memory was foggy, but I was in the woods, in the same spot I remembered it all happening. It had to be real, but I doubted any of them would believe me.

"That's what I was afraid of." Raffe ran a hand through

his hair and glanced at the nameless guy in the center. "You need to make her forget."

Red flags were appearing all around me. "Wait. You *believe* me?"

"I don't understand." The ruggedly sexy, thirtysomething man blew out a breath. His light-brown hair was gelled back to perfection, and his strong jaw tensed, giving his cheekbones more dimension. "He should've accounted for that before he bit her. He put all of us in danger by not following the law."

I laughed, surprising myself as well as everyone else, and scooted away from them. "You all knew he was out here biting people?" What sort of sick place was this? One I needed to get the hell away from.

"Lafayette," Raffe growled. "Fix this. She's about to have a full-blown panic attack."

Wait. Lafayette. As in the housing administrator? Surely not, but that name wasn't super common.

Keith and Adam shoved Lafayette closer to me.

"Dammit, mutts," Lafayette hissed, two of his teeth extending past his bottom lip like my attacker's teeth had. "Don't manhandle me. You aren't my leaders, and I don't have to submit to any of you three."

My attacker's face came back into clear vision, and my heart pounded. Worse, Raffe, Keith, and Adam didn't even flinch when Lafayette grew fangs.

What had I gotten myself into? I'd come here of my own free will to be the victim of vampires.

Vampires.

My blood jolted again as if it finally remembered how to work.

If I went home now, my parents would *definitely* put me in a psych ward.

"Maybe, but one of your own was reckless. Not only was

he too close to the damn campus to feed, but he attacked *her*." Raffe glanced at me, his face softening. "And she's petrified." He turned back to Lafayette, his ice-blue eyes glowing. "Either fix it now, or we'll punish you along with him since you're ignoring the issue."

Raffe's eyes were just like the wolf's. That was why the wolf's eyes had seemed so familiar—they had to be his. But accepting that made me question everything about this world.

"It's about him not wiping her memories, right?" Keith's tone held an edge as he glared at Raffe. "Not about him attacking her?"

What the hell? My blood jolted.

Raffe's jaw clenched. "Of course." The two of them engaged in some sort of stare-off.

Lafayette's mouth pressed into a thin line though his two canine teeth still hung out. "You really do push boundaries, *Prince Wright*."

Prince?

This night kept getting wilder, and I wished I hadn't come out here at all.

How selfish was that, given a girl had been *eaten* ... drunk from ... *whatever* these weirdos called it? My blood increased a notch to a fizz.

I had to get away from them.

Adrenaline pumped through me, and I climbed to my feet. "Don't come near me."

"Raffe, grab her, man." Keith shook his head. "Her voice is getting shrill, and after that weird noise that led us to her, my brain can't handle it. I get she's a human, but she'll be so much better off if we make her forget everything."

Adam snorted. "What brain?"

"The big one right here." Keith pointed at his head. "It's full of all sorts of information, which I'd like to retain by calming her ass down. Like, pronto. Besides, my tacos and pizza are getting cold, and I'm borderline hangry."

White-hot anger coursed through me, almost increasing the fizz to a hum. I couldn't believe they were *joking*.

"And you two are the ones Raffe chose for his second and third in command?" Lafayette rolled his golden eyes and lifted his hands as he approached me. With each step forward he took, I took one back.

"As much as I hate to admit it, Keith is right. If you'll allow me to help you forget everything, you won't be fearful anymore."

Raffe placed a hand over his heart. "Nothing bad will happen to you. I promise."

"Says a man who can change into a *wolf*," I spat out, wanting him to tell me I was crazy. That this was a bad dream I'd wake up from. This wasn't the first time I'd had that wish, but it was the first time I needed it to be true because of something I hadn't done.

He sighed and hung his head. "Lafayette, make her forget about us too, and tell her to avoid the woods as well. This is the second time something's happened to her, and she's only been here two days."

My fear climbed, and my blood hummed. "Someone *was* chasing me in the woods?"

Raffe oozed concern and determination while Keith and Adam showed varying degrees of annoyance. Lafayette emanated bitterness and hate, but I wasn't sure if that was directed at me or Raffe.

"Fine." Lafayette stepped toward me, the edges of his eyes turning crimson as they swirled in a hypnotic spiral like the other guy's had.

I flicked my gaze to the ground underneath the four guys, and the earth shook.

"What the fuck?" Keith yelped, and Raffe's eyes widened and locked on me.

I turned tail and ran.

I spun around, realizing that trying to outrun vampires and wolves was dumb, but I didn't know what else to do, nor did I know how long the earth would shake.

That fatigue weighed me down again, but I moved as fast as possible while I could. Every few steps, my body seemed to weigh even more.

I reached the area where the tree line thinned ... so close to campus.

My victory was short-lived as my legs sagged, the exertion too much.

Suddenly, Slade appeared in front of me like a mirage.

"Go," I croaked, not wanting him to be part of this awful encounter.

"Skylar?" His forehead lined with worry, and he hurried to me. "What's wrong?"

Before I crumpled completely, he caught me and anchored me to his chest. He rasped, "What the hell happened?"

"You need—" I started, but a loud growl from behind me cut me off.

CHAPTER SEVEN

I didn't have to turn around to know who it was. Unfortunately, I was attuned to his voice and unique noises already, and the tingle of awareness at the base of my neck further confirmed his presence. I hated how attuned I was to him and, worse, that knowing what he was didn't strangle me with fear like it did with the others.

"Let go of her *now*," Raffe snarled.

Slade tensed. "And let her fall? She can barely walk."

I hated how weak that made me sound, but I couldn't do anything about it. I wished I could push through the fatigue, but this exhaustion was different from before. It was as if my soul was drained as well as my body, the sensation eerie and cold.

"Well, you're relieved of duty," Raffe replied, his sizable hand clutching my arm and pulling me backward.

My breath caught in anticipation, and I craved to feel his strength once more. His chest was more muscular, and he felt safer than Slade, despite knowing he was part animal.

But Slade's arms tightened like a vise, keeping me within his embrace.

"Let her go," Raffe warned. "I need to take her back to Lafayette so he can alter her mind."

I whimpered, remembering sharp teeth sinking into my neck, and I yanked my arm free. "No, I don't want to do that. Slade, we need to go." I shook my head and buried my face in Slade's chest. Even though I desperately wanted to go to Raffe, I didn't have a death wish, and my survival skills had kicked in. Slade was on my side. I had to believe that Raffe wouldn't want another human exposed to his freaky-ass world.

My head bobbed as Slade inhaled and said, "What the hell happened out there?" His arms tightened around my waist, feeling weird.

"Edward lost his damn mind and attacked her and some other girl who goes to school here." Raffe kept his voice low and full of warning. "We came when he was feeding off her in the open. When I pushed him off, he went fucking rabid trying to get back to her."

"Shit." Slade huffed, and he leaned back, pushing me away slightly so he could examine me. "Did he bite her?"

The way he acted so casually about it made my blood run cold.

He *knew* about this world.

Slade joining the conversation to talk about me as if I wasn't here *again* pissed me off more. "Yes, *she* did get bitten, but most importantly, am I the only person here who didn't know that monsters are real?" My anger gave my legs strength, so I pushed out of his grip then stumbled a few steps.

Raffe placed his hands on my shoulders to steady me as Slade countered my movements.

Grimacing, Slade lifted his hands in front of him. "No. Over half the student population here doesn't know about the supernatural world. It's not just you."

That didn't make me not knowing any better. I leaned toward the trunk of the fir tree closest to me. Raffe helped me keep my balance, and I pressed my back against the trunk. Then I gritted out, "Neither one of you touch me." I couldn't trust either of them. They'd hidden what was going on here, but at least Raffe's warnings made sense. Some of my anger at him thawed. He'd *tried* to convey to me a need to be cautious.

"Yeah, whatever." Raffe shrugged and dropped his hands, but his face creased with hurt before smoothing out.

Not wanting more to analyze, I wrapped my arms around my waist and breathed. Being vulnerable pissed me off. I wanted to get away from these guys, but I didn't have the strength to walk past them and make it to the apartment.

Not that they would let me. Then I'd put Lucy in their crosshairs.

"He must have taken too much blood from her." Slade frowned and shook his head. "She can't even stand."

Lafayette, Keith, and Adam stepped into view. The two wolf boys wore scowls, but Lafayette tilted his head as he stared at me.

"What the *fuck* was that back there?" Keith scratched his head. "Where the hell did that noise come from?"

"Her." Lafayette stared at me. "She did it. Just before the noise increased, the scent of her blood changed. It smelled heavenly, more so than witch blood—which has proven to be deadly."

My heart stopped.

Had he just compared my blood to witch blood? How many sorts of supernatural people existed?

"You're a witch?" Adam's brows lifted to nearly his hairline. "But your underlying scent doesn't smell like herbs. You're more earthy and floral."

I blinked, trying to keep up with the conversation. "What? No. I'm not a witch." If I were, I'd be aware of that, surely?

"She's not. I would've sensed it." Slade wrung his hands. "She radiates human."

My mouth went dry, and a scream of frustration lodged in my throat, but screaming would take way too much energy. "Of course you're supernatural too." I couldn't keep the bitterness from my tone. The one genuine person I've met here, and he has a huge-ass secret.

"None of this matters." Raffe blew out a breath. "We need to alter her memory, and we *all* need to forget about what happened tonight."

Lafayette wrinkled his nose and huffed. "I'll alter her memories, and we'll go from there."

My mouth dried. I didn't want anyone doing brain stuff to me. "Edward tried when he attacked me, and it didn't work. I still remembered what happened when I came to with you four around me. Things went blurry for a bit then became crystal clear again."

"He probably didn't do it right," Lafayette said as he stepped toward me.

My heart raced, and Raffe moved between Lafayette and me.

"What the hell, man?" Keith groaned. "You asked him to wipe her mind, and now you're blocking him. I don't even know what's going on with you tonight."

"That was before we knew Edward tried to make her forget everything." Raffe's back was tense. "Whatever she *is* must make her immune to mind altering."

I snorted, and my body weakened. "You mean mind manipulation." Altering didn't sound as harsh, but they were playing with people's minds. It was sick, and I was glad that the worst thing my blood did was smell nice and cause weird things to happen around me.

"It's a necessary evil to keep the existence of supernaturals secret." Adam shrugged as if messing with people's memories was more than okay.

All five men needed punching. They were so arrogant and weren't trying to see things from a human's perspective. "Oh sure, humans who are being used as a food source shouldn't be aware it's happening. That girl was *really* enjoying being fed from tonight." I let sarcasm drip from my tone as bile churned in my stomach from the memory of the terror etched on her face. I'd have been a food source tonight, too, if Raffe and his friends hadn't come to my aid. "Whatever happened to her anyway?" My heart dropped. She could still be out there, hurt and bleeding. Some other vampire could find her and pick up where Edward had left off.

"She's fine. While you were passed out, I took care of her and had just returned when you woke up." Lafayette lifted his chin and sneered. "Enlighten me. What do you think we should eat? Unlike the movies, vampires can't live on animal blood. It lacks the nutrients we need. Should we just stake ourselves through the heart and die?"

That thought held merit, but I doubted I should agree. He might decide to eat me later.

"Calm down." Slade laughed a little too loudly. "She just learned about us tonight and was attacked. She has a right to be upset while she takes it all in."

Raffe jerked his head toward Slade, his eyes glowing.

When I thought I'd seen them glow before, I hadn't been imagining things. Worse, I found them more alluring. I now understood a small piece of a mystery that not everyone else did.

I was one of the few.

And so damn pathetic.

"He's right, man," Adam murmured. "But I'm not sure where that leaves us, so it's your call."

Slade wrinkled his nose. "Not just *his* call."

Clear animosity existed between the species, or whatever you called the divide between witch, wolf, and vampire. It seemed like Slade resented Raffe and his role in their world.

Raffe didn't miss a beat. He straightened and seemed to tower over me and the others, though he was only a few inches taller than Adam and Keith. "We don't have an option. We can't alter her mind, and I'd hate to try and have her react in a worse way than she did back there." He gestured back to where the five of us had come from. "And we've vowed never to hurt a human who isn't threatening us."

"But what if she tells other humans?" Lafayette pursed his lips. "It could lead to people coming here and digging for evidence. If she talks, that could be considered a *threat*."

Now they were debating whether they should *kill* me. And I was *right here*.

"Simple." Raffe turned to me, his ice-blue eyes locking with mine. He stepped close, his scent swirling around me, making me dizzy and adding to the haze in my brain. "Skylar."

The way my name rolled off his tongue made me tingly. I opened my mouth to ask him to say it again, but he continued before I could.

"Do you swear not to alert anyone about what happened tonight or about our existence, including your own magic?"

That last part snapped me back into the moment. He'd said my blood had surged magic, but I wasn't a supernatural.

I also noticed he'd said *alert*, not *tell*, meaning any sort of message—verbal, handwritten, or text. "I'm assuming, if I did, it would be off with my head?" I arched a brow, being ornerier than I'd intended. This probably wasn't the time to come off as if I was uncertain of my intentions.

Raffe grimaced, and Slade shook his head and covered his mouth with his hand.

When I looked at Lafayette, he narrowed his eyes and muttered, "You're rather odd."

A *vampire* had just dubbed me odd. I'd never thought I had a death wish until now. "Look, I won't inform, tell, text, video, stream, or anything else to anyone. I'll put this in the vault because, believe it or not, I *want* to live. I just don't want to be fed from or attacked."

Raffe sniffed me again.

What the hell was up with that? Did I stink?

"That's a fair request." Slade put his hands into his jeans pockets. "Besides, she has magic, so feeding off her is forbidden."

"Yes, but she's also *human*, so what rules apply to her?" Adam rubbed the back of his neck. "It's a blurred line. Humans aren't allowed to know about our existence, but she does, and she's human, so she shouldn't have any sort of magic, but she does. She's not even a hybrid, yet that sounds like what she is. She's an enigma."

That was why I'd never fit in.

I never had and never would.

And I still didn't have an explanation.

My heart ached, the wish that I'd find a way to belong here long faded out of reach. It had been a hopeless wish.

Raffe glanced at Lafayette.

The vampire tapped a finger on his chin as he scrutinized me. When his gaze slid to Slade, I noticed Slade nod slightly.

Lafayette dropped his hand to his side. "Fine. Adam is right. We need to figure out the rules and how they apply to her, but she's not lying. None of her vitals changed. But ..." He paused, moving closer to me.

Raffe tensed, and Slade's jaw clenched, but neither of them blocked his advance.

His irises darkened. "You need to understand that if you inform anyone of anything that even hints at the paranormal, we'll be forced to kill them. No matter how many people you tell. And our network is worldwide."

The threat hung in the air, covering me like an uncomfortably warm blanket. "Understood." I would never hurt anyone innocent. Not even my bullies deserved to die for this. What I'd seen tonight was inhumane. "I swear, I won't say anything to anyone beyond the five of you." I was very specific because I had a shit ton of questions I was determined to get answers to over time.

"Good." The tension left Raffe's shoulders. "That's settled. Now I need to meet with my dad and inform him of what happened tonight."

"*That* is a fucking good idea." Keith rubbed his stomach. "And I need pizza and tacos."

That was the second time he'd mentioned food. Even the thought had my insides revolting.

"Go on." Raffe placed a hand on my shoulder. "I'll help Skylar get back to her place."

"No." I straightened and almost cried in relief when my legs didn't give out. The ground still seemed to move under my feet, but I wasn't falling over. "I can make it back by myself."

He arched a brow. "I saw you fall into Slade. You're exhausted."

"Speaking of which ..." Keith trailed off and snorted. "I mean, the pun wasn't intended, but it works."

"I'm a warlock, not a witch." Slade scowled.

Keith raised his hands. "Which is weaker than a witch, so you're welcome." He patted his chest and waggled his brows. "Like I said, speaking of which ..." He paused, emphasizing it all over again. "Raffe, how the hell did you manage to function after that horrible humming sound before the rest of us could?"

Tapping his hands on his black slacks, Raffe chewed on his bottom lip. "I ... I don't know. It was painful, but when she began moving away, I was able to follow her. I covered my ears until Slade appeared and she dropped."

Now that I was standing, my legs were already wobbling. Exhaustion was slamming into me again, and if I didn't go, I wouldn't make it back on my own. I needed to show them I wasn't a complete weakling. "I'll leave you five to discuss ... whatever. I'm going to bed."

"I can walk you to your door." Slade smiled slightly. "I need to get back as well. My roommate will be worried."

"Are you—" Raffe started, but he clamped his mouth shut.

Adam and Keith furrowed their brows, watching him.

"That's a good idea," he rasped. "I'll see you two around."

Not wanting to stay but also not wanting to leave Raffe's side, I took slow and steady steps. Slade kept pace beside me, and I expected him to try to anchor me as Raffe had, but he kept his hands at his sides.

The two of us walked in silence, and after about twenty steps, I glanced over my shoulder to find the other four guys gone. I shouldn't have been surprised, but it still bothered me that I hadn't even heard footsteps.

"Are you okay?" Slade clasped his hands in front of his chest like he wasn't sure what to do with them.

"Not sure if *okay* is the right word, and I have so many questions." I yawned, and my steps became more sluggish. "But I don't have the energy tonight to ask any."

He chuckled, his shoulders relaxing. "That's fair. You had an eventful day, and it was also the first day of classes."

I'd been here a little over twenty-four hours, and my life had turned upside down. One question came to mind that I'd had my entire life, and for the first time, I was with someone who wouldn't think I was a freak and shun me if I asked. At least, not for that.

We strolled to the front of the apartment building, and I paused at the steps. "What exactly am I?"

"I don't know for sure, but I might be able to find an answer." He pulled out his phone. "Can I have your number in case I learn anything?"

That was a no-brainer, and that damn hope surged, expanding my chest. I rattled off my number. "Will you text me so I can save your contact on my phone? I don't answer calls or messages from strangers."

He winked, and my phone dinged in my back pocket. "Done."

I stumbled, my legs almost giving out again. It felt like I had weights tied around my ankles. "Okay. I need to go inside. I'll see you later."

"Are you sure you don't want me to help you inside? It's the girls' apartment complex, but you're allowed visitors."

I was tempted to let him help me, but after years of relying on myself, it didn't feel right to trust someone I'd just met. Besides, I didn't want Lucy to get caught up in any of this. "Nah, I'm fine. See you later."

I hurried to the door, the edges of my vision darkening. Somehow, I made it up the elevator and into the apartment before I blacked out.

Lucy jumped from the couch, her eyes wide. "Hey, are you okay?"

I didn't pause as I walked through the living room and headed to my bedroom. "I'm not feeling well. I need sleep."

"Uh. Okay." She sounded worried, but she remained in the living room, not pushing me for answers.

I shut the door and stripped down to my bra and panties, wanting the dirty clothes off me. Then I collapsed on the bed and fell asleep.

My phone dinged. I peeled my eyes open and stared at the ceiling. For a moment, I couldn't remember where the hell I was. Cold tendrils of fear clutched my chest, and I bolted upright. This wasn't my bedroom.

Reality crashed back in. I was at EEU ... and the events of the night before stole my breath.

It hadn't been a nightmare, and even though I didn't feel as exhausted this morning, my eyes were still heavy with sleep.

Another alert came from my phone, and I snagged my jeans from the floor and removed it.

Two things registered simultaneously.

The first was that it was nine thirty and I hadn't set my alarm last night. Thank God someone was texting me, or I might have slept through the morning and missed my eleven o'clock statistics class. The next was who was texting me.

Slade.

His message was short and sweet:

I found the answer. Meet me behind your apartment. I'll be there in ten minutes.

My pulse thudded and my blood jolted. All signs of fatigue disappeared, and my blood revved back to life. Being this close to an answer had me damn near doing cartwheels.

I snatched up clean underwear, a bra, a pair of jeans, and a violet sweater from my closet and rushed into the bathroom to take a shower. I needed to wash off whatever residue was left from last night.

Within ten minutes, I'd showered, put on a dash of makeup, and pulled my wet hair into a messy bun. Beggars couldn't be choosers, and my hair would dry fine this way.

Luckily, Lucy wasn't here to pepper me with questions. I slipped on my sneakers, grabbed my backpack, and hurried to the elevator, going faster with each step.

I made my way to the back of the apartment near the woods. Slade was already there with two cups in his hands.

He raised one and smiled. "I hope you like vanilla latte. The barista in the student center said most girls enjoy it."

"I don't discriminate as long as it's not decaf." I eagerly took the cup, not only because of the drink but also because I wanted to hurry through the pleasantries. "So, what did you find out?"

"Something that will blow your mind." He lifted his cup as if to toast me then took a sip.

My blood fizzed. I needed him to tell me, and fast.

But when he opened his mouth, fear strangled me. What if I didn't like what he had to say?

Before I could tell him to wait, the words were out of his mouth.

CHAPTER EIGHT

"I looked through one of the oldest witch's *Book of Twilight* and found references to someone with magic like yours."

My hands shook. I was at odds with myself, afraid that whatever I learned might make things worse for me. "*Book of Twilight*?" I needed to focus and make sure I understood what he told me and exactly how he'd gotten the information.

"Oh." He grimaced. "Right. Sorry. I didn't mean to make you feel like I was talking gibberish. A *Book of Twilight* is what coven members call their journals. It contains stories of their lives, their spells and dreams, and the wisdom they gained during their lifetime. If the book isn't destroyed upon their death, it's handed over to their coven, and it becomes coven knowledge. If a book survives ten generations, the individual coven is required to turn it over to the supreme priestess. Once that happens, if the supreme priestess determines it has information that should be shared with all covens, it's stored here at EEU, and students can learn about that history as part of their education. Of course, any witch or warlock tied to the supreme priestess is allowed to visit the library and research the books as well."

My brain had gone hazy. That was one hell of an answer for what I'd thought was a simple question. "Why here?"

"Because the supreme priestess lives nearby, and she's on the university board." He shrugged. "She's responsible for the books' safekeeping since they're no longer allowed to be taken off campus."

"Is there a guard?" That seemed like a costly venture, but hell, the United States government did similar things, and the documents and books were more secure than here.

He chuckled. "No, she spelled the books. They literally can't be taken past the perimeter, and if someone activates the perimeter spell, the witches and warlocks on campus are notified with a warning zap. The person wouldn't get far with a book, given where the library is located."

My head tilted. "The books aren't kept in the Wright Library?"

"And let humans stumble upon them?" He arched a brow.

"Where, then?"

Clutching his cup to his chest, he blinked. "I'd love to tell you, but I can't. You're not part of the organization."

"Organization?" I snorted. "Here I thought you called it a coven." Maybe that was what the collective covens were called.

Instead of replying to my coven comment, he took another drink and avoided my gaze.

Great. Clearly, I'd said something he hadn't wanted me to. The time had come to change the subject. I blew out a breath and steeled myself. "What did you learn?"

He licked a bit of foam from his bottom lip and stepped toward me. He whispered, "I need to use magic for a minute, so stay close." He lifted his free hand and held it out as he walked around me, murmuring, "Keep the conversation we're having away from nearby ears." The air shimmered where his fingertips touched and remained until the circle completed itself. He stopped where he'd been standing before.

My jaw dropped. I glanced through whatever spell he'd created and saw a faint gleam in the air, but I had to actively search for it to notice. "How did you change the air?"

"Since you have magic within you, you have the ability to see it." He stepped closer to me and ran a hand down my cheek. "To any human, it'll look like we're having an intimate conversation they can't hear."

"What about supernaturals?" At this point, I knew there had to be a reason.

"They'll know something is up but won't risk ruining the spell. What I have to tell you is something you shouldn't share with *anyone*. Even I will only share it with people I trust because, if what I suspect is true, you're something rare."

Being rare was never a good thing. People felt threatened by something different, someone they didn't fully understand. I'd dealt with that for most of my life. "I won't, but we have to come up with an explanation for the others who were there last night. I'm sure they want to know what I am too."

He nodded. "You're right, but I think I have a workaround."

Slade had been nicer to me than anyone else. If I was going to trust someone, he made the most sense. Even though I had a weird attraction to Raffe, he was all growly and douchey. He'd saved me twice, maybe three times, depending on who'd been watching me that first time in the woods. But he wouldn't hesitate to share whatever information he had with his best friends and father. They were a pack, and with my knowledge of wolves, I understood what that meant. They were a family unit. "Okay." I blew out a breath. "Let's have it."

I clutched my cup so hard the lid lifted on one side. My

blood fizzed as if it were rising as well, and I could sense the excitement rolling off Slade. Whatever he had to say, his eagerness had my blood *whooshing* in my ears.

"I believe you are what the witches and wizards of that time called an arcane-born." He lowered his head close to mine, his coffee breath hitting my face.

The closeness caught me off guard, and I took a step back.

"Stay close," he said, his free hand catching my arm. "We need to keep up the illusion that we're having a moment, so hopefully even the supernaturals will avoid us. We don't want people asking the wrong type of questions, do we?"

Right.

Our ruse.

But standing this close to him felt wrong ...

Pushing away the weird sensation, I concentrated on the one thing I'd always wanted to know. "Arcane ... born?" I hadn't meant for it to come out like a question, but my tongue had stuck on the words.

He nodded, excitement lightening his irises. "Yeah. It sounds sick, right?"

That wasn't the description I'd have chosen. "I can tell you no one understands me, especially when my blood does the humming thing."

"That's because you haven't been trained." He bounced a little, reminding me of a child. "I'm surprised your parents didn't tell you about this."

My blood went cold, the fizz fading away to nonexistence. Needing to regroup, I secured the lid on my drink and took a sip. The sweet milky coffee coated my mouth and warmed my throat as it went down, but the chill in my blood remained.

"Skylar?" His forehead creased.

There was no getting out of this revelation. A lump formed in my throat. "I'm adopted." The adoption was closed, and I had no idea who my biological parents were. But now I had a possible reason why they'd wanted to get rid of me, and it confirmed what I'd feared all along.

Knowing I was a freak, they'd pawned me off on my unsuspecting family, leaving me untrained and prone to chaos.

"Oh." His mouth held the O for a second longer than necessary. "That's unfortunate."

I snorted, startling him. But it was either laugh or cry, and I chose the former.

That stupid emotion called hope warmed my chest. "I was given to my adoptive parents the same day I was born. My biological parents couldn't have known I was ..." I trailed off. I was positive I would never be able to call myself *arcaneborn*. That didn't sound right. But maybe they'd given me up due to an unfortunate situation and not because of what I was.

"Actually, they would have." He flinched and rubbed a hand on his jeans. "There's this rare event that happens every two hundred to five hundred years that activates the dormant gene that contains the magic. It's called the Milky Way flash where, for a brief second, the stars in the Milky Way flare, but it happens so quickly that it's undetectable by human equipment or eyes. Supernaturals can see it, but only witches can track it. The last one happened twenty-one years ago on January nineteenth."

My body tensed. "Then it can't be me. My birthday is March nineteenth."

"The activation doesn't happen on the day of birth." He placed a hand on my shoulder. "It happens during the pregnancy, while the baby is still forming. After a person is born, the event wouldn't activate the magic."

A sharp pain pierced my heart. "Can the event be predicted?"

He shook his head. "That's one of the mysteries. It just happens, and no one knows why. Some say that it's Fate intervening."

"Fate?" I'd heard of gods and goddesses, and I'd heard fate was a bitch, but it sounded like he thought of it as a sentient thing and not a set of circumstances. "Like a person?"

"No, more of a being." He shrugged. "She's all-knowing and sets things into motion, but she doesn't have power like the moon goddess and Mother Earth do."

So my parents had given me up because of my blood. "So they gave me up instead of helping me with my blood. They must have known. Why would they do that to me?" I'd always hoped that finding answers would help me understand, but instead, I felt more broken.

"I ... I don't know." His lips pressed into a firm line.

I placed a hand on my chest, my blood dangerously close to humming. "I need to go into the woods in case I can't calm down." I took some deep breaths.

He nodded. "Come on."

We walked into the woods and stood in a grove of trees. I dropped my coffee, removed my backpack, and squatted. I had to focus on something other than the raw sense of abandonment deep in my heart—the cold void I suspected would never be filled.

I worked my hands into the mulch, needing to connect to nature. The damp earth on my hands centered me, and I remembered how running my hands through it felt.

"Uh ..." Slade stuttered.

I raised my head and saw a deer fifty feet away from us.

My heartbeat evened out as the animal took a timid step toward me. It wasn't the same deer as the first night. This one had large antlers. He didn't get close, likely because Slade was with me, but the two of us stared at one another.

It was a good thing since I'd rather no one else knew of my bond with animals.

When my blood calmed to normal, my body sagged. I'd managed to avoid a chaotic morning.

Slade cleared his throat, and the spell between the deer and me disappeared. "I hate to interrupt, but I need to head to class."

My head jerked upward. "What time is it?"

"Ten to eleven." He bit his lip. "But I don't want to leave you out here."

I stood and put on my backpack. "I have class too. I need to get going." When I glanced at his hands, I noticed he'd picked up the cup I'd tossed aside. I flinched. "Sorry, but the part I drank was really good."

"You have a lot going on. It's fine." He gestured for me to follow him. "Let's go before we're late."

We walked in comfortable silence, and when we crossed the road to the academic buildings, I waved. "I've got statistics, so I'll see you around."

He snorted. "No way. I do too. What are the odds?"

"Three classes together." I bobbed my head. "Those are strange odds, but I'll take them." It was nice to know there'd be a friendly face in class.

We headed into the Evergreen Building, and I followed Slade to the second floor, fourth door on the left.

As we reached the door, he grinned. "How are you in math?"

"I hold my own." A vet had to be good at math, chemistry, and biological sciences. "Why?"

"Because I suck at it, and I may need a tutor." He shrugged. "Sounds like I found the perfect one."

I rolled my eyes and smiled just as a tingle ran down my spine.

My attention immediately shot to the back of the room where Raffe sat, Adam on one side and another guy whose demeanor screamed *jock* on the other. Several girls sat around them.

We locked gazes, and Raffe's eyes glowed faintly, reminding me of the wolf inside.

Luckily, a desk in the front row was open, so I hurried over and claimed the spot.

"Seriously?" Slade chuckled and took the spot beside me. "The front again? Why not the side? I left my bag earlier, at the desk in the back corner, and there's an open spot beside me."

My eye caught the lone black backpack. So that was why he didn't have a bag.

But I wanted to be in the front row where I'd have to pay attention because the professor would see me. "Go for it. I'm sitting here."

"Fine." He chuckled as he walked over and grabbed his bag. I was surprised when he returned and slid back into the seat beside me.

I thought I could feel Raffe's eyes on me. It had to be my imagination. That wasn't actually possible.

Slade tapped his fingers on his desk. "You know what? I was thinking about what we were talking about earlier. Maybe I could get more information and meet up with you later. I might be able to help you with your problem."

"No." That was hard to say because I wanted to say yes. "You've done enough. I don't want to burden you."

"It's no burden," he said and leaned closer to me.

A groan that sounded damn close to a growl reached my ears.

Unfortunately, I knew exactly who'd made that noise, and worse, I liked that it had happened when Slade leaned toward me.

What was wrong with me?

Slade tapped a finger to his mouth. "Maybe I can help you get things under control."

Hope surged in my chest, and there was no squelching it. Someone with answers was willing to help me get whatever *this* was under control. "Really? Y—"

"Absolutely not," Raffe said loudly from behind me. He got up and stomped toward us.

The room went silent as Slade turned to Raffe. "I wasn't asking you, *Wright*."

The tension was palpable, and when I looked at Raffe, his eyes were glowing even with humans all around.

This couldn't be good.

CHAPTER NINE

I didn't know what had angered Raffe, but we were in a risky situation. Alarm rang through me. "He was talking to me, and it's my choice. There's no reason to get upset." I stood and placed a hand on Raffe's forearm to get him to glare at me and not Slade.

My hand buzzed where it touched his skin, and I jerked back. Raffe and I gasped.

For a moment, time went still.

I turned my hand over to find my skin unmarred. So strange. I glanced at his forearm, which looked smooth as well. No injuries to explain what happened.

Dammit.

With the cold weather, static electricity made the most sense, but I wasn't stupid.

That had been *way* more intense.

Raffe and I stared at each other, and the *tug* I felt toward him became a *yank*. I had to dig my feet into the tile floor to keep myself in place.

The sensation was as strong as the need to breathe and somehow scarier. This sort of attraction—or *whatever* this was

—could only lead to bad decisions and heartache. With his broody nature and *I don't give a shit* vibe, Raffe screamed "Closed-off player."

"Are you okay?" Slade asked worriedly.

I tried to turn my head to answer him but couldn't.

I was at Raffe's mercy.

What in the hell was going on? Was I losing my damn mind? I had to be.

"I'm ..." I didn't know what to say. *Fine* wasn't right. I was most definitely not that, but I didn't want to give Raffe the satisfaction of knowing how much he affected me. He had a big enough ego as it was. "Tired." That worked. I was more than tired. I was fucking exhausted, and I hadn't been here for two full days. I dreaded how I'd feel by the end of the semester.

"Man!" Adam called from the back. "Class is going to start any second. You should sit down. You know Professor Haynes doesn't tolerate disrespect."

I was glad he was getting involved. Since he was part of Raffe's pack, maybe he could calm him down.

Raffe gritted his teeth and swallowed. "Getting help from him isn't smart."

His dislike regarding Slade helping me had weird flutters shooting through my stomach. I winced. "That's *your* opinion —and *my* choice to make." I wouldn't let someone bully me out of having my potential first real friend. A friend who'd already given me answers about my heritage and weird blood. "I'll take your concern under advisement." Not that it would change my mind, but at least I'd acknowledged that I'd heard him. I had to do something to ease his bruised male ego.

"Wait. Did you and Josie break up?" a girl sitting two seats back from me and in front of Raffe asked. From the corner of my eye, I could see her russet-brown eyes widen and a grin spread across her face. "Because, you know, I'm single." She twirled a strand of chestnut-brown hair around her finger and leaned over the desk to get his attention.

Agony sliced through me, and my knees weakened as my blood fizzed.

He had a girlfriend.

Of course he did.

Keith had mentioned her in the bookstore, but I'd forgotten, too caught up in him and this weird draw.

He was the sexiest man I'd ever seen and, apparently, a prince heir to the wolf people. I bet he had all the women in their circle wagging their tails, begging to be the one at his side.

Raffe flinched, and I didn't want to think about what he'd seen on my face to react that way. His guilt and remorse slammed into me, probably because he realized I found him super attractive while he was committed to someone else. That guilt had to be about her.

The only somewhat silver lining was that he wasn't basking in my pain.

The hint of a decent man rose to the top, which made *this* even harder. Whatever *this* was.

The silence was deafening until Adam laughed, reminding me of a hyena, and said, "Do you really think those two will ever break up? That's wishful thinking."

"Then why is he so interested in *her*?" the girl asked, popping her gum. "He should be with a cheerleader like me, not her."

Raffe snorted and cut his eyes to the girl, his emotions surging more powerfully. His voice lowered, dripping with disgust. "I would never be with *her*. I want to make that very clear, and Josie and I are as close as always. Don't start rumors."

That was a kick in the gut, and my blood damn near hummed.

With Raffe's gaze elsewhere, I could finally look away, but I found Slade's face twisted with concern, which didn't help my anxiety. The hum vibrated, and I sensed it rising to the surface of my skin. At any second, the power would escape and cause something to happen.

Slade's attention flicked between Raffe and me, and I wanted to run from the room. I clasped my hands across my waist, hating that I looked like a broken and weak girl just because the hottest guy in school had a girlfriend.

I couldn't explain my strong emotions, especially since I didn't understand them myself.

Tucking a lock of hair behind my ear, I spun around and slid back into my chair. I needed to pretend that others weren't here so I could calm down. I glared at my desk, trying to focus on something ... anything else.

My desk shook slightly, causing my heart rate to skyrocket.

"What the fuck?" the cheerleader girl damn near screeched.

This was awful. Second day and I'd already made a freak of myself in front of the humans and disgusted the supernaturals.

I didn't have a place in either world. I wasn't a supernatural or fully human. I was some mix that didn't even have a species name.

Slade leaned over and rubbed my back. He took my hand in his, and I could feel tingles on my neck from Raffe's stare.

What the hell was his problem? I wanted to scream at him and shut this down, which meant getting my emotions under control.

Slade whispered, "Hey, I'm right here."

I'd never had someone be there for me during an episode.

I could feel the hum's intensity increasing, and I heard gasps behind me. At this level, I could sense everyone's emotions, though I couldn't pinpoint whose was which with my back to them. But intrigue, fear, and disbelief were the main ones. The one that screamed guilt, annoyance, and dread was Raffe. I had no doubt about that.

"Skylar, squeeze my hand and focus on me." Slade's breath hit my face, the sweet coffee scent filling my nose.

Slade's concern and excitement swirled between us. I wasn't sure why he felt excited, but I didn't want to focus on that. I wanted to focus on his concern for me. This was the first time anyone had openly shown that they cared about me in front of others.

The humming started to slow. My desk still teetered, but it wasn't shaking like before.

My gaze moved from the desk to his hand, and he tensed as his discomfort slammed into me, weighing me down.

"It's okay," he reassured me again. "Keep focusing."

His breath, so normal smelling in the chaos, helped my heart return to a normal pace. My blood lessened to a fizz, leaving behind an awkward silence.

"What the hell happened?" a guy asked from the back, and I wanted to disappear again, but I kept my grasp and attention on Slade's hand while remembering the scent of his breath.

"Come on." Slade lifted my hand and pulled me out of the classroom.

I shouldn't leave, but after what had happened, I wanted to run away and never return.

When we stepped into the hallway, we almost ran into a woman with dark, wavy hair. She wore a modest red suit with crimson lipstick and looked like she could have just exited a catwalk. Yes, she was dressed nicely, but it was more about the air she held.

"Why are you two leaving?" she asked, arching a perfectly sculpted eyebrow. "Class is about to begin." Her attention darted over my shoulder. She scowled. "What happened?"

"Something you're going to need to fix." Slade quickly filled her in, and the woman's dark-gray eyes scrutinized me.

"She's the human with magic." She sighed. "I'll alter their minds before someone posts about it online. You two stay here for a second." She marched into the classroom and shut the door behind her.

She was a vampire. Lovely. A vampire statistics teacher. What were the odds?

I rubbed my hands together, hating that everyone saw how badly Raffe affected me. "I'm sorry."

"Hey, he's a jackass and a bully." Slade turned so we were facing each other. "He says whatever he wants, thinking there won't be repercussions. He should never have interrupted our conversation. Maybe now he'll think twice about upsetting you after what happened in there. It's good for him to be uncomfortable."

Some of the worry in my chest unknotted. This was good. Slade thought I was upset because Raffe was bossing me around. He had pissed me off, but that wasn't what had set me off. "What's Professor Haynes going to do?"

"Alter the human students' memories and force them to delete anything they may have captured on their phones." He smiled. "Adam and Raffe were keeping an eye on things. They wouldn't let anyone do something that would risk exposing our world."

He was right. I rolled my neck. "Were you serious about helping me?" In my life, a lot of people had promised things that they never followed through on.

"Of course." He tilted his head, gaze steady.

"Good." I blew out a breath, not caring how desperate I might sound. "Because I need help." My blood jolted as my vision blurred.

"And you'll get it," he vowed, pulling me into his arms and kissing the top of my head. "I promise."

I cringed at his gesture, and my mouth went dry. I believed him, which wasn't normal for me. I often doubted people's sincerity, but he seemed genuine in his desire to help me. I had to hold on to that, or I would crumble, especially with everything that had happened in the classroom.

The door opened, and Professor Haynes waved us back in. Everyone in the classroom, aside from Raffe, Adam, and the professor, was frozen in some sort of daze. Raffe stood by my seat, and my legs moved way too quickly toward him.

The professor slipped out just as I sat back at my desk. Before she closed the door, she said, "And you remember everything that happens from this point forward."

The classroom buzzed back to life.

Raffe sighed, and I watched his body straighten. "You're nothing but an accident waiting to happen—so that's why I interrupted your conversation with Slade. You're nothing but trouble, and anyone who associates with you will be tainted by that."

My face burned, and I wanted to sink into the ground. He was continuing his original interruption as if nothing had happened. Was he trying to force me to mess up again so the board would revoke my scholarship?

Acid burned my throat. Here I was, at a new school, being treated the same as always—ridiculed and demeaned. Well, too bad. I refused to let yet another person run me off and make me feel unwelcome. My blood fizzed, and I realized we were coming dangerously close to creating another situation.

Everyone but Slade laughed, and I opened my binder and kept my body facing forward. I couldn't prove Raffe right and lose control again.

The star quarterback had just labeled me a social pariah.

Normally, the girls bullied me while the guys chuckled in the background. This was a whole new low for me, and of course, Raffe would be the person behind it. And that stupid *tug* still wanted me to move closer to him.

Because, you know, that was healthy.

Professor Haynes reentered the room as if she were arriving for the first time, and I got lost in something that made sense to me.

Numbers.

When class ended, I was out of my seat and running to the door. I didn't want to see any of the inevitable looks of pity people would cast my way. At least my next class was chemistry, which would keep me distracted.

I tromped down the stairs and out the front door, wanting to put distance between me and everyone back in that classroom.

"Skylar!" Raffe's deep, sexy voice called out. "Wait."

My feet damn near stopped. *Oh, hell no.* I gritted my teeth and continued to march to the Howling Building next door.

At least the theme of the building names made sense now.

A towering presence loomed behind me, and I knew who it was.

"Let me explain," Raffe almost pleaded, making my blood boil and fizz. "I'm acting like this to protect you, believe it or not."

I spun to face him and thrust a finger into his chest. "How is making sure no one will want to be friends with me protecting me?" I regretted it as soon as I'd said it.

He sighed. "Because you're causing a ton of uncertainty

in our world." His full lips and commanding presence distracted me from everything he'd done to me back there.

"As if I haven't had that uncertainty my entire life!" Was he seriously trying to turn this around and play the victim? "You *humiliated* me."

"I talked with my father last night, and we agreed that, with your inability to control your magic, it's too risky for you to be around humans more than you have to be." Raffe karate-chopped the air. "I was hoping to talk to you about it, but you lost control again, and I had to act that way. I'm sorry. I swear, I wish this was all different. *Believe me.*" His voice cracked as if he were in pain.

He'd labeled me a social outcast, yet he was acting like the victim. Part of me *still* wanted to soothe him! *And* he was taken, which made all this worse.

"You're a jackass." Rage overcame me, and the edges of my vision hazed red. I pushed my finger harder into his chest to make my point. But all I accomplished was hurting my finger. Well, la-de-fucking-dah. "That wasn't *your* decision to make. What you did back there affects *my* life, not yours. You can take your explanation and shove it up your ass, Raffe." I dropped my finger and marched away, discreetly flexing the finger to work out the slight ache. His chest was all muscle, no fat, and I'd expected more of a cushion, or I wouldn't have jabbed him that hard.

"It's my responsibility—" he started, but I merely lifted my middle finger over my shoulder, not making him read between the lines.

Though I walked off in anger, with my blood damn near humming again, I ached like I'd left a piece of my soul behind.

An hour and a half later, I shut my chemistry book. Once again, Slade was in my class, and I was relieved to have a friend by my side. He'd tried to talk to me about the whole Raffe situation, but I'd shut that conversation down, not wanting to give the jackass any more of my time than I already had.

Still, the betrayal and hurt stabbed just as hard as it had when it all went down. The only solace had been my classes, which were over for the day.

I wanted to keep myself busy.

My chem lab was on Thursdays, and I was free for the rest of the day. I was restless and couldn't go into the woods. I wanted to be around animals, but I hadn't done my training class for the animal shelter yet, so I couldn't go there either.

"You have another class after this?" Slade asked as we headed out the back of Howling and toward the apartments.

"No, I'm free until tomorrow." My voice dropped, revealing exactly how I felt about that.

He smiled. "Me too, so ... while the sun is high and less ... *unusual* activity is going on, do you want to go into the woods and have your first lesson?"

I stopped in my tracks. "Now?" Excitement bubbled inside me, but I squashed it.

"Sure." He nodded back to the building we'd been in. "After this morning, it might be best if we start right away so you feel more confident and Raffe can back off."

"*That* sounds like a plan."

He clutched the straps of his backpack. "Then let's go."

I followed him a while into the woods, and I'd expected to feel uncomfortable, but with Slade knowing how the supernatural world worked, I wasn't worried at all.

We stepped into a small circular clearing ten feet in diameter. Slade leaned his backpack against a fir then took mine and placed it next to his.

We stood at the edge of the clearing, facing the other side.

"The first thing you need to learn is how to summon your magic." He closed his eyes and held out his hands. "Make it rise within you. Find where it's stored and imagine tugging it upward. Your magic is similar to that of a warlock and witch, but our magic doesn't infuse our blood. Instead, it infuses our essence, which isn't as strong, but our bodies are supernatural. That means we can endure the magical drain better. There's always a weakness for every strength a supernatural has. So call your magic and let me know when you feel it."

I snorted. He couldn't be serious about needing to yank on his magic to feel it. I closed my eyes and hoped he could help me calm the storm once it started. Then something strange happened.

CHAPTER TEN

Nothing happened.
My blood didn't jolt.

The *one* time I wanted it to thrum to life, *this* was what I got?

Nada.

Zilch.

Not even a fucking twinge.

Maybe Fate was real and laughing her ass off, the bitch.

I opened my eyes, unsure of what I'd see, but it wasn't the breeze ruffling the tree limbs like nothing strange was happening.

Seriously, what the *hell* was wrong with me?

Slade laughed, and I snapped my head in his direction.

"If looks could kill, I'd be a dead man right now." His irises twinkled with mirth.

My limbs grew heavy. Slade was *laughing* at me. That burned, especially after he'd been a decent friend to me for all of a day, but you know, that was more than I'd had before.

Now my blood jolted.

His face soured. "Wait. I didn't mean to hurt your feelings."

I placed a hand on my hip. "Oh, and you thought I'd be happy with you making fun of me?"

"No." He lifted both hands. "That wasn't what I was doing. You were being adorable, and it made me laugh."

Did he think that would make me feel better? I'd heard guys were dumb, but I hadn't expected it to be so blatant. "So you're happy that I'm struggling?" The jolt upgraded to the fizz, and for once, I wasn't stressed about letting it go. It was just us out there, and he was a warlock and understood what was happening.

"I'm sorry." He dropped his hands. "I'm not happy that you're struggling, and I'm not laughing at you. I just think you're really pretty, and I'm clearly letting it affect my judgment. I'd never want to make you feel less than worthy."

Some of my anger thawed, effectively easing my blood. "I'm just supersensitive about being laughed at and insulted, so I may have overreacted a tad." I wouldn't apologize for it. If he'd lived my life, he would understand the baggage I carried. "And I'm frustrated. I've never had issues with it before."

"I'm not surprised. Summoning your magic is different from when your magic takes control."

I rocked back on my heels and crossed my arms. "You didn't think to warn me of that?"

He shrugged and put his hands into his jeans pockets. "In my defense, we have different magic. From what I read, your magic is called similarly to coven magic. My magic isn't like that. "

"What do you mean?" I clenched my hands, my nails biting into my palms. He was sharing what he'd learned, but I wished he would've told me more this morning. He might be holding things back, and I didn't like the idea of him controlling what and when I learned things. However, I didn't want to piss him off and screw myself out of learning as much as I could, especially since he wouldn't share where the library was.

"I'm not sure yet, but yours is more about vibrations, like most coven members use, except for the small amount that use elemental magic too." He rubbed the back of his neck. "That's why I didn't say anything earlier. I don't fully know, but I do have an inkling of which *Book of Twilight* to read next. A priestess might have been in a relationship with an arcane-born."

That was interesting, especially since Slade and I were forming a bond. "What sort of relationship?"

He shrugged. "I'm not sure. Just something this priestess wrote about near the end of her book. I plan on going back to the library and reading his book tonight, but I wanted to take you out here so you could practice controlling your magic."

"I'm so sorry." I hated that I'd exposed the supernatural world the way I had. I'd promised not to the night before, and not even a full day later, I'd nearly made my desk fall apart. If the professor hadn't been a vampire, I could only imagine who would've gotten hurt trying to mitigate the damage I'd caused. A shiver ran down my spine, and my blood jolted once more.

"It's not your fault," he said, taking my hand in his and squeezing. "You have these superstrong powers, and you were raised by humans who know nothing about this world. Of course you're going to have these issues."

My eyes stung, and my vision blurred. I'd never had anyone who understood me before. And he was attractive, which would be an added bonus if I'd felt anything beyond friendship for him.

But I didn't because of an unattainable guy who was a

jackass, and who also wasn't, depending on how the stars aligned.

When Slade held my hand for a moment too long, I took a small step back, needing to break contact. It felt weird and wrong to be holding his hand. That didn't make any sense, but I couldn't shake the sensation. "How did you learn to control your magic?" I asked, hoping he wouldn't pick up on my changing the subject.

He frowned a second before forcing a smile. "Everyone has a trigger. You have to figure it out. My mom has to pull the magic from the ground."

"What?" My jaw dropped. "Witches kill nature to perform spells?"

He shook his head. "She doesn't actually pull it from the earth, but that's how her magic manifests within her. My magic is like a void in my chest that I have to yank on. The amount of magic I release depends on how hard I yank." He tapped his chest right above his heart.

Weird.

"Mine feels as if it's in my blood." I paused, searching for the words to describe it. I never had before. "There are like three phases it goes through, though sometimes it can skip a phase, depending on what's going on."

Pursing his lips, he furrowed his brows. "What do you mean?"

"I'm assuming it's equivalent to your tug, but I can't control it ... not yet." I wrung my hands. "The first phase, which I consider a warm-up, feels like there's an extra jolt running through my blood. Sorta like adrenaline, but it doesn't make my heart pound."

He tilted his head. "Interesting."

"The second phase is what I consider a fizz. It's stronger than a jolt and reminds me of pop rocks—but in my blood."

That was the best comparison I could think of. It started out with a few pops, but as the intensity increased, it was like pouring a whole damn bag into your mouth.

When disgust or confusion didn't cross his face, I continued, wanting to get this off my chest. "The last stage is when my blood hums. That's when things happen, like the desk in the room—it shook in sync with my blood. Sometimes I feel as if my body is shaking too, but it could be my imagination." I wouldn't know. I ran to get away from people, and the one time Mom had witnessed a meltdown, I'd been too afraid to ask what she'd seen. She'd left the room, and we'd never discussed what had happened. I'd been five years old, and she'd looked at me differently after that day.

"That's what it feels like, but what *triggers* it?" He steepled his fingers.

Lungs seizing, I murmured, "Emotion." Of course that was my trigger. Every time I got upset, scared, nervous, or whatever negative, intense emotion that flooded me, my blood responded. "The negative kinds, like how Raffe made me feel earlier today. I've tried breathing exercises, but I can't stop it."

"It's resistant to positive emotions?"

"I ... I think so." Now I doubted myself. Most of the emotions I felt were negative, so maybe positive emotions didn't occur often enough for me to notice their impact.

"Your magic thrives on defending you."

That was not what I would say *at all*. "More like it makes my life harder and gets me labeled a freak and weirdo. I wouldn't call that defensive."

He bobbed his head. "Fair, but what I meant is, when you feel something negative, your magic thinks you're in danger. It sparks to ward off the threat, or that's what it's intended to do. It's just not trained yet."

I liked that idea. "It did react more powerfully than ever

when that Edward guy attacked me." I understood what he was getting at, not that I fully agreed with him. If my magic was meant to defend me, it'd been doing a shit job overall. "But how does knowing that help me?"

"Think about something that upsets you, and we can take it from there."

My mouth went dry. Purposely doing it might put me more in control, but I didn't know how to channel the magic or pull it back. "I don't think we should experiment until we learn more from the priest's twilight book."

"*Book of Twilight*." He chuckled. "Not like the shimmery vampire romance that was so popular years ago. For now, let's try to get it to jolt and not go straight to fizzing or humming."

The fact that he'd used my descriptions warmed my heart. He'd truly been listening to me and not just being polite. "Okay." I rubbed my hands together, trying to think about something that would upset me just the right amount.

Raffe's face popped into my brain along with the stunt he'd pulled in statistics. My blood fizzed at the memory, taking it a little further than I'd meant to go. "I didn't mean to, but it's fizzing." I gritted my teeth, already feeling like a failure. I couldn't do one simple task, and the fizzing escalated to a near humming.

"Okay." He cleared his throat. "Now think a happy thought."

That caught me off guard. "I thought we were trying to control it."

"We are. If you can think of a happy thought and calm yourself down, you'll have a way to get it to work when you want it to and go away when you don't."

A happy thought. I didn't have many of those. I closed my eyes and imagined the deer I'd seen here in the woods. I imagined their large brown eyes staring into mine, and just like that, my blood lowered to a jolt. "It's working."

"You calmed down?" he asked hopefully.

"Not fully." I remembered how I'd put my hands on the ground and how the coolness had covered my skin. I took in a deep breath, smelling the woods around me.

After a few minutes, my blood went back to normal.

When I opened my eyes, Slade was beaming at me. "You did it, didn't you?"

I nodded. I'd never been able to control it like that without it happening on its own.

"Good." He winked. "Let's go eat. That's enough for one day until I can learn more about your magic."

My stomach gurgled. "You know what? That sounds great."

We picked up our backpacks and headed across campus to the student center. And, for once, I felt like a regular college student hanging out with a friend.

Slade got a salad with nuts and fruits—apparently, coven members shied away from meat—while I grabbed a club sandwich.

We sat in the student center in the open dining area, a space with at least one hundred tables. I'd picked the back corner, wanting to fade into the background.

When we were done eating, we stayed and did our homework and compared notes for the three classes we had together. With both of us being science majors and juniors in college, we'd have most of our classes together until we graduated.

That thought comforted me. It was nice to have a friend.

People began glancing up from their phones and looking at us. At first, I thought I was being paranoid until someone pointed at me and laughed.

Unease filtered through me, jolting my blood. "Why do people keep looking at us?"

Slade glanced up from his microbiology book and put down his highlighter. "Who? I haven't noticed anybody."

I leaned across the gold-colored table. "Uh ... almost everyone near us."

"They are?" He scanned the room.

The pale bookstore clerk strolled up to the table. He arched a brow and shook his head. "I warned you."

"What are you talking about, Dave?" Slade asked, his eyes narrowing.

"Raffe and his minions." Dave slid into the seat next to me, forcing me to scoot over. "A few people have been posting on social media about a girl Raffe said was bad news. How he's never burned someone so publicly. The latest post included a picture, so everyone knows who she is." He turned his phone around so I could see the image. It was of Slade and me sitting here.

The news had spread faster than I'd expected. I'd honestly thought Raffe was overconfident about his campuswide reach, but I'd been wrong.

My face burned, and my blood fizzed to damn near hum level. This was superbad. I had to get out of here if I wanted any chance at calming myself down. No happy thoughts Peter Pan style would help when I felt on display for everyone's dissection. "Let me out."

"What?" Dave pouted, and he leaned way too close to me, sniffing. "I just got here."

Slade knew what was going on. "Trust her, man, or there will be more negative stuff that could get out for *us*."

The way he said *us* meant supernaturals. Of course, Dave was one as well. It seemed like most of the people I'd met here weren't human.

Dave's face twisted in agony, and he groaned. "Yeah, okay. She needs to get away from me." Dave stood quickly, and I hurried out, grabbing all my books and stuffing them into my backpack.

Dave clutched his head, and Slade said, "Go. I'll meet you outside."

An eerie sensation rolled down my spine, so I didn't argue. I took my tray and headed to the door.

Giggles and snickers followed my path as everyone watched me leave in a hurry, making my blood spike.

I pictured the deer's eyes in my mind and the way the wolf I'd helped back home had trusted me when I'd released it from the hunter's trap. Those were the three most recent encounters that I hung on to, and my blood dipped back to a regular fizz as I dumped my trash beside the glass doors that led down the hall.

Adjusting my backpack straps, I turned left toward the bookstore to head out the back way. Outside, I took a left and crossed the road to the parking lot, not wanting to walk through the greenway.

"Skylar, wait up!" Slade called out.

Because it was him, I slowed down but didn't stop completely. I wanted to get back to the apartment and hide for the rest of the night.

By the time he reached my side, I was already halfway through the lot.

"I'm sorry about that." He sighed. "Not sure what was going on with Dave, but I needed to stay back to make sure he didn't follow us."

"It's not *your* fault." I huffed, hating that my emotions

hadn't leveled out. Right now, Dave was the least of my worries. "You didn't do that."

"Let me be clear—I don't like Raffe. I think he's an arrogant, entitled prick who was born with a silver spoon in his mouth."

Laughter bubbled out of me. "Don't hold back or anything."

"Eh, he's a dick." He shrugged. "And what I'm about to say goes against my very nature."

I lifted a brow. "What's that?"

"His dad is his king and alpha." Slade wrinkled his nose, again making it clear how he felt about things. "And his dad ordered him to do something to keep you away from humans. I heard what he said this morning when he was trying to explain himself to you."

"Uh. Okay?" I didn't understand his point.

"He felt he had to obey."

I understood wolf pack hierarchy. "Maybe, but he's wolf *and* human, and he should understand both sides of his being. What he did wasn't very humane, and maybe he should've challenged his dad instead of blindly obeying."

Slade faltered then quickened his pace to catch up with me. "You know, I never heard anyone put it that way."

We were coming up to the apartment, and I couldn't get inside fast enough. "Yeah, well, that's what alienating humans does to someone's perspective."

After the day I'd had, I was tired, and it was already getting close to seven o'clock. I didn't usually interact with people this much. At the building door, I forced a smile. "I'm tired. I'm going to take a shower and veg out."

"You should." He bumped his shoulder into mine and said, "I'm going to drop off my bag and head back to the library to do more research so I can help you."

"I really appreciate that." I wanted to understand how I could control this so Raffe and his dad couldn't pull anything else like they had today. "I'll see you tomorrow."

"Don't hesitate to reach out if you need anything."

I headed inside, and within minutes, I was walking through my front door.

As soon as I entered, I stopped in my tracks. Something—Fate or whatever—had to be fucking with me.

CHAPTER ELEVEN

T he one place that should've been safe had turned into anything *but*.

There on the couch across from me were Raffe, a breathtaking girl I didn't know, and Lucy. On the other couch sat Adam and Keith.

Now Lucy's comment about running in the woods made more sense, seeing as this group only hung out with their own kind.

To my dismay, my focus refused to stray from Raffe's arm, casually draped on the back of the couch around the girl next to him.

She had to be *Josie*.

Raffe and I locked gazes, and jealousy flared through me so hard it stole my breath. My blood leaped into a fizz and teetered on a hum, and something cold and ugly clenched my heart. It felt as if it couldn't beat anymore.

His irises darkened, and his guilt swirled toward me.

Keith groaned and leaned his head back. "You've got to be fucking kidding me. The human you got stuck with is *her*?"

He emanated disgust, the kind I was used to feeling from people. He'd made his feelings about me very clear.

"Wait." Lucy tilted her head, examining me. "You're the human with magic?"

Yeah, this was already going *stellar*. I could feel the million questions she'd ask when we were alone.

The other girl tossed a lock of her dark, long, wavy hair over her shoulder and turned to Raffe. Something I couldn't name poured from her as she pursed her pouty lips and sighed. "When people learn she's rooming with your *cousin,* it'll make your public display this morning harder to believe."

Tearing his gaze from mine, Raffe focused on her. "Josie, you act like I knew about this. I knew Lucy was rooming with a human, but I didn't realize it was Skylar. We need to switch Lucy to another apartment."

Lucy's mouth dropped. "Excuse me, why am *I* the one who has to move?"

Out of *everyone* on campus, I'd been assigned to room with Raffe's cousin? I'd always had bad luck, but *this* seemed like some sort of demented karma. I was certain I'd never screwed anyone over even close to this. I might have exposed some kids' secrets by accident when I was younger, thinking I was helping them work through things, but I'd never purposely done anything mean. Nothing worthy of experiencing my own personal hell.

If Raffe and Josie were hanging out here, I'd be more than happy to go. "If you find somewhere else for me to sleep, I don't mind moving."

"Lafayette should be able to fix this." Adam lifted a hand. "One of them just needs to call him."

Scoffing, Lucy shook her head. "I already did. This is the first semester where there isn't any flexibility. Every person has a roommate, and no one else has called in yet requesting a switch."

"What about the residence hall?" Keith leaned forward. "I'm sure something could happen there."

I'd live there just to get out of here even though the thought of sharing a single room with someone and a bathroom with an entire floor had sweat pooling under my arms. If my magic got volatile and I needed to be alone to calm myself, I wouldn't be able to get away from prying eyes.

I closed my eyes and wrapped my arms around my waist to dampen the fizz. The vibration that occurred just before a hum was in my blood.

"It's the same problem with the residence hall." Lucy ran her hands through her hair. "But he's supposed to let me know when something opens. We can figure it out then."

I thought of the deer and locked onto that image to calm myself. Noises became muffled. Something creaked, maybe someone rising from the couch, but I didn't dare open my eyes. I was only just getting myself under control.

"It's a temporary problem. Better than a long-term one." That was Adam.

"That's a horrible idea," Raffe said, his voice closer to me than I'd expected. His scent filled my nose, and I opened my eyes as he placed his hands on my shoulders. His mouth pressed into a line, and his forehead creased with worry. "This is why Skylar can't room with another supernatural or human under any circumstances. She's struggling to control her magic."

The buzz that had happened earlier when I'd touched his arm vibrated through the sleeves of my sweater. It wasn't as intense, but it was enough to ease the intensity in my blood. The fizzing ebbed to a mere jolt.

Had his touch made that big of a difference? What did

that mean? Trying to regain some sense of control and balance, I straightened my shoulders. It was easier to get myself under control with Raffe next to me and away from Josie. How pathetic was *that*? "It shouldn't be a problem much longer."

He arched a brow. "What do you mean?"

"Slade helped me determine the trigger, and I now understand that the way I was trying to control it wasn't the answer." In fact, deep breathing and other things people advised me to try had made my anxiety run rampant. "But it's not coming naturally to me yet, so I need to keep practicing."

Raffe's jaw twitched. "Isn't that *nice*?"

"Maybe she should room with a witch," Adam interjected. "If Slade can help her, maybe a witch could—"

Raffe spun around and growled, "Absolutely not. Until we know more about what she is and what's going on, we keep her close. Maybe Lucy rooming with her is a good thing."

Once again, he seemed to have a split personality. "You just said that Lucy should move." I almost felt like he was playing head games with me, saying one thing and then contradicting it. Being nice one second and then blasting me in front of everyone because his daddy told him to.

"Yeah, I'm with her." Josie crossed her arms, an eyebrow arched. "What's going on with you? You normally don't change your mind within five minutes."

Raffe's shoulders slumped, and his brow furrowed. "You're right. At first, I agreed with you. I thought people might question why my own cousin was rooming with someone I said was trouble. Dad doesn't want it known publicly that she's someone of interest until we know more about her. We thought a public display of rejection would persuade the humans to stay away."

Hot anger swirled through me, and my blood fizzed again.

"You and your dad are just going to isolate me and watch me like I'm an experiment to see what I'm capable of?" No wonder Slade had told me not to trust anyone with this information. If they learned I had ancient, rare abilities, what would they do to me?

Blowing out a breath, Raffe lifted his hands. "No. You aren't an experiment, but we aren't sure how to proceed. You aren't a supernatural, but you aren't fully human either, so we don't know what laws and restrictions should be in place for you. Until we can determine all that, we need to limit who's around you."

In other words, I was a prisoner. *Fuck that.* "I came here to go to school. I can't not go to classes." My blood hummed, and the wooden coffee table shook like the desk had earlier.

"What the—" Josie's hazel eyes widened, and fear seeped from her, adding to my heightened emotions.

"That's not what I meant." Raffe's voice was calm. "You'll attend classes, but I'd rather you hang out with people who *know* about your abilities as much as possible."

If he thought that would calm me, he'd learn otherwise. He and his father thought they could control my life, and that was *not* okay with me.

Yet my body still wanted to be by his side, the attraction strong.

"Maybe we should lock her up." Keith snorted. "That's the second time she's lost control today. We should put a warning sticker on her."

His mockery hit right where it hurt. My emotions roared, and the table splintered, each piece continuing to shake.

"Dammit," Raffe snarled. "Adam, if he opens his mouth again, knock his ass out."

Knowing I was on the brink of making something worse happen, I closed my eyes and forced the deer to the forefront of my mind. I wrung my hands, pretending I was sinking them into the mulchy forest floor as the deer and I stared at one another.

"You know what?" Lucy said, and someone stood from their seat. "There's another way to resolve this. All of you, *out*."

I could get behind that.

The table settled slightly, and Lucy said, "See? *You* are the reason she's upset, so leave. I've decided I don't care what Raffe says. I don't want a new roommate even after everything is settled."

I could feel her concern and determination, and I opened my eyes to find her staring at me with a warm smile.

In the corner of my vision, Raffe flinched, but his face smoothed into a mask of indifference. If I hadn't known better, I would've thought I'd imagined the expression.

"That's good with me." Keith stood and gestured at Josie and Adam. "I'm starving."

"You three are *always* hungry." Josie chuckled and rolled her eyes. "It's bad enough that you're wolf shifters—add in all the exercise from football and you guys want to eat all the damn time."

"Sometimes, I wake up at night just to eat." Keith rubbed his stomach. "It's a perk of being who we are."

Now that some of the negativity had eased, my emotions dropped back to a high fizz. I'd have to be careful until Raffe, Josie, and Keith got out of here. The two people who weren't near-constant triggers were Adam and Lucy.

"He's not even lying." Adam hung his head. "One time, I got up and found him standing naked in front of the refrigerator door. Sometimes, I wish a vampire could alter my memories because that one is at the top of my list to forget."

I swallowed my laughter, not wanting to set Keith off. I

imagined that had been an unpleasant experience for Adam. Though Keith was attractive, I didn't like him at all as a person.

"Oh my gods," Josie groaned as she strolled toward me. "Why in the world did you put that image in my mind? That's disturbing."

"Don't knock it until you try it." Keith puffed out his chest.

I waited for Raffe to react, but he didn't. In fact, he kept glancing my way every few seconds.

Keith and Adam walked past me without acknowledging me, but Josie stopped in front of me.

She licked her lips. "I know we had a rocky start, but I hope we can get past that since you live with my best friend."

Any hope that this altercation would prevent her from coming over vanished. As long as I lived with Lucy, I was stuck being around Josie and Raffe. I nodded. "Sorry for breaking the table."

She snorted. "Not my table, so no wood off my back." She glanced at Raffe and arched a brow. "You ready?"

"I'll meet you at the student center in a minute," he said, authority lacing his voice.

"Yeah, see you there. I'll be in the bookstore to check something out while I wait for you." She marched out the door without giving him a kiss or hug.

Weird.

With the three of them gone, my blood settled into a low fizz, just enough to keep me uncomfortable. I was exhausted, especially after breaking the coffee table.

Lucy crossed her arms and glared at Raffe. "What do you want?"

"A chance to talk to Skylar alone."

"I don't know—" she started.

"It wasn't a request." His eyes glowed. "Go with the others to the student center, and I'll meet you in a few minutes."

She scowled and looked at me. "I'm sorry." Then she left Raffe and me alone.

The room closed in on me, and my mouth went dry. I didn't know what he wanted, but my hormones were going wild while my brain screamed a loud warning.

As soon as the door shut, his face twisted in apology. "Look, I'm sorry. I didn't mean to make it sound like you're a prisoner. It's just ... we're worried you could expose the supernatural world."

I placed my hands on my hips, needing to do something with them so I didn't reach for him. The soft look on his face had my resolve crumbling, and the *yank* in my chest made me want to close the distance between us. "Maybe you didn't mean to, but you did." I had to stand my ground and not be a pushover. I'd been one my entire life, and it had to end sometime. Right? "I'm not trying to cause problems. I just want to find somewhere to belong. I've never had that before, and even *here*, among supernaturals and humans, I still don't belong. You alienating me like that earlier made things harder on me."

He rubbed his temples. "I was a jackass, and I'm sorry. I saw an opportunity and took it."

"If Slade doesn't mind training me on how to control my magic, then I'm doing it." I lifted my chin, drawing my first boundary ever. "I think he can help me, given the chance."

"Be careful with him." He scowled. "He's not known for his generous nature."

I snorted. "He's been nice, trying to help me, and he hasn't publicly embarrassed me. So..."

Raffe hung his head. "Fair, but I *have* saved you. That counts for something." He smiled, now overly bright.

My stupid heart fluttered. When he was like this, it was hard to remember he was a jackass. "Why do you act so differently when we're alone?" The question came out before I could stop it.

His smile fell, and I swore his irises darkened with regret. We stared at one another, each searching for something in the other.

"It's best if we keep our distance." His voice was deep and raspy. "For both our sakes. I don't want to keep upsetting you."

I almost wished my magic was fritzing so I could read his emotions. He looked so conflicted, but knowing better than to ask why, I nodded. "That would be for the best." The words might as well have been a knife to the chest.

"Okay." He huffed and took a step toward the door. He grimaced as if in pain. "But the offer always stands, Skylar. If you need me, you've got my number. And I'll stop being a jerk to you in public."

At least there was that.

"I'll have Lucy bring you back something to eat." He opened the door. "See you around."

He shut the door, and a piece of my heart walked out with him.

A LITTLE OVER two weeks later, I hadn't gotten very far with training. I could get my blood swirling, but the little bit of control I'd gotten that first time had vanished, and I couldn't get the power to dissipate.

Slade and I spent almost every day together. He was still

searching for more information about my heritage—apparently, the priestess's book hadn't been fruitful.

At night, Lucy and I would watch a few episodes of *Criminal Minds* before we retired to bed. We were forming a friendship in our own right, though it was a slow process.

On Saturday, I got a call from the animal shelter. They had a volunteer class scheduled for the following Saturday morning that I could take. Having that to look forward to was the only thing that got me rolling out of bed this early Tuesday morning as I dreaded seeing Raffe in class.

True to his word, we hadn't spoken since that night, but even without speaking to him for over two weeks, I felt the same damn pull, my body begging me to eliminate any distance between us. At least Slade was in the class I had with Raffe. That was a blessing, especially since it was the one Raffe had embarrassed me in.

"Earth to Skylar," Slade said from my side.

The two of us were heading into Evergreen after having a quick biscuit and grabbing a latte, but my stomach gurgled more with each step I took closer to Raffe.

"Sorry, I was lost in thought." He'd helped me so much that I should have been hanging on to his every word, but I couldn't get Raffe off my mind. "What's up?"

"I asked if you wanted to go to the football game with me and a few other *people* Saturday night." He waggled his brows. "You know, my friends who you haven't wanted to meet yet. You came all this way—at least, get a proper student experience."

He was right. If we weren't in the woods practicing magic, I was holed up in my room, apart from very short trips to the student center to eat. But Raffe had asked me to hang out only with people I knew, and I'd been trying to respect that. "Raffe said—"

"Fuck him." Slade rolled his eyes. "Too many people hang on his every word. Besides, he hasn't spoken to you in weeks. I'll be there to make sure nothing happens, and if it does, we leave. It's that simple."

The idea of going somewhere with a friend and having a normal experience like a football game did sound exciting. I'd never done anything like that before, and I trusted Slade. "Okay. I'm in."

"Great." He beamed as we breezed into the room.

The nape of my neck prickled, indicating that Raffe's gaze was on me. Our eyes connected as Slade said, "I can pick you up at six, and we can grab dinner first."

Turning my head toward Slade was physically painful. My eyes wanted to stay locked on Raffe, but I forced a smile and said, "Great."

A few seconds after we slipped into our seats, Professor Haynes strutted in.

She held a stack of papers in her hands and began passing them out. "I mentioned there would be a few projects throughout the semester, and this is the first. I'm handing out the assignment along with your assigned partner."

My throat constricted. I'd hoped that we could pick our partners so Slade and I could work together. He was the only person I was comfortable with, especially in this class.

When the piece of paper landed on my desk, I flipped to the second page, found my assigned partner ... and laughed.

CHAPTER TWELVE

I f this wasn't proof that someone or something hated me high up in the universe, I didn't know what else could be.

Written there in a neat font was the last person I'd ever want to be paired with.

Raffe Wright.

My pulse quickened, and the tugging in my chest purred, trying to rear its ugly head. I refused to acknowledge that it was calling me a big, fat liar.

Slade's head jerked back. "This has to be a joke."

He pushed his paper toward me, and I read the name on his. *Keith Barron.*

Okay, I stood corrected. Maybe, just maybe, Slade had me beat in the bad karma department. At least Raffe could be civil, unlike Keith. Keith was nice to his people, but he spouted off shit to anyone outside of his group.

As the professor walked back past my desk after handing the wolf crew their papers, Keith asked, "Can we switch partners?"

"Absolutely not." She shook her head, back turned to them, but the corners of her lips tilted upward. "I was given instructions to assign pairs this term, and I handled it as best I could, given certain circumstances in this class." She schooled her expression and turned to address Keith and the others. "This is your assignment. Accept it, move on, and learn how to work with one another."

Slade and I being paired with Keith and Raffe was less than ideal, but I found some enjoyment in the fact that they weren't getting their way. I'd seen how everyone moved and navigated around Raffe and his closest friends, even Lucy. People treated them like royalty, including humans who didn't know that was actually the case.

Still, just because Raffe and I were partners didn't mean we had to physically work together. We could split up the assignment and email portions to each other without having to meet. At least that was my goal.

I flipped back to the first page and snorted.

Our project was titled, *How Does Sitting in the Front of the Classroom Affect Grades?* To make this work, we would have to do a lot of polling around campus and hope people were honest about their grades, which meant I would be required to talk to a lot more people. Unless Raffe decided he would handle all of it, which was likely. Either way, we wouldn't have to work together much and could break up sections of our report for each of us to write.

Professor Haynes began class, launching into specifics of the assignment. Raffe and I would have to give a presentation together, which would require us to work together. Some of my concern flared back, and my blood jolted.

I closed my eyes and placed my palms down on my desk. I imagined the coolness was from the earth and, for the first time in weeks, the technique worked. I exhaled a shaky breath, thankful that another disaster hadn't struck.

Then I pushed the assignment out of my mind and focused on class.

Later that day, after chemistry, Slade and I strolled toward the student center. After the disastrous assignment in statistics, I'd managed to get out of class without Raffe talking to me. Most likely, he didn't have any desire to speak to me. We'd gone two weeks without acknowledging each other, and I'd seen him several times around campus with Josie.

Last week, Lucy had asked if I was attending the football game, and as soon as I'd said no, she'd seemed relieved. There was no question why. Her king and her cousin both preferred that I not hang out with humans even though I had plans to do just that at this Saturday's game.

"This project is going to suck." Slade leaned his head back. "Out of all the people in the world I could get stuck with, it'd be the sociopath."

I snorted. "Keith may say uncouth things and appear to lack remorse, but he isn't like that with everyone, so I don't think that term really applies to him—but he's judgmental and abrasive."

"And you're defending him?" Slade arched a brow, a grin slipping through his mask.

"Hell no." I lifted a hand. "But we're science majors, so we should make sure we get terms right. I can't have you tainting my degree and all."

"Skylar, we're science majors, not psychologists." He patted his chest. "I get a pass."

I booped him on the nose and scrunched my face. "Nope, you're with me. That means the bar is set way higher." I almost choked, realizing how those words could be taken. I opened my mouth to clarify what I'd meant, but before I could mitigate the damage, Keith cooed from behind us, "Aww."

I tensed, hoping he was talking about someone else and not adding to my faux pas, but then the nape of my neck sizzled. I hated that I knew Raffe was there and his attention was on me. It made my stomach feel funny and quickened my breathing.

"It looks like Slade finally found a girlfriend," Keith continued. "I never thought he'd find someone he enjoyed spending time with as much as himself."

A lump lodged in my throat, and I couldn't swallow.

A group of guys walking by snickered, reminding me we had an audience. I glanced around, noting that the grassy area between classes was filled with students heading to and from class.

"Don't be a douchebag," Slade muttered as he turned in their direction. "You three made it clear that you didn't want to hang out with Skylar, but that doesn't mean no one else does. She's cool, and you're the ones missing out on getting to know her. Now, you better run along before someone thinks you're talking to us. They might get the wrong idea."

I mashed my lips together to keep from smiling. I loved how he didn't give a shit about these three. He was one of the few who always stood strong in front of them. The smart version of me would have kept my back to them, but that damn yank tugged me around, and my eyes immediately found Raffe's.

His nostrils were flared, and his hands were clenched tightly into fists. He stood between Adam and Keith, rage rolling off him. I could sense it without my blood humming.

Something had pissed him off, likely Slade, and worse, a part of me was thrilled that he was fuming. My attraction was taking on a life I hadn't experienced before. If we'd been alone, I'd have been rubbing my body all over him.

"Leave them alone." Adam pinched the bridge of his nose. "Do you want something to happen?" He gestured at me, referencing my wonky blood and not Slade's mouth.

I huffed, the insinuation hurting, though I hadn't been able to control the magic until earlier today. I had to believe that was progress. "Come on, Slade." I wouldn't stand here while they ridiculed me. I'd done that enough my whole life.

"Yeah, run off like a scared—" Keith started, but a deep rasp cut him off.

"Don't finish that sentence. It's in your best interest to shut up," Raffe said.

"What the *hell*, man?" Keith jerked back and crossed his arms.

With Raffe's angry gaze on Keith, I placed my hand on Slade's forearm. I nudged him and whispered, "Let's go."

As soon as my hand touched Slade, Raffe's gaze homed in. His breathing sped up, and he took a hurried step toward Slade.

My ears rang as the *yank* between us intensified.

"You're right." Slade wrinkled his nose. "Raffe needs to get a handle on his guard dog."

He took my hand in his and started to lead me away. The way our hands molded together didn't feel right. In fact, it felt as if I was doing something wrong.

"That's not who I need to get a handle on," Raffe damn near growled, and my head snapped back toward him.

Guilt crashed over me, suffocating me, and I released Slade's hand. The moment I stopped touching Slade, Raffe's body relaxed marginally.

The damage was done. Adam pressed a hand to Raffe's chest, holding him back and stepping between Raffe and me.

Slade grabbed my wrist and pulled on me harder. Finally, my feet moved as if whatever trance I'd been in had eased enough for me to move away from Raffe. My heart pounded, and my blood fizzed.

I'd been so caught up in Raffe, his anger, and my insanely wild attraction that I hadn't been aware of how close I'd been to combusting. Adjusting my backpack, I moved quicker, not needing to be dragged anymore, and Slade released his grasp on me.

Every cell in my body wanted me to look over my shoulder, but I fought the instinct. If I glanced back, chances were good that I would try to head back to him. I had to move forward in all ways and stop pining for a guy who was with another girl.

"You four don't get along." I shook my head, trying to say something, anything, to keep me from spinning and making more of an ass of myself.

"Uh ... yeah, but Raffe has never acted like *that*." Slade bit his bottom lip. "Normally, he would've stepped in like Adam to shut Keith up, but I wasn't sure who Raffe was more upset with, Keith or me."

I'd noticed that too, though for the last little bit, I'd been convinced he was going to kick Slade's ass. "But it was weird. They all stopped talking despite Adam blocking Raffe." The back of my neck tingled again, and I took another step away from Slade. I didn't understand why, but the urge was so strong I couldn't fight it.

"They were using their link to communicate."

We reached the back door to the student center, and I eagerly rushed through it. As soon as it closed, the tingling on the back of my neck stopped, and my heartbeat settled, allowing the fizz to downgrade to a jolt. Wanting to learn more about wolf shifters, I focused on that. "Link?"

"Let's grab some food, and I'll explain it to you." He gestured to the people walking past us.

I nodded, and we hurried into the cafeteria. It was loud and busy, so I went to the right side, settling on a slice of premade pizza to get out of the chaos.

After applying the food to my account, I found our usual table vacant in the back corner and eagerly took the spot. Even on a busy day, no one ever sat in this booth. I felt a slight vibration coming off it.

Strange.

I was opening my Dr Pepper when Slade arrived and slid in across from me.

"Did you do something to this table?" Between it always being open and the slight vibration, I figured it was spelled. "To prevent others from sitting here?"

He beamed and flipped his wrist, increasing the vibration.

"You did." I smiled. "Why didn't you tell me?"

"I wanted to see how long it took you to figure out." He leaned forward and winked. "But you can feel it. That's great. You're learning to sense other magic."

My chest puffed out, and I didn't even feel embarrassed. After failing almost every day for the last two weeks, I was ecstatic that I'd done *something* positive. "What spell did you do?" I wanted to know desperately.

"Nothing major. Just an aversion spell." He shrugged and snatched his fork then started stabbing at his salad. "I like this spot, and you seem comfortable here."

And Raffe and Keith had made it sound as if he wasn't a good guy. Everything he'd done for me proved the opposite of that. I took a bite of my pepperoni and sausage pizza, reveling in the moment. I had a real friend, and I enjoyed it.

"What?" He put his fork down and arched a brow.

I placed my pizza on the plate. "I didn't say anything."

"But you're over there smiling while you eat." Slade leaned back in his seat. "What gives?"

He was right. I was smiling. I probably looked like a weirdo, but I felt content. "Just nice, us being friends."

"Friends?" His smile dropped. "That's it?" His attention dropped to the table.

My stomach dropped too. Shit. This wasn't good. I'd hoped that the awkwardness between us on our way here was gone, but now he was asking about our relationship status. A year ago, I would've *loved* this conversation. It had seemed like a pipe dream. But now that it was happening, I'd give anything to skip it.

The best thing I could do was be honest with him. Leading him on would only make me a complete asshole. "Slade, you're a great guy."

He groaned, his head leaning back. "That is not a good sign."

"What?" I hated that he'd called me out, but dammit, I didn't want to move on without explaining the real issue. "You have no clue what I'm going to say."

"Oh, I do." He placed his hands on either side of his golden tray. "This is what my mom calls a bad-news sandwich. It's when you want to let someone down softly while maintaining a relationship with the person you're letting down. You start with something nice, then reveal the bad part, then end with something nice to ease the negative news you sandwiched in the middle."

I'd never heard that before. Worse, that was exactly what I'd been doing. "Okay, fine." If he wanted direct, I'd give it to him. "I don't want to ruin our friendship." I left out the part about me being borderline obsessed with a sexy, mysterious wolf-human prince. That would only upset Slade and had no redeeming explanation because it would imply I liked the star quarterback even though he ignored me and hurt me every chance he got unless we were alone.

"Who said it would?" Slade leaned forward. "There's a reason Keith is giving me hell. I rarely give girls much attention and definitely not the amount I've been giving you. I obviously think we have something special."

He wasn't making this easy on me, but I couldn't budge. I didn't want to lose him. "You may be right, but Slade, you're the first friend I've ever had. I don't want to risk losing you. You mean too damn much to me." I feared this might push him into walking away from me, but if he did, I'd know his interest in me had been shallow.

"You're right." He ran a hand through his hair. "You've told me about the shit you've gone through, so I understand why you feel that way. Don't worry." He winked. "You just need more time to see how good things could be between us."

That was definitely *not* how I wanted him to react. He was still hopeful we would wind up together, and I was afraid to push it. At least he was giving me space, and I *didn't* want to lose him. I decided to change the subject and focus on my burning questions about what a pack link was.

I could figure the rest out later, but right now, I had to make sure I didn't lose a friend.

SLADE and I had been practicing for hours, and sweat coated my body. The sun was setting, and my blood hummed within me.

"Focus on calming down," Slade murmured, barely loud enough for me to hear. "You've been doing it for the last hour."

My body sagged with fatigue, but with the pride and awe

rolling off Slade, I couldn't quit. I didn't want to disappoint him, so I pulled up the image that actually quieted the power that hummed through me.

It wasn't the deer or mulch that did the trick.

It was something wrong. Something I shouldn't even think about.

When I felt close to imploding, only one image calmed me.

Raffe.

Unlike the deer and the mulch, I could summon his image immediately, and when I remembered the way my skin tingled from his touch, the humming faded away.

"You did it *again*!" Slade lifted a fist. "I think you got it, Skylar."

At least, he hadn't said *finally*. I would've deserved it. "I hate to do this, but I need to head back to my apartment. I'm worn out." My legs felt weighed down, and I even struggled to breathe. Just like the night of the vampire attack, I felt like I might pass out from exhaustion.

"Are you sure you can't go another round?" Slade pouted. "I thought we could get you to channel your magic into something again ... like a rock, tree, specific branch, anything you choose."

I swayed on my feet. "I'm sorry. I can't. I'm not feeling well."

He sighed. "Okay, let's get you home."

I could hear the disappointment in his voice, and it gutted me, but I was too exhausted to continue.

We headed back, and I gritted my teeth, putting one foot in front of the other. A few times, I truly thought I'd topple over.

"Shit, Sky," Slade said and slid his arm around my waist. "I didn't realize you were so far gone."

Honestly, I'd been struggling for the past hour, but I was more exhausted than even I had realized. Adrenaline must have kept me going longer than I should have. "I'll be fine," I mumbled, the words barely coherent.

"You don't sound like it."

We continued our trek, my body weight mostly on him. I could barely stay upright, that was how far gone I was.

At the apartment building entrance, I steadied myself to go inside. The last thing I needed was for him to come to my room and have him and Lucy get into it. When Slade had learned who my roommate was, he had manifested a look of pure disgust.

A group of girls watched us with unabashed interest. They could tell something was wrong with me. When Slade opened the front door, he moved to help me again, but I shook my head and almost toppled over.

I didn't want to get a worse reputation or be run through the gossip mill more than I already had been. "I've got it."

"But—" Slade said, but I pushed off him. My legs shook like noodles, but I stayed upright.

"See you in the morning." I took slow, steady steps into the building. I didn't want him to argue. I didn't have the energy to spare.

I shuffled inside and heard someone ask, "What is wrong with her?" right before the door closed.

Lovely. I hoped he would make up a reasonable excuse.

Luckily, no one was around as I stumbled into the elevator. I leaned against the car wall and used it to support myself then pulled up my last text, which was from Lucy. She'd asked when I was getting home. I hoped like hell she was there and sent two simple words: *Help. Elevator.* Or I hoped that was what it said. The words were blurry.

Time ticked by, oh so slowly, as I rode up. I leaned my

head against the wall, and the world spun around me. I'd done too much. I felt too sick. Just like the night before.

When the door opened, I tried to get out, but the floor vanished under my feet as I fell forward.

Something was wrong. A shiver ran through me a moment before something caught me.

CHAPTER THIRTEEN

Ginormous arms scooped me up and cradled me against a freaking brick wall with the sandalwood-amber scent and the faint buzz where my skin touched my savior's soothing me.

Red flags flew everywhere in my mind, but my body wasn't listening. I *melted* into *his* embrace.

Raffe.

He always seemed to be near when I needed him most. A troubling fact that only strengthened my feelings toward him. Deep inside him, there was a nice, caring guy even if he was good at hiding it.

The world spun as he marched down the hallway, and even though my eyes were closed, I could feel the anger coiled in his body. He was *pissed*.

Buttons to our apartment lock beeped as he entered the code to get inside.

I groaned. I hated that he knew the code, but I couldn't fault Lucy for sharing it with him. He was her cousin.

At the noise, his breathing quickened. My head moved

with each ragged breath, helping me stay awake. Inside the apartment, he marched straight for the couch.

The door shut behind us, and I took a deep breath, wanting to hold his scent inside me a little longer after he deposited me on the couch. But I didn't feel cloth underneath me. Instead, Raffe sat down, still holding me in his arms.

My eyes fluttered open. His face was right over mine, and his gaze was examining me all over.

He grumbled, and his ice-blue eyes glowed, making him more breathtaking. I blinked a few times, wondering if this was a dream. But if it was a dream, I'd rather he not be scowling at me.

"Are you gonna answer me?" he rasped, his eyes brightening.

I blinked. "Whuh?" My eyelids grew heavier, and it was a struggle to keep them open.

"What did he do to you?" Raffe gritted out, his nostrils flaring.

"Nuttin'," I slurred. No matter how hard I tried, I couldn't stay awake. "Halp." Between my fatigue and being in his arms, I fell fast asleep, warm and safe, feeling like I'd finally come home.

"You ready to go?" Lucy asked from a few feet away.

Go? Where? I didn't have a clue what she was talking about. I tried to pry my eyelids open, but before I could do anything to respond to her, Raffe said, "I'm not going. I'm staying here."

Raffe. What was he doing here? Then my memories came crashing back. He'd seen me exhausted again, and he knew I'd been drained. He'd come to the elevator, instead of Lucy, to help me into the apartment.

Silence stretched between us, but after what Slade had said, that didn't mean they weren't communicating.

After a sigh, Lucy murmured, "I sure hope you know what you're doing." Then a door shut.

He scoffed. "So do I."

I turned my head toward him ... and a soft pillow touched the side of my face.

A sour taste filled my mouth, and my eyes fluttered open.

My purple butterfly mobile hung right over my head. I was in my room.

The bed dipped beside me, and the *yank* happened. I turned my head and locked eyes with Raffe. He lay on his side, facing me with his hair messier than normal, his expression strained. The worry in his irises had weird sensations flipping through me.

I expected him to inundate me with questions, but he remained stoic. The only sounds I could hear were the pounding of my heart and his steady breaths.

My eyelids were still heavy, but not like before. His nearness had awakened something strange inside me. I cleared my throat. "Thank you."

He lifted a brow. "For?"

"Helping me," I said slowly to make sure my fatigue didn't slip through. He'd been angry earlier, and I didn't want to reignite that. "I expected Lucy to come, not you." I was still confused about why he'd been there, but I could ask Lucy about it later, after I got more rest.

"Then you should try texting *her* next time." The corners of his eyes wrinkled, and his scowl deepened.

Shock kick-started my brain. "Wait. I texted you? I thought—"

"Here I thought you were actually taking me up on my offer to help you." He laughed bitterly. "I should've known."

Maybe I was super exhausted to the point of misreading signals, but it sounded very much like I had hurt his feelings. My chest constricted. I hated that I'd made him feel that way. "She texted me earlier, and I just replied to my last text because my vision was blurry and I couldn't see straight." Leaving out that last part probably would've been better.

As expected, his jaw clenched. "I texted you about thirty minutes before your message, so you messaged me instead of her. And what the *fuck* did Slade do to you to get you in this condition? I swear, I'm going to kill him."

"No one saw anything." That must be why he was this upset. "He put a perimeter spell around us and set some aversion spells between the campus and where we practice. You don't have to worry about exposure."

A vein bulged between his brows, somehow making him more attractive. "That's *not* what I'm upset about, Skylar. Look at you. It can't be healthy to wear yourself down like this. He has to stop pushing you."

I was equal parts livid and flattered. The two emotions collided like hot and cold, but unlike ice cream and hot cake, this wasn't pleasant. "*I* do what I want. You don't get to blame him for this."

"He didn't pressure you to keep practicing today?" He cocked his head, waiting for my answer.

The bastard. I hated to make his point for him, so I straightened my shoulders, which wasn't very effective since I lay in bed, but beggars couldn't be choosers. "Nope. It was *all* me."

He grimaced. "Oh my gods." He waved a hand in front of his nose.

I froze. I hadn't farted, right? Surely I'd know if I had.

"That was a stinker." His eyes watered.

That was it. I needed to die. Forever. He would never let me live this down, and if he told Keith ... my blood fizzed. "I swear, it wasn't me. It must have been you."

Now I was wide awake from shame. I sniffed, trying to smell the offending odor, but I didn't smell anything other than his alluring scent.

My face flamed.

It *had* been me. I was immune to my own stench.

"What?" His forehead wrinkled, and he burst out laughing. "No, you didn't fart. Is that why you turned bright red?"

My body sagged against the bed. "It *was* you. Thank God."

"No, it was definitely you." He smiled dazzlingly. The indifferent man I knew slipped away into someone who had my heart sputtering.

In that moment, he was being genuine, and the happiness he radiated made me feel almost whole. With my blood fizzing like it was, I could sense his emotions, and they were different from the times I'd sensed them before.

I shook my head. "Not buying it. You just told me I didn't fart."

He rolled his eyes, but the grin didn't disappear. "When people lie, it smells like sulfur."

I sat up so fast that the world spun, but all I could focus on were his words. "No *way*. I've never smelled anything like that before, and I've known when people were lying."

"Humans and coven members can't smell lies." He tapped his nose and winked. "But shifters and vampires can." His expression dropped. "So I know Slade pressured you to continue whatever it was the two of you were doing."

Shit. That had gone sideways. "I'm my own person, Raffe." I placed my hands on the mattress to steady myself.

Sitting up had been a mistake, but I wasn't willing to admit it. "Unlike you and your crew, Slade didn't bend my will to his."

His head jerked back. "What is that supposed to mean?"

I guess we were having this conversation. Fine with me. It was overdue, if pointless. Like a warning shot before a war started, it wouldn't change a damn thing. "You know what I mean. You're not stupid. Your group—especially you and Keith—bark and expect everyone to roll over and show their belly."

He smirked, catching me off guard. "Really, Sky? Dog jokes?" He shook his head. "I thought you'd be more original. You don't think shifters hear that all the fucking time?"

Those weird somersaults returned at his use of my nickname. "Not really." I bobbed my head, which was a huge mistake because the room spun faster. Acid inched up my throat, burning. "With you all being wolf humans, animal behavior plays a big part in your roles. Wolves submit the same way dogs do, so I'm not making dog jokes. Besides, dogs and wolves are a ninety-nine point nine percent DNA match, so you're definitely relatives." Being with Raffe and talking about my passion—animals—had returned my blood to normal.

It was his turn to blink. "I'm not comfortable with the turn this conversation took, and I think I might want to erase it from my mind. Please tell me that ninety-nine point nine percent DNA match was you talking out of your ass like Keith does."

I giggle-snorted because, you know, snorting wasn't embarrassing enough. "Nope. I'm pre-vet, and that's a fact. But I'm sure your DNA isn't *that* close a match, with your human side and all."

"First off, it's wolf shifter." His shoulders shook. "Second, let's get back on topic. You're making it really hard to stay mad at you, which is unusual for me."

A shiver shot through me. Even if it wasn't the same sort of effect he had on me, at least I'd challenged him. "Look, I'm not trying to be rude or mean, but what I'm saying is true. You have a wolf pack hierarchy, and you, as the prince and all, are at the top. If Adam and Keith are the ones you lean on, that means they're strong too. You expect everyone to fall in line. That's not how I work, nor do I want to. I've met enough bullies in my lifetime."

"Everything I'm doing is to protect you." Raffe stood and turned to me. "Don't you see that? Yet you're determined to get yourself into trouble."

"You're protecting me by trying to control me and my blood issues?" I understood others called what I had magic, but that didn't feel right to me. The power felt like a lifeline, just like the blood running through my body. "Slade is helping me so I don't lose control in front of humans. You should *support* that." That was the part I didn't get. Raffe didn't want me to risk being around humans, but he didn't want me to learn how to control the ancient power flowing through me.

He placed a hand on his chest. "I do support that, but you don't need *him* to help you."

"Maybe not." I shrugged. Now that I'd had some guidance from Slade, maybe I could figure things out on my own. He hadn't found any more information, so it wasn't like he had inside knowledge of how my power worked. "But I do need a friend, and with your little temper tantrum about not being associated with me, Lucy and I can't hang out, and none of the other supernaturals will approach me. So maybe I don't *need* him to help me, but I *want* him to as a *friend*."

Raffe rubbed the back of his neck. "Is that all you two are? Friends?" His bicep bulged with each stroke of his hand, and the muscles in his jaw twitched. He bit his bottom lip, and the show of insecurity made my mouth go dry.

The yanking between us strengthened more than ever before. The only reason I remained sitting on my bed instead of crawling to him was, if I moved too much, I'd get dizzy.

For some reason, he seemed invested in my answer. I could've just said yes, but my relationship status shouldn't matter to him. "Why do you care?" He had Josie. I needed to know if what I felt was one-sided. Needed it confirmed so I could take the rejection and move on.

His hands fell to his sides, and he sat back down on the bed. He'd moved closer to me, and our faces were a foot apart.

"I shouldn't care." His focus settled on my lips. "But seeing you and Slade together like that earlier ... it tore me apart."

Without thinking, I licked my lips. His minty breath hit my face, and I had to fight to keep myself from leaning toward him and pressing my mouth to his.

I needed to keep a clear head. If I already felt this strong of a connection with him, I didn't need to add a kiss to the mess. That could ruin me.

Still, he had someone, and I refused to reassure him about Slade when Raffe and I meant nothing to one another. "What are you saying? You told everyone you didn't want to be around me."

"I wish that was the problem, Skylar." He sighed, and his face inched closer.

The *yank* between us was so palpable that my chest ached. "Then what's the real problem?" He needed to say the words. He loved Josie. It was the slap in the face I needed to wake me up.

"We *can't* be together." His features twisted in agony. "No matter how much I want it."

Wait. My heart fluttered even though it needed to remain cool and calm. All it heard was that he wanted to be with me. It didn't comprehend the *can't be together* part. "Why not?" I tensed, waiting for the barrage of insults. I was a weirdo, a freak, unworthy. All the things everyone had told me my entire life.

"You're human, and I'm a wolf shifter." He winced. "It's forbidden for shifters to be with anyone who isn't supernatural and frowned upon for us to date someone outside our own species. I'm the future king, so we ... *us* ... it can't happen." But even as he said the words, he inched closer. "If I wasn't the king's heir and hadn't been preparing for the transition my entire life, things would be different."

My eyelashes fluttered. His mouth was inches from mine. I wanted him to close the distance.

He must have read my mind because his lips brushed mine. Electric sparks sizzled on my lips, the shock enough to make one word flash into my mind.

Forbidden.

He'd never be with me. This would only demolish my already fractured heart.

I touched his chest and pushed him back slightly. As his eyes opened, a subtle glow within them hinted at something supernatural that I couldn't quite grasp, but at least I understood his position.

"I can't." I shook my head. "We can't. It's not fair to either one of us." I couldn't bring myself to mention Josie.

"Yeah." He climbed to his feet and tugged on the hem of his shirt, smoothing out the wrinkles. "You're right. I should go. It's not smart for me to be here."

A stupid part of me wanted to beg him to stay, but the survivor in me said he needed to leave *now*. "You should."

He frowned like he'd hoped I'd have a different answer.

"Lucy's bringing you something back to eat. You should get more rest."

I nodded. "Okay. Thanks."

The silence became unbearable.

He walked to the bedroom door and glanced over his shoulder. "Nothing changes. If you need me, text or call. I'll be there for you." Then he left.

With each step he took, a cold void opened wider near my heart.

When the front door opened, I called out, "Thank you, Raffe," knowing he could hear me.

The moment I was alone, I lay back with tears streaming down my face. I shouldn't have felt half this much for him, but Raffe had somehow weaseled his way into my heart. I needed to stay far away from him. Seeing him got harder and harder every time, especially knowing he was also drawn to me.

I touched my lips, the sparks now mere tingles.

Resolved, I grabbed my phone and pulled up Slade's name. I'd made my decision and knew I couldn't go back, so I typed out a message.

CHAPTER FOURTEEN

I read my text to Slade one more time. I already knew this wouldn't go over well, but I couldn't handle Saturday.

Me: Hey, I can't go to the game after all. Something came up.

I was being a chicken, but the thought of attending the game with Raffe on the field and everyone's eyes on him, especially Josie's, made me want to throw up. I'd already overheard them talking about how she wore his jersey.

When my phone didn't ding back, I tossed it on the bed. Just sending the text had the room spinning again. I needed rest, especially after what had transpired between Raffe and me.

As my eyelids grew heavy, my heart squeezed so tightly I wanted to squirm. With my lips still tingling, I fell into a restless sleep.

ALARM BLARING AND HEAD POUNDING, I stirred from sleep. Nausea churned violently in my stomach, and I patted the side of the bed sporadically for the blasted phone to stop the noise. When I finally found it, under the pillow and up against the headboard, I almost chucked it against the wall.

Gritting my teeth, I swiped, waiting for the blessed silence, but even when the noise stopped, the pounding in my head got worse.

Ugh.

I wanted to clutch it and curl into a ball, but that wouldn't accomplish anything. I needed to get ready for class. The only thing that would tame this beast was food and headache medicine.

With every ounce of control I had, I forced myself to put my feet on the floor and stand. The world tilted around me, but it didn't swirl like yesterday, so that was a win.

I shuffled to the closet and snatched some clean underwear, a bra, a teal sweatshirt, and jeans, and then made my way to the bathroom. In the mirror, I couldn't believe what I saw. I had dark circles under my eyes and was sickly pale like I had the flu or something.

Lovely.

I needed a shower, but I didn't have the energy. My whole body was weak, so I changed into my clothes and ran a brush through my hair. I didn't brush my teeth. The toothpaste would make me more nauseous.

Back in my room, I tossed my clothes from yesterday onto the floor and grabbed my backpack and phone. The backpack weighed a ton, but I needed it for class. When I headed into the small hallway, Lucy popped her head out of her room.

She wore a loose gray shirt and black sweatpants, and her hair was a tangled mess, but when she looked at me, her eyes bulged. "Are you sick?"

"I ... I don't know." I adjusted the straps on my shoulders

and stumbled into the wall. "But I need something to eat and medicine." Even talking had my head splitting in two.

"Shit. Let me go with you." She stepped back into her room and shut the door. "Give me one minute."

"You don't need to go with me," I whispered, knowing she could hear me. In that moment, the wolf *shifter's* kick-ass hearing was beneficial. "I'll be fine. You can even come out here and smell that I'm not lying."

Her door opened, and she joined me in jeans and a tight-fitted EEU sweater, her hair smoothed to perfection.

I blinked, thinking it had to be an illusion. "That didn't even take you a minute." I had to be losing track of time.

She snorted and took my backpack from me.

I sighed. It felt like the weight of the world had been lifted from my shoulders. Something *was* wrong with me.

"Do you want me to get you something and bring it back?" She bit her bottom lip. "I don't mind. I wish I hadn't eaten what I brought back for you last night, but I went out for a run and came back hungry, and you were still passed out, so …" She grimaced.

Though I wasn't one-hundred-percent positive, I assumed she'd run in her wolf body. Normally, I'd ask, but I didn't want to exert the energy. "I need to go. I'm not sure what I can actually handle eating." The thought of almost anything damn near had me heading to the bathroom.

"Okay." She held out an arm. "Do you want to lean on me?"

That sounded way too tempting, but I forced myself to shake my head. "Don't want to risk you getting sick if I'm contagious."

"Supernaturals rarely get sick, and when they do, it's not human diseases." She winked. "I'll be fine."

Ugh. Why was she making this so difficult? I almost

wished she would swoop me up in her arms and carry me like Raffe had last night.

Raffe.

A sharp pain streaked through my chest. I had to stop thinking about him, especially in this condition. "Let's go."

My phone buzzed in my hand, and I glanced at it to find a text.

Slade: Everything okay? You never answered me last night. Still on for breakfast?

Shit. He'd messaged me last night? I hadn't heard it.

"Everything okay?" Lucy's query echoing Slade's felt ominous as she arched a brow and opened the door to the hallway. She had her own phone in her hand, and I noticed her screen was lit up like she'd been on it.

"Yeah, it's Slade." I inhaled, focusing my energy on getting to the student center. It wasn't that far, but it might as well have been *miles*. "Can we go?"

She mashed her lips together. "Yeah, sorry. Let's go."

We walked down the hall, and by the time we reached the elevator, Lucy's face was lined with concern.

When we settled into the elevator, I leaned against the wall, pulled up Slade's message again, and replied.

Me: Not feeling the best. On my way to the student center now.

Before I could put the phone down, it buzzed.

Slade: On my way.

A knot formed deep within me, adding to my discomfort. Here was this handsome, nice guy who was going out of his way to help me and who'd made it clear he was interested in me, and I was hung up on someone who would never be *anything* to me and who had a girlfriend. What kind of pathetic girl was I? *Pathetic* didn't even capture how horrible I was.

"Hey, are you going to barf?" Lucy's nose wrinkled. "If you are, we'll be outside in a few minutes. Try to hold it until then because, if you do, I will too, and that won't be good for anyone."

I snorted, surprising myself. "I thought *supernaturals* didn't get sick."

"We don't ... *usually*. But it would be what's called sympathy vomiting."

"Fair." I put my phone back into my jeans pocket and laid the side of my head on the metal elevator wall, enjoying the coolness.

Of course, that was when the door opened.

I groaned. The time had come to walk again, so I pushed myself off the wall. The sooner I got to the student center, the quicker I could eat and take something for this wretched headache. I had to get myself together enough to attend classes today. The small silver lining was that it was a day with shorter classes, unlike Thursdays, which typically had longer classes and a lab at the end of the day.

Outside, I almost ran into a solid chest again. I managed to slow down enough so I didn't slam right into Raffe.

My pulse quickened, and my chest tightened, squeezing all the organs inside as it tried to yank me to him. I nearly sobbed. Why, out of everyone I could run into, did it have to be *him*?

I could feel his gaze on me, and I *hated* him seeing me this way. I wished he were struggling with this damn connection the same as I was, but seeing me like *this* guaranteed he wasn't.

"Let's get you something to eat," he rasped, sounding

more gravelly than normal. He bent as if he was going to carry me.

Oh, hell no. The last thing I needed was for him to touch me, especially since the yanking in my chest hurt worse than my head.

I stumbled back into Lucy.

"Whoa." Lucy placed her hands on my shoulders, steadying me. "Are you okay?"

My blood barely jolted, but I felt it simmer slightly from the stress swirling through me. Worse, with the jolt, my body felt more sluggish. "I don't want your help. You should go." I hadn't messaged him, so how'd he know ...

Lucy.

I glanced over my shoulder and frowned. "Did you *tell* him?"

She winced. "He told me last night that if anything happened to let him know. I just—"

"You don't have to explain anything, Lucy." Raffe's voice deepened to almost a growl. "You did *nothing* wrong."

"You're right." I faced forward, anger giving me a boost. "*She* didn't. She doesn't know that, after last night, I want nothing to do with you!" I waited for him to wrinkle his nose and call me a stinker again.

Instead, his eyes flashed with hurt.

And I realized I'd meant it. Not because I didn't want to be with him—unfortunately, I did—but because I refused to play his game. To have special time alone together, only for him to act cold and indifferent around others, then to have to see him with Josie, my heart couldn't handle it. And if I allowed it to continue? I would have no one to blame but myself.

I would *not* be that girl.

"Raffe, you should go," Lucy said softly behind me. "If she doesn't want your help—"

"She can't make it to the student center like *this*." He waved a hand at me, his face twisted in either disgust or agony. Either way, it didn't change a damn thing.

"Watch me." I lifted my chin, something stirring inside me. I'd never cowered before the bullies, and I refused to do it now. Even if I had to crawl to the student center, I would get there as long as it meant he didn't touch me and win whatever battle we were having.

Straightening up as much as I could, I walked past him. My pace wasn't fast, but I stayed on my own two legs, which was all that mattered.

Raffe growled like a true wolf-sounding noise.

Pure animal.

And my blood warmed, but it wasn't due to my power.

Yeah, no. I wasn't going to analyze that.

The two of them didn't say anything, but I heard soft footsteps hurrying to catch up to me. After a second, Lucy appeared at my side, her lips pressed into a thin line. She kept stealing glances at me. Even in my state, I could see the questions running through her head, but she kept her mouth shut, and I understood why.

From the way my neck was tingling, I knew Raffe was following us. Again, I hated how attuned to him I was.

Students milling around between classes and ambling toward the student center glanced at me. Luckily, most didn't stare, but my state drew more attention than usual, or maybe it was the girl at my side.

"Skylar!" Slade called out from behind me. "Hey." The sound of quickly approaching footsteps released some of the tension within me, which normally would be a good thing, but not today. My body wanted to sag with it, and that made it harder to stay upright.

"Hey." Lucy wrapped an arm around my waist, pulling me to her side. "I got you."

I hated that I needed her, but I would've been crawling if she hadn't been here.

"You should leave," Raffe rasped, his voice almost the growl it had been before. "You're the reason she's in this condition."

"What?" Slade replied coldly. "I didn't make her sick. I'm *healthy*. *You* know that."

Those two were going to get into another pissing match, and I didn't have the energy or the patience to deal with it. My head was still killing me, and I felt like I was overheating, which further upset my stomach. I needed to eat something pronto, and the student center was *right there*. "Let's leave them."

"Agreed."

We continued as they began to argue. I wasn't sure they even realized we were walking away, but I didn't give a damn.

Five years later, though it was probably mere minutes, we entered the cafeteria. It was a few minutes after eight, and several students were choosing their breakfasts, but it wasn't too busy. Early classes had started, and most people had classes later in the day.

When the smell of eggs, grease, fried chicken, and all things breakfast hit my nose, I waited for my stomach to revolt. Instead, it gurgled ... *loudly*. I was *starving*.

Lucy flinched. "Do we need to find a bathroom?"

"No, I need food." I licked my lips, my mouth salivating.

"Can you sit on your own or do you want me to walk you to a table?" She nodded toward one.

"I've got it." If that got food to me faster, I'd take it. "Can you get me hash browns, coffee, and a bacon, egg, and cheese omelet?"

She winked. "You got it."

The smell of food had somehow given me more energy. I shuffled to the table where Slade and I always sat. As I got settled, Raffe breezed into the room and headed straight toward me.

A lump formed in my throat when I noticed Slade was missing. Had Raffe scared him off? Surely, he wouldn't do that to me, but I wasn't so sure.

"Seems like your *buddy* doesn't care as much as he pretends to." He arched his brow and paused a few steps away. He sneered. "Are you fucking serious?"

That was when I remembered Slade's aversion spell. I couldn't hide my smile, but I tried to school my expression. It was hard with my head pounding in sync with my heart. "Just sit over there. You don't need to be near me anyway. Remember, you don't associate with *trouble*." I threw his words back at him and placed my head into my hands. I just wanted whatever this was to be over. If Raffe was right, I felt ill because I was still drained from using my magic.

"Dammit, Sky," he gritted out.

Flutters came to life at that damn nickname. It never rolled off someone's tongue like it did his, and I hated it. I did. "Skylar," I corrected him.

"Here we go," Lucy singsonged.

I glanced up and truly fell head over heels in love with her. She was my hero, bringing me the very sustenance I needed to survive. She strolled toward us, and Raffe said, "Wait."

Lucy breezed right past the point where Raffe had stopped. She set the tray in front of me, and I swiped up the fork and dug into the omelet. The taste exploded in my mouth, and I shoved in another bite before I finished the first.

I was *famished*.

Lucy lifted a brow. "That's how I feel after a run."

"Because you use so much of your *energy*." Raffe emphasized the word as he sat at the neighboring table. "Obviously, she didn't eat the dinner you brought her."

Lucy's gaze fell just as Slade's laugh interrupted us. He said, "Looks like my plan worked."

I took a bite of hash browns and glanced up to find him smiling at Raffe with two lattes from the coffee shop in his hands.

He hadn't abandoned me.

"Asshole." Raffe sneered as his eyes homed in on the lattes. "Why is she okay?" He nodded to Lucy.

"Because Sky likes her, and *I* didn't want to get in the way of a friendship, unlike some people here." Slade arched a brow as he slid into the spot across from me. He handed me a latte, and I didn't hesitate to grab it and take a huge sip.

Slade cracked open his lid and blew on the coffee. "How can you drink it that hot? You always kill me."

"That's my *superpower*," I shot back like we always did each morning.

"It seems like you're okay now." Lucy glanced at my food and then my face. "You actually look like you have a pulse and aren't a corpse."

I took another bite of food and cringed internally. Clearly, I'd looked as bad as I thought. I covered my mouth since it was full. "I feel better, and I know your class is later. If you wanna go back to the apartment, please do. I have class at nine, so I'll head there after I eat."

"You sure?" Lucy tilted her head and wrung her hands, unsure if she should stay or not.

"Promise." I nodded. "By the time I take some headache medicine, I'll be golden."

The tingle at the back of my neck increased to a tickle-like warning.

"Oh." Lucy pulled a packet of Advil out of her pocket and put it on the table. "There."

"You are my hero." I lifted my latte and took a huge sip. "Followed by Slade with the latte."

He waved a hand and bowed, making me laugh.

"Don't worry." Slade kicked me gently under the table and said, "We have both classes together today, so I'll take care of her."

"Uh ..." Lucy bit her lip.

"It's fine," I assured her. "I'll text you if I need anything." Her concern made me realize that we were closer friends than I'd been aware of, and despite her cousin, she was a really good person.

"Fuck this," Raffe spat and banged his fist on the table. The entire room went quiet.

CHAPTER FIFTEEN

My heart jumped, and my blood jolted back to life. It would've been fizzing if I hadn't been weak.

Unfazed by the attention, Raffe stood, his olive skin turning a faint shade of pink. Nostrils flared, he looked every inch the broody man he portrayed to the world, except for last night when he'd let his guard down with me.

Ugh. I had to stop remembering that.

"You truly want to surround yourself with as much trouble as possible." He grimaced and shook his head. "When you get hurt, don't say I didn't warn you." He spun on his heel and strode toward the exit.

Chest tightening, I tried to remain indifferent. I didn't want him to know how much his anger and words hurt. Hell, I purposely didn't analyze the impact he had on me because I had no doubt if I dug deep, the answer would petrify me.

The handful of people sitting near us had watched the entire debacle with wide eyes. Their attention locked on Raffe as he stalked out of the center. Even when angry, he moved gracefully and with confidence.

But the truth hit me hard.

He'd made more of a spectacle here than he had in the classroom, leaving me in his wake as if I were nothing.

I had to force my hands to stay flat on the table so I didn't clutch my heart, which hurt as if it had been broken into two. How I felt about him had to stay secret. I didn't want Slade or Lucy to know. I suspected that would cause more problems.

Staring after her cousin and frowning, Lucy shook her head.

"Uh, what's his problem?" Slade leaned back in his seat. "No one forced him to come here."

"No clue." Lucy laughed humorlessly. "That was weird, even for him." She paused and turned to us. "I should go, but seriously, text me if you need anything. I don't care if Slade is with you—if you need something or want my help, message me. Got it?" Her attention flicked between Slade and me.

Interesting. She wasn't a fan of Slade either. She just wasn't obnoxious about it, unlike Raffe and Keith. And those two were supposed to be the future leaders?

"Understood." I laid a hand over my heart and smiled. The pain had eased from knowing that not only did Slade have my back, but Lucy did too. I'd hoped to find a friend here, and somehow, I'd made two. Take that, Lizzy from kindergarten.

"Good." Lucy nodded and pointed at Slade. "And do you?"

He lifted both hands in front of him. "You didn't have a problem getting *here*, did you?" He tapped the table, making his insinuation clear. "That should tell you more than enough unless you start to act more like your cousin."

A knot formed in my stomach, and the food I'd eaten sat uncomfortably. That was a veiled threat. "Slade," I chastised, wanting my two friends to tolerate one another.

Lucy scoffed and looked at me. When she bit her lip, I knew she was having second thoughts about leaving.

"It'll be *fine.*" I karate-chopped the air, not wanting her to feel obligated to stay. She'd woken up early to help me, and I didn't want her to miss out on the nap she wanted. "If I need to text you about how Slade gulps his latte and it's getting on my last nerve, I'll do that," I teased, trying to lighten the mood.

"Please don't." The corners of her lips tipped upward. "I meant if you feel bad, strange, or need amazing company, message me. Don't just tell me all the annoying things Slade does. I'd get no rest."

His forehead creased, and he tilted his head. "You know I'm right here, right? Or did I become invisible in the last few seconds?"

"Oh, believe me." Lucy rocked back on her heels. "You did *not* become invisible. Or mute."

Okay, maybe she wasn't as forceful about her dislike, but she had no qualms about making it clear he wasn't her favorite person.

"Go, take a nap while you still can." I made a shooing gesture. The longer these two remained together, the snippier they got. "I have you on speed dial."

She yawned. "Okay. See you later."

As she walked off, other people watched her as well, although they weren't gawking like they had with Raffe. Still, they kept flicking their gazes back to me.

Yeah, this was something I was all too familiar with. They wanted to know what had happened but weren't willing to talk to the outcast that someone popular had shunned. Good, they could remain clueless for all I cared.

When Lucy was far enough away, Slade muttered, "Damn wolf shifters."

We didn't have much time, but with him referencing the

species as a whole, I had a question. "Is *that* the problem, or is it those particular people?" From what the vampire in the bookstore had said, it seemed to be Raffe and his group specifically.

"That species in particular, but that *group* is the worst of them by far." He clutched his latte again but didn't raise the cup. "They're the ones who call the shots, but most of them go along with it, so ..."

I couldn't blame Slade for feeling that way. That was how popular kids and bullying worked. The ones who let it happen and didn't stand in its way were as bad as the antagonists. "What do they do that's so bad?"

"Raffe and his family aren't supposed to have authority over *all* of us." He scanned the room, likely looking for any eavesdroppers. "But they do."

That was interesting. I opened my mouth to ask more questions, but he subtly shook his head and glanced over my shoulder toward the cafeteria.

That was all the hint I needed to close my mouth tight. I didn't need the supernaturals watching me more closely. I shivered, thinking about how Edward had attacked me.

"Even though that's true, Raffe is acting moodier than usual." Slade played with the cardboard sleeve around the cup. "Did anything strange happen before I joined you three?"

"Nope." I popped the *p*, wanting to end this conversation. I felt like the moment Raffe and I had shared last night had made today's encounter more volatile, but that was something I wouldn't share with anyone ... not even my two friends. I needed to forget it even happened.

At that thought, my mouth tingled faintly, remembering the way his lips had felt as they'd brushed mine.

We needed to change the subject pronto.

"From what I've heard, King Jovian is putting a lot of pressure on him." Slade tapped the table with his free hand. "Apparently, shortly after Raffe graduates, a transition is expected to happen."

That would be quite a burden to carry. I struggled to keep my blood under control. I couldn't imagine taking over a position with that level of responsibility, especially when all the other supernaturals resented it.

I laughed bitterly. "My volatile ass must be making it harder on him." Maybe that was why he'd joined Lucy and me. He was afraid I'd lose control and cause another scene, one he'd have to clean up.

"Don't worry about him." Slade reached across the table and placed his hand on top of mine. "Raffe is a jerk, and that's putting it politely."

His touch was warm and comforting, but that was all. I wished my skin would tingle or buzz when he touched me. It would make things so much easier, especially since he liked spending time with me. I smiled, and the gesture eased some of my pain. "You're right. That is putting it mildly."

When he didn't remove his hand, the warmth vanished and changed to discomfort. I slid my hand out from under his and removed my phone from my back pocket. We had ten minutes until class began. "We need to get moving, or we'll be late." Though I felt better, I wasn't back to one hundred percent, and I doubted I could walk quickly.

Thankfully, the caffeine and Advil were kicking in, so I should be able to make it through our classes.

"You're right." He stood and grabbed my backpack and his own.

I held out my hand to take mine from him, but he took a step back. "Let's not push it. You're pale and a little shaky. Let me carry your backpack to our first class."

Once again, I didn't understand why Raffe kept warning me off him. He made it sound like Slade wasn't a nice guy, but here he was, offering to take care of me. "Okay."

He winked, and we headed to class.

All the while, I tried like hell to focus on the moment and push a certain sexy wolf shifter from my mind.

THE NEXT WEEK and a half blurred together, but one thing changed drastically. Raffe kept his distance from me, and worse, Josie started showing up more often, walking with him to classes. Each time I saw them together, a fresh wave of pain swamped me, and it wasn't getting better. My blood was fritzing again. Thinking about Raffe to calm myself down was *not* working anymore, and not being able to walk in the woods alone meant I didn't have any release. Slade had refused to train me, stating he wanted to wait until Monday to be sure I was back to one hundred percent. He hadn't found any more answers, and it seemed like what little control I'd gained was being stripped from me.

There had been one highlight, however—my volunteer training class at the animal shelter. This Saturday, I'd get to actually work and take care of the animals.

Last Tuesday, Professor Haynes went over the highlights of the first group project and said it would be in our best interests to get started because the data collection would take time.

So as Slade and I strolled into stats this Tuesday, I dreaded the inevitable conversation Raffe and I would be required to have.

"Be reasonable, Professor Haynes," Raffe said.

He was standing in front of the room, talking with the professor.

Haynes lifted her chin and stared Raffe right in the eye. "I informed everyone when the assignments were handed out that there would be no changing partners."

A lump formed in my throat. Not being paired with Raffe would be the best thing for me, but that didn't dampen the hurt. My blood fizzed, reacting to my emotions.

"There are extenuating circumstances—" he started.

"Let me make myself *very clear*, Mr. Wright. I don't care who you are or who your father is. In this classroom, I'm the law, and everyone is treated equally. You will *not* get special treatment. I'm not sure how much clearer I can be."

If that didn't put him in his place, I wasn't sure what would.

Raffe's jaw clenched, and I took my seat, forcing myself to unpack my binder and not watch the altercation. I had to get my blood under control.

After a second, his voice rattled, "Understood. Enjoy this moment."

Knowing what he was, I heard the growl he was trying to control as he headed past me. I stared at the binder on my desk, and my neck tingled, informing me that he was looking at me for longer than a second as he brushed by.

The fizz increased to almost a hum, and the emotions I read from Raffe were conflicted. I sensed guilt, anger, and longing, which didn't make sense. He hadn't talked to me in nine days. I'd kept count.

It was almost physically impossible not to look at him, but thankfully, Professor Haynes started class, so I dove in, ready to focus on my notes.

She emphasized that if we didn't start our project soon, we wouldn't complete the assignment on time. We could not procrastinate.

My phone buzzed, and I turned it to silent.

But I saw the message that had come through.

Raffe: Don't worry about it. Josie and I will begin the data collection this weekend. I'll email you the data, and you can write the report.

I didn't respond. I didn't need to. He'd told me how things would happen.

I tossed my phone back into my bag, my blood damn near fizzing. I focused on taking notes, hoping it'd calm the storm brewing inside.

My cheeks hurt from smiling so much. I'd been at the shelter since eight this morning, and it was now five. I would've stayed longer, but the place was closing, and the lead volunteer was about to physically kick me out.

For the first time since I'd had to stop going into the woods alone, I felt a semblance of peace.

In the woods, I enjoyed the solitude of being surrounded by nature without any prying eyes. The trees, mulch, grass, animals, and even the drizzly mist that almost always surrounded me there brought me such calm.

At the shelter, the calm came from making a difference. The leader of the volunteers had noticed that dogs that were scared and aggressive calmed down in my presence, which eased something inside me as well.

As I climbed into my car to head back to the apartment, I received a text. I started the car and swiped the screen.

Slade: It's homecoming tonight. I won't take no for an answer. Be at your place in an hour. Dress for the football game and a bonfire.

My gut screamed *no*. Raffe had told me not to come. But

why should that matter? He got to do everything, and Slade would be there with me. Maybe I could sneak away to the edge of the woods and decompress a little.

My blood jolted, the peace I'd found at the shelter already in my rearview mirror.

I put the car into drive, knowing I didn't have to answer right away. I didn't want to do something stupid, but I wanted to scream at the idea of being alone in the apartment when I had a chance to hang out with Slade and others who were as similar to me as I could find.

Hands tightening on the steering wheel, I followed the roads back to campus. With every mile, my decision became clearer.

Why was I letting Raffe control my life? I wasn't a supernatural and hadn't I allowed enough bullies to control me? That's essentially what he was. He wanted to keep me isolated while he got to be with friends and Josie. In other words, he got to live his life.

None of it was fair.

It ended now.

When I pulled into my spot in the parking lot, I replied to Slade.

Me: You know what? I'm in, but I'll meet you at the stadium.

I didn't want him to get the impression it was a date. He'd been touching my hands and arms more often, so I had to make sure I kept my boundaries.

Slade: Fine, I'll save you a seat.

Noting I had an hour to get ready, I hurried into the apartment. I'd been around animals all day, so I wanted to take a shower.

Forty-five minutes later, I was frowning at my makeup. I

rarely wore any, so when I tried, it never looked right.

Lucy came out of her room and stopped at the bathroom door. Her hair was pulled into a twist, with pieces of hair framing her face, and she wore an EEU crop top that stopped about an inch from the top of her jeans. She arched a brow. "What are you doing?"

I'd hoped to sneak out before she caught me. I dreaded her reaction, but she'd know if I lied. I'd learned that the hard way with Raffe. "Slade told me I didn't have a choice but to go to the game and bonfire, and I said okay." My voice rose on *okay*, turning my statement into a question.

Her face softened. "That's excellent. You need to have a life."

My jaw dropped, and she rolled her eyes.

"I know what Raffe says, but despite what people *think*, he and his dad aren't always right." She shrugged. "Slade will be there, and though I don't love that you two are so close, I will be too. You'll have two people who'll make sure nothing bad happens. You deserve to have friends and do things like the rest of us."

That was what I'd been thinking. I blew out a breath and looked at myself in the mirror. "You don't think I'm being crazy or reckless?"

She entered the bathroom and picked up my foundation. "Let's not go wild, but I will agree you aren't being reckless." She got a sponge and squirted makeup on it. "Since you've been staring at this like it's foreign, I'm going to do your hair and makeup."

"You don't—"

Before I could finish, she began working on my face, biting her bottom lip as she applied each layer. I almost wanted to complain but didn't want to ruin the first girl moment I'd ever had.

When she was done, I was afraid to look in the mirror. But after a moment, I did and couldn't believe what I saw. She'd made my makeup look so natural I could barely see it, except my features stood out more.

My cognac-brown eyes seemed to glow, and my lips were painted a light red that wasn't overbearing. Add in the way she had my dark hair waving down my back and I almost wouldn't recognize myself.

She laughed. "Were you expecting to look horrendous?"

I cringed. "You were putting a lot of makeup on me, so I wasn't expecting this. Thank you."

"For someone who doesn't normally wear makeup, less is more, so I opted for a natural look to start you off."

"You did amazing. I never could've achieved this." I let my sincerity lace each word.

"We aren't finished yet." She took my hand and dragged me into her room. "I have a shirt you can borrow."

"But ..." I sighed, not wanting to put her out.

"No buts." She wagged a finger. "Of any kind. I want to do this, so come on."

Keeping with her personality, her bright-yellow comforter reminded me of the sun. She strolled to her closet, and I noted both an Xbox and a PlayStation under her television. She had a remote on her bed with a gamer's headset. She'd told me she liked gaming, but this seemed way more intense than just *like*.

"Here," she said and tossed me an evergreen EEU sweatshirt.

Obliging her, I slipped it on then realized it was a crop top.

She clapped. "Perfect."

I placed a hand over my stomach, feeling self-conscious. "I'm not sure—"

"If you don't wear it, I'll never help you get ready again."

She crossed her arms and leaned back. "That looks amazing on you, better than it does on me. Also, isn't it important to show other women not to be ashamed of their stomachs? Flaunt it."

I snorted, realizing she was right. Besides, I was young. It was okay to act like it once in a while. "Fine, but only tonight."

"Works for me." She grabbed my hand and tugged me to the door. "Let's go. We need to get there before all the good seats are taken."

My body felt light. I hadn't expected us to walk over together. "Your friends—"

"—know the way." She winked, opening our door. "They'll be fine. I'll let them know I'm meeting them there." She tapped her head, and her eyes glowed.

I wanted to ask questions, but for once, the hallway had people in it waiting for the elevator. Everyone was decked out in their EEU clothes, no doubt heading to the same place we were.

Soon, we were walking outside in companionable silence, enjoying a cloudy night without a drizzle, making our way toward the all-brick Howling Stadium.

The gates were open, and people went through security to get inside. Lucy led us to one of the shorter lines.

I bit my lip as my blood jolted. "Are you sure about walking in with me? I don't want to cause problems. I won't have hurt feelings."

Lucy scowled. "I'm sure. Look, Raffe and I might be close and family, but he doesn't get to dictate every decision I make in my life, like who I'm friends with. You're the most authentic friend I have."

Blinking, I tilted my head back. "I see you with people all the time."

"They're my ... *friends*." She emphasized and tapped her

head. "But they hang out with me mostly because of who I am. You don't care about that. Even when you learned everything, you never tried to use me to get something for yourself."

That was a sentiment I understood. "I get it but from a different perspective. Everyone's always treated me like I'm a freak, but you don't."

"Who says we both aren't and that's why we get along so well?" She stuck out her tongue, and I laughed. "But we seem to have a few things in common."

It was my turn to get her back. I leaned toward her ear, trying to keep from laughing, and whispered, "Yup. I like animals, and you turn into one."

"Shut up." She pushed me playfully as we reached the front of the line.

The security guards were all dressed in EEU colors, and after scanning our student IDs, they allowed us inside.

I stopped short when I saw a huge banner of a football player on the wall. Unfortunately, I had no doubt who it was with his muscular body and piercing eyes, even under a helmet.

Raffe.

A group of girls stood in front of it, taking pictures with him behind them.

For some reason, that made my blood fizz.

I had to pry my eyes away before I had a meltdown. I looked around, taking in the vendors and all the people milling around inside the cement walls that were standard for a stadium.

None of that helped because I wanted to fixate on the picture of Raffe.

"Skylar?" Lucy asked with concern.

I shouldn't have come here. Raffe was playing tonight, and

Josie would be here, wearing his jersey. Why had I thought this was a good idea? "I need to—"

"Lucy." A booming, commanding voice sounded from behind us.

Lucy's eyes widened, and she mouthed, *Oh shit.*

Now, my blood damn near hummed.

She plastered on a smile and turned around, her voice sickly sweet. "Hey, Uncle Jovian. Are you here to see Raffe play?"

Oh no. This was Raffe's father, the man who didn't want me here and who had a lot of say over the supernatural world. I needed to get away before he realized who I was.

As I started to step away, he said, "And who is your friend? I don't think I've met her."

There was no escape.

CHAPTER SIXTEEN

I didn't know what to do. My blood was close to humming, but running would make things far worse. The king didn't want me around humans, and this was the worst possible place for him to meet me, but I shouldn't run off and act guilty, especially since I'd be leaving Lucy to handle the mess alone. But I shouldn't meet him either.

"Oh, this is someone new to the school," Lucy said flippantly.

I turned and got ready to scurry away, but someone knocked into me, keeping me trapped.

The king cleared his throat. "More reason for me to meet her since she's spending time with my niece."

He wouldn't let it go, and the longer we put off the introduction, the stranger it would seem. Worse, my blood could cause chaos if I didn't get through this, get away, and calm down. Between the king and all these people milling around me, I felt close to exploding.

Gritting my teeth, I turned back around. I wasn't prepared for his commanding presence and the power he radiated, similar to Raffe's but more refined.

I couldn't swallow as more people brushed past me.

His lips pressed together, emphasizing his trimmed brown beard. His brows furrowed as his steel-blue eyes scanned me. "I'm Jovian Wright. And you are?"

With my blood nearing catastrophic levels, I read suspicion rolling off him in waves.

I wanted to lie, to say another name, but he'd be able to smell it. Instead, I straightened my shoulders to give the illusion of confidence. "Skylar Greene." I held out my hand, hating how it shook, but it wasn't like he couldn't hear my heart pounding. Could he?

He ran a hand through his longish salt-and-pepper hair, and his gaze hardened. Slowly, he gave my hand one shake and dropped it.

Anger and frustration funneled off him and slammed into me, confirming he'd put who I was together.

"I understood from Raffe that you were staying in for the evening." He stuck out his chest, causing the school emblem on the jersey I assumed had Raffe's number on the back to stretch tight.

I heard a feminine laugh, and over the king's shoulder, I noticed a middle-aged woman with dirty-blonde hair wearing the same jersey. She came up beside him and looped her arm through his then laid her head on his shoulder. She radiated happiness.

My mouth went dry. That was Raffe's mom. The queen.

She assessed me. "I'm sure there's an explanation. Our son has been busy with football, helping to handle affairs for you on campus, keeping up with his political science degree, and spending time with Josie and his friends. Besides, why wouldn't a student be here supporting the football team? It's homecoming!" Her gray eyes twinkled with kindness. Then she sniffed, and her head tilted. Her smile faltered, and confusion mixed with intrigue barreled into me.

She must have figured out who I was, or maybe what I was and was not.

As Raffe's parents stared at me uneasily, their emotions mixed together and blanketed me. My chest clenched, and my blood began to hum.

The fluorescent lights above our heads flickered, and the queen glanced up, eyes widening.

The king scowled, and a group of girls near me shrieked.

I had to get away. Past a concession stand was a women's bathroom. "If you'll excuse me, I need to run to the restroom."

I spun on my heel and darted away, my emotions peaking.

A light cracked overhead, and I glanced over my shoulder to see sparks flying while people stumbled away.

The king didn't budge, his eyes locked on me until I found refuge in the bathroom. My pulse thudded as my blood coursed with power.

I ran down the row of evergreen stalls, finding the one at the very end vacant. I rushed inside and slid the door into place as the stall around me shook from my magic.

"What the hell?" an older voice a few stalls down exclaimed.

My ears pounded in tune with my heart rate. Being stuck in a small stall was *not* helping.

I had to find a way to calm down.

Trying not to overthink, I closed my eyes and laid my forehead against the metal door. The coolness felt good against my hot skin.

Focusing on the chill, I conjured the image of the woods in my mind. I brushed both hands along the door, picturing myself in the forest to calm the shrieks and the rattling.

Someway, somehow, my blood quieted a notch into a fizz.

With myself somewhat more under control, I pushed off the door, trying not to think about what I might have pressed my face into, and flushed the toilet. I opened the door and went to the line of sinks.

After washing my hands, I splashed water on my face. I had to cool down more, but I didn't want to mess up my makeup.

I dried my hands and patted my face with a paper towel then looked in the mirror. My skin was flushed but settling back into my natural color.

"What the hell was that?" an older lady asked as she strolled to the sinks. She glanced back at the stalls. "That was the strangest thing. I would've thought it was an earthquake, but only the last few stalls were shaking."

Shit. Having a vampire in here would have come in handy, but I wouldn't know one if they were standing beside me.

"I don't know what you're talking about." I shrugged, trying to keep my blood from fritzing again.

"Are you serious?" She rolled her eyes. "The stalls shook so hard that—"

I couldn't stay here. "It seems like everything is fine now." I cut her off and left via a second exit. I removed my phone and texted Slade.

Me: At the bathroom near the front. Not sure where you are or where to go. I met King Jovian and he's near. SOS.

I kept my phone in my hand and tried to blend in with the crowd. Luckily, the line to the concession stand was long, but I could still see King Jovian, Lucy, and the queen standing where I'd left them. A stadium worker swept up the glass from the lights I had ruined.

King Jovian's attention cut to me, and my blood kicked up

again.

Yeah, I couldn't stay here.

When a couple of human guys I recognized from stats walked by, I followed them. The seating section numbers kept increasing as we reached what had to be midfield.

"Sky," a familiar voice called, and the weight lifted from my shoulders immediately.

My gaze landed on Slade, and tears burned my eyes. I was so damn happy to see him.

His forehead creased as he jogged over to me. "Hey. I thought you were near the front."

"I ... I was, but things went bad with *them,* and I had to get away." I bit my lip.

When he placed his hand on the center of my back and fell into step beside me, I didn't pull away. I needed comfort ... someone who had my back. Lucy couldn't be that person right now with the king and queen being her family and all.

"What do you mean, bad?" He arched a brow. "Like what we've been working on bad?"

I nodded. "Something happened." I removed my phone and sent him a short text summing it up as best I could. When I hit send, he paused to read the text then frowned.

"This is why I should've picked you up." He hung his head and turned to me. "I'm sorry, Sky."

I breathed easier, knowing I wasn't overreacting. "It's not your fault, and you're right. I just ..." I trailed off, not wanting to finish that statement. I didn't want him to think this was a date, and I was putting up boundaries to make it clear, but saying it bluntly seemed cruel.

"Hey, it's fine. Don't worry about it." He winked and took my hand. "Next time, I'll come get you."

Next time. I was certain there wouldn't be a next time, but before I could say so, he pointed to the stairs in front of us and said, "This is us."

When we entered the open arena, I saw we were near a goalpost. I followed him down the stairs, noting a section full of people our age. We took a left and walked down the right side of a stair rail that split the section of students in two.

I could tell the stair rail was a division between humans and supernaturals even if it wasn't on purpose. The humans were to the left, looking plain like me compared to the supernaturals to my right. Whether it was right or wrong, the supernaturals had an air of beauty and grace that, no matter what a human did, they'd never achieve. Something woven into their beauty made them stand apart from us mere mortals.

As we passed, many other supernaturals glanced my way, probably noting I was with one of their own even though I wasn't a coven member.

My blood fizzed under the scrutiny, and a girl's head snapped in my direction. She hissed. Slade glanced over his shoulder at her and picked up our pace.

Finally, three rows from the front, Slade stopped. He winked at me and sat first. "This is us."

That put me on the end, and I was grateful I didn't have to sit beside someone I didn't know. Dealing with people in front of and behind me was hard enough. I wasn't used to going out in public like this or being around so many people.

The football team was on the field warming up, and unfortunately, my gaze went straight to Raffe. He turned his head at the same time, and our eyes met. The tingles at the base of my neck started, and the damn *yank* in my chest made me want to climb over the gate and rush to him.

"Sky," Slade said, pulling my attention away from Raffe. "This is Gavyn." He pointed to the man next to him with ash-blond hair some women would kill for. "And that's Hecate." He gestured to the woman on Gavyn's other side. She reminded me of a grown-up version of Merida from *Brave* with vibrant, wavy red hair. Her pale skin was flawless, and she had jade-green eyes that made the stone look boring. "And the bored-looking guy beside her is Cade." Cade had light-brown skin and warm, friendly brown eyes. "Everyone, this is Skylar."

"Oh, we figured that out when you vanished without a word." Hecate pouted and twirled a piece of hair around her finger, cutting her eyes to me.

Well, that was *not* a warm welcome.

"Don't give him hell for running off to meet a girl." Gavyn chuckled. "It's nice that he's taken an interest in someone other than himself for a change."

Slade tensed, and I wondered why his friend would make a comment like that.

"Ignore these two." Cade leaned over and extended his hand to me. "It's very nice to meet you, Skylar. Those two are jealous because he hasn't hung out with us as much since he met you."

Jealous. That was a new one when it came to me.

"Speak for yourself." Gavyn placed his hands behind his head, his forest-green eyes on the field. "I find it refreshing."

"Maybe *you* do." Hecate bit her lip and edged behind Gavyn toward Slade. She almost purred, "But I rather miss our alone time."

"Hecate," Slade warned, shifting closer to me and placing an arm around my waist. He pulled me to his side. "You promised."

She'd *promised*? I didn't have to hear the story to know something had happened between them, and Hecate wasn't happy that it was over. My stomach churned. I hoped I hadn't messed up Slade's relationship by needing help with my power and my heritage.

I wrung my hands. Coming here had been a mistake.

"Heads up," someone called from the front row, and I jerked my head forward in time to see a football sail into Slade's stomach.

He grunted, releasing my waist, and picked up the ball that thudded at our feet.

On the field, Raffe stood at the gate with his hands raised. "Sorry about that. The ball slipped when I was tossing it." His tone was gravelly and amused.

It was a problem that I was familiar enough with his voice to know his intent.

Slade tensed and tossed the ball back. "Hopefully you won't have butterfingers during the game."

Raffe removed his helmet and winked at me. "My hands work just fine when I want them to."

My body warmed at the insinuation, and I had to force my brain not to head down a dangerous path.

The coach shouted for the team to head to the locker room, and Raffe continued to stare at me as he headed off the field. The tingle on my neck became alarmingly intense.

"Uh ... what the fuck?" Hecate scoffed. "Was that over *her*?"

My heart ached, and my blood fired up again, strong enough to read Hecate's dislike for me.

Between this and running into the king, I could only think of one smart choice to make. "I should go."

Slade turned to me and took my hands. He lowered his voice. "No, don't. Please." He bit his bottom lip. "I really would like you to stay, and I'm sorry about Hecate. I didn't realize she'd be like that."

I freed one hand and tucked a piece of hair behind my ear. "She doesn't like me, and I'm struggling ..."

"She and I had a thing, but it was never serious. She got more invested than I realized, but I swear, if you give her a chance, she'll come around. I promise." He placed a hand over his heart. "Stay for the first quarter, and if they make you feel uncomfortable or things act up, we'll cut out."

"I can leave. You don't have to." Having friends was important, and I didn't want to come between Slade and his.

He shook his head. "You're not leaving alone. Just give me a quarter."

I blew out a breath. He'd done so much for me, so I could give him fifteen minutes. "Fine."

"Good." He smiled. "One second." He turned his back to me and moved so the four of them could talk quickly.

I had no doubt what he was saying, especially when Hecate glanced at me with a frown. The other two guys raised their brows and tried not to make it noticeable that they were looking.

My skin crawled. I wished I had shifter hearing, but from the way he was holding his hands, he'd cast a spell so no one could overhear them.

That was strange, but I didn't want to overanalyze it. He had to be protecting me.

Hecate smiled tightly at me, and Slade moved back beside me.

Her expression was fake, but it was better than the animosity she'd thrown my way.

I leaned toward him and asked, "What did you say?"

"Nothing you need to worry about." He booped my nose, and the band began to play.

It was football time.

I stayed for the whole game because Gavyn and Hecate were being polite. I didn't talk to Cade much since he was three people down from me, but things were okay enough for me not to tear Slade away from his friends.

Though I didn't want to admit it, I'd enjoyed watching Raffe play. He, Keith, Adam, and two others on the team were clearly supernaturals. Their extra speed and grace stood out from the other players, but they held back enough not to raise too many questions about their abilities.

Barely.

Every throw Raffe made was perfect, and Keith and Adam scored almost all the touchdowns, leaving the final score 63–0.

I had to close my eyes to avoid one thing though. After every touchdown, Josie ran from her spot with the cheerleaders to give Raffe a huge hug.

Each time, my heart broke. I didn't understand how that was possible. It was so stupid.

The five of us left with the hordes and headed to a section of the woods behind the residence halls where the bonfire would be held. Apparently, this was tradition and a way to keep the faculty from learning about the party.

I felt uneasy with so many humans out here hanging out with supernaturals, especially vampires. This seemed like a potential buffet for them, and the thought upset my stomach.

"Skylar, how do you like EEU so far?" Cade asked, coming up beside me. He put his hands into his jeans pockets and smiled. He was the most personable of the group, maybe more so than Slade.

"It's been good." I shrugged. I wasn't sure what to say. I'd been attacked by a vampire, been stalked, and the king of the wolf shifters didn't like me even though he'd never met me until tonight, yet I'd made friends for the first time. And a certain wolf-shifter prince had control over my heart. It was a mixture that was good and bad. "I wouldn't leave." When I spoke those words, I realized how true they were.

Gavyn chuckled and muttered, "Not that you could if you wanted to."

My step faltered. "What? Why wouldn't I be able to leave?"

"Don't listen to him, Sky." Slade bumped his shoulder into mine but turned to Gavyn, giving him the stink eye. "He likes to stir up shit."

Hecate smirked but remained quiet.

If it weren't for all the people around us, I would've pushed the issue. The four of them knew something I didn't.

Silence descended among us, and soon, we stepped into a large clearing that had four log fires burning and four large kegs in the back, with red Solo cups stacked on a portable table nearby. Most seats around the fire were taken, and people were already swaying from having started drinking early.

Needing to get away from Slade's friend, I smiled. "I'm going to get a drink. Does anyone need one?"

"Sure, I'll go with you." Hecate came over and grabbed my arm. "You guys go find us a spot before they're all taken. We'll be right back."

Slade frowned, but before he could intervene, Hecate dragged me toward a keg.

Had I known this was how it would wind up, I wouldn't have offered.

When we were away from the others, she sighed. "You need to be careful with that one."

I lifted a brow, finding it odd she would say something

about one of her own. She sounded like Raffe. "You aren't listening to your own advice with how you're pining for him."

She pressed her lips together. "That's fair, but it's also why I'm warning you. He'll do *anything* to make sure his mommy stays happy with him."

"What does that have to do with me?" Slade hadn't talked about his family, other than to reveal he was an only child and his parents were still married.

"More than you know."

I wanted to ask more, but a guy stumbled in front of the kegs and bowed. "Hello, gorgeous ladies. Are you lost? Because I—" He lifted a finger. "No, wait. Let me try again. Are you lost? Because my eyes—" He shook his head and huffed. "No. *I'm lost*. Because of—"

"Yes, you're lost." Hecate laughed, snagging four cups and handing me two. "And it goes, 'Can you tell me where I am because I got lost in your eyes?'"

"Fuck." He groaned, running a hand down his face. "That. Dammit."

Hecate smacked his ass. "Practice. I'm sure the next girl you think is hot will be here in a few minutes."

"Yeah, okay." He nodded and headed over to the edge of the clearing.

I filled up my two cups and glanced around. No one was nearby. "When you say his—"

"Hey." Slade sidled up. "What's taking you two so long?" He took a drink from my hand and smiled. "We've got a spot over there. Let's go."

As Slade guided me away from Hecate, I glanced over my shoulder, and she shrugged.

Something strange was going on. Slade wanted me to hang out with his friends, but he was hovering over me.

Not wanting to think anymore tonight, I guzzled the beer.

"Hey, you didn't tell me she knows how to party." Gavyn grinned as Hecate handed him one of her cups.

Slade laughed. "I didn't know either."

When everyone had a drink, I lifted mine in the air. "Empty." I needed another cup. I turned back to the keg with Slade by my side.

This was going to be a long night, but beer would get me by.

After two more cupfuls, the world began to tilt. But I was relaxed, and my blood wasn't raging. Maybe drinking was the answer.

The five of us sat on a log by one of the fires with people on the other two makeshift benches. Slade had me on one end of the group again, and he sat next to me, but when the tingles started on the back of my neck, I knew what that meant.

Raffe was here.

Before I could stop myself, I turned and locked gazes with him and saw Josie standing between him and Lucy. They weren't holding hands, but Josie was wearing his jersey, which about fucking ripped out my heart.

Why the hell was I pining for him? It had to be because he'd saved me twice.

Keith held up his phone and a speaker. A few seconds later, Nirvana blared into the clearing.

"Come on, football star." Josie held out a hand to Raffe. "Let's dance and wear off the adrenaline."

The five of them moved toward another bonfire, and Adam went to grab them some beers. People watched them, but they didn't acknowledge anyone else.

I tried not to watch them dance, but every few seconds, I found myself staring at them.

Slade turned to me. "Hey, are you okay?"

I hadn't noticed how close we were, but his face was only inches from mine.

How did that happen? I tilted my head back to put distance between us. "Yeah, I'm fine."

Laughter sounded from Raffe's group, and my blood jolted. "I'll be right back. I'm going for a quick walk."

I wobbled trying to stand, but when I made it to my feet, I hurried to get away from it all.

I needed to connect with nature. It'd been too long.

When I reached the edge of the clearing, Slade wrapped an arm around my waist. He said, "You shouldn't go out here alone."

"Go hang out with your friends." I forced a smile and removed his arm. That damn tingle at the nape of my neck was happening again. Raffe was watching me, or I hoped he was, which was pathetic. Josie had his undivided attention.

"Nope." He took my hand and guided me into the woods. "I'd rather be with you."

That was the problem.

We walked in silence, the music quieting as we went deeper, and the tingling dissipated. I stopped and leaned against a tree, the world tilting. "I need a minute."

"Are you going to be sick?" he asked with concern.

Some of my annoyance toward him vanished. He was taking care of me ... *again.* He was a good guy.

"I don't think so." I waved a finger. "The world went sideways for a second."

"Which means you're done drinking." He chuckled. "Though it's nice to see you let go."

"Never have I let go before. We'll see if it's worth it in the morning." I'd heard hangovers were a bitch, and honestly, the damn alcohol didn't numb the pain of being around Raffe. I wanted to not feel *anything* for once.

I needed to connect with the woods and animals while I could. I stood ... and stumbled. Slade caught me, pulling me flush against his chest.

Our faces were only inches apart again, and his eyes flicked down to my mouth. "We'll get you something to eat, and you'll be okay."

If he'd been Raffe, I would have melted into his arms and allowed him to close the distance between us. I wished like anything I could feel that way about Slade, but even drunk, the attraction wasn't there.

A tingle shot down my spine as Slade lowered his mouth toward mine.

"Slade. Stop." I shook my head, not wanting to hurt him, but also not wanting to lead him on.

He sighed. "Look, I get it. You don't want to ruin things between us, but let's share one kiss and see how it goes."

"I can't." I placed my hands on his chest and pushed.

His grip tightened, and I stayed in place. He tilted his head and pouted. "If you don't feel anything, we don't have to do it again."

My back straightened. He was pressuring me, and even drunk Skylar knew that. "No."

"Just once."

Fear clawed at my chest, and I stumbled back to gain distance. But he countered my move, pulling me closer.

A snarl came from behind us. Then suddenly Slade was gone.

CHAPTER SEVENTEEN

I stumbled forward, reeling from the sudden loss of Slade's support. The ground tilted under my feet, and for once, it wasn't from my blood.

"She said *no*," Raffe growled.

My heart rate picked up, but my blood didn't jolt or fizz. It was like it was broken, not attuned with emotions for once.

The fir trees closed in around me. I balanced myself on a trunk and looked to my right to find Raffe gripping Slade's shirt collar. Raffe's free hand was fisted, and the veins in his neck bulged.

Once again, Raffe was here to help me out of a horrible situation.

Slade puffed out his chest despite Raffe clutching his shirt and towering half a foot over him. "You don't know what you're talking about," Slade spat. "What are you even doing here? You're supposed to be with your friends, not spying on me."

"I wasn't spying on you, dickhead." Raffe's jaw clenched, his muscles working. "I was keeping an eye on Skylar."

My heart pitter-pattered. I liked the idea of Raffe

watching out for me a little too much, but even in my drunken haze, I understood it was less about his feelings toward me and more about making sure I didn't cause a scene.

After all, he had Josie and had never been an option for me.

"You don't need to. Besides, you made it clear you don't want to associate with Sky." Slade glared down at Raffe's hands. "Release me."

For the first time since coming here, I *hated* Slade using my nickname.

"Fine, but if you make one comment or even *look* in Skylar's direction, I'll kick your ass." Raffe's chest heaved, and his irises glowed. "Do you understand?"

"Why don't you go back to your friends and *Josie*?" Slade sneered. "Sky and I were doing fine until you appeared."

I laughed then cringed when Raffe's eyes flashed at me and the glow grew brighter. I swore dark fur sprouted on his arms, and then he punched Slade in the jaw. Slade's head snapped back, and he groaned.

Shit. Being drunk and in this situation was a nasty combination. I'd officially become one of *those* girls I judged.

"What the *fuck*," Slade rasped, clutching his jaw. "Wait until the school board learns about this."

School board? A chill ran down my back. I didn't want Raffe to get into trouble with the board or his father for protecting me.

"I hope you do tell them." Raffe bared his teeth, and they looked sharper than normal. "I'd love to tell them *exactly* what I stumbled upon and why I felt the need to intervene. No one, human or supernatural, should be pressured into anything, especially something physical."

My face burned, and I wrapped my arms around my waist. The thought of having to stand up in front of the university board and detail what had happened turned my stomach into knots. I didn't want to get Slade into trouble, especially since I hoped that alcohol was partly to blame for his actions, but I absolutely refused to throw Raffe to the wolves, no pun intended, for getting me out of the situation.

"And what exactly is that, mutt?" Slade stood straight, but it didn't make a difference because Raffe was larger than him in every way.

"I'm the mutt?" Raffe laughed harshly. "You're the one trying to force a woman to kiss you. She told you no two times, but you were still going for it. That's what a real dog would do, warlock or not. At least my morals aren't fucked."

Slade's hands quivered. "You traipsed after us instead of keeping an eye on the bloodsuckers?"

"Unlike you, I have friends I trust." Raffe tilted his head. "But that's what happens when you burn every relationship to the ground by doing shady things and getting information to make *Mommy* happy."

"Don't speak as if you know us." Slade shook his head, but his gaze landed on me.

Raffe shoved him back, and Slade tripped over his feet and landed on his ass. Raffe took the opportunity to tower over him and rasp, "I said don't fucking look at her."

Eyes tightening, Slade lifted his hands.

He was going to perform magic. I had to stop this before something awful happened, especially with innocent bystanders—humans—close by.

"You two, *stop.*" I pushed myself away from the tree, trying like hell to balance. If I swayed or stumbled, that would only prove how dire the situation had been. "I'm going home, so there's no need to continue *this.*" I waved a hand in front of me too hard and stutter-stepped.

"You heard her." Slade stood up and smoothed his shirt. "She's fine. Go back to your friends and leave us alone."

Raffe curled his lip. "So you can pressure her again? Not happening. I'll take her home, or she can join my group back at the bonfire."

"Fine, we'll go back." Slade started to turn to me.

Raffe caught his arm. "What did I tell you *not* to do again?"

I realized the crux of my entire problem. I wasn't sure if it was my drunken haze or this moment that made everything click into place. Overall, Slade's friends seemed nice, but I didn't fit in with them. I didn't belong with humans or supernaturals. With my body and emotions, I was human, but my blood held power, so I danced between two worlds, belonging to neither.

No wonder my parents had abandoned me, especially if they knew the type of magic I had.

The cold void inside me that seemed all-encompassing at times gaped open. I'd thought that learning about my heritage and finding friends had mended it some, but I'd been so wrong. Or maybe reality was ripping it back open.

No one understood me.

"I don't want to go back to the party." My voice shook, so I paused to get my act together. "I want to go back to my apartment." If I couldn't enjoy being in the woods without drama, I wanted to be in my bed, wallowing in self-pity. I needed to break down and accept the truth that it had taken me way too long to realize.

Raffe frowned and glared daggers at Slade. He pointed at me and said, "You've upset her and made her feel uncomfortable. Is that what your goal was tonight?"

"No!" Slade shook his head. "I wanted her to see that we

make sense together. But every time I feel like I'm making progress, you intervene."

"That wasn't *progress,* idiot." Raffe's voice hovered between words and a growl. "You're going to learn, one way or another."

I hurried to Raffe, my feet slipping, and caught his arm before he could punch Slade again. The buzz zipped between us, and Raffe relaxed enough to lower his arm. I didn't dare look at Slade. Focused only on Raffe, I murmured, "Don't. He's been drinking, and this isn't worth it."

"Sky, get away before he hurts you too," Slade said urgently.

The bit of headway I'd made with Raffe reversed, and he tugged me behind him, blocking me from Slade's view. The muscles in his back strained against his polo shirt. "I would *never* hurt her."

"Bullshit," Slade retorted, not valuing his health at all. "You've hurt her multiple times, blasting her in front of the class and with all your snide comments. Don't act like you're the hero when you've been the villain the whole fucking time."

It was true enough that I wouldn't argue with him. With Raffe, I wasn't sure what attitude I'd get when we were around other people. But one thing I knew without a doubt—when it came to my physical health, he'd been my main protector, and I felt safe with him. When he'd almost kissed me and I'd told him no, he'd stopped without hesitation, a huge contrast to how he treated me around others.

He'd explained himself, though his actions weren't truly justifiable. I was forbidden and, worse, an unknown.

So having Slade, the person who'd been kind and helpful, try to force himself on me had changed something deep within me. I'd been foolish to come out here alone with him.

"Slade, you need to go back to your friends." I stepped around Raffe, needing him to see my expression as I said it. I didn't want Slade to blame this on Raffe. "I'm going home, and I don't want you near me for the rest of the night."

His mouth dropped open. "Are you serious? He pays attention to you one time, and you're panting after him like all the other pathetic girls?"

I inhaled sharply. "That's not what I'm doing." Any other time, that accusation would have been valid. This time, I didn't feel safe with Slade. "You're not yourself tonight."

Raffe snorted. "You sure have her fooled."

"Fuck you," Slade said loudly, and he turned his hand over.

"If you cast any magic this close to humans, there will be consequences." Raffe crowded Slade and said slowly, "Holding my wolf back when all I want to do is sink my teeth into your throat is the hardest thing I've ever had to do. If I can do that, you better not touch me with your magic, or not only will you have to answer to Dad and me, you'll have to address it with your mother too."

His mother.

He'd mentioned her in passing a handful of times. She was the priestess of their coven and busy, but when he spoke about her, respect shone in his eyes. Now, two different people had brought her up and made it clear she was *very* important in his life. Something about the context nagged at me. I was missing something important.

"Fine. I can see she's drunk and can't see reason." Slade rolled his shoulders. "I'll let your friends know you took off with her."

Raffe tapped his temple. "Don't worry about my friends. I'll take care of it. Got it?" More power than usual radiated off him.

Despite not being a supernatural, I could feel it, and I understood why all the supernaturals feared him and his father. Slade didn't have half that amount of power within him.

"Fine." He sneered as if he smelled something bad then glared at me. He didn't say goodbye as he stalked past me toward his friends.

With his face twisted in disgust and the coldness in his eyes, he looked like another person. Not even close to the guy I knew. The one who'd catered to me, helping me and joking around. This Slade was a stranger.

The tingles on my neck started again. I hated to think what expression Raffe saw on my face, but a pain throbbed in my chest. One I was all too familiar with.

Betrayal and loneliness.

Raffe cleared his throat. "You ready to head back to your apartment?"

No, I wasn't. I wanted to go deeper into the woods, away from all these people, and enjoy the cloudy night and lie on the ground surrounded by nature. Back home, I'd spent time in the woods behind our house each day, and not connecting with nature daily had thrown me off center. I glanced longingly at the surrounding trees.

"We either need to join the others or head to your apartment." He moved in front of me, his expression soft and eyes the warm cobalt I'd seen a handful of times. "With vampires out here, it's not safe for you."

I swallowed loudly. "They're feeding off humans?"

He nodded. "They are, but that's why the witches and my friends are here. We make sure they don't make a scene or get out of line. With how crazy Edward was for your blood, I'd rather not risk your safety."

I became queasy. These humans thought they were

heading to a party, but they were coming to get feasted on. I shivered, wondering how many victims they'd have before the night was over. Even if the victims didn't remember the attack, they still suffered during that moment.

I swallowed my words. I understood what it was like for people to view you as weak and take things from you. Way back in kindergarten, Lizzy had broken my trust and destroyed my innocence when she'd decided to attack me. But I was too drunk to have that conversation, and all it would do was piss Raffe off and not change anything.

Raffe held out his hand, his face softening. "Let's go."

The *yank* in my chest had my legs moving closer and my hand taking his before I knew what was happening. The comforting buzz channeled between us.

A lump formed in my throat. "If you walk me to the tree line, I can get the rest of the way back without ruining your night with—" I stopped, unable to say *Josie* even though I *needed* to say it to remind myself of her existence and make her real. "Friends." Of course, that was the word I'd settle on.

He groaned, tossing his head back. "Dammit, Skylar. You're gonna be the death of me."

"That's why I'm trying not to cause you more problems." I averted my gaze, waiting for him to take the excuse and leave me.

"You're stuck with me," Raffe whispered as he put a finger under my chin, tilting up my face so we could look each other in the eyes. "Let's go before Slade changes his mind and comes back looking for you."

That was enough to get me moving.

Walking in stride with Raffe, I hated that I stumbled every few steps.

"How many drinks did you have tonight?" He arched a brow and glanced at me. I hated that every expression he had was somehow as sexy as the one before. There were no bad angles, which made trying not to be attracted to him more difficult.

Knowing I couldn't lie without smelling like rotten eggs to him, I sighed. "I lost count. But after meeting *your* parents and causing a scene, I stopped thinking clearly." If I'd known I'd get this bad and make worse decisions, I would've abstained.

"Yeah, I heard you fried some lights." He winced. "I'm sorry about all of it."

"Sorry?" He hadn't done anything. He'd been on the field, warming up with his team.

"Dad was angry that you were there and asked if I was aware you were coming." He bit his bottom lip, which wasn't normal for him. "I get that he's worried. I mean, you did break the lights, but luckily, it could be blamed on electrical shit. But I didn't realize until tonight that our request wasn't fair to you either."

Once again, the kind and understanding guy from the other night reappeared, and dammit, I needed him to go away before things got more strained between us. It was better when he was a jerk because then I could pretend to hate him. "I won't make that mistake again."

"You deserve to have a college experience too, though." He shrugged. "And it was nice that every time I made a play, I turned and saw you watching me."

My pulse quickened, and the lack of my blood responding made my skin crawl. I wanted to say I'd enjoyed that part of the night too, but I didn't need to encourage more strangeness between us.

"Don't get me wrong." He squeezed my hand. "I understand my dad and where he's coming from. But it's tricky. As king, he has to think about what's best for the most people, and it's not safe for you to be around humans or supernaturals with how unstable you are."

I opened my mouth, ready to tell him where he could shove his and his daddy's opinion, but he continued, "But asking you to isolate yourself feels wrong, so I'm not sure what that says about me as the future king. I don't want to do that to you anymore, and honestly, that scares me."

All my anger whooshed from me. I blinked, trying to understand what was happening.

He was talking to me about his concerns and problems.

"You want friends." He smiled sadly and stepped closer. "And you picked one of the worst ones possible, which I tried to warn you about."

I tried to glare at him, but turning my head had me almost falling to my knees. He wrapped an arm around my waist and caught me before I could hit the ground.

Every inch of me buzzed where he touched me, even through my shirt. I caught my breath, getting more lightheaded.

When he helped me up, our chests touched, and the tingles coursed throughout my body. I moaned, unable to hold the sound in.

His eyes glowed faintly. "What's wrong?"

My drunk tongue spoke before my mind registered the words. "Wherever you touch me, my skin buzzes." I winced. I sounded pathetic.

His brows lifted. "What do you mean buzzes? Is it because you're drunk?"

I'd already said it—might as well own it. "At first, it was just when our skin touched. Whenever you touched me over clothes, I felt nothing. But now—"

His irises glowed brighter, transfixing me.

"That's impossible." He shook his head. "You're *human*."

His words were like a cold shower. I was forbidden. "Sorry. I know it sounds weird. Forget I said anything." My eyes burned, and I wanted to kick myself. I tried to release his hand and move away, but he held me tightly.

"You don't understand." He held me in place and gazed into my eyes. "I feel it too."

My lungs seized. I must have heard him wrong. "How is that possible? What is it?"

He smiled. "I don't know. I've never experienced anything like it before."

"Me neither." I turned away, needing distance so I could think straight. He had Josie, and I had to remember that.

He didn't say anything as he fell back into step with me.

The silence turned awkward, so I decided to fill it. "Your eyes glowed a lot tonight. What does that mean?"

"I bet they did." He chuckled. "That happens when our wolf magic surges forward. When we get angry, feel threatened, or use our pack link, our eyes glow more. The brighter it is, the more magic we're using, and the harder it is to hold our wolf back."

"Pack link?" Slade had mentioned it, but I wanted to hear it from Raffe.

He nodded. "It's how wolves communicate telepathically, using wolf magic."

Wow. "You can talk to everyone that way?"

"Anyone in the United States if I wanted to because they all roll up to my dad and me. But I can't talk to any of the wolves overseas because they're separate packs. Only our alpha—my dad—can link with their alpha, if they have one, and all the US pack members. There's a whole hierarchy, so the lowest pack alpha can link only to his pack members and his alpha. His alpha can link to all the lowest-level alphas and all those pack members, and that alpha links to his own alpha, who can link to all the packs below him, and then to the alpha above him, and so on up to me and my dad."

I snorted. "It's like a pyramid scheme?"

"Ugh." He tilted his head back. "Seriously? No one would ever dare say something like that to me ... until you."

"Good. Someone needs to keep you humble." I wrinkled my nose. "But no, I get it. Even better, maybe some of my knowledge about animals will come in handy around you all."

"Animal knowledge, huh?" He moved closer, our arms brushing. "What do you know?"

"Do you have all night? Because I'm applying to vet school and taking all the required science classes."

He beamed. "A vet. Really?"

The way he smiled had warmth spreading throughout my body. "Yeah. That's why I came to school here." I paused and lifted my free hand. "Well, that and the scholarship. I've been told animals are unusually drawn to me."

I both loved and hated how natural this whole conversation was between us. Talking to him was easy, more so than talking with Lucy.

"It's your calming presence." He scratched the back of his neck. "It's easy to feel comfortable around you."

"Doesn't seem that way when I'm around you and Keith." I laughed dryly. "Or your dad."

"Well, yeah." He shrugged. "We can sense you have some sort of influence over us, which makes us wary. We have stronger wolves, and we aren't used to anyone affecting us like that. But I have to admit, I'm glad you've been able to help Lucy. She's always felt like she has to be perfect—you being assigned as her roommate has been Fate's blessing."

"What?" I tilted my head. "We don't do anything special."

"Nah, and that's what makes it nice. She can be herself

around you. She said after you two watch *Criminal Minds* together, she can go to sleep without issue."

That sentence alone would scare most people. Who would find watching a show about murders relaxing? Apparently, Lucy and I did.

We reached the tree line, and I expected Raffe to take the opportunity to split off from me, but he didn't slow down or release my hand as we continued to my apartment.

He rubbed his lips. "Lucy felt bad about not following you earlier, after the situation with my parents, but she stayed with them to keep Mom from going after you and asking questions."

"I'm glad she didn't find me." When I got like that, it was best for me to be alone. "It would've been weird if she'd come into the bathroom stall with me."

He laughed, the sound deep and carefree. "That's fair."

At the apartment entrance, he opened the door for me. He released my hand and followed me inside.

I tried to hide my smile. He was walking me to my door.

I wasn't sure what to say, but the silence wasn't tense. It was as if we'd known each other for years.

Outside my door, I turned to him. "Thank you for everything tonight."

He pursed his lips. "Are you trying to get rid of me?"

My hands stilled. "You said you were taking me to my apartment. I figured you'd want to go back and hang out with your ... friends." I still couldn't make myself say *Josie*.

"I thought we could hang out." He shrugged and fidgeted. "I told them I wasn't coming back."

"Oh." My jaw dropped a little.

He smirked, wrapping one arm around my waist and punching in the code.

The door clicked, and he pushed it open. He shuffled me backward into the apartment.

My skin prickled with awareness. We were alone.

When the door shut, he spun me around and caged me between his arms and the door.

"It's about damn time I got you alone," he murmured, his breath fanning my face and mixing with his unique scent.

My head fogged, and it had nothing to do with the alcohol.

He lowered his head, his eyes on my lips.

Everything inside me screamed to let him kiss me. If my lips tingled from just a brush, I could only imagine how intoxicating a full kiss would feel.

With his lips an inch from mine, I breathed out, "But Josie."

His entire body flinched. "Dammit, Skylar." He pulled back. "Do you not want to kiss me? *I* know that no means no."

"Is that a serious question?" My hands fisted in his shirt, and I wasn't sure if I was pulling him closer or pushing him away. I feared it was the former. "Of course I do. But not when you're with someone else."

He sighed. "You won't like it, but I've got something to tell you."

My heart nearly stopped. What had he been keeping from me?

CHAPTER EIGHTEEN

I clenched my hands, trying to contain my frustration. He'd better start talking *now*. "Are you engaged to her?" I didn't know why that was where my mind had leaped. She was gorgeous, and not forbidden to him, so why wouldn't he settle down with her? But then why the hell was he here with me? Was I some conquest he wanted to make before they exchanged vows? Not that I was anything to brag about, but that was all I could come up with.

"What? No," he replied hurriedly, cupping my face with his hand. "Not even close to that."

Some of the pressure squeezing my body lifted, but cold fear still strangled my heart. "Then what?"

One side of his mouth tipped upward. "Josie and I are *just* friends. Nothing more."

I could breathe again, and something warm expanded in my chest—hope. "You jackass. That was the last thing I expected you to say."

"Yeah, I got that after the engagement comment." He snickered. "But I figure this news is just as bad in a different way."

"What do you mean?" The thought of him being with Josie these past weeks had been hell. At least it wouldn't torment me anymore.

He placed his hand on the door beside me and leaned closer. "It's hard enough to stay away from you and appear indifferent, but I played up the Josie angle to make you want to stay away from me." He pressed his forehead to mine. "We've been friends since forever. She's part of my dad's pack, and we support each other, but that's it."

My stomach dropped. I *had* been using her existence as a reminder to stay away from Raffe. "I'm still forbidden to you."

He grimaced. "I know. Believe me. But I'm finding it hard to care about that, especially when I'm with you like this." He stared at me with those warm eyes that were my undoing.

Maybe the alcohol was influencing me, but Raffe was here in front of me, wanting to kiss me. He wasn't with anyone, so it wasn't wrong. There was no reason to say no if he tried again, right? Other than him stealing my heart.

Wolf peeking through, he licked his lips. "I'm going to try to kiss you again, but if you still don't want me to, all you have to say is stop."

My head spun, and I nodded. "Okay."

He smiled, and then his lips were on mine, urgent yet soft enough that I still had control. My skin sizzled as I followed his lead. I'd never been kissed before, and this was the most amazing experience ever.

Something came over me, and my tongue glided across his mouth, begging for entrance.

He growled, the sound warming my body and making my brain hazier as I wrapped my arms around his neck and pulled him closer.

I needed more of him, his taste, his smell. Everything about him was so damn tempting and perfect.

Responding in earnest, he deepened the kiss, his hands sliding down to my waist, where he touched my bare skin.

A desperate moan escaped me. I should've been embarrassed, but with the way he was touching me, I couldn't think past how good his touch felt.

"Fuck," he rasped, pulling away from my mouth and trailing kisses down my neck. His lips hovered over the main artery in my neck where my pulse pounded, but I didn't feel any panic or fear like when the vampire had bitten me.

An overwhelming desire came over me, and I tilted my head back, giving him better access to my neck. My heart pounded, and my blood jolted, finally waking up from the night.

His teeth raked against my skin, and I whimpered and grabbed his hair, pressing him into my neck while heat flooded my body.

It wasn't enough. I needed *more*.

He stilled and kissed my neck softly in the same spot where his teeth had grazed me, and then he untangled my hands from his hair. He leaned back, putting distance between us, but one hand remained on my waist, anchoring me in place.

Oh my God. He didn't like what I'd done. Why had I tried to get him to bite me? I wanted to become invisible and never look him in the eye again. Had I suffocated him by shoving his face into my neck? Did he think I wanted to dominate him? I was certain an alpha wouldn't like that. "I'm so sorry." I closed my eyes, not wanting to see the disgust on his face.

He laughed huskily. "What the fuck for?"

My eyes flew open. "For smothering you."

"For *what?*" His head tilted and his forehead creased.

He wouldn't make this easy for me. "I shoved your face in

my neck, and you stopped." My face was on fire. I wanted to die right here and now. Death would be better than having this conversation and then seeing him every day after my heart was ripped from my chest.

A smile took over half his face, and he looked nothing like the broody man everyone saw. "First off, you weren't smothering me, and even if you had been, I wouldn't have fucking stopped. I liked it ... *a lot.*"

"You did?" I asked, placing a hand on his chest. I didn't want to stop touching him, which was hugely problematic. "Then why *did* you stop?"

His hand tightened on my waist as he leaned down, his nose brushing my neck where he'd kissed it. "Because I enjoyed it way too much. And you aren't sober."

My face flamed again but for a whole different reason. "If I was sober, I would've done the same thing."

"Maybe." He kissed the spot one more time and straightened. "But I'd rather confirm that for myself. You also had a bad experience tonight, and I want to make sure you're thinking clearly." He tucked a lock of my hair behind my ear. "In fairness, I shouldn't have kissed you until tomorrow, but it's so damn hard to control myself around you."

I must have misunderstood him. "I doubt you'll be kissing me tomorrow after we've both had some sleep and wake up refreshed." That damn pain shot through my heart again. Kissing him had been foolish. He'd made it clear we would never be together, and it had been hard enough to stay away from him before we kissed. This would only make things unbearable.

"Oh, I'll be kissing you. Trust me." He pulled my body to his. "If you still want to in the morning, that is." He cleared his throat and bit his lip, not looking like the confident man he usually was.

"But why?" Not even two weeks ago, he'd told me we would never, ever happen. "You said—"

His face fell. "I know what I said, but I'm tired of fighting this connection." He shivered. "Seeing Slade trying to kiss you, I almost fucking lost it. And when you said no, I was able to breathe again ... until that douchebag pressured you and kept doing it."

Tingles spread throughout my body, making me feel as if I could fly. "But your father ..." I hated to bring up all our issues, but the more time we spent together, the harder it would be if we didn't face them.

"If you think I don't know every obstacle we'll have to face to be together, you're wrong." He pinched the bridge of his nose and took a step back. "That's why I put distance between us so hard the past week and a half, but tonight, everything changed. In a way, I have Slade to thank for that because, Skylar, I wanna be with you."

This had to be a dream. I'd wake up, and the cruel reality would crush me. But the way my heart pounded, I faced only one true choice. "I want to be with you too." And I did, so desperately.

He exhaled in relief like he hadn't expected that answer. "Here's the thing, though. Until I can figure out how to handle this with my dad and the wolf shifters, I'd like to keep this a secret."

A secret.

I liked the sound of that. If people knew Raffe and I were dating, they'd watch me closely. That was the last thing I needed. "Fine, but I have two stipulations. First, we're exclusive, public or not. I don't share."

"Yeah?" He smirked, taking a step toward me again. "Good, I don't either. As long as you agree to be exclusive with me, I accept your first term."

"Agreed." I nodded, my heart skipping a beat. That had been far easier than I'd expected.

He pulled me flush against his body and nipped my earlobe. He murmured, "Good. I'd hate to have to kill every damn man who thinks they have a chance with you."

I took a shaky breath. What type of person was I to find his threat so damn sexy? I had to keep going before I forgot myself. "Second, you don't get to be a dick to me anymore."

"Sky—"

"I get that, if we're secret, we can't be super friendly, but no insults or public humiliations, including from Keith." I lifted a brow. I needed to know he was in my corner even in public. Also, I was tired of my life being a living hell.

He took my hand in his and put it over his heart. He vowed, "I swear, and I'm sorry. I—"

"Don't." I didn't want him to apologize. "That's not the point. I understand the position you're in, but if we're in this, then respect has to be given ... both ways."

"That's all I want to give you."

I arched a brow. "All you want to give me is respect? What happened to all the promises of what you'll do to me tomorrow when I'm sober?"

Raising my fingers to his lips, he kissed each one, and my body sizzled.

He winked. "You're right. I want to give you a lot more than just respect."

Aaand I needed a cold shower. I'd never been aroused like this before.

He closed his eyes and took a step back. "Dammit, Sky. You're going to be the death of me."

"What did I do?" We'd been flirting, and now he seemed flustered.

"Your scent." He opened his eyes, his irises glowing. "I

can smell your desire, and it's taking every ounce of control I have not to touch you."

I wanted to convince him that was exactly what he should do, but he'd made it clear he didn't want to do anything more while I was tipsy, and we had agreed to respect one another.

Of course, that was when my stomach gurgled. I hadn't eaten dinner.

He smirked. "Now *that* gives me an idea."

"My growly stomach?" I rocked back on my heels. "Really?"

"Yup." He removed his keys from his jeans pocket and lifted them. "Wanna go for a ride and grab something to eat? I'm starving after the game. There's a Taco Bell close by that's open late."

I wasn't a huge fan of Taco Bell, but I could stand to eat something. From what I'd seen, food helped with not winding up with a hangover. "Okay."

He laced our fingers again and opened the door. "Let's ride."

That was an odd way to put it, but whatever. I was down to go anywhere with him.

Hand in hand, we headed to the elevator. It was surreal walking with him like this, and my cheeks hurt from smiling so big.

As we rode down the elevator, he pulled me into his arms and nuzzled my neck. I gasped as desire surged through me again, making him groan.

I smacked him away and laughed. "Why do you keep doing that if you're going to complain?"

"Believe me, I'm not complaining." He pecked my lips and pulled back. "It's fucking hot."

The door opened, and he led me out the front to the parking lot. We headed toward a fancy black motorcycle and a white Navigator. Of course, I'd expect nothing less than the best for the future wolf king.

When we got close, he released my hand and went to the back of the bike. He unlocked the storage container and removed two black full-face helmets.

I glanced at him and then the Navigator. I hadn't expected him to own the bike.

"You're sober enough to hold on tight to me, right?" He held a helmet.

"Are you serious?"

"If you're feeling dizzy and don't mind me driving your car, we can take that." His nose wrinkled, but he smoothed out his expression in a clear attempt to hide his disgust.

"I'm almost back to normal." My head had stopped spinning, though my blood still wasn't acting normal. I'd gotten all hot and bothered by him, and it hadn't fizzed or hummed. "This is your bike?"

He cut his eyes. "Is that so hard to believe?"

Actually, no, now that I thought about it. "How fast does it go?"

"Fast, but it's a cruiser bike, so it's comfortable." He ran a hand over it. "I got it this summer. It's a Dark Horse."

Whatever that meant. I could tell it was one of the more expensive bikes. "Yeah, okay." I took the helmet from him. "And you're comfortable having a second rider?"

"We're about to find out, but I'm confident we'll be okay. Otherwise, I wouldn't risk it." He put his helmet on and flipped up the glass then helped me with mine.

It slid on without issue. "You've never ridden with anyone before?" That was hard to believe since he had two helmets.

"Nope. I've never wanted anyone to ride my baby with me before." He slung his leg over the bike. "This is my hobby that I've never shared with anyone until you. I ran out and got a second helmet the next day, just in case I ever got the opportunity to ride with you."

My vision blurred, and my chest ached but in a good way. He'd acted like such an ass this whole time, but he'd been pining for me as much as I had for him. "Well then, let's ride." I slid on behind him.

When I wrapped my arms around him, he glanced back. "You better hold on tight."

And then we were off, and I'd never felt so free.

The next morning, I woke up tingly, warm, and completely content.

In other words, I'd found my home.

I peeled my eyes open to find myself nestled between Raffe's arm and body, my head on his chest, rising with each breath. His face was relaxed in sleep.

After he'd gotten me to eat three tacos while he'd eaten three big boxes of food, we'd ridden back to my apartment. Lucy hadn't returned home, and the two of us had passed out in my bed, cuddling.

My stomach fluttered as I finally understood what I'd been feeling on my drive here that first day. This place wasn't meant to be my home—being in Raffe's arms was.

I closed my eyes to settle back into sleep, but someone knocked at the front door.

My body tensed. Who would be here this early on Sunday? They must be here for Lucy. There was no way I was getting out of this bed.

Just as I began to drift off, I heard another round of banging.

This time, Raffe moved and then kissed the top of my

head. He murmured, "Stay here. I'll be right back."

I wanted to pout, but I noticed the skin around his eyes was tight. I swallowed it back. Maybe it was one of his friends, someone who knew he was here and wasn't happy about it.

Not wanting to pressure him, I moved away from his side, and he was out the door before I could register it.

"Shit!" Lucy shouted from her room just as the front door opened.

Raffe growled so loudly even I could hear it. "What the fuck do you think you're doing?"

CHAPTER NINETEEN

My blood jolted as my heart raced. From Raffe's reaction, it could only be one person. But surely Slade would've texted me before showing up here, especially after last night.

"I'm here to see Sky," Slade snapped. "What are *you* doing here?"

Dammit, there was my confirmation. I had to get out there *now*.

I tossed the covers off just as Lucy charged into my room. Her eyes were wide, and her hair was tangled, indicating she'd been asleep. She yanked on her oversized sweatshirt and blinked several times. "What's going on?"

"It's none of your damn business why I'm here," Raffe rasped. "Now leave."

My stomach dropped. "Raffe didn't tell you?"

"Tell me what?" Her brows furrowed.

"You don't live here, and you aren't *my* boss, so you don't have any say in the matter," Slade retorted.

I had no time for this. "I'll tell you in a minute."

I headed into the living room where Raffe was blocking

the entryway into the apartment. Slade had his fists clenched and his shoulders back, making it obvious that he wasn't leaving. His jaw was bruised from where Raffe had punched him, and he had to tilt his head up to stare Raffe in the eyes.

My blood fizzed. I could sense Raffe's raw anger and Slade's determination and annoyance.

They were going to make a scene if they didn't cool it. The last thing we needed was humans witnessing this confrontation.

"You two get in here," I demanded, grabbing Raffe's arm and tugging him farther back into the living room.

His head jerked in my direction, his nostrils flaring as he stared at me. The buzz between us spurred to life and calmed my blood to a jolt. "What?" he gasped.

And people said women were the dramatic ones? I rolled my eyes. "Unless you want to make a scene." I gestured to Slade and the hallway.

"Sky—" Lucy started.

Raffe huffed. "Fine, but he comes in only enough to shut the door."

Slade smirked. "You heard her." He entered the apartment, his shoulder slamming into Raffe's in a *fuck-you* move. He must have thought he'd won with me.

What was it with these two? Slade had more animosity toward Raffe than anyone else, and I still hadn't put all the pieces together.

Slade tried to come farther into the apartment, but I dropped my hand from Raffe and stepped in front of Slade as Raffe closed the door.

As soon as I stopped touching Raffe, my blood started to fizz. Dread pooled hard in my stomach. Slade emanated triumph and confidence, and I regretted letting him in. But I'd done it more for Raffe than for him, and he needed to know that. "To be clear, you're not staying. I only invited you in so you two didn't cause a scene in the hallway."

Slade flinched, and shock and anger took over. "Are you serious? You're going to let him boss you around too, like you're one of his pups?"

Wow. He'd never talked to me like that before, and it stung.

"You son of a bi—" Raffe started and moved to get between Slade and me.

There was no way I was letting Raffe interfere, especially after *that* comment. I stepped forward and poked my finger into Slade's chest.

I spoke slowly and clearly to make sure he understood my words since whatever asshole had taken over his body last night had struggled with that. "Me not wanting you here has *nothing* to do with Raffe. It has to do with your lack of respect last night and how you showed up at my door uninvited, demanding to talk to me. You say he's arrogant and expects to be obeyed—how do you think you're coming across right now?"

Slade's expression changed, but the emotion wasn't remorse. In fact, he looked more calculating. "We're *friends*. I didn't think that—"

"Are we?" I crossed my arms, noticing Raffe's deep frown. "I'm pretty sure last night changed that."

"Anyone going to fill me in?" Lucy asked from behind me.

I glanced over my shoulder at her. "Slade tried to kiss me." I'd leave it at that. I didn't need to embarrass him or myself further with more specifics.

"Tried to force her to kiss him is more like it," Raffe growled.

Slade huffed. "She wanted to. She just—"

In a blur, Raffe had Slade pinned against the wall by the

neck before I could blink. Raffe's entire body was as rigid as a statue.

"Do not even attempt to *finish* that sentence." Raffe took a ragged breath. "She said no twice, and you ignored her. Now you come here after I told you not to look at her? You should be glad you're not fucking dead. I'm about to change my mind if you keep pushing."

My blood came close to humming. I needed to get it under control, but I wasn't sure how with Raffe about to snap as well.

"That was you?" Lucy asked as she came to my side, blinking. "Raffe didn't name names, just said he had to get involved."

My heart ached, and Slade laughed.

His emotions changed to vindication and bitterness. "Why am I not surprised that he'd leave that out? We can't disappoint *Daddy*." He threw a parental reference at Raffe like he had last night. I wondered if Slade was pushing Raffe to make him snap.

I touched the center of Raffe's shoulders, my skin buzzing and my blood calming a notch. "He's not worth it." I wished I could pack-link with Raffe so Slade couldn't hear our conversation.

Raffe's breathing evened out, my touch impacting him as well.

"She's right." Lucy cleared her throat. "He's a punk, and if you do something, you're the one who'll get into trouble, especially since Skylar's human."

Her insinuation was clear—If King Jovian learned that Raffe had been here, protecting me, he'd know we were spending time together. Raffe had asked for time to figure out how to tell people about us. I could give him that.

Releasing his hold, Raffe took a step back, allowing Slade to land hard on his feet.

I couldn't believe how much I'd misread Slade. I'd thought he was a good guy and trustworthy, and in the blink of an eye, everything had changed. "You need to leave. I don't want to talk to you. Today or any time in the future."

He huffed. "Sky, can we talk without an audience?" He gestured at Raffe and Lucy as if I didn't know who he was talking about.

Like he thought I was stupid.

"It's Skylar to you," I corrected, and the corners of Raffe's mouth tipped upward. "And no. We have nothing left to say to each other. I'm too upset to talk to you. You need to go." Not wanting to drag out this visit any longer, I dropped my hand from Raffe and turned to my room.

Lucy stood a few feet in front of me, her eyes on the hand that had stopped touching Raffe.

Not even twelve hours in, and I might have blown our secret. I'd have to be more careful.

"You heard her." Raffe sounded so happy. "Leave ... or I'll fucking make you."

I heard the sound of a scuffle as I reached the hallway that separated Lucy's room and mine. When I turned right to go into my room, I glanced back. Slade was brushing off his shirt with Raffe hovering over him. Slade said, "I'm going."

I went into my room and shut the door. I needed Slade to see I was serious. He'd know Raffe would never let him anywhere close to my room, especially after last night.

Now that I was alone, the sting of betrayal attacked my heart, and my vision blurred. All this time, I'd believed that Slade was my one loyal friend. At times, his friendship had been the only reason I didn't feel so alone here, and I'd trusted him implicitly. To have that ripped away made me feel exposed.

My blood fizzed close to a hum. I didn't want Raffe to see me like this. Not after he'd decided that he wanted us to be together. He might take it all back if I lost control again ... and I couldn't handle that after Slade.

The front door opened and closed, and I lay down on my bed and closed my eyes. I needed to pull the image of the deer and the woods into my mind to calm myself down.

Footsteps headed toward my room, and Lucy called out, "Raffe, what the—"

My heart clenched. She was going to ask questions, and he didn't want anyone to know about us.

"Not now, Lucy," he commanded. Then his footsteps were outside my door.

"Don't—" I started just as the door opened.

I opened my eyes, but I couldn't see anything through my tears.

"Sky—" Raffe closed my door. "Dammit. Don't cry."

I wished that was my only problem.

He was at my side in seconds. He lay down next to me, scooping me into his arms, and anchoring me to his chest. The danger level of my blood lessened in his embrace as the buzzing soared to life between us.

Surrounded by his touch and scent, I felt safe and comforted, which made me cry harder. How did that make sense? I was a complete and utter mess in front of Raffe, but I didn't have it in me to pull away.

I was a train wreck.

"Hey, what's wrong?" Raffe kissed the top of my head. "Why are you crying? Did he do something I didn't see?"

His concern and tenderness made the emotions pour out more. "No," I croaked.

"Then what?" His fingertips trailed up and down my back.

I sniffled and wiped the tears from my cheeks, but more replaced them. I managed to clear them enough to see Raffe's face.

His forehead was creased, and his brows were furrowed. He was worried, and I wasn't answering him.

"That's it. I'm fucking killing him." Raffe blew out a breath. "He doesn't deserve to live after hurting you like this."

"Don't." I took a deep breath to get myself together. The sting was there, but I needed to explain why I was so upset. "I trusted him. That's all. I thought he was my friend. The first one I've had since ..." I trailed off, agony stabbing my heart again. "Since kindergarten." I sounded pathetic.

"I should've punched his ass again," he snarled, and I laughed.

The sound hurt my raw throat, but despite being a snotty, crying mess, I found myself smiling. Who would've thought someone wanting to hurt a person for me would make me happy? "You just want an excuse to hit him."

His eyes warmed to the color that was quickly becoming a favorite. "I do regularly wish to kick his ass, but this is different. I want to kill him. He's an opportunistic asshole, and I hate that he set his sights on you."

I bit my bottom lip. "Why did he? I don't understand."

"There's no telling with him." He pressed his lips together and cupped my face. "It doesn't matter. I won't allow him to hurt you anymore." He moved to kiss me.

I turned my head into the pillow, and he stiffened like something was wrong.

Crap. I hadn't meant to hurt his feelings. I rubbed my face in my pillow, wiping off the excess tears, and turned back to find his jaw clenched.

"You don't want to kiss me right now. I'm a snotty mess."

He relaxed and arched a brow. "I *always* want to kiss you." He moved toward me again, and his lips landed softly on mine.

The sizzle took over, and I was so glad he'd tried again.

A knock sounded on my door. "Hey, I'm coming in."

The doorknob turned, and I tried to move away from him, but he held me in place. My eyes widened as Lucy stepped into my room, and Raffe lay on his back, keeping me in his arms.

Lucy snorted. "Why am I not surprised to find you two like this?"

My jaw dropped. "You're not?"

Raffe tilted his chin. "You better not tell anyone else until I decide how to tell Dad."

She lifted a hand. "I won't say a word, but why tell me?"

"Because I'll be around here a lot, and you would have figured it out anyway." Raffe shrugged.

A huge smile spread across my face. I loved that he already planned on spending more time with me.

"Don't interrupt our girl time." Lucy placed her hands on her hips.

"If I want to be here—"

"He won't." I refused to limit my time with a real friend, and Lucy was definitely that. "I'll make sure of it."

Raffe blinked like he couldn't believe what I'd said.

Lucy winked and said, "That's my girl. All right, I'm heading back to bed." She left the two of us alone.

"As fun as this is ..." Raffe untangled himself from me and stood. "I need to run back to my apartment and change." I damn near pouted, but he added, "I'll meet you in thirty minutes at the edge of the tree line behind this building."

I sat straight up. "Are we going into the woods?"

"You bet." He pecked my forehead and headed to my door.

I jumped up and hurried to get ready, truly excited.

Yesterday had been amazing. Raffe had changed and grabbed some food, and we'd spent all afternoon in the woods. I hadn't expected it to be as rejuvenating as it was when I was alone, but with Raffe, it was even better.

Slade had always talked or led the way, but Raffe was different. Half the time, we didn't speak, just enjoyed each other's presence, and I got to lie on the ground, absorbed in nature with him beside me.

He'd left to go hang out with Keith and Adam, not wanting them to become suspicious, but that was fine. Lucy and I got to watch *Criminal Minds* together.

I'd woken up an hour earlier than usual before class this morning to get coffee and breakfast before the time I usually met up with Slade. I didn't bother bringing my backpack since I'd be coming back to the apartment before class.

As I walked out of the apartment building and headed toward the student center, Slade stepped out of the woods.

My throat went dry, and I removed my phone from my pocket and sent Raffe a text. He'd made me promise to let him know if Slade showed up when he wasn't around.

Me: Slade is outside my apartment.

I put my phone back in my pocket. Raffe would be on his way soon, and he could smell my scent, so I took off toward the student center.

"Sky ... lar!" Slade called out. "Wait."

He had some balls approaching me like this after everything. I picked up my pace, giving him my answer. I wouldn't even acknowledge his presence.

"Dammit, why do you have to make things so difficult?" he muttered.

If he was trying to fix the issues between us, he was handling the situation horribly. As he caught up to me, my blood jolted, and a scream lodged in my throat. What was it with him and not taking no for an answer?

"I found something out!" he called, stopping me in my tracks.

My blood fizzed. "What is it?" I kept my back to him, ready to take off if it was something I wasn't interested in hearing. I didn't like that he kept pushing me to talk instead of waiting for me to come to him on my own terms.

"You know what I mean. I learned more about what you are. If you want to know what it is, you'll have to talk to me."

CHAPTER TWENTY

I fought the urge to beg him for the information. It took every ounce of my self-control.

My blood fizzed at that dangerous level that meant a hum and havoc weren't far behind. But dammit, Slade knew how important this information was to me. I could only hope he was telling the truth and not playing games. "Why should I believe you?" I couldn't give in too easily, but my suspicion was all for show. I was certain he knew that. He had me right where he wanted me.

"When have I ever lied to you?" he answered.

The one benefit of my magic stirring to this level was that I could read his emotions, but they weren't helpful. Determination and annoyance.

Needing to see his expression, I turned around. Slade had come here to dangle a carrot in front of my face, and he wanted to push me into talking to him instead of waiting until I was ready. Disappointment sat heavy in me, making it hard to breathe, but I didn't want to risk missing out on important information. "And?" I arched a brow, refusing to give him more than that after the shit he'd pulled Saturday night and yesterday morning.

He smirked, and I regretted asking.

He took a step closer. "I think we should—" He cut himself off and glanced toward the apartment buildings at the exact moment the base of my neck tingled.

Raffe was here.

My heart jolted, but my blood didn't surge. I didn't take my eyes off Slade. I needed to read every damn expression on his face.

"Did you text them?" Slade's nose wrinkled, and the skin around his eyes tightened. "Or is Raffe stalking you?"

Them?

Unable to stop myself, I looked in Raffe's direction to find him, Keith, and Adam stalking over.

Raffe had on EEU evergreen-colored sweatpants and a black T-shirt while Keith wore boxer shorts and a white tank top. Adam was dressed in jeans and a polo shirt, indicating he'd been up, unlike the other two. My gaze immediately went back to Raffe and the noticeable bulge in his sweatpants. The cold weather had no effect on him, or if it did, any future physical interaction we might have together just got way more intimidating.

My body flooded with warmth. What the fuck was wrong with me, having these thoughts at a very inappropriate time?

For a split second, Raffe's irises warmed to cobalt as our gazes connected.

I wanted to die all over again. He'd told me he could smell my arousal. I could only assume ...

Oh God, no.

Then his eyes cooled back to their icy shade as he took the spot next to me and faced Slade. He growled, "What did I say about fucking looking at her?"

Knowing I was dangerously close to combusting, I stepped closer to Raffe. The moment my arm brushed his, the fizz calmed to a nonthreatening level.

Slade crossed his arms and frowned. "If she doesn't want to talk to me, *she* doesn't have to."

"Then why are you waiting for her outside the women's apartments?" Raffe rasped, radiating power.

Adam and Keith looked at each other quickly before stepping up behind Raffe, presenting a united front.

"None of your damn business." Slade tilted his head back and squared his shoulders. "I have nothing to say to *you*. Only *her*."

"Then I suggest you get your ass moving." Raffe stepped forward, edging in front of me. "Because she texted me about what you were up to."

Slade flinched and focused back on me. "Fine. Forget what I told you." The corner of his mouth tilted upward.

Jackass. He knew he had power over me, and I resented it. I wondered if this was retaliation for me rejecting him or if it was because of Raffe's involvement. Slade hadn't acted like this before.

Worse, I was about to do what he wanted. "Can we talk later?" Slade would refuse to talk to me with Raffe here, and Raffe would refuse to leave, knowing Slade had been waiting for me.

Raffe's head snapped in my direction, and he narrowed his eyes. I could hear his unspoken question—*what the fuck?*—and I deserved it.

"Are you talking to me?" Slade pointed at himself and blinked several times.

He wanted me to reinforce that I'd meant him, and I regretted that I'd fallen for his tactic. But I could either snub the one person who could give me answers and help me with my magic *or* bend my pride to get the answers I desperately needed. That didn't mean I would play the entire game with him. "Don't be a jerk. I think you've been enough of one the past two days."

His face creased, which would normally scream guilt, but his emotions didn't change. This had to be an act, and I couldn't call him out on it. My ability to read emotions was something I hadn't shared with anyone, and I planned to keep it to myself. "You're right. We can talk about it in microbiology."

In other words, when Raffe wasn't around. But it wasn't like I could say no. We'd be seeing each other in an hour and a half.

Raffe growled, not even attempting to hide the animal within since there weren't any humans around …well, other than *me*. From the way his body vibrated, I feared he would shift if Slade didn't leave.

"Fine." I wanted him to leave *now*. "See you then."

He winked at me, and I could read that Raffe was about to snap. As he walked off, I placed my hand on Raffe's forearm, knowing I needed skin-to-skin contact with him.

Slade whistled as he strolled toward the student center like he didn't have a care in the world, Raffe watching him the entire way.

Once Slade was across the road and heading between the Evergreen and Howling buildings, Keith snapped, "Can someone please tell me what the fuck is going on?"

"I have the same question." Raffe turned to me and arched a brow. "What do you mean you're going to talk to *him* later? It looks like I'll be attending micro-fucking-biology with you now."

Unable to stop, I snorted. I didn't understand why, but

Raffe's protectiveness made me happy. "That will be hard to do when you aren't on the roster."

"Uh ... why does it fucking matter if he talks to her?" Keith's face twisted in disgust as he looked at me. "She talks to him all the time. I'm all for him locking her down so there's one less thing for us to worry about. The witches can have that burden."

In the blink of an eye, Raffe had pivoted on Keith and shoved him in the chest. Keith stumbled back several feet but righted himself before he could fall over.

"Whoa, Raffe." Adam stepped between them, his attention flicking between Raffe and me. "What the *hell*? He's just pissy because you woke him up by slamming your door and busting out of the apartment without explaining what was wrong."

"I didn't ask either of you to come," Raffe snarled. "And if you talk about her that way again, I will kick your ass. Do you understand me?"

Even though I *loved* the way Raffe was acting, I didn't want to come between him and his friends. I scurried next to him and touched his arm. "Hey, it's okay."

"It's *not* okay," Raffe bit, but his tone softened when he talked to me. "You aren't Slade's. And no one talks about you that way. I'm done trying to force you to hole up and not have a life."

"What?" Keith's jaw dropped. "Please tell me this is a joke. Not even two nights ago, your father—the *king*—almost blew a fuse just because she was at the football game! Now you're telling her she's free to go wherever she likes?"

Raffe nodded but kept his attention on me. "That's exactly what I'm saying."

If I hadn't felt my blood running through my veins, I would've believed that my heart had stopped. He was saying all this again in front of his friends, and I fell a little more for him.

"Man, I'm not normally one to interfere." Adam lifted both hands. "But I'm kinda with Keith on this. I don't think it's smart."

My lungs didn't fill as much as fear crept inside me. With Keith and Adam talking to him like this, what if he decided that being with me wasn't smart?

Raffe crossed his arms. "Why do you think Slade is so desperate to lock her down, and his mom isn't interfering like my dad is? They need her for something. I just don't know what. So do you think it's wise to hand her over to them? Maybe we should go buy some fucking ribbon, tie a bow around her neck, and deliver her to their door."

Adam's and Keith's faces fell, but not as much as my heart. Was that the real reason Raffe wanted to be with me? Was he keeping us a secret because he was ashamed and doing whatever it took to put distance between Slade and me? I didn't want to believe that was true, but how could I not after *that*?

"You know ..." Adam tapped his finger against his lips. "I hadn't thought of that, but you're right. Priestess Olwyn and Slade only do things to further the coven's agenda."

"Maybe, but King Jovian would be aware of that." Keith adjusted his boxers. "So—"

"Dad's worried about being held accountable if she outs the supernatural world." Raffe scanned the area. "Not about the other stuff, but that's where I step in—to handle what he can't see, even if it incites his wrath."

My eyes burned, and I had to leave before I had a meltdown. My blood fizzed, and a hum was close behind. "Okay, while you three catch up, I'm going back to my apartment."

There was no way I was going to the student center. Since Slade had gone that way, Raffe would no doubt follow me. I'd skip breakfast, which wasn't a problem because I'd lost my appetite.

I'd been so stupid. I'd honestly believed that Raffe was interested in me.

Not wanting to seem completely off, I nodded at Keith. "You three should go back to your apartment. You've gotta be chilly."

Raffe's forehead creased as Adam waved.

Keith glanced down at his crotch and frowned. "It's not small or shriveled at all, *thank you*."

I paused, blinking. Then understanding crashed over me. "I didn't say that to insult your dick size." My face burned, and tears filled my eyes. Not only had I learned that Raffe was with me just so I wouldn't get with Slade, but now they thought I was making fun of someone's dick. What sort of hell had I woken up in? I'd been so happy. Now it was all stripped away.

"Damn straight." He wiggled his hips. "Because you can't. It's huge."

"Shut up, Keith," Raffe growled. "And she's right. We should go back inside."

"Thanks for coming." I stared at the ground, praying I could make it back to my room before the tears fell. "I'll see you guys later." Without waiting for a response, I strode off to the apartment.

I headed straight to the elevator. The front door opened a few seconds behind me, but a tear ran down my cheek, and my blood started humming, so I didn't turn around. I could feel the hum throughout me. It was only a matter of time before something happened.

When a hand took mine, the buzzing sprang to life, and I

was tugged around and into a strong chest. Just like that, my blood simmered to a jolt.

"Hey, why did you take off like that?" Raffe asked.

I shuddered in the safety of his arms. Even though I knew he didn't want to be with me, his arms felt safe, like home. How pathetic could I be? A sob formed in my chest, and I forced myself to pull away.

"I need to go to my room." I somehow said it without breaking down. "I need to be alone."

The elevator door dinged, and Raffe followed me inside.

"Sky, what's wrong?" He blocked the elevator door. "Did Keith upset you with his dick comment? Because I punched the dickhead after you left for embarrassing you and even thinking you'd be looking there."

I opened my mouth, but he lifted a hand.

"To be clear, even if you were looking." He flinched and jerked his head as if he had a tic. "Which you weren't. Don't tell me because I won't be able to not kill him."

For some reason, that made me lose it. I laughed and cried simultaneously, which I hadn't known was a thing. I felt like there were two people inside me. My blood hummed again, and I didn't know what to do to stop it.

The elevator door opened just as the floor under our feet began to shake.

"Sky," he breathed. "We need to get out of here."

My mouth went dry as the humming increased and the elevator shook harder. Raffe lifted me into his arms and stepped into the hallway of our floor. Like before, his touch soothed my blood, and it settled back into a high fizz.

He didn't say anything as he carried me down the hallway and into the apartment. Once inside, he headed to my room, but I shook my head. I couldn't handle having him in my room after what I'd learned. "Put me down."

He immediately stopped and placed me on my feet. I blinked through my tears and saw concern all over his face.

"What's wrong? Why are you so upset?" He reached out to touch my face.

I took a step back, though the yanking in my chest sprang to life, pissed that I'd put distance between us.

He dropped his hand, respecting my boundaries, and I almost hated him for it.

"Why do you want to be with me?" This time, my voice broke. I couldn't hide the pain. The fizz thrummed so strongly that it would turn into a hum again at any second.

His brows furrowed. "What sort of question is that?"

"So the witches don't *claim* me? That's not a good reason, Raffe."

"What?" He shook his head. "Is that what Slade told you? Babe, that's not it at all."

It would've been nice to be able to smell a lie so I could tell him he stank. "*You* said it! Down there! To your friends. Did you think I wasn't listening?"

His shoulders sagged. "No. Shit. Sky, believe me, if that was the reason, I wouldn't *be* with you. Not like this. Not the way I want to. Being with you, even in secret, makes this harder for me ... for both of us. I swear to you, even if you didn't have whatever power you have, I'd want to be with you."

Luckily, my fizz was so high I could read him—and he was being honest and raw. Unlike Slade, whose emotions could be construed in many different ways, Raffe was straightforward, leaving no doubts.

"I'm so sorry I made you think that." He lifted his hands and winced, closing them. "That is the last thing I'd ever want to do."

The vise around my chest loosened as I took in his kindness and transparency.

"Can I please fucking touch you now?" He bit his lip uncertainly.

I nodded, and he wrapped his arms around me, pulling me to his chest. His lips found mine, claiming me, and I opened wide, eagerly letting him in.

All the pieces of me that had felt fractured were slowly coming back together, thanks to him.

He groaned and pulled away, making me pout. He laughed. "I'm sorry. I don't want to stop. But I need to know what happened and why you agreed to talk to him."

I sighed. "Slade told me he discovered more information about my heritage." I wasn't supposed to share what I was with Raffe, but after the shit Slade pulled, I wasn't sure if this was another way to manipulate or isolate me. And it'd be nice to see Raffe's reaction.

"What do you mean?" He tilted his head. "How is that possible? If he learned something, he should have told everybody. We're all trying to figure out what you are and how we can help you."

"You are?" I had thought only Slade was helping me look for answers. Another piece of information that had been concealed from me, but at least Raffe was telling me now.

He nodded. "My dad and I are invested in figuring out what you are to help you control your magic. The other supernaturals are using their resources to find answers and will report back to us. If Slade knows something and is keeping it to himself, that's a fucking problem. Where is he getting this information?"

Raffe was being honest with me, so I could reciprocate but the warning of not sharing the name of the book replayed in my head. If Slade found more answers, I needed him to be willing to tell me so I'd share enough to not prevent me from finding out more from them. "Some sort of coven history books. He's been scouring it every night."

"I bet he's been reporting to Priestess Olwyn and they aren't sharing." Raffe huffed. "We'd heard rumors that she might have a coven library hidden here somewhere."

I stepped toward Raffe again, needing to be closer. "Why does she have that power?"

"He didn't tell you?" Raffe laughed humorlessly and placed his hands on my waist. "She's on the university board."

Of course she was. You'd think he would've shared that with me. "Nope. He didn't."

"That's not surprising." He wrinkled his nose. "But, babe, he's probably saying that to get you to talk to him again."

I nodded. "I figured that too, but what if he knows something new?"

"We can figure it out. Together," he said softly.

I really liked the idea of that. But the *Book of Twilight* had said that one of the rare coven priestesses had had a relationship with an arcane-born. The only place it was documented that we knew about was there, and I couldn't give up the chance to learn more. I hoped he'd understand. "I'd like that too, but I'm sorry. I can't risk it."

He frowned and rolled his shoulders, his hands tightening on my waist. "Fine, but if you're going to talk to him, I better damn well be near."

"That I fully support." I kissed his cheek. "I don't want to be alone with him ever again."

"Good, because you never will be again." He kissed my lips, and we got lost in each other.

During microbiology, Slade and I had agreed to talk in the woods after our classes, but first, we, including Raffe, had economics. I'd switched seats in both classes and was sitting next to Dave, the bookstore guy, who'd quirked an eyebrow at the change but hadn't commented aloud.

Raffe was still a few seats behind me. Today, I didn't hesitate to glance over my shoulder at him, and we gave each other quick smiles. I'd texted Raffe about meeting Slade afterward, and he'd let me know that he, Adam, and Keith would be near my normal training spot with Slade in case something happened.

Dave side-eyed me. "Trouble in paradise?"

I blinked at him. "What?"

"You and Slade. You two break up?"

My eyes widened. "We were never together." How many people had thought we were?

"Interesting." He pulled out his laptop and set it up for class. "Don't get me wrong. Slade's more my speed than—" He nodded back toward Raffe. "But still a little self-centered."

Oh, had I ever learned that. I felt foolish for not listening. "Thanks for the warning."

He shrugged. "Didn't want to get on Slade's bad side. Supreme Priestess Olwyn tends to take things out on people who piss her off if they're students here." He tapped his head. "Food for thought."

Great.

The teacher started class, and I wondered how screwed I was.

After class, I left a little after Slade, not wanting to walk with him.

Raffe, Keith, and Adam hung back, but I could feel the buzzing on my neck informing me that Raffe was watching me.

That was a handy sense to have.

In the clearing, I felt something tingle around me. Probably my nerves.

Slade was already there. I saw him, and my phone dinged. I glanced down and read the message from Raffe just as Slade laughed.

He said, "Something wrong, *Skylar*?"

CHAPTER TWENTY-ONE

Raffe: Come back. The area is spelled. We can't get close or hear anything.

I huffed. That tingle hadn't been from nerves but from the perimeter spell Slade had cast. I should've considered the possibility, but damn, Slade had been in the same class as me for the past hour, so he shouldn't have had time to set up a spell. He would've had to walk the entire area, and I'd hurried here separately from him with Raffe, Adam, and Keith following half a mile behind to make sure Slade didn't know they were watching.

Obviously, he'd accounted for everything.

My blood took off straight into a fizz. After Saturday, I didn't feel comfortable being alone with Slade. That was why I hadn't argued with Raffe about staying close. Even though Slade wasn't drunk, I didn't know what to think about him after he'd shown up Sunday and ambushed me outside the apartment this morning. He was acting like a different person.

I scanned the area, avoiding looking at Slade. I quickly replied to Raffe, not wanting to leave him hanging.

Me: I'll head back

"Skylar, will you please look at me?" Slade asked gently, sounding more like the friend I knew.

Against my better judgment, I obliged. It wasn't like I had many options. He had information I wanted to know. I despised the power it gave him over me.

What I saw had the walls I'd built around my heart crumbling.

His expression was soft, and his emerald eyes were warm like they used to be when we'd hung out and things hadn't gotten so complicated. "I'm sorry about everything, and I didn't spell the area to piss you off."

I extended my arms at my sides and snorted. "Well, I'm pissed about it, so forgive me if I don't believe you."

His shoulders slumped. "You know it's spelled only because Raffe followed you. If he hadn't, we wouldn't be having this conversation."

I gritted my teeth to prevent my blood from humming. "Because I wouldn't *know*. You still did it, and that's a separate problem. If I don't feel comfortable coming here and talking to you alone, you shouldn't trick me into doing it. You tried to pressure me into kissing you the other night."

He ran a hand through his blond spikes. "You're right. I was a douche." Sincerity and regret wafted from him. "I was in the wrong. I get it, and I hate that it's straining our relationship. But I'm crazy about you, and I want you to be with me."

I scoffed. "Do you think that makes it better? Because that's a horrible way to make me see you in a positive light. Most importantly, I already told you I want us to remain friends for *this* reason. I didn't want things to change between us, but it's too late now."

He shook his head. "Why? We could be good together."

Exhaling, I tried to stay calm. My blood was dangerously

close to humming, and I hadn't agreed to come here and talk about this. "What information did you find?"

"We'll get there." He placed a hand on his heart. "I promise. I just want—"

"I'm not ready to have this conversation with you." My stomach roiled. I hated confrontation. "And here you are, pushing. You say Raffe is spoiled and always gets his way, but how do you think you're acting? Maybe Raffe is right. Maybe you've always been pushy, and I didn't see it until now. The last time we trained together, I barely made it back to my apartment, and I felt awful that next day. You pushed me to keep training after I told you I was spent."

I wasn't sure that was completely fair, but our entire relationship was in question. As I replayed our interactions, I didn't see him as particularly pushy, but the change in his attitude had started that day.

The pain of losing a person I thought was a friend throbbed deep within my heart. But I wouldn't let him push me around. "If you won't tell me what you know, I'm out of here." I spun on my heel and marched back the way I'd come from.

"Wait!" Slade huffed. "Please don't go."

I paused but kept my back to him. "Are you going to share the information?"

"Yeah," he answered in a gravelly tone. "I promise, okay? Just stay."

Some of the tension in my neck released, but my blood remained at that high-level fizz. I wasn't sure I could trust him, but I could read the defeat and frustration rolling off him.

I slowly turned around. "Fine. Start talking, or I'm gone."

He raised his hands in front of his chest in surrender. "Do

you remember the arcane-born who had a relationship with the priestess centuries ago?"

"Of course I do." As if I'd forget anything he'd shared about my heritage.

"I finally found a second *Book of Twilight* of hers, and it had information about the arcane-born. Apparently, they were close friends." He stepped toward me. "The arcane-born lived in the priestess's coven since witches and warlocks have the closest supernatural abilities to your power."

That ... made sense. "The wolf shifters and vampires were probably thrilled about that."

He shrugged. "It was irrelevant and didn't matter. Back then, there were more witches than wolf shifters and vampires. That's one reason we have more detailed notes—because of the time the arcane-born spent with our species."

I flinched. Slade hadn't mentioned the arcane-born's family. "Was he alone? No relatives?"

Slade nodded. "He was."

I wasn't the only one who'd been orphaned. Maybe the journey between this previous arcane-born's life and mine was similar.

"Like you, he struggled to control his power, and the coven helped him."

Hope expanded in my chest. "Does the book detail any of that?" I took a few steps forward, eagerness swirling through me. I'd give damn near anything to see the book for myself and devour every word. This was the closest I'd gotten to answers, and I needed them more than oxygen to live.

Not that I was dramatic or anything.

"I haven't learned the details yet—I found the book late last night and read the first five pages, but I plan on heading back to the library today to see what else it reveals." He lifted a finger. "There was one thing on the first page. The priestess detailed the way she discovered Foster, the arcane-born. He was near death when she found him. He lost control of his power in the middle of the town, but he escaped. He continued to panic and caused a mild earthquake that alerted the witches to a magical presence. They found him near death from exerting so much magic."

Shit. I couldn't imagine the panic he must have felt. I understood the blood humming and all the sensations that went with it, but causing an actual earthquake was hard to fathom. I'd shaken the ground under my feet and nearby, but nothing that would register on the Richter scale. "How did they know he caused it?"

"They carried him back to their coven and let him rest in one of their houses. When he came to, he reacted much like you did the other day. He could hardly stay awake, and he was famished. But he told them about his *blood jumping*. He knew he'd caused the quake, and the signature around the center of where his magic was released had the same magical essence that was within him."

Jumping. I didn't describe my magic like that, but it made sense. He must have been talking about his blood vibrating. After I'd gotten so worn down, I hadn't felt it anymore.

"And the priestess also spoke of Foster's death five years later. His magic took a toll on him. The book is all about him and their story."

The fizzing in my blood felt ominous. "Is it the same for witches?"

"No." His lips pressed into a line. "If we use magic, we get drained, but our bodies heal. It doesn't take the same toll on us as it does on you."

I kicked at the ground. "So, I could've died the other day." Though I hadn't released a huge burst of power like Foster had, I had used mine for hours.

He licked his lips. "I didn't know that, and I'm sorry. I'm not sure if you were close to death or if you were severely drained, but either way, once you feel fatigued, we need to stop."

A bitter laugh escaped me. I had told him I needed to stop, but he'd pressured me, and I'd trusted him. I couldn't believe how foolish I'd been. I hadn't wanted to disappoint him, which was why I'd pushed through. I'd been so desperate for a friend.

"In my defense, when I saw how bad off you were, I refused to train you for the rest of the week, remember? We weren't supposed to restart until today because I wanted to make sure you were recovered." He clasped his hands and shook them in front of him. "You have no clue how upset I was last night. I stayed up all night, knowing I hurt you."

I sighed, reading how guilty he felt. But he was right. I'd begged him on Thursday to train me again, and he'd pushed back, wanting to make sure I was ready. How could I hold getting drained against him when he hadn't known and refused to train me until I'd recovered? "It's not your fault. It's just easier to be angry at you for everything, but I could've said no. It was my fault, not yours." He'd put my needs first, more than I had. That was one reason it had hurt so much when he'd turned into someone else this past weekend.

He put a hand on my shoulder. "I'm partly to blame too, but it's good to know you don't hate me for it." He frowned. "I wish I could redo this weekend and not be such an asshole to you. I don't even know what I was thinking. I was drunk, and the way Raffe took off with you ... I was afraid I'd lost you, and I've been doing stupid shit since then."

My blood settled to a jolt, the remorse coming off him lending truth to his words. Maybe we could salvage our friendship, even though that would take time. "Stop acting that way and quit giving me reasons not to talk to you."

"Really? You'll give me another chance?" He grinned and bounced on his feet like a little boy.

I lifted a hand. "I don't know, but I do need help to control my power." Raffe and the others couldn't assist me with that, and though I might not have the best life in the world, I didn't want to *die*. "But we can't go back after what you pulled this weekend. You'll have to prove to me that this weekend was a fluke and not how you treat everyone." Hecate's attitude also gave me pause. She didn't think too highly of him, though she clearly wanted to date him. Maybe she was trying to get me out of the picture?

"That's fair." He bit his bottom lip despite his smile growing wider. "What if I can make it up to you?"

Here was the charming man I'd felt a connection with and trusted. But the memory of him trying to force himself on me kept popping up in my mind. "It's going to take more than one thing. It's going to take time."

His smile drooped slightly, and he nodded. "Fair. But a sign of good intentions can't hurt. Right?"

I clutched my phone harder. I didn't know how to respond to that. It felt like a trap.

"What if I talk to someone and see if you can visit the coven library with me?"

That was unexpected. I rocked back on my heels, but the word *someone* repeated in my mind. He was still keeping stuff from me, making me wary of him all over again. "You mean your mother?"

He snorted, the lines of bitterness falling back on his face. "Raffe told you. You *have* been spending more time with him, haven't you? You know, he's not a great guy. He's using you to get to me." Maliciousness and hatred flashed like a beacon from him.

The thing was, I didn't believe that about Raffe. Yes, we had our challenges, but he cared about me. We had a connection, and that couldn't be faked ... unless the buzzing was wolf magic. I hadn't felt it with Lucy, but we were the same sex. Would the buzzing happen if I touched Adam or Keith? Now I couldn't help but wonder, but regardless, I'd felt a connection with Raffe the first time I saw him, and nothing for the other two. I could always touch Adam or Keith and see if I felt the buzz.

I didn't want Slade to know that his seeds of doubt were working on me, so I shrugged. "He says the same thing about you. So far, you've proved him right."

Slade jerked his head back like I'd slapped him. He rasped, "He's been an ass to you."

"He has been, but so have you." I wouldn't let him conveniently forget about this past weekend. "Unlike *you*, he's saved me from threats and helped me out of a bad situation with a drunk guy. Also, he's never lied to me or withheld information from me. He's been doing what he thinks he has to do to make his father happy. Is that why you didn't tell me about your mom? She didn't want you to?"

Blinking, Slade ran a hand down his face. "Wow. You're defending *him*?"

"You're deflecting." I crossed my arms. "Why didn't you tell me about your mom? Hiding stuff from me and pushing yourself on me are two separate things that have nothing to do with Raffe."

He exhaled noisily. "Fine. When we met, you were skittish and unsure why you were here. I worried that if you knew my mom was the head of the board at EEU, you wouldn't want to be friends with me, so I didn't tell you." He avoided my eyes like he was still hiding something, but I didn't want to call him out on it while he was coming clean.

"It's been over a month. Why didn't you tell me before now?" We'd gotten close, and he knew things about me. It didn't seem right that he'd hidden that his mother worked here.

This time, he met my gaze. "I didn't know how to tell you, and our friendship was founded on how well we got along together. It had no bearing on who my mother is."

I wasn't letting this go. He'd skipped around the truth when we'd talked about family. "You wanted to go out with me yet didn't want to tell me who your mother is?"

He hung his head. "I was trying to figure out how, but every time I thought about telling you, we were having a good time, and I didn't want to ruin it. But you're right. I should have told you. Gods, I've fucked up so many times."

At least he was admitting he was wrong. Some of my anger melted away, and my blood returned to normal. I understood not wanting to ruin something, and I wasn't an asshole who would drop a friend over something like that. "I wouldn't have gotten upset, and I would've understood if I hadn't learned it from someone else. I need a friend who's honest with me, respects me, and doesn't hide things, which is the opposite of how you've behaved."

"You're right. Let me make it up to you. Let me talk to my mom and see if I can get you access to the library. Then we can look through the books together, at least for a night, and you can get an understanding of our coven and how it works. You'll see that what I'm telling you is true, especially since you feel like you can't trust me anymore." He touched my shoulder. "I want to restore what we lost, and I vow to tell you everything I can."

That he *could*. Not everything he knew. The wordsmithing was purposeful, and I knew he wasn't being completely honest with me.

The thing was, I wanted to get into that damn library, which meant I had to play along. "Okay, I'd—"

Something vibrated over my skin, stealing my breath. My blood responded with a loud hum as Slade's attention homed in behind me.

CHAPTER TWENTY-TWO

I spun around, searching for a threat. I hadn't realized I'd stepped over the spell perimeter last time because I'd been more focused on the meeting. This felt as if two different magical signatures were warring with one another.

"Shit," Slade hissed, and my blood leaped into a hum.

I was going to blow soon.

I shouldn't have come here. The woods by this school were not my friend, even if it was my solace.

Squinting, I looked harder. One of the magical signatures vanished, but now that I could sense the magic, I focused on the new magical presence.

It vanished, and the air around me returned to normal. But the sense of impending doom weighed on my shoulders. Something was coming.

And Raffe was out there.

What if something happened to him? The thought sent me over the edge, and the trees several feet in front of me shook in tandem with my blood.

I could only hope Raffe had sensed the threat before it arrived. I wanted to text him, but with the way my body shook, I couldn't. All I'd wind up doing was to mess up my phone.

A woman with long, light-blond hair and wearing a hunter-green dress suit stepped into view.

A residual hint of the unfamiliar magic wafted from her. I read anger and speculation from her as she tilted her head and stared at the shaking fir trees.

I couldn't let her hurt Slade and me. I crouched, pressing my hands into the mulchy earth. Instead of concentrating on the feel of it to calm myself, I felt my blood funnel into my hands.

The ground shook in sync with the trees and my blood. It surged from my hands to where the woman stood. The trees cracked, and she looked up and raised her hands.

"Sky!" Slade exclaimed as the tops of the two trees fell toward the newcomer. His voice was cut off by a loud grunt and a thud.

Wind blew from the woman's hands, tossing the tree limbs several feet away from us.

Shit. I'd have to do something else to keep her from reaching us. I gritted my teeth, trying to keep my eyes open. I focused on my fear, needing my blood to do more to protect us. I didn't know how to fucking control it. My chest heaved, and I bent another tree, hoping to crack it in half. Then the ground underneath her feet split open.

Her eyes bulged as she lifted her hands.

My body sagged, and my breathing turned ragged as fatigue hit me. I'd never channeled power like this before.

"I'm not here to harm you," the woman called, keeping her arms raised as if I had a gun trained on her.

I wanted to laugh. That was exactly what somebody who wanted to harm me would say. I'd been dumb enough for one day, and I wouldn't be made a fool of again.

But then Raffe stepped from the trees behind the woman, and my blood calmed some. The last person I wanted to harm was him, but I needed to keep the woman distracted.

"Sky," he rasped and stood beside the woman. "She's not here to attack you. She came here to help us reach you." He stepped in front of her, his attention on me.

"What the hell, man?" Keith shouted from somewhere behind them, still hidden by the trees. "She's unstable and will hurt both of you now!"

My strength gave out, and I dropped from my hands onto my elbows. The fatigue was hitting hard again. The trees were still swaying, but the ground had stopped shaking. My blood jolt petered out as if it also didn't want to hurt *him*.

The information I'd learned from Slade emerged in my head. I'd drained myself again.

Raffe didn't pause. He continued to close the distance between us, and the closer he got, the more my blood settled within me.

"Raffe, are you trying to get yourself *killed*?" Keith snapped.

My blood fizzed, and I could read Raffe clearly. He was concerned but not scared.

He continued as if Keith hadn't spoken. "This is Slade's mom, Priestess Olwyn. I called her to come and take down this perimeter since you asked us to be nearby and you're uncomfortable being alone with Slade."

Not wanting to meet the head of the school board as a limp mess, I tried to sit up, but all I could do was lift my head a little more and scan her over.

Now that Raffe had revealed her identity, I could see the resemblance to Slade. He had the same eye color as her, and they shared high cheekbones. I could hardly believe she was old enough to have a son my age because she barely looked forty, but that had to be due to her supernatural genes.

She nodded, a faint smile on her mouth. She radiated awe and intrigue.

A shiver ran down my back.

"Like Prince Raffe said, I'm not here to harm you or my son. I came to check on you." She spoke as if I were a child.

I frowned, not liking the tone she'd taken with me.

Raffe squatted next to me, blocking her from my view. His scent filled my nose, making me feel like nothing bad could ever happen. When he touched my arm, my blood settled into a jolt. I leaned my head on his arm, unable to hold myself up any longer.

"Thank goddess, she's calm." Priestess Olwyn sighed and hurried past me.

Wait. Slade.

He hadn't said or done anything since his mom arrived.

Concern gave me the strength to look over my shoulder, and I wished I hadn't.

Slade lay on his side, unmoving.

His mom dropped to her knees beside him and ran a hand over his head.

My body sagged even more. "Oh my God. What happened to him?" Even though I was mad at him, I still cared about him. I didn't want him hurt, and I was clueless as to what could have caused him to collapse ... unless *I* had.

"I don't know." Priestess Olwyn pursed her lips as Keith and Adam stepped into the clearing. She placed her hands in her lap. "What was he doing when he fell? Me taking down the perimeter spell wouldn't have done this to him since we're part of the same coven and blood. Something else must have happened." She glanced at me and back at Slade.

I remembered him saying my name and coming toward

me. "I think it might be my fault." A sob built in my chest. "I'm so sorry."

"You have nothing to feel bad about, dear. It was a mere accident." She smiled tightly at me and turned her attention back to him.

He didn't move. Fear strangled me, cutting off my air.

"Hey," Raffe said gently. With his free hand, he reached out and turned my face toward him.

He was being kind and gentle, everything I didn't deserve. I'd lost control of my power again, and I'd hurt Slade and almost hurt his mom. I'd attacked people who weren't a threat, and Slade wasn't moving.

Warm cobalt eyes met mine, and Raffe said, "He's breathing, and his heart is beating. He'll be fine."

Relief had my body giving out. I slumped back. I hadn't killed Slade, but I'd hurt him. I couldn't believe my blood had dominated me all over again, especially when I thought I'd made progress.

"Yes, dear. He'll be fine," Priestess Olwyn assured me. "He probably had the wind knocked out of him and passed out. Nothing appears to be broken."

"That's a damn shame," Keith grumbled loud enough for me to hear him.

A faint growl rumbled from Raffe, and when I looked up, his eyes were glowing.

There was no telling what Raffe was saying to the other two.

"She's exhausted." Priestess Olwyn sighed. "Why don't you take her back to her apartment, and I'll take care of my son."

I should have demanded to stay here and make sure Slade was okay, but I was having a hard time keeping my eyes open. "I'm so sorry, ma'am." I had no doubt my ass would be thrown out of this college tomorrow, and I would bow out gracefully. I'd have to explain to my parents what I'd done, which would be problematic, but I deserved it.

"Stop. I've already told you I'm not angry." Light footsteps headed our way, and Slade's mother crouched in front of me. Her lips pressed into a line, and she patted my arm. "You have immense power, and no one taught you how to use it or harness it. Of course you're going to be unbalanced. I'm just glad my son was able to help you until he got stupid this past weekend." She rolled her eyes and frowned.

From her comment, I realized Slade had been updating her about me, and he hadn't told me a damn thing about her. He'd told me we shouldn't share what I was with anyone, but she'd made those comments so nonchalantly that I suspected she knew more than she let on. After all, she was in charge of the library that housed the books Slade was researching.

"Keith, help Priestess Olwyn get Slade to his room." Raffe stood slowly, helping me up with him.

I put a little weight on my legs, and my knees almost buckled. Raffe bent to pick me up, and I shook my head.

If he picked me up, I'd melt into his embrace, and we were supposed to keep our relationship status secret. Keith already seemed alarmed enough about Raffe's actions toward me. We were under scrutiny already without adding more to the mix.

He frowned, unhappy about my refusal, but huffed in surrender.

Raffe respected me whenever I said no. He didn't push even if he was unhappy with what I wanted.

"Adam, can you walk on Skylar's other side to make sure she doesn't fall over?" His neck tensed as if that had been hard for him to say.

"Sure." Adam flanked me, and we started walking.

Keith and Priestess Olwyn were talking, but all I could

focus on was putting one foot in front of the other as we headed back toward the apartments.

Our pace was slow but steady, but suddenly, my right ankle gave out, and I fell toward Adam. He clutched my arm, steadying me.

"Dammit, Sky," Raffe growled, and he slipped an arm around my waist, anchoring me to his side. "You should let me carry you." His jaw was clenched as if in anger, but I had no clue why.

"Man, it's fine." Adam lifted his brows. "I caught her."

Raffe's chest rattled. "If I'd been carrying her, you wouldn't have had to."

Wait. Was he mad that Adam had caught me? That was strange. But my stumble had answered one of my questions. When Adam touched me, I felt no yank, tingle, or buzz. Not even a hint of one.

As if sensing Raffe's anger, my chest yanked me toward him, pressing our bodies more firmly together. At that adjustment, he relaxed.

After a few steps of silence, Adam blew out a breath. "Look, I'm not trying to be a jerk."

"Then shut up," Raffe snapped. "Problem solved."

I snorted, catching myself off guard. But I had to agree with Raffe—whenever someone said that, they were about to act like one.

"Nah, it's better coming from me than Keith." Adam cleared his throat. "Man, I understand what you said earlier about the witches needing her for something. Priestess Olwyn's reaction just proved it. But if your dad finds out that Skylar had another magical meltdown—"

"Dad's not here, and I'm your alpha." Raffe's arm tightened around my waist. "I get that he's nervous about what she is and doesn't want her to make humans aware of us, but his plan isn't working. That's why she was meeting with Slade today. He said he had answers."

My pulse skipped a beat. Raffe was standing up for me like he'd promised. He wouldn't force me to remain a recluse, and I could've kissed him—if the world hadn't been spinning so strongly and I could actually find his lips, that was.

"Did you learn anything?" Adam asked.

I had no doubt who that question was directed at.

"She's exhausted and can barely stand," Raffe bit out. "Back the fuck off."

A faint smile spread across my face at his protectiveness. "I can try to stand. It might help me not to focus on how tired I am." My words held a faint slur as if I'd been drinking.

"Ba—" Raffe cut himself off. "But you don't have to."

I was confident he'd almost called me babe. My legs shook more with each step, the exhaustion catching back up to me. "But if I tell you, I need you two to swear it stays between us. I don't want Slade to know I'm sharing this in case he stops providing information."

Raffe huffed. "Fine. I swear."

"Me too," Adam answered. "But what about Keith?"

"He's kinda hotheaded, so—" I hated talking ill of their friend, but Keith was a wild card.

"We won't tell him." Raffe lowered his head so our eyes met. "I'll alpha-will Adam if I have to."

"No need." Adam sighed. "I'll keep it quiet."

With that settled, I filled them in on what I'd learned tonight.

"Wait." Raffe's tone lost its warmth. "You're telling me that using too much of your magic can *kill* you, and you had the earth fucking cracking open tonight? What were you thinking?"

His words were like a slap, but even though my blood wasn't doing anything, I understood the reaction.

Fear.

"I couldn't control it. I thought someone was attacking us." I refused to feel bad about that. I needed to focus on learning how to control it. "Believe me, if I could help it, I wouldn't have made a scene in front of your dad or made the desk shake in class when you labeled me a pariah."

Adam chuckled. "She has a point, man. But what you should be pissed about is Slade knowing all this and not sharing it with us."

"Yeah, you're right." Raffe huffed. "I'm sorry, Sky. About everything."

My heart melted. I needed to tell him everything when we were alone. I couldn't trust Slade anymore, and my gut said I could trust Raffe. Maybe together, Raffe and I could figure all this out and Slade wouldn't be able to hold knowledge about me over my head.

As we stepped from the woods, Raffe said, "Adam, will you go grab something for her to eat and bring it back to her room? Snag something for me too. I want to make sure Slade doesn't try something else."

"Yeah, okay," Adam replied. "I'll be back soon."

Raffe and I continued to the apartment, and when we stepped into the elevator, the edges of my vision turned dark. Raffe swooped me into his arms, and no matter how hard I tried to stay awake, snuggled into his chest and feeling safe, I succumbed to sleep.

I woke up blanketed in Raffe's arms again. I glanced at the clock. It was five a.m. Unlike last time, I felt almost like myself since Raffe had forced chicken noodle soup, a grilled cheese, and a chocolate chip cookie down my throat for dinner before carrying me to bed.

I lifted my head from his chest and stared at his face. He was always handsome, but like this, when he didn't have the pressure of being what everyone expected him to be, he looked like a different person. Still handsome, but not as haunted and stressed. Add in his rugged good looks, delicious body, and protective, loyal, and smart characteristics, and I was certain I'd found my perfect guy. Which should scare the hell out of me.

His eyes cracked open, and one side of his mouth lifted up. "Are you watching me sleep? Because that's fucking creepy."

I laughed, my cheeks hurting. "If you think it's creepy, why are you smiling?"

"Who said I didn't like creepy?" He winked, but his smile dropped as worry creased his face. "Are you feeling okay? Do you need anything? I can get you something to drink or eat. Just tell me what you need."

For the first time in my life, I felt cherished. My body warmed, and I nodded. "I can think of one thing I need."

"What? Anything."

I kissed him, startling him, but he recovered within a second, and his mouth responded to mine. I licked his lips, begging for entrance, and he opened, allowing our tongues to collide.

My hand slipped down under his shirt, touching the curves of his abs. I wasn't sure what to do since I'd never been with a man before, but the way his stomach quivered at my touch made me think he liked it.

I traced every curve, lowering my hand to his jeans, and dipped my finger inside his waistband.

He hissed as his hands swept over my back. The buzzing between us intensified, and I got light-headed, but not like when I was tired after my blood exploded with power.

This was different and new, and a knot of need was tightening within me.

I pulled my mouth away from his and kissed my way down his neck like he'd done to mine before, and his hand slipped up and over my bra.

As I grazed his neck with my teeth, he growled, but it was full of need instead of anger.

"Can I touch you?" he rasped, his hand gently squeezing my breast.

I nodded, unable to speak. I wanted him to touch me everywhere, but I wasn't brave enough to say it.

His hand slipped underneath my bra, and my breathing turned ragged. As his finger rolled over my nipple, my back arched, and I unfastened his jeans.

"Can I touch you?" I repeated.

"Only if you want to. You don't have to."

That answer, right there, was all I needed. I slid my hand into his boxers, and I paused when I reached his dick. Damn. He was large and hard, and that both thrilled and scared me.

Unsure what to do, I stroked him, and his hips jerked in rhythm with my hand. He groaned as he propped himself on his elbow and lifted my shirt then unfastened my bra. He bent his head and sucked my nipple into his mouth as his hands slid between my legs. Soon, he was circling between my folds as I panted and stroked him faster.

I'd never done anything like this before, and when the friction built inside me, all I could do was focus on the new sensations rippling through my body. I panted and murmured, "Faster."

He obeyed, taking me over the edge. My body clenched as

pleasure like never before slammed into me, and my body shook. I moaned loudly, and he chuckled, placing his mouth over mine to drown out the sound.

As I was coming down, his body jerked, and he finished, our tongues still working in tandem together.

He pulled away, eyes glowing, and rasped, "Mine."

Maybe I should've argued, but all I did was nod and repeat his claim, needing him to know it went both ways. "Mine."

"Damn straight I am."

After we cleaned up, the two of us went back to sleep.

Two hours later, I was still tired but felt energized in a different way. Raffe had gone back to his place to change, and he would be here soon to walk me to the student center. We'd decided we couldn't pretend to be enemies anymore, so we'd be friends. At least that way, we could be seen talking in public together.

I'd finished brushing my hair, putting on makeup, and getting dressed when a knock sounded on the door.

Raffe!

I hurried into the living room, eager to see him. To kiss him. Though it'd been only an hour, it felt like days had passed since he'd been here, especially after what we'd done together this morning.

When I opened the door, ready to attack him with kisses, I paused.

It wasn't Raffe.

It was Priestess Olwyn with a huge frown on her face.

Shit. Something must have happened to Slade, and it was all my fault.

CHAPTER TWENTY-THREE

"Did he not wake up?" My voice shook, and I wrapped my arms around my waist. I'd never forgive myself if Slade wasn't okay.

The priestess's eyebrows rose, and panic clawed at my chest. My blood jolted to life, although not as strong as yesterday.

She blinked. "Slade is fine... or will be in a day or two. That's not why I'm here."

That didn't relieve my panic. Instead, my anxiety strangled my lungs until I couldn't breathe. This was it. She was going to tell me I had to leave EEU. Between my exhaustion and exploring Raffe's body, I'd forgotten all about this pending threat, but now that it was here, my heart raced. If I left, what would that mean for Raffe and me? How would I learn more about my blood and supernaturals? I had to face the consequences of what I'd done, but I had so much to lose. "Oh, right." I blinked, trying to hold back tears. "I can be out of here by the end of the day."

Her brows furrowed. "Why are you leaving? I don't think that's best for any of us."

I tilted my head. "Isn't that why you're here? To kick me out of the university for what I did to Slade?"

Face softening, she smiled slightly. "Of course not, Skylar. I want you to remain a student here. But may I come inside?" She glanced around the hallway. "I'd rather not have this conversation out here."

Oxygen filled my lungs again, making me light-headed. I didn't have to leave. Instead of becoming a melted mess of goo, I needed to get my head on straight. I forced myself to take a step back and waved her into the apartment.

Part of me didn't want her here, especially with Raffe coming back any second. But what could I do? Tell her no? I doubted that would go over well, especially after I'd hurt her son.

When I shut the door, Lucy shouted out from her bedroom, "For the love of the gods, you two better be quiet or I'll come out and kick both of your asses. Getting woken up at four in the morning with—"

"Priestess Olwyn is here!" I needed Lucy to shut up *now*.

Priestess Olwyn arched a brow and rocked back on her high heels.

Silence stretched between us. Then Lucy cleared her throat. "Oh, okay. So it's not Josie? My bad. I'm just going back to sleep, then."

I wanted to kill her, but instead, I forced a smile.

The way Slade's mother tapped a long, crimson fingernail on her bottom lip screamed she wasn't buying it. "I didn't realize you were close to Josie as well, especially after Raffe's public display about you being trouble."

That was equivalent to a punch in the gut. That particular memory caused my old wounds to resurface. That memory was fresh, but I still felt the need to defend him. "He was doing what he thought he had to. And Raffe has stepped up to help me several times when no one else did."

She *tsk*ed. "Not even my son?"

Yeah, I wasn't sure how to answer that or if I wanted to. "He's helped me in other ways—well, before this past weekend."

"That's why I'm here." She strolled to the center of the living room, scanning the area. She wore another suit, this one black, and a pentagram necklace that settled within her cleavage. "To apologize for my son's actions. After what Keith told me last night when he was helping me get Slade home, well ... it made me sick. I've never been so disappointed in him before, especially since wolf shifters had to step in because of his actions." She wrinkled her nose as if the words were disgusting to say. "I wanted to let you know that none of that will be a problem going forward, and I hope you can trust me enough to allow Slade, and myself, to train you to control your power."

My legs almost gave out. Had the supreme priestess of the covens just offered to train me? This had to be a dream ... or nightmare. I wasn't sure which. "*You?*" I squeaked, sounding most definitely not chill.

"If you would rather I not ..." She trailed off and bit her bottom lip.

I gulped. "No, that's not what I meant. It's just, I struggle, and I would hate for you to waste your time with me. I'm sure you have better things to do."

"Well, yes, I'm busy, but Skylar, I'd like to think of you as one of my own." She placed a hand over her heart. "I hope that doesn't sound too presumptuous."

My jaw dropped. Had I heard her right? She wanted to think of me as part of her coven? I'd never had anyone be so welcoming before. But if I aligned with her, it would cause more issues between Raffe and me. We had enough stacked against us without me adding another wedge between us. "I'm honored. Truly." I wrung my hands, unsure what to say or how to proceed. "But I want to focus on controlling my power before committing to a group of people. I hope you understand. I'm still trying to find myself, and I don't want to put the burden on anyone while I'm off balance."

"The first problem I see is that people are making you feel like you're a burden." She shook her head. "It's a damn shame that certain people—especially kings—could be so jaded toward someone they simply don't understand."

She wasn't holding back. I had no doubt she was referring to King Jovian.

"I'm not asking for a decision today." She took a few steps closer and placed a hand on my shoulder. "The offer still stands, and I'm confident you'll feel comfortable soon and see where you belong."

Now I knew where Slade got his pushiness from, but unlike her son, Olwyn was subtle. If I hadn't grown up with bullies and learned how they escaped trouble, I would've missed the signs.

I had to play along. Otherwise, I could wind up on the wrong side of her wrath. "Thank you, and I would be honored if you and Slade would train me." I needed someone to help me get myself under control before I accidentally killed myself.

She smiled. "Excellent. You'll need to rest this week, but you should be ready to train soon."

I hated to wait that long, but staying alive was sort of a priority, so I nodded. "Sounds good."

I heard the lock buttons being pushed, and I tensed. *This* was Raffe. I should've known he wouldn't have knocked earlier. I turned to the door as it opened, and Raffe entered with a coffee from the campus coffee shop and three closed to-go plates.

Priestess Olwyn clasped her hands together. "Prince Raffe, I didn't realize you were doing deliveries on campus."

He didn't seem surprised to see her as he moved into our small kitchen and set the plates on the square wooden table against the wall. Granted, why would he be? His wolf nose had probably detected her presence.

An ability that would've come in handy before I'd opened the door.

"Nope, this is an exception," he answered smoothly. "After the fatigue that hit Skylar last night, I wanted to make sure she ate before heading to class. How's *Slade*?"

If I hadn't been listening so closely, I might have missed the slight edge.

"He's doing well. Thank you for asking." Priestess Olwyn dropped her hands and focused on me again. "I'd better head back to the office, but I look forward to seeing you soon."

"Thanks for dropping by." I didn't know what else to say, and I doubted she wanted me to rehash our conversation in front of Raffe. "And please let Slade know I'm sorry."

Raffe growled. "You have nothing to be sorry for. He caused everything that happened last night. He should be apologizing to *you*, not the other way around."

Priestess Olwyn's expression seemed strained for a moment before it slid back into neutral. "He'll be in class today, so you can tell him all that yourself." She patted my arm. "If you need *anything*, please call me. I want to make sure you feel welcome and at home here."

Another dig at how the wolf shifters had handled my presence.

Raffe inhaled sharply, likely realizing the same thing, but she wasn't wrong. Slade was the only person who'd been nice to me at first. "I appreciate it." If she didn't leave soon, I'd be pushing her out the door.

The tension in the room was so thick that I wanted to run and hide. I needed to understand why these two groups hated each other so much.

Priestess Olwyn left, and when the door shut, Raffe closed the distance between us. He cupped my face and stared deeply into my eyes. Between the buzzing and the way he looked at me as if I were his entire world, my head became foggy. The yanking in my chest strengthened, and I wanted to touch him all over like we had this morning.

"Did she threaten you?" he asked, examining me. "Fuck, I should've never left."

Okay, horny Sky needed to retreat because Raffe truly was worried. I shook my head to clear it and remember how to speak. I gave him a rundown of what Slade's mother had said.

I'd expected him to relax, but the more I spoke, the more his muscles tensed.

I was missing something. "What's wrong? She was nice."

"Her interest in you is unsettling." He dropped his hands and huffed. "She has to know something more than what you told me last night, and she hasn't informed us as she should."

Guilt weighed me down. I'd promised Slade I wouldn't share this information, but that didn't feel right. Not with Raffe protecting me and the two of us being in a relationship. I needed to trust him, and he hadn't given me a reason not to.

I grabbed his shirt and dragged him into my room.

I trusted Lucy, but I didn't want to get her caught up in whatever *this* was ... this grandstanding between the witches, Raffe, and his dad.

"Babe, I'm all for touching you again, but I'm more worried about what the priestess is using you for." His forehead creased with worry.

To me, it felt like a challenge, so I shut my door and pushed him onto my bed.

When I straddled him, his eyelids hooded, and he gripped my hips and pulled me against him.

He was already hard, and my back arched, but I had to remember the real reason I'd brought him here. I moved so my lips were right by his ear and whispered, "I know what they know, but I need to know you won't tell anyone. I can't risk them not sharing things with me, and your dad won't tolerate it if he learns it." After my brief meeting with him and with the way others talked about their king, I understood his dad would do what he wanted.

He stilled. "I swear. Just tell me."

"Slade found a book a few days after I got here with some information about my heritage. He called me an arcane-born."

He froze. "What sort of *book*?"

That was a strange question. "He called it a *Book of Twilight*."

"Are you fucking serious?" he hissed, his body coiling. "Those were supposed to be destroyed."

My heart dropped into my stomach. "Please don't say anything. It's the only thing that's giving me answers, and I need to learn so I can get my blood under control."

He hung his head. "Sky—"

"Listen, *please*." Then I told him about the cosmic event that triggered the power within the fetus of a pregnant woman. When I finished, I leaned back to see his face. "Have you heard anything about that?"

"No." His forehead wrinkled. "I haven't, but shifters weren't great at keeping records centuries ago, and the covens weren't supposed to either."

"Raffe." I wasn't above begging. "Don't tell your dad until I have time to find everything I can. I need answers." Maybe I shouldn't have told him because I'd never seen that expression on his face before. Even though it was the last thing I wanted to do, I moved to get off him.

He gripped my hips tighter and asked, "Why are you getting up?"

"I ..." I wasn't sure what to say, but my body warmed from him making me stay put. "I thought you might feel different—"

His mouth claimed mine, and he ground against me.

I gasped as he pulled back and smirked. "Does it seem like I feel differently about you?"

My body felt light ... happy. "If I say yes, will you do that again?"

"Oh, you started something. And yes, I'll keep your secret because you're not getting free of me now." He kissed the tip of my nose. "I was upset—not because of the books they're hiding but because I think they know a whole lot more about you than they've let on. It's just now coming out, and it makes me wonder what their ulterior motive is."

I shrugged. "You now know everything I do."

"You promise to keep me in the loop?" he asked, tucking a piece of hair behind my ear.

"As long as you keep your promise," I replied breathlessly.

"Good." He then ground against me again. "Now, I'm going to get you off then force you to eat the food I got you."

Before I could say anything, his mouth was on mine, and soon, we were making each other pant again.

THE NEXT TWO weeks flew by, mainly because Raffe and I had begun working on our stats project. We surveyed students each afternoon, documenting where they sat in class and their grades, and then he'd head off to practice while I compiled the data. As expected, our data collection validated the theory that people who sat in the front earned slightly better grades.

By the time I got done updating our data and our report, I'd completed my other homework just when he'd be heading over after practice, clean and changed.

When I wasn't working on the project, I met Slade to train. Each outing was tense, and we went over the same things, but I couldn't control my blood. Each day, I left more flustered, wondering if I was meant to die.

It was Tuesday night, and Lucy, Josie, and I headed to the student center to meet up with Raffe, Keith, and Adam after their practice.

"It's still strange to have a human hanging out with us." Josie chuckled, standing beside Lucy in Raffe's jersey. "What's next? Hanging out with witches?"

I almost missed a step.

"Josie." Lucy's eyes bulged. "That's rude."

"Oh." Her jaw dropped. "I'm sorry, Skylar. I didn't mean for it to come off that way. I'm still not used to it is all. This is the fourth time, and we're actually going to the student center." She flinched. "That was a bitchy thing to say. It came out all wrong."

That was the thing. I believed her, which made it hard to dislike her. "It's okay. I bet it's weird since I shouldn't know about you." I shrugged.

"Hey, if it's any consolation, I think you're cool." She winked. "I've never said that about any human, and if Raffe trusts you, that's further validation in my mind."

"Thanks." I forced a smile. "I like you all too ... except Keith."

Lucy and Josie burst out laughing and said, "Same," in unison.

It was really weird when they did things like that.

As we entered the student center and passed the bookstore, Josie crossed her arms like she was covering up the fact that she was wearing Raffe's jersey, and glanced into the bookstore. Dave was checking out a customer, but his attention darted toward us and landed on her.

As soon as their eyes connected, she forced her head forward. "We should hurry. The guys are here."

I was about to ask what that was all about, but she sped up and found the guys already at a table. They had food and drinks spread all over it.

I went to go get food for myself, but Lucy grabbed my hand and said, "They got enough for everyone."

I noticed a spot open by Raffe, but Josie hurried over and took it. I expected him to tell her that the seat was saved for me, but she leaned over and touched his arm, her eyes glowing.

They were pack-linking.

He glanced at me and waved then turned back to her, dismissing me.

Little things like that happened whenever Raffe and Josie were both hanging out at the apartment, but I'd escape to my room. I couldn't ignore them in the middle of the student center as easily.

Lucy frowned, taking my hand and tugging me into the seat between her and Adam, putting me directly across from Raffe.

At least it wasn't Keith.

I understood that Raffe had to spend time with his friends so they wouldn't suspect why he was spending time alone with me, but I wondered why I needed to be part of the equation. At first, I'd thought it was to get them used to seeing us together so we could come out with our relationship, but so far, he'd barely acknowledged my presence.

It wasn't that I didn't want him to have friends, but I'd like for him to include me.

"What is she doing here?" Keith grumbled from his spot across from Lucy.

"Friends, remember?" Lucy smiled too brightly and took a hamburger from one of the trays then started stuffing her face.

I felt weird, but I took a sandwich just as Raffe and Josie burst out laughing. She laid her head on his shoulder, and I expected him to tell her to stop, but all he did was laugh with her and push her back.

Something unusually strong surged through me, and my blood jolted.

It slipped right into a fizz, the magnitude taking me by surprise. I clutched the table, trying to rein it in.

Adam leaned toward me, worry creasing his brow. "Are you okay?"

"Yeah." I forced myself to take a bite of the sandwich. I wasn't even sure what was on it. I just needed to do something to forget about my rage. The bread stuck to the roof of my dry mouth, and the others continued to talk.

Once again, no one included me.

I tried not to watch Josie and Raffe, but it was hard with them sitting right in front of me. Occasionally, they would join in on the conversation, but Josie would say something that focused his attention right back on her. She touched him, and he always moved away from her, but he didn't tell her to stop.

It was driving me insane.

After ten minutes, I wasn't just angry but upset too, and my blood was rising nearly to a hum.

I had to leave.

Leaning over to Lucy, I swallowed to get the last pieces of bread down my throat. "Hey, I need to head out."

She nodded, taking my hand in hers and squeezing comfortingly. She understood. Of course she did. "I'll bring you something back in a bit."

Even though the last thing I wanted to do was eat, I needed to. Slade and I were training tomorrow.

Not bothering to say anything to Raffe, I saluted Adam and scurried outside.

I'd hoped to make it to the apartment before I cried, but as soon as the cool evening air hit my face, the tears fell down my cheeks, and the magic hummed within me.

I wrapped my arms around myself and headed across the road to walk into the tree line for coverage. I didn't want anyone heading to and from the student center to see me like this.

I'd been feeling off, but tonight, being in public with Raffe but not being *with* him really hit home. I felt lonelier than ever before and somehow more pathetic than that girl I'd hoped I'd left behind.

I sensed a presence following me, and my heart raced.

It had to be Raffe.

When I spun around, though, my breath caught. It was definitely *not* Raffe, and I needed to run.

CHAPTER TWENTY-FOUR

My blood jolted to a hum as Dave's face twisted in agony.

His teeth protruded from his mouth, and he groaned. "Dammit, you smell so fucking delicious."

The limbs of the fir tree over his head began to shake, and he took a few steps back.

"What the—" Dave glanced overhead and scowled. "Is that Slade again?"

Slade again? I wanted to ask, but not when he was like this. "It's me, so back away. If you attack me, you'll get hurt." My blood hummed with the power flooding from my body. Dave had been nice to me, and I didn't want to hurt him, especially when I could read that he was struggling against his natural inclination.

"You're doing that?" He blinked a few times then hunched over. "Why do you smell so damn *good*? You did once in the cafeteria, but nothing like *this*."

Lafayette had said the same thing about my scent when my magic went wild. He'd assumed that the vampire who'd attacked me hadn't been able to control his urges. If I didn't want to be a beacon for vampires, I needed to calm my blood. "I ... I don't know." My panic surged, and the trees whipped and bent like they had the other night.

The tingles at the nape of my neck flared, and I couldn't get an image to surface in my mind to soothe me—deer, the shelter animals, especially not Raffe. It was as if my blood was keeping me focused on my pain and the vampire in front of me.

"Can you stop it?" He wheezed as his face contorted. "You need to go. I don't want to hurt you or Josie."

He didn't need to tell me twice. I spun and started to run, hoping that distance would get me back to a controllable level.

"Don't fucking *run*," Dave snarled. "The predator in me will take over, and I will chase you. Walk slowly."

He couldn't be serious.

The trees to my left cracked, and a section of branches crashed to the ground. I gritted out, "You tell me not to run and say something like *that*?" Everything inside me urged me to get away from him as quickly as possible.

Something blurred past me, and I thought my life was over.

The three firs to my left trembled behind me in the direction of the threat, and an arm wrapped around my waist and pulled me aside.

I fought, desperate to get away. Then I noticed the buzzing where the person was touching me and calmed.

"Run to the apartment," Raffe said, his voice a mixture of an animalistic growl and a human voice. "I'll handle this." He set me behind him and stepped between Dave and me.

His back muscles bunched, and fur broke out along his arms.

"Wait." I touched his back, wanting to make sure he heard me. "Dave didn't attack me." Or I didn't think he had. "He told me to leave. That he didn't want to hurt me." Or Josie, which was odd, but not relevant, because she wasn't even here. His mention of her was odd, but he was struggling, so he probably had no clue what he was saying.

"What?" Raffe clenched his arms, but his fur had stopped spreading.

Dave hissed, and from what I could tell, he hadn't moved from where he'd been standing. He said, "Get her out of here. If you don't, I'll lose control. Wolf shifter here or not."

"I can't risk you attacking her later." Raffe's clenched hands shook.

Without thinking, I smacked him in the back. I didn't hit him hard, but my hand hurt as if I'd punched a brick. How the hell was that possible? "You're going to kill him? Don't be stupid. Let's get out of here. My blood is going haywire. Once I calm down, he'll be fine." I hated how my heart leaped at the fact that Raffe was here.

"Fuck yeah, I'll kill him. He wanted to hurt you. That's unacceptable." He answered the question so simply, like we were talking about what to eat for dinner, not someone's life.

Trusting my instincts, I touched his back. The contact wasn't solely for him but for me as well, and my blood settled into a fizz. I didn't understand why Raffe had such an influence over me, but touching him helped me control my blood more than anything else did.

I'd also expended a lot of energy, and I sagged into him. "Raffe, please. Can you take me home?"

He exhaled and reached behind him, placing a hand on my waist. His body was still tense, but luckily, my words were getting through to him.

"Man, I'm sorry." Dave sounded more like himself. "But I didn't attack her. That has to count for something. Hurting me would cause questions from everyone since I didn't actually attack her."

"Not after the story I'd tell everybody. Just because you didn't attack her now doesn't mean you won't later." The edge returned to his voice. "That's not a risk I'm comfortable taking."

I loved that he cared about me that much, but Dave hadn't done anything to justify Raffe's retaliation. "But I am, so leave him alone."

He glanced over his shoulder at me, and whatever he saw wasn't good because his face was lined with worry.

"Fine." He pulled me to his side. "But if this happens again, he won't get another chance."

I didn't have enough energy to argue with him. Instead, I remained silent, which he must have taken as agreement.

"Dave, clean up the branches before any humans come by," Raffe commanded, authority ringing in his voice, and I was sure he expected Dave to obey.

I dreaded the questions that would circulate about what had happened here. It was bad enough that I'd had an episode in front of King Jovian. Now I'd had another one while dating his son, the very person who wanted to keep our relationship a secret. Here I was, proving to him that his reasons were valid.

Would I ever get my shit together? Every time I thought I'd made progress, I did something to prove I hadn't made any at all.

"On it," he replied without any resentment. Then he cleared his throat awkwardly.

Here it was, the inevitable question that would trigger everything.

"I don't know what happened here, and to be honest, I don't want to. But Skylar ..." He paused.

Raffe snarled, "Don't fucking talk to her."

I cut my eyes to Raffe, arching a brow. He was going to act like *that* after he hadn't told Josie to stop touching him? Yeah, that didn't work for me.

Lifting my chin, I glanced over my shoulder just as Dave bent to pick up part of the tree trunk.

"Yes?" I asked.

Dave jerked his head up as Raffe growled angrily.

Well, good. He deserved to be upset, the same way I'd been. I kept my gaze on Dave.

Smirking, Dave shook his head like he couldn't believe what I was doing. "I just wanted to say don't worry about anyone finding out about this. I understand secrets and needing them to stay that way. I also know rumors have been going wild, and I won't add to your burden."

Ah, that was why he hadn't been shocked when he'd realized it was me. He'd heard rumors. I appreciated the olive branch he was handing me. "Thank you ... for everything." Maybe he'd fought his urges so he wouldn't get on the witches' bad side, but that still meant something to me. He could've attacked me and hidden the evidence.

Dave smiled genuinely. "No problem. And thanks for stopping smelling so damn tempting."

I smiled back then let Raffe guide me toward the apartment. I hated how good it felt to be in his arms after he'd hurt me. Part of me wanted to get angry and tell him to back the fuck off, but a more substantial part wanted to forget about it and sink into his arms.

After a few steps, Raffe huffed and grumbled, "Did you seriously thank him for not feasting on you or killing you?"

I snorted. That was one way of putting it. "Yeah. He didn't want to hurt me. I know it." I'd read him when my blood was strong, and he'd put up one hell of a fight. Something most couldn't do.

Raffe scowled. "I still want to kill him. He could attack you at any time."

"Are you going to kill *all* vampires?" I snuggled into his side, allowing him to take more of my weight. Though I wasn't as exhausted as I'd been the other day, I was a little wobbly.

He arched a brow. "You know what? Your plan has merit."

I rolled my eyes and fought the smile that was threatening to break through. "You know you can't. That wouldn't just piss off your dad but all the supernaturals."

"It'd be worth it as long as you were safe. How drained are you?" He examined my face.

My stupid, traitorous heart leaped, and all my hurt and anger left me. "I'm a little tired, but not too bad. You showed up almost as soon as it started." How could I be upset with someone who cared about me so thoroughly?

Then my stomach soured. I suspected he'd act the same way toward Josie. Jealousy churned within me, and I wanted to cry and scream and hate a woman simply for being close to the man I loved.

Wait.

Loved?

No.

It was too soon ... and loving *him* could destroy me.

I couldn't handle these thoughts, so I pushed them out of my head and focused on Raffe's arm around me.

"I didn't notice you were gone until I glanced over and Lucy linked with me to tell me you left." He bit his bottom lip. "I'm glad I got here when I did. You should've texted me."

The heat of my anger flowed back into me, and my skin jolted despite his touch. I welcomed it. A jolt I could stand, and I needed my anger to remain rational. "Don't you dare blame me." I stepped away from him, ignoring the way my chest yanked me toward him. "You're the reason I had to go, so if it's anyone's fault, it's *yours*." I was tired of being a pushover.

He blinked so much that I thought he was rehearsing for a fucking comedy—like he was waiting for the punch line or something. "My fault? What the *fuck,* Sky. Are you serious right now?"

I turned to face him and crossed my arms. "Deadly."

This time, when he growled, it was channeled toward me. He rasped, "Not fucking funny after what happened back there."

"I'm not trying to be funny. I don't appreciate your insinuation that I did something wrong by leaving an uncomfortable situation and running into trouble I couldn't have predicted, and not texting you immediately while standing face to face with a hungry vampire!" A deep, throbbing ache shot through my heart, and my blood pulsed into a fizz. "So spare me the lecture and let it go."

His head jerked back, and he scratched the top of his head. "Is this from exhaustion because—" Then he froze.

"Hey guys," Keith called from behind me.

Of *course* his friends would appear now. It was probably for the best. I'd been about to say a lot of things that wouldn't have gone over well.

Josie ran up and jumped on Raffe's back, laughing.

Those damn tears sprang back into my eyes.

"Hey now," Raffe said, straining and dropping her back onto her feet.

Again, he didn't tell her to stop touching him. If it didn't happen so often, I could probably handle it, but she did it all the damn time, and they had so many private conversations. It felt like he was dating her, and I was his side girl.

I turned away and almost ran into Adam.

His eyes met mine, and he frowned. "Is something wrong?"

"Just tired." I inhaled, trying to keep my act together. "I better go inside. See you guys later."

I stalked past them all, not glancing at Raffe. If he didn't know what was wrong, then he was dense and stupid.

"Hey, I'll come with you." Lucy jogged to catch up to me. She was frowning as she looped her arm through mine. "It's *Criminal Minds* time anyway."

I could've kissed her. Raffe wasn't allowed to join us, and I needed time away from him. Clearly, hanging out with this group wouldn't work out for me.

I could feel the tingle on the nape of my neck, and it came damn close to shattering me, but I kept moving, focusing on putting one foot in front of the other.

The two of us didn't speak again until we'd made it into our apartment. As soon as the door closed, Lucy groaned, "I'm so sorry. Raffe is an idiot."

My eyes burned, and a tear broke free and rolled down my cheek. I wiped it away. My one rule was to never cry in front of anyone because bullies thrived on it, but I felt I could let my guard down with Lucy. "I'm not being stupid?"

"If a guy touched you like that even once, Raffe would lose it." Lucy mashed her lips together. "I've seen the way he looks at you when he thinks no one is watching."

I glanced at the ceiling, trying to keep myself from sobbing. "Then why does he let *her* do it? And he ignores me when they're together."

Lucy took my hand and led me to the couch. I sat down, and she turned her body toward me.

"The five of us grew up together, and Josie's parents are Raffe's parents' best friends." Lucy clasped her hands together. "They've always been close, and in high school,

Raffe had problems with all the human girls wanting to date him, so they came up with the plan to have Josie pretend to be his girlfriend." She rubbed her palms on her jeans. "They've been pretending since the eleventh grade, and Raffe isn't willing to tell anyone about you two. So ..." She trailed off and cringed.

"He's keeping up the ruse." I laughed bitterly. "Great. That's just swell." I sniffled, my nose stuffy from holding back tears.

"Look, I know it hurts, and it doesn't seem this way now, but he *has* been shrugging off her touches, and I can see how uncomfortable he is with her attention." Lucy sighed.

I bit the inside of my cheek. "That doesn't make it okay. If I did something like that with Slade, or even Adam, he'd come unglued."

She nodded. "You're right." Then her eyes glowed. "He's on his way up here."

That was my cue to head to my room ... alone. "Tell him that my outburst with Dave exhausted me and I went to bed." I needed space, and I couldn't think straight around him.

"Okay."

I forced a smile and wiped away another tear. "Thanks. And please don't say anything about me being upset." The last thing I wanted to do was cause things to be more difficult for Raffe.

She saluted me. "You got it."

I rushed into my room and locked the door. I'd never handled a problem like this before, but I was certain of one thing: When I did date someone, they wouldn't be ashamed of me. I'd felt unworthy enough my whole life, and at some point, I had to start loving myself.

I put in my earbuds, turned on music, and lay down. Closing my eyes, I wished like hell sleep would come.

I'D BEEN DRIFTING for a while when my phone buzzed. I glanced at the message, hoping pathetically that it was from Raffe. It was near ten p.m., and I hadn't heard a peep from him. It didn't surprise me—if he thought I was asleep, he wouldn't chance waking me, knowing I needed rest after my encounter with Dave. But it wasn't him.

Slade: Hey, I know it's late. Mom thought tonight would be a good night for you to visit the coven library, but it's off if you tell Raffe.

My pulse raced, and I sat up. Slade had mentioned that he'd try to set this up, but I'd never expected it to happen. The slight nap I'd taken was enough for me to be alert now.

Me: I'm in. Where do I meet you?

Slade: Behind the men's residence hall. I'll come from the library to meet you.

Interesting. That was in the direction of where the bonfire had been held. I'd expected the coven library to be behind the apartments where he and I often trained.

Me: Give me twenty.

After running a brush through my hair and changing into a thicker sweater, I headed downstairs, and when I exited the elevator, Raffe was standing in the lobby in front of the door. His eyes snapped to me, and he immediately pulled me into his arms. "Hey, I've been gathering the nerve to come to your room and talk to you."

Like always, my anger and annoyance vanished. His touch had a way of making me feel safe and loved. It was when he wasn't touching me that was the problem. "What are you doing out here? You could've texted or called me."

"I know, but I needed to talk to you, and I was afraid you

wouldn't answer the door. Babe, I'm so damn sorry." He pulled back, cupping my face. "I've been beside myself all night. I'm such a jackass."

I inhaled his scent and forced myself to step back. "What do you mean?" I didn't want to assume he'd figured out what had upset me.

"It was the second time that put it into perspective." He bit his bottom lip. "Seeing how hurt you were when Josie jumped on my back. I felt uncomfortable with it, but until I saw your face, I didn't realize how badly it was hurting you. I was stupid."

Okay, so he did have a clue. "Look, I get that you and Josie are friends, and I don't want to come between that, but when you two are together, it's like you're with *her* and not me. You sit next to her and have private conversations with her, and she constantly touches you like I want to do." My chest tightened. "I—"

"It won't happen anymore." He pulled me to his chest. "I swear it. You're the *only* woman who will touch me, and I'll make sure you're the one who feels special, not hurt."

I tilted my head. "But you don't want anyone to know about me."

"I'm still figuring that out, but I'll tell Josie we need to cut the act." He kissed my lips. "I'd rather deal with that fallout than see you hurt like that again."

Even though part of my heart *loved* his answer, the other part was in agony. He still didn't want his closest friends to know he was with me. I wondered if whatever we had had been doomed from the start.

I didn't have time to worry about it, not with the story of my heritage dangling right in front of me. "I hate to cut this short, but I need to go. Slade reached out, wanting me to meet him and see the library. He'll wonder what's taking so long."

"Shit. Well, I'm going to follow you, and when you're done, I get to come back here with you tonight, right?" He stared into my eyes, brow creased, not looking like the confident man I knew.

My heart ached, hating that I'd made him feel that way. "Of course. I always sleep better in your arms."

He exhaled and winked. "I feel the same."

"About sleeping in your arms?" I teased.

He laughed, carefree and happy, my favorite sound and one I heard only when we were alone.

"Cute." He booped my nose.

"He told me not to bring you." My body tensed. I didn't want to ruin my one shot at answers.

"You didn't. I found you, and he won't know. You go out first. He could be watching. I'll follow behind you in the woods. Keep your phone on and text me if you need me."

I nodded. "Okay."

I turned to leave when he grabbed my hand.

"Most important of all, be careful." He kissed me, his tongue sliding into my mouth. "If he hurts you or pushes you in *any* way, I'll fucking kill him."

I tilted my head and snorted. "That's the second time tonight you've threatened to kill someone for me. Should I be worried?"

"Babe, where you're concerned, I'll kill anyone who's ever done or will do you wrong."

A shudder ran through me. That probably shouldn't turn me on. There was something horribly wrong with me.

He smacked my butt and said, "Go before I change my mind. I'm not happy about this, but I know you want answers."

This was the kind, caring, supportive, and sexy man that I

lov—cared for. I kissed him once more, not wanting to leave, and forced myself to walk out the door.

No other students were out, which wasn't surprising given it was close to ten thirty. Everything on campus was closed. I turned left and walked past the men's apartments toward the library and residence halls.

The sky was dark and cloudy, and a light drizzle had started—a typical Washington night. I wrapped my arms around my waist and shivered.

After a few minutes, I felt a tingle at the base of my neck. Raffe was in the woods, watching me. That eased a bit of my tension.

I walked past the massive six-story library toward the all-brick residence halls. The men's hall was at the edge of the campus, with the woods facing the back and one side. My breathing became more labored. I wasn't sure what I was getting myself into.

I made my way to the back and noted Slade's presence. He was standing in the middle of the back wall of the building. He waved at me to join him, and when I got close, he scanned the area.

He smiled, reminding me of the Slade I used to know.

"Right on time." He winked.

"Sorry. I took a nap and needed a minute to get myself back together." I bounced on my feet. "Where to?"

"You're here." He waved a hand, and his magic pulsed from him.

Then the strangest thing happened.

CHAPTER TWENTY-FIVE

A section of the brick wall separated and moved to the side, creating a doorway. What was even stranger than the hidden door was that the wall didn't shake or make a sound, as if it was purely an illusion.

I sucked in a breath and raised my hands, my fingers slipping through the opening.

Nope. That was real. It truly had happened.

"It's neat, isn't it?" Slade smiled. "You should feel special. Not many people know about this, and we're asking that you not share this with anyone." He placed a hand on my back, guiding me forward.

His touch felt *wrong*, and I took a hurried step into the darkness to move away from it. My neck tingled more as if I could sense Raffe's rage, but I didn't want to argue with Slade while he was taking me somewhere I wasn't supposed to go.

As I stepped through the doorway, magic brushed against my skin, and the darkness transformed.

I stepped into a hallway of books and hanging lanterns. The ceiling of the library was cement but buttressed by carved wooden arches with twinkle lights strung through them, adding to the glow. A strong musty odor hit my nose, which wasn't surprising given how old these books were.

I scanned the books, each one bound in old leather with handwritten names on the spine, followed by what appeared to be a coven name. There had to be thousands—the hallway seemed to go on for miles.

"It's amazing, isn't it?" Slade asked from close behind me.

I jumped and spun around. The door had closed, and we were almost chest to chest. I took a step back, needing more distance.

As I stepped deeper into the library, more vibrations brushed my skin from both sides. My breath caught, and I jerked my head from side to side. It felt like people were crowding me, but I couldn't see anyone.

"Hey, it's okay." Slade extended his arm again, but when I flinched, he stopped. He frowned but lowered his hand. "The books contain spells, so what you're feeling is the remnants of each person's magic. It can't do anything to you—it's just their signatures that were left behind."

A shiver ran down my spine. "A warning would've been nice."

He shrugged. "I wasn't sure you'd feel it. You don't seem to feel the magic in us, but maybe that's because our bodies are barriers, whereas the books don't have one."

I pursed my lips. "You can feel another coven's magic?"

He nodded. "It's how we identify ourselves without ever saying a word. It came in very handy during the Salem witch trials. We knew who to protect and who we could be ourselves with."

My head tilted back. I'd never considered how much of the history I'd learned might not be accurate. Now I couldn't help but question almost everything I knew. How much had the supernaturals influenced things without us humans ever realizing it? I hated to think about humans as their prey and how easily we might be manipulated. I probably didn't want to know the answer.

"Come on. Mom and a few others from our coven are waiting for us." He pointed down the hallway to stairs that led to a second level.

Strange.

Turning around, I felt trapped. When Slade had mentioned there was a secret coven library, I'd assumed it was in the woods, somewhere Raffe could easily reach if I got into trouble. I wasn't sure I could escape from here if something happened. I'd let my eagerness to learn about my heritage taint my judgment, and now I might have gotten myself into a world of trouble.

That sounded about right with how things went for me.

As I walked toward the stairs, a different sort of vibration brushed my skin, scraping like sandpaper. I gritted my teeth, feeling more raw with each step. I didn't want Slade to know I was bothered since I wasn't sure what they had in store for me. I didn't trust him anymore, and his mom wasn't much better. Unfortunately, they had the one thing no one else did.

Answers.

I reached the cement stairs and took them slowly, the vibrations becoming downright painful. Slade knew how desperate I was, and I didn't want to validate that knowledge by hurrying. He already had enough control over me.

At the top of the stairs, I entered a sizable room. Two long rectangular tables ran parallel to one another, and a large lantern-style chandelier hung from the center of the ceiling, lighting the room.

Three women and one man sat at the middle of the table on the left. Priestess Olwyn sat on the side nearest to the wall, facing me with the two women on either side of her. The priestess gestured at the seat across from her, next to the man. "Skylar, please join us." She placed her hands on an old, worn book in front of her.

My head spun, and I wanted to run over and snatch the book from her grasp. But I'd learned a lot from Lizzy and other bullies I'd known throughout the years. If they knew they had something I wanted, they'd use it against me at every opportunity. The thing was, I suspected Slade and his mom were bullies, only better at hiding it to manipulate me.

The closer I got to the table, the more my skin felt as if it were being pulled away from muscle. And when I sat next to the middle-aged, blond-haired man, unease made my skin crawl and my blood jolt.

He looked at me and tugged at the black suit coat he wore, his slate eyes scanning me. "This is the arcane-born?" He quirked a brow.

My mouth went dry. Slade had told me not to tell anyone, and now I was sitting in a room with five people who knew about me. I swallowed and lifted my chin, trying like hell to appear confident and not terrified. "This is now public knowledge?" I looked at Slade as he sat next to me.

Slade winced, but Priestess Olwyn ran a hand over the closed leather book. "He didn't share the information. I did. But there is a reason he recommended you keep silent. You see, the wolf shifters—in particular Prince Raffe and King Jovian—would want to use you to further their power. They shouldn't even be ruling since all the decisions they make benefit them and not the rest of us. It's essential to keep the knowledge of what you are limited to a handful who have *everyone's* best interests at heart." I heard that tone of disgust in the priestess's voice.

It was the same tone Slade sometimes had, especially when talking to Raffe.

Something she'd said nagged at me.

The brown-complected woman across from the blond man tossed her dark-brown hair over her shoulder. I estimated she was in her thirties. "Don't worry, Skylar." Her dark-brown eyes warmed as she placed a hand over her chest. "This won't go beyond our trusted circle."

I wasn't sure I believed them. The jolt changed to a fizz. Maybe I shouldn't have come here. "Why do you say the wolves shouldn't be leading?"

"Witches were in charge centuries ago, and we did the goddess's bidding." Priestess Olwyn tapped her finger against the book. "And this particular *Book of Twilight* is part of the history of when the shift in leadership happened."

I snorted. "No pun intended, right?"

All five of them stared at me blankly.

"'Shift in leadership.' Shift." Wow. This was a tough audience, and my anxiety was getting the best of me. *Lovely.* "Wolves shift, right?" I mean, they were called wolf shifters for a reason. If they didn't shift, how did they—

The woman on Olwyn's other side, a caramel blonde close to my age, laughed. "Oh, that makes sense." Her giggle sounded like bells chiming. "Because you're right. They do shift. It's so weird, and I'm hardly ever around them."

"That's a blessing if you ask me." Slade scowled and leaned back in his seat.

At least one person here appreciated my horrible joke. "Sorry. I'm a little nervous." There was no point in lying. I ran a finger along the seam of my jeans, hoping to work out a bit of excess energy. "Look, I appreciate you allowing me to come here and learn about my heritage, but why are you telling me all this? I'm not a supernatural."

"You need to understand your history, which is entwined with that of the witches and the wolves." Priestess Olwyn steepled her fingers. "The fall of the covens came with the death of the last arcane-born."

My breath seized, and my blood increased to a solid fizz.

"Now you have her attention." The man glanced at me with a smirk.

Now that my blood had enough power, I could read his emotions. He was intrigued by me but also disappointed as if he'd expected something more. I couldn't blame him. Calling me an arcane-born was like calling a chihuahua a wolf. There was no comparison. I shivered at the slightest provocation, tried not to pee my pants when frightened, and had to pretend to be somewhat ferocious.

"Well, I should, Priest Alastor." Priestess Olwyn sat up straighter and spat, "Especially with her growing friendship with Prince Raffe and his cronies." Hatred and frustration poured off her like cancer.

Priest? I hadn't expected that. And cronies? Had we gone back in time? "My friendship with Lucy and the other shifters isn't your concern." I'd come here to learn about my heritage, not get lectured about who I chose to hang out with. "EEU put Lucy and me together as roommates."

"*What?*" the woman with dark hair gasped. "Supreme Priestess, you didn't tell us that."

"Because, *Priestess* Eva, it was none of your concern." Priestess Olwyn's face looked strained, and anger dominated her emotions. "When I learned of it, I talked with Lafayette. Apparently, the old vampire was bored and wanted to give Raffe's family hell by matching a human with someone of the royal line."

A knot formed in my stomach. I was pretty sure she was angry with me, but she was lashing out at her people.

The fair-skinned blonde smiled kindly. "I understand wanting to keep things civil with your roommate, but you must understand; if the wolf shifters find out what you are, they'll kill you in an instant."

She was petite compared to the others, her cobalt irises shone like beacons ... and something malicious emanated from her.

I had to be reading her wrong.

"Priestess Sabrina, that's easier said than done with the mutt panting at her heels." Slade's lip curled back. "Even though King Jovian has declared that we keep our distance from Skylar until we discover what she is, he must have directed Prince Raffe to get close to her. He publicly humiliates her at every chance, following his father's directive, but he's always lurking close by. They're clearly trying to figure out what she is, and Prince Raffe has doubled his efforts since King Jovian witnessed her surge of power in the stadium. They must realize she's special."

My chest ached. Once again, doubts grew about why Raffe was spending more time with me. He'd pretended for years that he was dating Josie—maybe he was doing the same with me. But that didn't make sense. Between the yank in my chest and the buzz whenever we touched, he couldn't be faking his attraction. Had he lied about dating me being forbidden and was actually keeping our relationship secret to do what Slade had suggested? My heart ached at the thought.

"Something you said upset her." Priestess Olwyn tilted her head, examining me. "You didn't think Prince Raffe was truly interested in befriending you, did you?"

I bit my bottom lip, my fizz nearing a damn hum.

"That's how wolf shifters work." Priestess Sabrina frowned and leaned across the table. "They manipulate people to get what they want, and they don't care who they screw over. That's what happened to the last arcane-born and why we're warning you."

Ears ringing, I tried not to physically react. "What do you mean?"

Priestess Olwyn opened the book and spun it around, allowing me to read.

Foster met the princess of the wolf shifters under the full moon. He was taken with her, despite our warnings about the dangers the wolves posed to the coven. Though our magic is stronger, the wolves are more resilient. They've learned that if they force us to use our magic for long periods of time, they can overcome us. That's why the goddess blessed us with him—to keep the wolf shifters in check. Yet Foster isn't listening. The wolf shifter has entranced, I suspect, another coven's magic, though I can't read a signature from him. I keep warning him that all relationships with wolf shifters end in great disappointment, but he thinks she's different.

Unlike the other books, this one didn't have any vibrations coming off it. I almost wished it did to distract me from the dismay screaming within.

Those were the only words written on that page, and I suspected the coven members wanted me to think I knew how the story ended, but I refused to be manipulated. "What happened?"

When Priestess Olwyn flipped toward the end of the book, fear strangled me.

Eventually, the wolves attacked. Foster used his magic to slow the wolves, which is the only reason some of us survived. But I watched as he crumpled to the ground, and I felt his magic release back into the world. Though he learned to harness his rare magic, in the end, it took his life. We owe him ours for eternity. Either way, our coven has fallen, and I fear that savage men will now lead the supernaturals.

I sucked in a breath. "Foster died protecting the witches?"

Slade placed a hand on my arm. Every cell in me wanted

to pull away from his touch, but I didn't want to disrespect him in front of his mother and their people. "Yes. That's the last entry, and the fall of the coven is detailed in the priestess's *Book of Twilight*. But this book contains insights into how Foster controlled his magic."

I couldn't believe this was the ending to Foster's story. None of it added up. "What happened to his friendship with the princess?"

"It ended in his death." Priestess Olwyn shut the book. "You read that, and now you know. We're the only people you can trust, and more so, we need your help, Skylar."

"Need my help?" My skin crawled. "How can I help? I can't control myself, let alone help you accomplish anything. Besides, Lucy and I are friends. I don't want to ruin that relationship." Or the one I had with Raffe, though it was best that I exclude that particular fact.

"We don't want you to hurt anyone." Priestess Olwyn pulled the book to her chest. "Just be willing to listen to the struggles we're facing … both vampires and witches."

The world spun, and I gripped the arms of my chair. "I'm not sure what you expect from me, but my goal is to become a vet and help animals. I don't want to get involved in a supernatural civil war."

"No, dear." Priestess Eva shook her head. "We don't want a war, and you won't have to hurt anyone or put yourself in danger. We are in different times. You've been lured in by the wolf shifters, and we want a chance for you to see things from our perspective. If you open your eyes and listen, you'll see the struggles we face while we teach you about your power like our kind did for Foster."

Every single person here was determined to influence me. Even though I certainly didn't trust them, they had the *Book of Twilight* with all the details about Foster. If I told them to shove it, I wouldn't have anyone to train me, and I wouldn't be able to read more of the journal. They clearly wanted something from me too; otherwise, they wouldn't have been so determined to win me over. I'd learned the hard way that everyone had their own best interests at heart, and once again, I was doubting Raffe.

Keep your enemies close was an unfortunate mantra I needed to implement, both with the covens and with Raffe.

Priest Alastor snorted humorlessly. "She's struggling with the decision. That's quite insulting."

My blood warmed to a hum. I cut my eyes to him just as his chair began to vibrate so hard that his teeth clacked together.

Priestesses Olwyn, Sabrina, and Eva jerked back in their seats, watching the debacle.

"Forgive me if I need time to process everything," I spat, knowing that losing control again confirmed my answer. "I need your help, and I'm open to seeing things from your perspective. I was always willing to listen to Slade until recently."

The priest's chair splintered into sharp shards, and he crashed to the floor. Fatigue hit me, but it wasn't incapacitating since I hadn't lost control for long.

Silence descended.

Priestess Olwyn grinned. "It's great to have you as part of our coven."

I hadn't meant *that*. The words hung over me like a heavy blanket, and I didn't know how to respond.

Sabrina and Eva beamed while Alastor scowled and climbed to his feet.

"Let's get you home." Slade stood and nodded in the direction we'd come from.

Before we reached the stairs, Priestess Sabrina said, "Oh, and Skylar. It's great to call you *sister*."

I glanced over my shoulder and saw her bright eyes and matching smile.

Throat constricting, I forced a smile. "Thanks. I'll see you around."

I swore she whispered, "Yes, you will." But her lips didn't move. Great, I was going crazy.

I followed Slade back through the library. At the end of the hall, he waved a hand, and the hidden door opened. The night sky greeted me.

The cool air was exactly what I needed. When I stepped outside, my blood settled to a jolt, and the urge to go home and to bed nearly knocked me over.

"Are you okay?" Slade asked as the door shut behind us.

I looked at him, and I saw my old friend. His face was lined with concern, and he rubbed his hands together like he wanted to do something to fix my exhaustion.

"It was a lot." I didn't want to lie to him, and I wanted to go to bed. Waking up in the morning with a fresh perspective might be the very thing I needed.

"If you need to talk about it—"

I shook my head. "And a priest? What's up with that?"

He chuckled. "It's rare but not unheard of. Over ninety-five percent of the time, the person who runs a coven is a woman. There've been only a handful of priests throughout the past centuries. He's been deemed worthy to be one."

Maybe he shouldn't have been. Alastor was volatile... maybe even more so than my blood. I forced myself not to shiver and yawned. "Interesting. Well, that little power burst made me tired."

"Yeah." Slade waved a hand. "Right. Let me walk you home."

The tingle at the nape of my neck broke through. Raffe was waiting for me. I sighed. "No, I'm good. But thanks." I smiled, trying to come off as sincere. "You didn't get rid of me yet."

"I'm glad. I was nervous." He kicked at the ground. "And I'm sorry for being a jackass. I got jealous, but tonight, I realized you'll soon understand everything, and that won't be a problem anymore."

I hated how hopeful he looked, and I didn't want to encourage him. "I'll see you around."

"You'll see me tomorrow." He winked. "We have class together, remember?"

"Oh, I remember." No matter how often I tried to forget. "See you then." I spun on my heel and headed back to my apartment.

As I thought through what I'd read and heard tonight, my heart raced, and my head whirled. How would understanding the plight of the witches and vampires help me? It wasn't like I could do anything about it. Did they expect me to fight against whatever allure Raffe had for me?

I stepped through the entrance to my apartment, expecting to see Raffe, but he wasn't there. Confused, I headed to my room, desperate for bed.

After changing out of my jeans and into pajamas, I received a text.

Raffe: I'm staying out here to see if anything else happens. Unless you need me.

Even though I was disappointed, I could use some time to myself to think without any influence.

Me: I'm good. Just tired. See you tomorrow. <3

Raffe: Counting the seconds until then. :*

My heart skipped a beat, but I pushed the sensation away and crawled into bed. I needed rest. That should help me think clearly. I expected to struggle to fall asleep, but within seconds, my eyelids grew heavy, and I was out.

THE NEXT MORNING, Lucy was already gone when I woke up. As I got ready and headed to the student center, I wondered what had gotten her out of bed so early. I grabbed a vanilla latte and a biscuit then spotted Lucy sitting at a table with a deep frown on her face.

My heart picked up.

Something was wrong.

I hurried over, intending to check on her before heading to class, but then I saw the people sitting across from her and checked my stride.

Josie, Adam, and Keith.

When Keith's gaze landed on me, he stood and snarled.

CHAPTER TWENTY-SIX

My heart pounded as my blood took off at a fizz. Keith was upset with *me*, and I had no clue why.

I didn't want another public scene. One was more than enough for a lifetime, and Raffe had provided that opportunity.

When Keith stepped toward me, an arm looped through mine, tugging me toward the exit. I held on to my biscuit tightly and realized Hecate had come to my rescue. A sweet scent that reminded me of cotton candy drifted into my nose from my right side where a paler woman I'd never met before flanked me.

I expected Keith to chase after me, but glancing over my shoulder, I found him standing at the edge of the shifters' table with a sneer. If looks could kill, I'd be dead.

"Are you asking him to tear into you?" Hecate jerked me so I couldn't see Keith any longer. "Staring at him like that will make him think you're challenging him."

Shit. My stomach clenched. I should've known that based on my animal studies. "Right, because I'm asserting dominance."

The new woman to my right chuckled, her pale-green eyes twinkling. "Or not backing down, though you are letting us carry you off." Wavy burgundy hair hung down over her white, lacy shirt. Her lips were a dark red that contrasted starkly with her pale complexion. She pressed them together. "At least they haven't completely brainwashed you *yet*."

"Brainwashed?" I didn't understand what was happening. Hecate wasn't a huge fan of mine, and now she was coming to my rescue along with a stranger. Between that and Keith's animosity, I felt as if I'd walked into an alternate reality.

"Yes, the wolf shifters' allure and power are intoxicating." The woman shrugged and sighed. "It's a damn shame since it's an advantage they often use to get their way."

"Zella, let's make sure we're far enough away from prying ears before you say anything else." Hecate rolled her eyes. "We don't need Keith reporting what we say back to King Jovian. You know she's on their radar."

That was enough to get my brain functioning again. "*She's* right here." Any warmth I'd had toward Hecate was gone.

"Don't be such a drama queen." Hecate arched a brow. "I was talking to her, not you, and what pronoun would you suggest I use?"

I blew out a breath. She had a point, but I refused to admit it and have her gloat. "You could've talked to both of us."

"Really? You're going all sensitive *now*?" Hecate waved a hand. "Raffe rejects you and marks you as a social outcast, yet you practically sniff his ass, but I talk to Zella about you in front of your face, and you get all butt hurt. *Please*. Now isn't the time to lose your thick skin."

A lifetime of people treating me as if I didn't exist was the sort of baggage she'd never understand. "I don't want to argue or seem ungrateful, but why are you helping me out?"

The three of us walked outside, and I shivered in the cool September morning. I detangled my arm from Hecate's and unwrapped my biscuit from the foil then took a huge bite.

"Slade informed me that you're part of the coven now." Hecate shrugged. "We might not be a pack like the wolf shifters, but we protect our own."

I glanced at Zella to see if I could feel the magic inside her. From what Slade had mentioned, I should be able to feel it, but I couldn't sense a damn thing. "Are you from the same coven?"

Zella snorted. "Uh. No. Not a witch here."

Okay, I hadn't expected that. With her pale skin, my second guess was ... "Vampire?"

She nodded. "It's so weird that someone who knows about us can't tell us apart."

"In fairness, your complexion reminded me of Dave's, but you're hanging out with a witch, which threw me." All the species seemed to stick with their own and were wary of one another, so Hecate hanging out with a vampire didn't make sense.

"Some vampires and witches are friends." Zella winked. "The wolf shifters have a way of bringing us together."

The past twelve hours'd had a constant theme. "That's what I keep hearing."

"It's true." Zella straightened. "Wolf shifters mess up *all* the time, and they get so many chances. If a vampire makes one wrong move, like feeding off Skylar here, they kill us. No talking, no trial, no anything. Just death."

I tensed. Raffe had threatened Dave, but I'd thought he was grandstanding to assert his strength. If what she said was true ... "Are you saying the vampire who attacked me in the woods is dead?" Now that I thought back on it, I remembered Raffe jumping on his back, though I hadn't realized it was Raffe then.

Zella became unnaturally frozen. "You didn't know?"

The bite of biscuit I'd swallowed threatened to come back up. "No. I passed out when a wolf jumped on his back." I couldn't bring myself to say Raffe's name. If they weren't aware which shifter had killed him, I'd rather it stay that way. "He was gone when I woke up, and so was the woman he'd been feeding on, so I assumed ..." I wasn't sure what I assumed. I'd been exhausted and traumatized. Any time I thought back on that day, I remembered the vampire's teeth sinking into my neck. The sharp stabbing pain was something I wished I could forget. Books and movies had it wrong. There was *nothing* pleasant about it.

"Raffe, Keith, and Adam killed him because he lost control." Zella snorted. "That was the first time it *ever* happened, and he was two hundred years old. That should've counted for *something*."

We were approaching Evergreen, which meant I needed to peel off soon, but I now had questions. "Why would a two-hundred-year-old attend college?"

"Vampires are weird," Hecate said and bumped her shoulder into mine.

I stumbled, some of my latte spilling out from the hole of the lid. I hadn't expected her to do something that friendly.

Zella took my arm to steady me. When I straightened, she answered, "Because living for centuries, if not thousands of years, causes boredom. Every now and then, we want to learn a new career or find something more stimulating. Edward came back here to study political science and work with the wolf shifters to change laws so everyone could live with the same rights and freedoms."

Knowing what little I did, I could see that the wolf shifters did take advantage of their power, and I'd wondered why someone hadn't tried to change that. Clearly, Edward had shared the same thought.

"He was foolish." Zella wrinkled her nose. "All it did was get him killed."

I exhaled and took a sip of my drink. The latte was already lukewarm due to the temperature outside. "Well, that's a good idea—to talk with the wolf shifters about the issues you have."

"You say that as if we haven't tried it." Zella lifted both hands. "So many of us have over the centuries, and we've been brushed aside and punished. Edward was relatively young and still naive enough to believe he could make a difference."

"Witches learn at a young age that things will never change." Hecate smacked her lips. "The wolf shifters think they're right, and they punish anyone who disagrees with them."

The buzzing on my neck alerted me that Raffe was watching me. These two had helped me avoid a confrontation back there, and I didn't want them to say something incriminating and chance Raffe overhearing. "Hey, I need to go inside. I'm almost frozen." I looked toward the apartments and saw Raffe heading toward us from across the road.

Hecate and Zella followed my stare then looked at me strangely.

"Okay, see you around." Hecate tilted her head. Then they turned around and headed back toward the student center.

I bounced on my heels, waiting on Raffe and trying to stay warm. He picked up his pace, and when he got closer, his brows furrowed. "What was that about?"

I forced myself to stand still in front of him, which was damn hard with the yanking in my chest.

I wanted to ask Raffe about Edward, but that wouldn't be smart after he's seen me with those two—Raffe would wonder why I was asking right after hanging out with them. I'd have to figure out how to talk to him strategically so he wouldn't be defensive, especially if Hecate and Zella were right about how wolf shifters treated witches and vampires.

Luckily, I could answer his question without lying. "It's weird. I went to get breakfast and a latte, and I saw Lucy, Josie, Adam, and Keith together. They all seemed upset, and when Keith noticed me, he stood and snarled at me. I have no idea why. Hecate and Zella intervened and got me out of there before Keith reached me."

"Shit. That's what I was afraid of." Raffe winced. "This is why I didn't want to tell Josie, Keith, and Adam that I was done pretending to date her."

I stopped in the middle of the hallway and turned to him, ignoring the bodies bumping into me as they passed. "What?" I must have misunderstood him.

"Last night, Josie, Adam, and Keith went for a run and found me ..." He paused and glanced around. "Outside. We hung out for a while, but nothing caught our eye."

He was talking in code in case there were any listening ears.

"When we headed in, I walked Josie to her apartment and broke it off with her." He put his hands into his pockets and scuffed his shoe on the tile floor. "They must not be taking the news of our supposed breakup well, which was why I didn't push it before."

I snorted. "This is my fault?"

"What? No." He reached out a hand for a second before dropping it.

And it stung. Even though we were together and he'd "broken it off" with Josie, he still wanted our relationship to be a secret.

Whispers of doubt shifted through my mind again. Was this Raffe's attempt to keep me under control?

"That's not what I was saying." He hung his head. "I keep messing this up. I just meant they know something is changing, and they don't like it. I worried they would blame you."

I huffed. "I mean, what do you think will happen when everything comes out?" Or maybe that was the point. It never would. He was already struggling with his friends' reactions and how his father might respond.

My heart throbbed, stealing my breath. I would always be a secret. No one would ever be proud to be with me. I'd be the person they wished had never been born.

"Sky—" Raffe groaned.

That right there confirmed it. He didn't think about it because we would never go public.

I hated that the pain swirling through me was so intense. I should've never expected anything different. "We better head to class." That was the one thing I had going right for me. I would graduate, become a vet, and submerge myself in animals—the only living things that enjoyed my company and for whom I could make a difference.

He sighed, but I turned my back and made my way to class. When would I love myself enough to not be okay with such poor treatment? I wanted to be accepted so much that I threw myself out there to be hurt, over and over again. Raffe could be the very thing that destroyed me, and by agreeing to this sort of relationship, I'd opened myself up to him, and there would be no repair.

"Wait. Skylar," he called again, but I hurried into Howling.

"I'm going to be late," I said normally, knowing he'd hear me. I walked into the building and tossed my biscuit into the trash. I'd lost my appetite.

In microbiology, I took my seat next to Dave. He lifted his head, and his eyebrows shot up.

Great. He didn't want to sit next to me. I shouldn't be surprised after yesterday. I swallowed around the lump in my throat and readied myself to get up. "Sorry. I can sit somewhere else. I wasn't thinking."

Dave cleared his throat. "No, please stay. I'm just a little surprised that you'd want to sit next to me after ... you know ..." He shrugged.

Oh, right. He'd wanted to eat me yesterday. "I can move. I didn't think." My brain had to be short-circuiting.

"It's fine, seriously." He sniffed and smiled. "There's nothing great smelling here."

My blood was only jolting, and I hadn't noticed until now. But it wasn't high-fizzing, which seemed to be the issue. "Okay then."

"Did Raffe tell the others what happened?" Dave snagged a book from his bag, but I heard the concern behind his words.

I shrugged. "I think so, but I wasn't around when he did."

He winced, and his comment about Josie popped back into my mind. Did he have a thing for her?

Not wanting to get involved in any more drama, I kept my question to myself. I unzipped my backpack and removed my notebook and pen then took a sip of my coffee. I was ready for class to begin so I could, for a few minutes, forget about my life and get lost in microbiology, one of the few topics in my life that made sense.

I LAY ON MY BED, staring at my purple paper butterfly chandelier. I'd avoided Raffe in economics by coming into class at the last minute. Luckily, we'd broken into separate groups to do our work today, and I'd made sure my group got our stuff done early and I was out the door before his group completed the assignment. I'd been hiding in my room ever since, knowing he'd be at football practice with Adam and Keith.

I'd done my homework, and now I was bored out of my mind. Lucy wasn't home, and I feared her absence had to do with Raffe and Josie.

My phone buzzed beside me, and I started, nearly falling off the bed. Great, when did I get so jumpy?

Mom's name rolled across the screen, so I swiped. If I didn't answer, she'd get worried.

"Hey, honey." Her voice was chipper, way more chipper than it had ever been when I'd lived with them. "How are you doing?"

"Great. You?" Good thing a wolf shifter wasn't here, or they'd be smelling my stench right about now.

"Well, other than your father and me missing you like crazy, we're doing okay." She launched into a story about her accounting job and the TV series she and Dad were watching together. Some sort of house-swapping reality show she enjoyed. Then she paused. "Are you sure everything's okay? You seem distant. Did anything weird happen again? Do you need us to come there?"

Her concern eased some of my pain. She hated when my blood went crazy, but the fact that she was willing to come here and support me meant more than she'd ever know. "I'm just stressed. Classes are hard, and I don't want to get behind." At least that wasn't a full lie.

"Oh, honey. You won't struggle. You never do."

Buttons beeped on the keypad, and my heart stuttered. That had to be Lucy, and I wondered what she'd say after avoiding me for so long.

But when loud, sure footsteps headed my way and my chest did the yanking sensation, I realized who it was.

"Sky, we need to talk," Raffe said then knocked on my door.

Mom gasped. "Is a boy in your apartment?"

Shit, I should've said something so Raffe realized I was talking to Mom. "Uh ... yeah. He's my stats partner. I forgot we were studying."

My door opened, and Raffe stepped inside, smirking.

He was having way too much fun with this. "All right, Mom, I need to go. Talk soon. Love you. Bye." I hung up and sat on my bed, glaring at him.

But with his wet hair and the way his polo shirt molded to his chest, it was hard to remember why I was angry. It was clear he'd taken a shower after practice before coming here.

When he stepped toward me and tried to wrap his arms around my waist, I stepped back, the yank damn near keeping my legs from moving.

He frowned and sighed. "I'm sorry about earlier. I could see you thought I was blaming you, and I wasn't. Keith was harassing me via the pack link to get to the student center, and when I saw you talking to a witch and a vampire, it threw me. I'm a complete jackass and not worthy of your forgiveness, but I'm hoping you give it to me anyway." He held my gaze steadily.

I wished that was the only problem, but my heart was turning to mush at his sincerity. "Fine. But you seem intent on making this a habit."

"In fairness, I didn't expect to meet *you,* so we have to

figure this out together." He leaned over and kissed my forehead. "I'm just so damn glad you're willing."

Together.

He knew the word to use to breach my defenses, but I couldn't ignore what had happened to Edward and almost to Dave. "Did you kill Edward?"

He flinched and straightened. "I see Hecate and Zella didn't waste any time filling you in. Frankly, I was surprised Slade hadn't."

I crossed my arms, my blood skipping the jolt and heading straight to the fizz. "That's not an answer." I didn't like him speaking in riddles. "Why didn't you tell me?"

He ran a hand over his face. "I didn't want you to blame yourself for Edward's death. You were already exhausted after damn near imploding. I wasn't trying to hide it or lie to you. I just wanted to protect you."

Some of my anger thawed. Unfortunately, he was right—knowing what really happened could have tipped me over again. "Still, why did you kill him? It was the first time he'd ever gone crazy like that, and my blood made Dave struggle."

He lifted both hands. "Babe, when a vampire loses control like that, it's easier for them to do it again and risk exposing our entire world. We can't chance that. I know it seems brutal and believe me, it brings me no joy. But if a vampire becomes blood-crazed and we don't end them, we risk not only outing our world but humans getting hurt horrendously and becoming blood slaves."

When he put it like that, it created a different image. I could read his sincerity and regret.

I exhaled. "But still—"

"You weren't thrilled about vampires feeding on humans, remember?" He tilted his head and tucked a piece of hair behind my ear. "We understand that they need food, but if we let one vampire get out of control to save someone who can't be saved, the vampires with control will start slipping. Wolf shifters are in charge of protecting humans and the secrets of the supernatural. I'm not saying our methods are perfect, but they are necessary." He stepped toward me again.

I placed a hand on his chest, still needing one question answered. "And Dave? What about him? You threatened to kill him, and he didn't lose control."

"He was going to hurt *you*." Raffe's nostrils flared. "He was damn close to stalking you, which is when the predator in them comes out. The thought of you being in that situation again …" He trailed off, his emotions so strong I could feel them. Devastation, fear, and anger. He moved to me again, and I let him wrap his arms around me. "I'd do anything to protect you."

"But I need you to promise you won't unless someone actually harms me." All the reasons I had to stay away from Raffe had slipped my mind. He was being honest, and if he was playing me, he could've called them liars. "Dave was trying so hard not to hurt me, yet you still threatened him."

He snorted. "Not ending him goes against my very nature and wolf when it comes to you."

I smiled tenderly, placing my hands on his chest. "But that's what I'm asking."

"Fine." He kissed my forehead. "For you, I swear to try." He moved to my lips and kissed me softly and sweetly.

His scent mixed with soap made my head swim, and I deepened the kiss. He opened his mouth, allowing my tongue entrance, and I pressed my body against his.

Growling, he grabbed my ass and lifted me against him, and I wrapped my legs around his waist. My body buzzed and my heart pounded. Each kiss was better than the last.

He cupped my breast as he pulled away from my mouth

and kissed his way down my neck. I hadn't even realized we'd moved until he laid me down on my bed and hovered over me. I unwrapped my legs and began pulling at his shirt.

He chuckled and removed his shirt then tossed it on the floor.

I would never tire of this view. His bare chest was muscular and beautiful, and his six-pack curved in dangerous ways. I wanted to do things with him that I'd never done with anyone before. He edged my shirt up my torso, the faint glow in his eyes surging, which turned me on even more. I loved the idea of him needing me so badly that his wolf peeked through.

He slipped his hand under my bra and rubbed my nipple, and my body arched just as I heard steps heading toward my door.

I hadn't heard the front door open.

Raffe jumped from the bed and had reached for his shirt when my bedroom door burst open. He stood in front of me and blocked the person's view as I adjusted my clothing.

Someone barged into my room, and I shrieked as Keith snarled, "I fucking *knew* it."

CHAPTER TWENTY-SEVEN

I yanked my top down, and Raffe's back tensed. I could see every muscle before his shirt covered him again.

This was bad.

Raffe bellowed, "Get the *fuck* out now, or I'll make you." I was surprised he didn't attack Keith, but when he backed up closer to me, ensuring that Keith couldn't see me, I realized why.

He was protecting me from one of his own.

My heart fluttered while my entire body felt weighed down. Keith wouldn't let this go.

"I'm stepping outside so you two can get your shit together," Keith snapped. "Then you better join me in the living room. Lucy, Adam, and Josie are on their way here. It's time for a fucking intervention."

"Get out before I lose control and kill your ass," Raffe seethed, his body shaking with each deep breath.

My blood was almost at a hum.

When the door shut, Raffe turned to me, his face strained. His emotions were anger, regret, dread, and fear.

For the millionth time, I wished I couldn't read emotions.

The last three sensations nearly ripped my heart into pieces all over again because he felt that way about being with *me*.

"I'm so sorry." He hung his head. "Stay here, and I'll talk to them."

The words knocked the breath out of me. "Are you serious? You want me to hide in my room while you face the firing squad about us?"

He cleared his throat. "It's better this way. You won't be visible, adding—" He stopped like sense had been knocked into him.

"Adding what?" I laughed, but the noise made my raw throat feel as if it were bleeding. "What will my presence make worse, Raffe? Please tell me." I'd thought that when we came out to his friends, he'd want to face them together, but instead, he wanted me to hide in my room as if my absence wouldn't remind them that I was a human freak with power.

"Fuck, Sky." He leaned his head back. "I can only deal with one irrational person at a time, and I need to focus on Keith and the others. If they call my dad ..." He trailed off and popped his neck. "Can you just listen this once, for fuck's sake?"

Here was the asshole I used to know. I'd seen glimpses of him since we'd started dating, but nothing like the jerk standing before me. I stepped forward, my blood humming. "You want to see irrational?" The wall where my favorite painting hung started to shake. I was losing control, but I didn't care.

His gaze darted to the wall as my picture crashed to the floor, the glass front shattering. He flinched and placed his hands on my shoulders.

Immediately, my blood calmed, despite the anger growing within me. I forced myself to step back, the backs of my knees hitting the bed. I almost fell onto it but somehow stayed upright.

"Sky—" He groaned. "Look, I'm—"

"No." I karate-chopped the air, my blood back to a high fizz. "If you say sorry one more time, I'm going to scream. Doing the same thing over and over again negates any apology. You don't respect me, and you know what's worse? I've been allowing it." The reality of what I just said crashed over me, waking me up from whatever stupor I'd been in.

"Babe, look, I'm being an ass. I get it, and you're right." He lifted his hands in surrender.

The front door opened and slammed shut. Then Keith shouted, "She's messing with his mind *again*. That's it. I'm done waiting."

Raffe clenched his hands, and I could read his emotions. He was flustered, and for some reason, he hadn't felt that way until I'd defended myself. Yet another negative reaction concerning me.

"Man ..." Adam sighed. "Wait."

Loud steps came toward my room, and Raffe spun around as the door opened.

"I swear to *gods*, Raffe." Keith stood there, his face turning red. "If you don't knock this shit off right this second, I'm linking with King Jovian. Something needs to be done about her because you've lost your damn mind where she's concerned."

Adam, Josie, and Lucy stood in the small hallway behind Keith. Lucy cringed while Josie's mouth hung open. Adam rubbed his temples as if he had a headache.

"Wait. Is this why you said you wanted to stop pretending to date?" Josie's brows furrowed. "You want to be with a human?"

"No." Raffe lifted his hands to his side.

I gasped, and my blood hummed in tune with the repeated stabbing of my heart. I'd thought I understood pain, but nothing compared to this.

"I don't *want* to be with a human." Raffe glanced over his shoulder at me. "But I want to be with Skylar."

Keith laughed. "Same thing. She's human, even if not completely. *Different* isn't good where the prince is involved."

Different. Weird. Outcast. I'd heard all the various synonyms tossed around to describe me.

One of the most common words directed at me throughout my childhood. I'd thought I'd grown immune to people calling me that, but no. After feeling somewhat accepted here, being labeled that way had tears sprouting in my eyes like they had the first time Lizzy had tossed the word at me, ending our friendship.

"So what if she's *different*?" Lucy spat, her nose wrinkling. "Not any more than any of us. She has magic. She's just not supernatural."

Now I was teary for another reason. Lucy was coming to my aid.

"Oh, gods." Keith shook his head. "She's gotten to you too. I wonder if manipulation is part of her magic."

"Shut up, man," Adam said and shoved him in the shoulder. "You're making this way more dramatic and acting like an epic ass ... even for you."

"Yeah, talk about her like that again, and we won't be friends." Raffe cracked his knuckles, stepping in front of me. "I get this isn't ideal, but I care about her."

The fizz calmed as some of my pain eased. I'd needed to see Raffe invested in our relationship; otherwise, we wouldn't have made it beyond this moment, and that scared me.

"I get it." Adam blew out a breath. "Skylar is a nice girl. Yeah, we don't know what her power is or if she can ever control it, but she's never done anything to purposely jeopardize our world or harm us."

Adam saying nice things about me was unexpected, but I'd take it. With his and Lucy's support, maybe Keith would follow suit and accept us. My chest expanded with hope.

"But man." Adam moved right in front of Raffe so I could see his face. He placed a hand on Raffe's shoulder and said, "Your dad will never accept this. Is she worth risking your relationship with your father and the throne as well? No one will follow you if you're in a relationship with a human."

Raffe went still.

And my heart shredded into pieces. He cared about me; that much was clear, or he would've denied me as soon as Keith had burst in on us. But he wasn't willing to risk alienation from his people for me. And could I live with myself if I asked him to? Even if he agreed, that ultimatum would lead to resentment.

"Adam's right." Josie edged into the room. "I like Skylar too, and I don't think we should ignore her. I want you to be happy and find someone, but you'll be risking *everything* if you commit to a human. A human you'll outlive by at least a century. You'll wind up alone."

Raffe groaned and covered his face.

That was my answer.

Though my heart had shattered into shards so small I doubted I could ever repair it, I blew out a breath. "It's not only up to him."

"Figures." Keith barked out a hateful laugh. "Here we go. Make the decision for him. Please, ruin his life."

I stepped aside so I could see Keith when I said this. The truth was, I would be the only one ruined. Raffe would be just fine. "Raffe and I aren't together."

"Please." Keith rolled his eyes. "I know what I walked in on."

"You're right." There was no point in lying. They'd all smell it, and Josie's truth had merit. What sort of selfish person would I be to want him to choose me—*barely*—and expect him to, what, be alone after I died? I wasn't sure how the aging thing worked, but it made sense that supernaturals would live a lot longer than humans.

Besides, who was to say we'd even stay together long term? Maybe Raffe didn't feel the same connection I did, the one that told me he was *it* for me.

"Since Raffe is having a hard time deciding, I'm doing it for us. You won't have to tell King Jovian anything because as of this moment, there's nothing to tell." Black spots filled my vision, and the walls closed in on me.

Raffe's head jerked around to me. His face twisted in agony. "Sky—"

"Don't." I held up a hand, not needing to hear the end of that sentence. He was conflicted, and being unsure about a huge decision like this wasn't fair. "Don't make this harder than it has to be." I had to get out of here, or I might change my mind and beg him to pick me.

I snatched my keys from the nightstand and breezed past Raffe. The fizz was again close to a hum, and I needed to get out of here before I caused the building to collapse on us.

Adam and Josie pressed their lips together as I passed them while Keith beamed in victory.

"Sky," Raffe groaned, grabbing my arm and tugging me toward him. The buzzing grew more intense, as did the *yank* in my chest. But his touch calmed my blood, which I desperately needed.

When our eyes met, his glistened, and his face twisted. The confident man I always saw wasn't there, and that destroyed me further. "Please don't. You're not sure, and I need to go."

His bottom lip quivered.

Keith knocked his hand away from me and growled, "You heard her."

I turned and stumbled into the hallway. I was surprised when Lucy fell into step beside me and walked out with me.

In the elevator, my vision clouded. I needed Lucy to stay here so I could go to my car and drive somewhere I could fall apart without anyone watching.

Once again, I was alone.

"Don't give up on him," Lucy whispered, taking my hand and squeezing. "You make him a better person."

I snorted, the sound rough and bitter. "I don't buy that. And Lucy, he couldn't decide. It's over."

"But you need to understand—"

"Stop." She wasn't making things easier even though she was being a friend. I needed to be alone and grieve everything I'd lost. Again. "I *do* understand. Believe me. People only want me in their lives for a short time if at all. Then they realize I'm not worth the cost." I was destined to be alone, and I had to accept that. "He's your cousin, I get it, but I need to take care of myself and get my emotions under control." My blood was already near a hum.

The elevator dinged, and I slowly released her hand, not wanting to be a jerk to her. She'd stood by me. "I'll come back soon. Text me when they all clear out?"

"Where are you going?" She bit her lip.

"Not the woods, if that's what you're worried about." Even though I wished I could be there. "I'm going for a drive to clear my head."

She huffed. "Okay. Be safe. If you get more upset, pull over. I'll text you soon."

"Promise." My voice cracked, indicating how damn close I was to losing it.

The doors slid shut, finally leaving me alone. With the tears already pouring down my cheeks, obscuring my vision, I realized I couldn't drive. Not like this. But I needed a way to calm down.

I had the number of the only person who wasn't associated with Raffe. I texted Slade.

Me: I need to go into the woods. Can you come with me?

Even if I was desperate, I wasn't suicidal and didn't want to be attacked by a vampire unable to resist my blood. Not only would it put my life at risk but that of my attacker.

My phone dinged, and I started. With how tense things were between us, I wouldn't have been surprised if he hadn't texted back.

Slade: Already in the woods in our usual spot. I'll meet you at the tree line.

Thank God. I took deep breaths to calm my blood, but it didn't help. Not wanting to rush and cause more adrenaline to course through me, I moved steadily toward the woods.

No one was outside. Most students would be either in their rooms or at the dining hall since the night air was cold. But I couldn't feel it.

I was numb, and inside, I was broken.

I hated meeting Slade while I felt like this, with my insides shredded as if I were near death. And my blood hummed.

All the tree branches around me shook in tune with the hum of my blood. I stiffened. My agony was stronger than ever before. It felt as if I'd left part of me behind with Raffe.

"Oh goddess, Sky." Slade stepped from the tree line, his brows furrowed. "What's wrong?"

"Nothing." I sniffled. "Just wolf shifters being themselves."

"Come on. I want to show you something," Slade murmured, taking my hand. It felt wrong, but I didn't have the energy to pull away.

I followed him, my power pulsing out and moving the trees closest to us. It was as if each tree I passed waved under my spell.

Then I felt the thrumming of other magic, and it eased my blood. The hum settled into a fizzing strength I was more comfortable with.

We stepped into the clearing where Hecate, Cade, Gavyn, and Priestess Olwyn waited. Priestess Olwyn was in the center of the others and smiled at me. "Skylar, I'm so glad you messaged Slade. You can see what it's like when we practice our magic." She held out her hands, palms up, and a storm cloud formed overhead and poured rain into her palm where it disappeared.

My eyes widened. So far, I'd seen Slade use magic only to spell a barrier to keep people out or others from overhearing us. "That's amazing. Can all witches do that?"

She closed her palms, and the rain stopped. "Only the strongest of the covens have an elemental magic they can control as well as the routine spells every coven member can perform. Slade and I both control water. Gavyn controls air."

At that prompt, Gavyn rotated his arms, and a small tornado whirled up in front of him. The needles on the ground rose and swirled into it. After a moment, he stilled his hands, and the tornado vanished.

"Cade controls earth."

Lowering his hands to the ground, Cade conjured a

mound of mud from the mulchy floor. He let it grow to about five feet high before lowering his hands, and the mud flowed back into the earth until the ground was back to normal.

"And Hecate, she's fire."

Flipping her hands over as the priestess had, Hecate concentrated, and flames erupted from her palms and danced over her fingers. The heat soared to me, and some feeling returned to my face. She then closed her palms, extinguishing the flames. When she opened her hands again, her skin was unburned.

"I had no idea." I took a shaky breath and realized my blood was now at a jolt and the branches near me weren't swaying anymore.

"Well, you're human and uninformed." Priestess Olwyn smiled sadly. "But you're one of us now, so you can ask us anything."

With that, some of my loneliness left me. At least this group wasn't disowning me. "Do you mind if I sit down and watch you?"

"Not at all." Slade moved to a spot beside Hecate. "Maybe watching us will help you control your own power."

I sat on the ground and got comfortable, ready to hang out here and forget the heartache of the night.

Despite the calming way last night had ended, as I headed to stats the next morning, I was beside myself. I dreaded seeing Raffe, and my blood was almost at a hum. I'd spent hours with the witches, watching them, but as soon as I'd returned to my room, all things Raffe had crashed over me again.

I'd put in my earbuds and played classical music, and I

slept on the living room couch since I had fewer memories of Raffe and me there.

Lucy didn't come out of her room to talk, but she'd texted to say good night when she heard me come in.

Now, I squared my shoulders and marched toward the classroom, Slade by my side. I refused to let what happened between Raffe and me jeopardize my future.

"Listen, everything will be okay," Slade assured me for like the hundredth time. "We're arriving early, and we'll sit as far from him as possible. I'll be there if he tries to talk to you."

The witches had asked why I was so upset, but I hadn't divulged details. All I'd told them was that I'd had a huge falling out with Raffe and Keith. I swore I'd seen a smile flicker across Priestess Olwyn's face before she forced her expression into a frown, but I couldn't be sure.

Today, we had to turn in our projects and give our presentation, and luckily, Raffe and I had completed ours a few days ago. Otherwise, last night would've been more awkward.

As expected, the room was empty when we entered, and Slade and I took seats in the far back corner to the left. I sat against the wall with Slade right next to me. I'd learned there were two other witches in the class with us, and Slade had messaged them to take the spots in front of us, blocking Raffe from sitting near me.

Not that he would.

I hadn't been able to eat, but I was able to drink a latte. Time passed slowly as I doodled in my notebook.

Raffe and Keith entered as class was about to begin. I felt the moment Raffe arrived, and when I glanced up, I expected to lock eyes on him.

But he didn't look my way—didn't even pause when he walked by the seat I usually sat in.

He was laughing with Keith and talking to some of the

football players, acting like the confident and standoffish guy he always had been.

It was like he and I had never happened.

Maybe to him, we never had.

My heart crushed itself into smaller pieces, turning to dust with no way of ever fully healing. My blood fizzed, and I bit the inside of my cheek to prevent myself from crying.

I *had* to keep it together ... for myself. Raffe had already taken so much from me—I'd be damned if I let him take my dignity.

I pressed my palms to the desk, trying like hell not to focus on him.

Just as I felt like I might lose control, Professor Haynes entered, and I used every ounce of self-control to focus on the lecture.

THE NEXT TWO weeks were excruciating, each day worse than the last. Lucy didn't come back to our apartment—she was staying on Josie's couch to give me space, per her text, and Raffe never looked my way once in any of our classes. All the damn time, my blood was at a fizz, and each day, I got closer to losing control. Slade and Hecate took turns bringing me into the woods and casting spells to keep people away so I could let the surge happen, and each night, I fell deeply asleep on the couch from the fatigue.

Pathetically, most of the time they went with me, I imagined I felt a tingle on the back of my neck like Raffe was watching me. I'd search the tree line for him, but he was never there. I was fooling myself. He'd already forgotten I existed.

With it being October, I started to keep my jacket on all the time, anticipating the need to rush into the woods. I always had a witch near me, watching me until they knew I was exhausted and ready to pass out.

I couldn't be alone.

My Saturdays at the animal shelter left me feeling more even-keeled for the rest of the day. Today, at the end of my shift, I went to the cat section to visit a skittish Scottish fold. The cat, true to the breed, didn't like most people, and I was the volunteer she was most comfortable with.

Despite the cat being a girl, the shelter owner had named her Keith. For me, she was the most loving animal at the shelter, and the irony of her name was not lost on me.

As I opened the cage to tell Keith goodbye, the shelter owner, Natalie, came up behind me. "You should take her home with you."

I laughed, rubbing Keith behind the ears. "I wish I could."

"If you don't, we'll have to find another place for her. She's been here too long."

I froze. She wouldn't do well with most people, nor did she care for other animals. Moving her was the worst thing that could happen to her. At least, here, she had her own cage and privacy. "When?"

"Next week."

My heart fractured. I wouldn't be here again until next Saturday, which meant this was the last time I'd see her ... unless I took her home. I turned to find Natalie's normally warm-brown eyes dark and the crow's-feet around her eyes deeper.

She'd been holding on to Keith longer than she was supposed to.

I thought about it. Keith wasn't high energy and would be relatively easy to hide in my room. Even better, she would help calm me. The animals had the same effect on me that I did on them. When I looked back at Keith, I knew there wasn't actually a decision to make. "I'll take her."

"You *will*?" Natalie's voice rose, and I looked to find her smiling.

"Yes, I will." I just hoped I could sneak her into the apartment without anyone noticing. With Lucy pretty much not living there right now, once I got Keith inside, everything would be fine. No one would be the wiser. "Do we need to complete the paperwork?"

She pulled out the completed form from behind her back. "Already did. You just need to sign it."

I laughed genuinely for the first time in days. "In other words, you knew I was a sucker."

"No, but I know how much you care about her, and I think you two need each other." She winked.

To stop her gloating, I signed the form and opened the cage. Keith jumped into my arms without hesitation and began to purr. I laughed, nuzzling her back, then asked, "Can I borrow a litter box and take some litter and food with me until I can run out and get some?"

"You sure can."

Within minutes, I had Keith and the items loaded in my car, and I was headed back to EEU.

As I got closer, my emotions grew more turbulent, and my blood quickly escalated to the point of no return.

Keith crawled into my lap, and I reached down and petted her behind the ears. My blood leveled out into a low fizz.

This had definitely been a smart idea.

I pulled into my spot then reached behind me and grabbed the bag of Keith's things that Natalie had given me. There was enough room for Keith to hide inside it as long as she didn't try to get out. With no other options, I coaxed the cat into the bag and darted to the apartment.

Keith meowed, and a few students stared at me, but I made it into the apartment without causing a huge scene.

Quickly, I punched in the numbers, threw open the door, and stepped inside. I shut the door and opened the bag to let Keith out ... and all hell broke loose.

CHAPTER TWENTY-EIGHT

Keith leaped from the bag in a way I'd never imagined possible. She lifted into the air, as if my blood were humming and controlling her, and launched across the room onto Lucy's chest. Lucy stood there with eyes as wide as saucers.

The cat hissed and clawed into Lucy's EEU shirt, going for blood. The shock must have worn off because Lucy growled and smacked Keith in the head, throwing her off and into our small kitchen wall with a solid *thud*. The cat slid down the wall and lay limp on the floor.

Holy shit. Had she killed my cat?

"Keith!" I shouted and dropped the bag as I fell to my knees on the laminate tile floor and scooped the cat into my arms. My mouth went dry, and my blood jolted, but when I sensed the cat's heartbeat, some of the panic ebbed.

I spun around, glaring at Lucy, and spat, "What the *fuck* is wrong with you?"

She blinked, taking in the cat in my arms then looking at me. "What's wrong with *me*?" She pointed to her ripped shirt where a small trickle of blood dotted one spot. "You brought a cat home when you live with a wolf shifter! How did you expect *that* to go?"

Cuddling Keith to my chest, I tried to steady my breathing. "You haven't been home since Wednesday, and I've been struggling. I need something to ground me. Keith does that."

Lucy sighed. "I'm sorry. Raffe asked me to give you space, and I didn't want to argue with him after that whole *thing*. And I thought he might be right ... that maybe you wouldn't want to be around us after Adam, Keith, and Josie pressured you two into splitting."

Pressured. That was a nice way of putting it. They'd held our relationship hostage, threatening to out Raffe to their world. What sort of friends did that to someone they supposedly cared about?

What sort of guy let them? Although, Raffe wasn't struggling with the decision the way I was, which was an answer in and of itself.

I stared at the floor and leaned against the wooden chair closest to me. Then I met her eyes. "You had my back, and that meant the world to me. And then you vanished, so ..."

"You thought that, after the confrontation, I decided that being your friend wasn't worth the hassle?"

I nodded. That was the usual reaction. I was the problem.

"I'm so sorry, Sky." She groaned. "I didn't think about it that way. I just didn't want to make things harder for you by hanging around. Believe me, I'd rather sleep in my own bed and hang out with you instead of Josie and her roommate. Don't get me wrong, Josie's great, but she's more of a girly girl than we are."

Raffe.

My heart squeezed, and the desperate need to see and touch him almost had me insisting that Lucy take me to his apartment. But that would make everything worse.

The throbbing in my chest increased. I was damn sure that, at some point, I wouldn't be able to fight it, and I dreaded the day that happened. "You do realize we became friends *despite* Raffe, right? So why would we stop being friends because of him?" I wanted my friendship with Lucy back. I felt more at ease with her than anyone else ... besides Raffe, but I now knew how that ended.

She laughed. "You know what? You're right. I should've talked to you before vanishing. So you're cool with me coming home?"

I smiled but then it froze. "Of course I am, but I can't take Keith back." I held on to her tighter. "They were going to get rid of her, and she helps keep me balanced."

"Ugh." Lucy leaned her head back. "Fine, but she needs to stay in your room. I don't want to be attacked every time I come into the living room."

Keith lifted her head, and relief flooded me. I'd been worried that I'd need to take her to the vet after that fall. "That works." She'd been living in a cage that was three feet long and two feet wide—my room would be like a mansion to her. "Believe it or not, she's really sweet and well-behaved."

"Yeah, I'm not buying it." Lucy scowled and looked at her tattered shirt. "This was one of my most comfortable shirts too."

I winced. "I'll buy you a new one. I didn't realize you'd be here, and I didn't consider how Keith would react to you being a wolf and all."

"It's fine." She snorted. "Naming a female cat Keith is payment enough."

When I rubbed Keith behind the ears, she purred, and I chuckled while replying, "I wish I could take the credit, but the shelter owner is the one who named her. Apparently, she had a boyfriend back in high school who was kind to one or two people but a complete jerk to everyone else. That's exactly how Keith is, so she named her after her ex-boyfriend. My takeaway is that all men named Keith are dicks."

"Maybe, but our Keith isn't usually a dick the way he's been to you." Lucy shrugged. "He's actually super loyal and protective, and when he perceives something as a threat, he eliminates it before the people he cares about get hurt."

My body warmed with anger, but I tried to control it. Luckily, with Keith in my arms, my blood merely jolted. I had to remember that Lucy was friends with wolf-shifter Keith and that they were a pack. Of course she was loyal to him. "Maybe that's the case, but I wasn't a threat to anyone. None of it matters. Keith got what he wanted. Raffe's back to his usual self and doesn't seem to remember we ever spent any time together."

He'd made it clear that I was nothing to him, and our time together hadn't meant a damn thing even though it had meant everything to me, fool that I was.

"Everything isn't what it seems, Sky." Lucy wrung her hands and paused like she was searching for words. "But the one thing that is clear now, even to Keith, is that you aren't a bad person. You ended things with Raffe because it was in *his* best interest. Not many people would've done that, especially when the person in question is a prince."

If Keith thought of me differently, he had an awful way of showing it. Unlike Raffe, he didn't ignore me—he threw glares and scowls at me as if I needed a reminder to stay away. "Let's agree to disagree." Cat Keith's eyes opened, and I didn't want to stand out here and wait for round two to happen between her and Lucy. "She's waking up—I'm taking her to my room."

"Gods, *please*." Lucy wrinkled her nose and took a step back. "Get that mangy thing away from me."

I rolled my eyes. "Don't be so dramatic. She's not mangy. I

gave her a bath earlier today." I was the only one she somewhat tolerated a bath from.

"All cats are mangy," Lucy grumbled.

Having something to focus on was helping me already. I snatched the bag off the floor, went into my room, and shut the door behind me. I'd been avoiding my room due to the memories of Raffe, but with the cat living here now, I'd create new ones.

Raffe's scent was still on my sheets, and tears sprang to my eyes. I couldn't make myself wash them. They might be the only way I could smell him ever again even if doing so was pure torture.

Placing Keith on the bed, I checked her over, and soon she was back on her feet, stalking the room. I set up the litter box, and when I was done, I heard a knock on the front door.

My heart galloped. Lucy was back, and the last thing I wanted was to face wolf-shifter Keith, Adam, or Josie. Apart from Lucy, I didn't want to see anyone who reminded me of Raffe.

Lucy's footsteps moved toward the door, and I placed my ear to my own. The door opened, and Lucy said, "What are you two doing here?"

Two.

I hoped hard that Raffe wasn't one of them. My blood jumped straight into a fizz until I realized that the guys would be warming up for tonight's football game, which started in an hour.

"Uh ... we're here to see if Sky wants to eat with us," Hecate said.

My body slumped with relief.

"What are *you* doing here?" Zella interjected. "The last we heard, you skipped out on her."

Shit. This would turn ugly if I didn't go out there. Cat

Keith rubbed against my leg, and I reached down and scratched behind her ear then picked up my wallet and phone. "I'll be back soon, and I'll grab you some tuna."

I slipped out my door, making sure to shut it firmly, and found Lucy frowning as she blocked the doorway so that Hecate and Zella couldn't come inside.

"Hey, I'm in for eating." I slid on a jacket. "Let's go."

Even though Lucy and I were settling back in with each other, she was part of Raffe's pack and needed to be loyal to them. Me eating with the witches and vampires would make things easier on her.

Lucy pouted. "Sky, I thought we'd hang out."

"Go eat with your friends." I forced a smile. I didn't want to give wolf-shifter Keith any reason to come after me again, thinking I was trying to get between Lucy and their pack. "Besides, don't you have a football game to go to? We can watch *Criminal Minds* tonight."

It was another home game, so I didn't have to worry about running into any shifters at the student center.

Like Josie.

My stomach dropped. Would she be wearing Raffe's jersey again? Were they back to pretending to date? Even as pain stabbed through my chest at the betrayal, I second-guessed myself. How was it a betrayal when we weren't together? Something was desperately wrong with me.

"Yeah, okay." Lucy exhaled. "That sounds like a plan. I should get to the game."

My blood surged into a high fizz, ready to hum.

Hecate's eyes widened, and she pulled me into the hallway. She could sense my power and how close to the edge I was. "Let's go," she said urgently to Zella.

"What's wrong?" Lucy asked with concern.

"The usual here, lately." Zella scoffed. "I swear, we hang out more in the woods than we do anywhere else."

Thankfully, the elevator was on our floor, and soon, the three of us were heading down to the first floor.

Zella twirled a piece of her hair around her finger. "Shouldn't you be gaining more control by now? It's like you're getting worse each day."

I felt the same way, but every day, the yanking in my chest, coupled with the need to see Raffe and touch him damn near overpowered me. I hoped bringing the cat home would keep me calmer from now on. "I don't know." I turned and pressed my head against the cool metal wall. "I just need to be out in the woods."

When the elevator door opened, Hecate took my hand, but I could feel her annoyance. I was getting on everyone's nerves, and I couldn't blame them.

"Go get us something to eat," Hecate called back to Zella. "I have a feeling we won't be able to sit down for very long."

I rushed into the woods. The hum flowed through my blood and out of my body, and a fir at the front of the tree line cracked in half and crashed to the ground. Still, my blood kept humming.

The next tree shook, and the entire trunk fell to my left, causing the ground to shake.

"Dammit, Sky," Hecate growled, "You need to calm down."

As I reached the edge of the trees, my legs gave out. I dropped to my knees and rolled onto my side. I tried to pull up a memory to calm myself, but all I could picture was Raffe's face, and my emotions rioted harder. More things broke and cracked, and my eyelids grew heavy. I'd never exerted power like this before.

My eyes closed, and exhaustion overtook me.

Mutters filtered into my mind.

"She's getting worse, and he keeps watching her," a voice that sounded a lot like Slade's replied. "What's going on?"

"Nothing good," Priestess Olwyn's strong female voice replied. "We need to make sure he stays away and figure out how to help her. I'm heading to the library to see if we've overlooked anything in a *Book of Twilight*. Get her up, feed her, and take her back to her apartment so she can rest. She'll need it after this. Cade and Eva are restoring the trees, so no one should notice. Luckily, most everyone is at the game."

A shiver shuddered through me, and I peeled my eyes open. Slade and Priestess Olwyn stood five feet away, and Hecate was sitting next to me on the ground, flames dancing in her hands. We were deeper in the woods than when I'd passed out, and I felt like a freight train had run me over. At least the flames explained why I wasn't freezing.

"She's awake," Hecate said.

I sort of wished my blood were fizzing so I could read everyone's emotions, but when Slade and Priestess Olwyn glanced at me, I could see the concern etched in every crease on their faces.

"Good." Priestess Olwyn moved toward me, her long emerald dress flowing behind her as she squatted beside me. "We were worried. You radiated quite a magical blast."

"I know." My eyes tried to close again, and I forced them open, feeling the burn of fatigue. "I'm sorry. I don't know what happened."

"We'll figure it out, dear. You just need rest." She patted my hand and looked at Slade. "Once she's settled, join me in the library. We have a lot to learn."

He nodded, and she rose and strode away.

Hecate and Slade helped me stand, and Slade wrapped an arm around my waist. My vision blurred from unshed tears. I wished the arm around me was Raffe's. I'd give almost anything to have him here.

Knowing that wishing was a waste of energy, I leaned all my weight on Slade. He placed his other arm under my knees and lifted me to his chest.

It was firm, but nothing like Raffe's chiseled chest. And his herbal scent wasn't tantalizing like Raffe's. Heartache choked me, and I gasped.

"Make sure no one comes near here while they work. I only put up a quick ward," Slade commanded, and he carried me away.

Without Hecate's flames, I shivered. At least I thought it was from the lack of heat, but maybe it was from feeling so wrong in someone else's arms. I tried to push the thought away, but wishing wouldn't accomplish anything. Raffe wasn't mine.

Not anymore.

My blood jolted, but my eyelids grew heavy once more, and sleep took me hard.

"Damn cat," Lucy growled from somewhere nearby.

A threatening hiss responded, and something shifted on top of me.

What the hell was going on? I opened my eyes to find the cat's back arched as she bared her teeth at Lucy, who was peeking through my partly open door, holding chopped-up meat on a plate.

"I'm trying to make sure you don't starve since Sky has been passed out since last night," Lucy spat as she opened the door wider and set the plate on the floor. "So we're clear, this is only because Sky needs you."

I laughed despite feeling like I had the flu. My body ached, and my head spun.

Lucy's gaze snapped to me, and she frowned. "Fine. I take it back. I'm not feeding you."

"No, thank you, really. I just think it's funny that you're talking to her like she can understand you." I lifted my head, but the room spun harder, so I lay back down.

"Hold on, let me go grab you something to eat." She disappeared, and I heard her rummaging around in the kitchen.

I had to get out of bed. She couldn't enter the room with Keith protecting me so vigilantly. Slowly, I braced myself on the wall and stood then shuffled to the door. I sidestepped the cat's food and made it into the living room.

Lucy turned around, holding a paper plate with a slice of pizza on it. She put it on the couch cushion because we never replaced the coffee table I'd destroyed, and hurried over to help me sit down.

I was certain I was going to vomit.

Somehow, I made it to the chair, and she handed me the pizza, which I devoured. After several bites, I began to feel better, like I had last time.

"Slade refused to talk to me, but it was obvious. Did you have another meltdown last night?" She tilted her head.

I laughed. If she only knew this wasn't the only time since Raffe and I ended things. Instead, I shrugged. "I'm fine. That's all that matters."

"Maybe you should talk to Raf—"

"Please don't finish that sentence." I was having a hard enough time not texting, calling, or rubbing my body all over him. The last thing I needed was encouragement to do any of those things. "The coven is helping me."

"Are you sure that's what they're doing?"

I didn't want to have this conversation. "Yeah. Their magic is similar to mine." I shrugged, not wanting to tell her about the *Book of Twilight*. I was thankful Raffe hadn't ratted out that secret, though I wondered why. Maybe he'd forgotten, though I doubted it.

At the thought of him, pain blasted throughout my body, just as I'd feared. My blood surged like it wanted to jolt, but it couldn't—the one benefit of having a meltdown.

She pursed her lips. "That doesn't mean they're helping."

The walls started to close in on me. I had to get out of here and away from her probing questions. Maybe Lucy coming back wasn't a good thing after all. "They're all I've got." I sighed and stood. "I'm going to grab my phone and run down to the student center for a coffee."

"I can go with you." Lucy stood.

Having her with me would be problematic. I wanted to learn if Slade and Priestess Olwyn had discovered anything that could help me. "I'm going to see if Slade can meet me. I need to talk to him."

She frowned. "He's probably busy."

I lifted a brow. That was an odd thing for her to say, especially since she didn't know him or his habits. "I'll find out."

As I went to my room, I could feel her gaze on me.

I slipped inside and found Keith eating the food. I smiled and grabbed my phone. "I'll be right back," I told her, doing what I'd made fun of Lucy for doing. That was karma for me.

I looked at the time and realized it was two in the afternoon. The coffee shop would be closing in thirty minutes. I had to hurry, so I shot a message to Slade and Hecate.

Me: I'm going to get a coffee. Anyone around?

As usual, Slade responded within seconds.

Slade: I'm held up, will be there soon.

A few seconds later, another text came through.

Hecate: On my way. See you there :/

One of them was all I needed in case I got in trouble. I shut the door behind me and headed to the front door. Lucy watched me with a deep frown.

I wanted to kick myself. She was back, and I was putting distance between us. "Hey, I'm really sorry about last night. I'll be back in an hour or so, and maybe we can actually watch our show for the rest of the day and order takeout?"

She smiled. "That sounds great."

Some of the guilt eased, and I opened the front door.

"Oh, and Sky," Lucy called out.

I paused and glanced at her. "Yeah?"

"I'm sorry too." She rolled her shoulders.

I wasn't sure what she was apologizing for, but I needed to leave before she tried to come with me. "You haven't done anything to apologize for." I stepped out the door. "See you soon." And I left.

Outside, the cool air invigorated me. Once I got some coffee, I should feel more normal.

Then I noticed Josie leaving the men's apartment building with Raffe's jersey in her hand.

Though it should've been impossible after last night, my blood didn't even fizz—it hummed immediately, and the pain of heartache and loss burned inside me. I truly felt like I was dying.

This was it.

The moment I imploded.

The moment I died.

CHAPTER TWENTY-NINE

I took off for the woods as fast as I could. I stumbled, and my knees hit the ground. The impact jarred me, and my blood hummed so hard that my body shook.

If I was going to die, I wouldn't do it publicly and out the supernaturals. The last thing I wanted to do was create any hardship for anyone.

Gritting my teeth, I stood.

"Skylar, wait!" Josie called from behind me.

My blood surged and became more volatile. It wasn't her fault; it was the situation, and I didn't want to risk harming her. "Stay back," I gritted out while attempting to run toward the woods.

The ground started to shake, and I wasn't sure if it was from my power, my lack of balance, or a combination of the two. I had to move faster, but no matter what I did, I kept stumbling over my damn feet, which had turned into lead.

Suddenly, an arm wrapped around my waist, and someone helped me stand upright.

Josie.

With her help, I was able to move faster, especially since she was pushing me toward the woods while helping me keep my balance.

"Are you causing the ground to shake?" she asked when we neared the tree line.

I needed to get deep into the woods.

"Yes, and that's why you need to *go*." I didn't want to hurt her. That would destroy Raffe. He loved her in a way I wished he cared about me. I could read her emotions so clearly, though. She was determined to help me. "If you stay, you will get hurt."

We reached the tree line, and the ground cracked under my feet.

"If I left you, Raffe would never forgive me," Josie rasped. "So how do we get it to stop?"

I stumbled deeper into the woods and dropped to my hands and knees. I slid my hands through the cool mulch and tried to focus on the earth, but my heartbreak kept my emotions too volatile to calm down.

There was no way I would get over it, not when Josie and Raffe had picked up where they'd left off. Maybe it was an act, but it wouldn't be forever. Those two made sense in a way Raffe and I never would.

"Skylar," Josie said louder and rubbed my back, bringing me out of my thoughts.

"I ... I don't know." I focused on the mulch and hoped some animals would come, but at the same time, I hoped that they wouldn't. Nothing else needed to get hurt, and I feared I was past the point of no return. "You need to go. Please!"

The ground split under my hands, and fear squeezed my heart on top of the pain. This must be what Foster had felt when his life came to an end.

"Thank gods you're here," Josie sighed and dropped her hand from me. "I don't know how to help her."

It must be a coven member, but how had they known I'd be here?

"Go," a deep, raspy voice I hadn't heard so close in days said, making my stomach flutter.

Raffe.

"But—" Josie moved back just as his sandalwood-and-amber scent surrounded me.

"Don't argue," his voice held something extra like power. "Leave *now*."

Arms scooped me up and cradled me against that chiseled chest. I buried my face in Raffe's shoulder and focused on the buzz from our touch as it sprang to life. If this was how I died, at least he was holding me one last time.

Josie scoffed, but I heard her stand and run away, the earth still quaking underneath us.

The buzz strengthened, like electricity surging between us, and the shaking of the ground lessened.

He kissed the top of my head and held me so tightly it hurt.

But I didn't care.

"Babe, I need you to calm down. You can't die on me." He rocked me like I was something precious, and his voice broke. "I can't live in a world you're not in."

A sob shook my chest, and I wrapped my arms around him desperately. Those were nice words to hear, but they weren't real. He was just trying to calm me down to save his people. "Don't lie to me. You haven't even looked at me since you ended things."

"Me?" He scoffed, and his chest shook. "You're the one who ended things and walked out. I've been trying to make it easier on you, but don't fucking accuse me of not looking at you. I've watched you every fucking night as you snuck out to meet those damn witches."

The pain in my chest receded, and my blood calmed to a faint hum. The branches still swayed like crazy, but the ground stilled. I pushed away from his chest and squirmed until he put me down. I didn't want him to hold me while he repainted what had happened. I felt sluggish, but my anger and frustration with him got me on my feet. The damn *yank* in my chest nearly had me stumbling into him, but I held my ground ... for myself. I was tired of letting people run over me. If I was going to die, I'd do it with dignity.

His crystal-blue eyes widened, and he stepped toward me, eliminating the distance.

I placed a hand on his chest, forcing him to stay back. The touch kept my blood in check.

"You need me," he growled.

I noticed the dark circles under his eyes, and his normal complexion was much paler than usual. He wore rumpled clothes like he hadn't changed since yesterday, and the image of Josie leaving the men's apartments sprouted in my mind.

The ground quivered underneath us again.

"Maybe, but not like this." My heart had been ripped from my body and stomped on. I felt as if I was coming apart. "I didn't break up with you. Your lack of knowing what you wanted broke us. And now Josie is wearing your jersey again, and you show up in wrinkled clothes, not having slept. I saw her leaving the men's apartment building, so don't act like you're innocent!"

His brows lifted as if he no longer noticed the ground quaking under our feet. For the first time in weeks, I had his full attention.

And I hated how it thrilled me.

"I haven't been in my apartment all fucking night, Sky." He stepped so close that our chests touched. "Ask me why."

I wasn't sure I wanted to, but I needed to hear the truth before I died. "Why?" My voice was barely a whisper, but he heard me.

"Lucy linked with me last night, telling me what happened, and I lost it." His breathing turned ragged. "She came home after the game to check on you and found Slade standing over you on the couch with you sacked out. She made his sorry ass leave so I could come over, and I paced your living room all fucking night. When your color started to return and your breathing became steady, I left and confronted Slade and the *supreme priestess* about what the fuck was going on with you. Whatever they're doing isn't working and, from what I can tell, has made you worse. The reason I'm here now is that Lucy told me you left the apartment. I was on my way to the student center to keep an eye on you when a fucking earthquake happened. Josie linked to me that I needed to get my ass over here because my girl could barely walk and was causing the phenomena."

My girl.

My blood eased to a high fizz. "You ...weren't with Josie?"

"How many times do I have to tell you that she and I are *just* friends?" He cupped my cheek. "You're the only woman I can see now, and no matter how long we're apart, nothing will fucking change that."

I couldn't stop myself from pressing my cheek into his palm. I'd been craving his touch for weeks. I could read the concern and fear swirling from him.

"But you never look at me anymore." I hated how broken I sounded, my voice quivering so much that my words were barely understandable. The past two weeks had been atrocious. "And you're always laughing."

"It was an act to make things easier on you. I didn't want to guilt you for ripping my fucking heart out." His thumb brushed my skin. "You said you didn't want us to be together, and I was respecting that."

My vision blurred, which pissed me off. I couldn't see the perfectly sculpted face that had been haunting me. "You weren't sure about us. I didn't want to come between you and your pack and have you resent me. And Josie's right—I'll only be here for a short while compared to you, and I'll get old. And we never discussed if there's a way to make me one of you, and I didn't want to force you—"

He laughed humorlessly. "If I could turn you, my wolf would've forced me to do it so our being different species wouldn't be a problem. But our bite doesn't turn humans, Sky. We can't do that. All the stories got that part wrong, which is why getting involved with humans is forbidden. They can never be part of our world."

That was my luck. "In other words, nothing can change between us. We're doomed to stay apart." The throbbing ache returned with a vengeance, and my blood surged with power.

"*Everything* has changed between us. If you walked away from me because I was unsure whether to risk everything to be with you, well I know without a doubt what my answer is. I can't live without you. I *won't* do it—it's pure agony. You're fucking *it* for me. If my dad, my friends, and my people can't accept that, screw them. I don't care if we have only eighty years together—they'll be the best of my entire life." He lowered his forehead to mine, staring right into my soul.

My blood became a mere jolt, and my chest warmed with love and hope. "Even when I'm wrinkly and need to be wheeled around because I need new hips?" I wasn't trying to be funny; I wanted to paint an accurate picture.

He laughed in that carefree way that was better than any

song. "Shifters do live longer than humans, yeah, but we aren't immortal. We live for two hundred years, max, so I won't be as young looking as I am today. When you're eighty, I'll at least look fifty, so you won't look like a complete cougar."

I rocked back on my heels and almost fell over. I was so damn exhausted. But as I expected, he caught me.

"Let's finish this talk after you rest," he said then lifted me and carried me like a princess.

After all our time apart, I didn't want to sleep. I wanted to enjoy being back in his arms and kiss him. This had to be a dream.

"It's not a dream."

His response made me realize that I must have said that last part aloud.

"You're stuck with me." He kissed my forehead again. "I'm never giving you a reason to push me away again."

With that reassurance, I drifted off to sleep.

My body buzzed from the strong arms wrapped around me. I moaned, not wanting to wake up from this heavenly dream, and heard a soft chuckle.

Wait. I stiffened as what had happened earlier flooded my mind. I opened my eyes and saw Raffe's face inches from mine. His eyes were fixed on me with that warmer blue I saw only when we were alone together.

"You're here," I breathed. This couldn't be real. But even with this dreamlike sensation, something was off, like I was forgetting something important, but Raffe's touch and smell forced the nagging sensation from my mind.

"I told you, there's no getting rid of me now." He smiled sweetly. "Especially since you broke up with me because I was hesitating, but I need you to know—I always knew the answer was you. I was trying to come to grips with everything that might change for me, but seeing you walk away, and having to watch you with the witches every night, made me realize how stupid I was. I felt like I couldn't breathe the entire time we were apart."

My heart pounded. "What do you mean, watching me with the witches?"

He winced. "I probably should've kept that to myself, but yeah, every time you went into the woods and I wasn't in class or training, I was out there, making sure you were safe. And let me tell you, I wanted to kick Slade's ass every time he got near you, so that tells you how much I was respecting your decision. Thank fuck that's over and I can punch him anytime he gets too close."

All this time, I thought I'd been imagining the tingles, but Raffe *had* been watching me. "I made both of us miserable."

"Yeah, but you gave me a much-needed wake-up call. I have no doubt at all anymore about what we are to each other, even though it shouldn't be possible." He tucked a lock of hair behind my ear. "Fuck everyone who tries to stand in our way."

My eyelids fluttered, and I reveled in the warmth of his touch. "I'm sure more humans and wolf shifters would fall in love if it weren't forbidden." My stomach clenched, and my eyes popped back open. Shit. I hadn't meant to say love, but now that I'd said it, I had no doubt that was what I felt for him. I'd been miserable and off balance without him.

"Love?" He smirked and arched a brow.

I groaned and slapped my palms over my face. Within hours of us getting back together, I had to go and drop the *L* bomb.

I peeked at him. "I mean, yeah, but you don't have to say it back. I don't want you to feel pressured. But I know I don't want to live without you either, and I want to give you everything I have." My face became uncomfortably hot as I held his gaze.

"You're so adorable when you get flustered. I kinda want to see you like this more often." He kissed me quickly and leaned back, serious now. "What we have is something most people would kill for. It's so damn rare and special, and not even love describes what I feel for you. You own me, babe, my heart and my body, and you're the other half of my soul. When I say I'll kill anyone for hurting you and any man for touching you, I fucking mean it."

That should have petrified me. Any normal person would be scared off. But I guessed it was a good thing I'd never been normal because everything he said—including the threats—thrilled me. "Are you saying we're soul mates?" I could believe it. From that very first night when I'd run out of the woods into him, I'd felt safe and treasured around him.

"That's one way of putting it, but we supernaturals call us fated mates." He took my hand in his and intertwined our fingers. The buzzing thrummed between us. "That's why, when we touch, our skin tingles. It's as close as we've gotten to our souls being complete once more."

It defied all logic, but what he said rang true in my heart. "Will we ever fully connect?"

He nodded. "When we complete the bond ... as much as we can with you being human."

"How does it happen?" I wanted to learn everything about our connection.

"When it's two wolf shifters, they have sex and bite one another. The sex merges their souls into one, and the biting bonds them so they can link with each other, and the weaker of the two join the stronger one's pack."

Why did that sound so damn sexy?

My every sense became attuned to the way our bodies were pressed together. I was done talking. I wanted to connect our souls and see what it was like. If touching him felt this great, I wanted to know what sex with him was like. My body warmed, and I could tell the moment he smelled my arousal.

He closed his eyes. "Babe, I wasn't trying to talk you into being physical with me. Besides, we need to get you something to eat. You expelled so much magic out there, and I need you to stay healthy."

He was right. I probably should eat, but there were more important things that needed to be taken care of first. Instead of answering, I kissed him gently. If he realized my intentions right away, he might resist me and demand that I eat. He was caring and amazing like that. So I'd have to distract him into it.

Clutching my hand a little tighter, he kissed me back. After a moment, I licked his lips, asking for entry.

Gently, he pulled away, his eyes glowing. "You need to eat."

"I will," I promised, and a desperate urge overtook me. I pushed him onto his back and straddled him. He was already hard between my legs, and need knotted in my stomach. The urge to connect with him this way was taking over, and though I didn't understand why, I wanted it to happen more than I wanted to breathe.

"The last time—" he started.

"Look, I don't feel sick, and the room isn't spinning." I hadn't realized that until now. I leaned down, my hair falling around us like a curtain, and kissed him. I took my time enjoying his taste and the way our mouths moved together. As soon as he tilted his head, I responded like we shared a mind.

He groaned. "You're making this really hard for me."

I snorted. "That's kind of the point, or do I have the way sex works completely wrong?"

"Ha ha." His chest shook with silent laughter. "Here I am concerned about your well-being, and you're making pervy jokes."

"You'd know if I were lying about not feeling well." I raised my head, wanting him to see my sincerity.

Something flipped in his eyes. They darkened, and he lunged up and deepened our kiss, devouring me. I tried not to grind into him, not wanting to take things too fast, but my body had a mind of its own. I pressed my core against his hardness, and he growled, gripping my hips and thrusting against me.

My breath caught, and need pooled deep within me. I moved so I could slide my hands under his shirt. As my fingertips traced the curves of his muscles, his body shuddered. I'd thought I'd never be able to do this with him again, and now that we were entangled, I couldn't fathom not doing it every day until I died.

As our kisses became more desperate, he slipped his hands under my shirt and bra, his fingers caressing my nipples. I sucked in a breath, the sensation causing pressure to build inside me. His firm touch, combined with his mouth sucking on my tongue, made me dizzy.

As he worked my body into a frenzy, I couldn't take it anymore. I needed to get rid of any barriers between us, so I broke away and sat up, then removed my shirt and bra. He watched me, his irises glowing, and when I tossed the clothes to the floor, he growled.

"You're so damn gorgeous," he breathed and grabbed my waist then twisted us so I landed on my back. He hovered over me, scanning me slowly.

He made me feel powerful and sexy.

I giggled as he sat up and pulled off his shirt. But the laughter died when I took in every inch of his chiseled body. We'd touched and pleasured each other before, but we'd always kept our clothes on. This was heading in a far more intimate direction, and I couldn't wait to experience it with him. The yanking inside me grew stronger than ever, like I *needed* us to connect.

He rolled onto his side and covered my breast with his mouth. His hands unfastened my jeans, and he slipped one underneath my panties between my legs. His fingers found the spot that drove me wild, and he circled.

"I don't want to finish like this," I protested weakly. That damn *yank* was almost painful with the strong need I had for him. "I want *all* of you."

His free hand clutched the sheets hard, and his mouth released my breast. His chest heaved as he said, while still rubbing between my folds, "If you're saying that because of how we merge souls—"

"That's not the only reason why." I panted, growing close to release. "I love you, and I want to spend the rest of my life with you. I know it. I feel it."

"Fuck, Sky. Are you sure? You're human ... and I've been careful with you. If we have sex, there won't be anything casual about it. If you think I'm possessive now, once we—"

"I love your possessiveness." I kissed him, wanting him to sense the depth of my emotions. "It never upsets me, and I may be human, but my heart and body want *you*. But if you aren't ready—"

His fingers didn't relent. Instead, he moved them faster. "I wanted you the first night we kissed. From the moment I saw you, Sky, I haven't felt any attraction to another woman. I've never yearned for anyone else's touch. I might have struggled with you being human, but I've always *wanted* you. I've made sure I didn't lose control by keeping our clothes on because my wolf has been *begging* me to claim you."

As I heard his words, my body tightened. He lowered his mouth to my nipple, his tongue flicking over it, and he drove me over the edge.

I moaned as ecstasy exploded within me. My body quivered, and he slipped two fingers inside me, making the sensations stronger.

My mouth found his, and I kissed him as I came back down to earth. But the deep need and yanking in my chest were even more desperate than before. I didn't want to pressure him, but I wasn't sure I could stop the desire coursing through me without fully becoming his.

He sniffed and growled. "You're ready to go again. Gods, I've never smelled you like this before, and it's driving me wild."

My face heated, but I nodded. "I'm sorry. I—"

He sat upright, gripped my jeans and panties, tugged them down my legs, and tossed them on the floor. "Tell me when you want to stop. My wolf will respect you. All you have to do is say no. I don't care what we're doing."

"I know." That was the thing; I trusted him implicitly.

He slid his fingers back inside me, his thumb hitting that spot between my legs as his free hand caressed my breasts. He hovered over me, watching my responses as he worked my body.

Never in a million years would I have thought I'd like this so much, but as we stared into each other's eyes, ecstasy assaulted my body again, hard and fast, taking me by surprise.

Wanting to see all of him, I sat up and tried to remove his pants, but my hands shook too hard, and the knot of desire tightened within me, despite him already bringing me to release.

He chuckled and removed my hands. "You're struggling. Let me." With that, he stripped off his pants and boxers.

Then he stood at the edge of my bed, naked, letting me look my fill, and my chest squeezed. I'd never seen him like this, only touched him through his clothes, but he was more than handsome. I couldn't come up with a word to describe how attractive I found him. I reached out and stroked him where he stood, and he shuddered.

"Dammit, Sky." He slid back onto the bed next to me. "I need to touch you too."

As he lay down next to me, I continued to stroke him. He thrust his hips in time with my hand, and his fingers slipped back inside me. Our mouths collided, but as my orgasm neared again, I whimpered with the urge to feel him inside me. "Raffe, make love to me."

His body stilled as he gripped my arm. He lifted his head and looked into my eyes. "Are you sure?"

"Yes, but only if you—" I started, but he cut me off with a kiss.

He settled between my legs and cupped my face. "I want you so damn bad, but I need to make sure you're okay. That you're certain. If we do this, we'll need to go slow with you being a virgin."

"I have no doubts. I want you forever. I promise," I said, feeling that vow with every ounce of my heart. Then I realized something. "Wait. How did you know I'm a virgin?" We'd never talked about it because I tended to lose my head around him, but clearly, he knew.

He smiled tenderly. "Call it intuition."

"What about you?" Great. I wanted to talk about his past conquests while desperate for him?

His smile slipped. "I won't lie to you. I've slept with people, Sky, but I swear I'm negative. Shifters can't get sick like that, and ever since our first kiss, I haven't thought about any of them. It's like no one but you has ever existed. If I could go back—"

I hadn't meant to make him feel guilty. "Let's make sure you really forget." I would pleasure him so many times he wouldn't even remember that he'd been with anyone before me. I was determined. I arched my hips against him, and he hissed.

"Forget what?" he rasped as he pushed against my entrance.

"Right answer," I said and leaned forward, claiming his lips.

Our bodies moved, and he inched inside me and paused, waiting for my body to adjust to him. Then he slid in a little more, taking his time. Each time he went deeper, it ached more, but with his mouth on mine, it was hard to feel anything but the pleasure of his body.

Soon he was all the way in, and he raised his head and asked, "Are you okay? Are you hurting?"

"Just give me a second." The warmth and pressure were nearly overwhelming, and I clung to the new sensations.

"However long you need." I heard the reverence in his voice. Then he peppered my face with kisses and cupped my breast.

My body was so alive, and when the discomfort was gone, I moved my hips.

We moved slowly, and soon my body tingled and quivered, needing more of him.

"You feel so damn good," he growled, his mouth trailing down my face to my neck. "I won't be able to last much longer if we don't take a break."

"No break." I turned my head more, giving him access to my neck. "I need you too much."

Our bodies moved in unison, and he quickened the pace. His teeth raked my neck, and I whimpered with need as a different urge slammed through me. "Bite me."

"Babe, you don't have to let me do that," he groaned, and his teeth scraped my neck harder. "Don't say it again, or I won't be able to stop myself."

"You don't understand." My body clenched as my release neared again. "I *need* you to bite me." I needed us to release together and for him to claim me so much that it hurt.

His teeth sank into my neck.

My body convulsed, and it was more than an orgasm. It was all-consuming and something I would only be able to experience with him and like this.

His body shook with his release, and sensation flowed into me, making my body warm. I felt stronger.

It had to be our souls merging.

When the sensations dissipated and my pulse calmed, he pulled me into his arms and stroked my back. My heart felt so full … so warm. I'd never been so happy.

"You're mine in all ways now." Raffe kissed my neck where he'd bitten me. "There are no take backs. Everyone will know you're mine and that we're both taken."

"Good." I loved the finality of it. No one could drive us apart … not even Keith.

Shit.

Keith.

That was what the nagging feeling had been about earlier.

I sat up and scanned my bedroom for the cat. I didn't understand how Raffe had gotten in here without Keith going psycho.

"What's wrong?" Raffe surveyed the room as if trying to find the answer for me.

"Where's Keith?" A lump formed in my throat. "I need to check on Keith."

If I thought I'd seen Raffe move fast before, it was nothing compared to now. Pure rage lit his eyes, and he yanked on his clothes. "Fucking *Keith*. Why are you thinking about *him* after making love with me? I'm going to *kill* him."

CHAPTER THIRTY

I sat up quickly, my breathing rapid. Something uncomfortably warm slammed into my chest and tightened it. "Cat Keith. Did Lucy not tell you about my cat?"

"*Cat* Keith?" Raffe paused, the waist of his jeans still unbuttoned around his hips. Then he burst out laughing. "You named the cat *Keith*? Lucy forgot to mention that."

His body relaxed, and the uncomfortable sensation in my chest vanished.

I filled him in with the story of how he got his name.

"That sounds about right, even with this Keith." He rolled his eyes and sat down next to me. "But *Keith* is fine. Lucy let her out into the living room to give us some alone time." He arched a brow. "But seriously, you brought a cat here to live with a wolf shifter? How did you expect that to go down?"

Fair point. "For the past couple of weeks, I've been struggling more than ever with my power, and animals calm me. She was about to be removed from the shelter and her future was uncertain. I'm the only person Keith likes, so when Natalie said I should take her home with me and why, I didn't even think about Lucy being part wolf. I only see her in human form, anyway." Come to think of it, I've only ever seen the guys in wolf form, not the girls.

He sighed and wrapped his arms around me, pulling me onto his lap. I gasped because when he touched me, it was so much more than a buzz now. It was like electricity, but not painful. The sensation was overwhelming, causing an overbearing, warm sensation that I never wanted to not feel again.

"Babe, I'm so damn sorry I put you through that," he rasped and kissed the top of my head. "If I'd known—"

Even though I didn't want to remove my head from his chest, I forced myself to, needing to comfort him. I might also wind up licking him if I wasn't careful. For now, I touched his face, his scruff prickly under my fingertips. I stared into his eyes and said, "I didn't say that to make you feel bad. I was explaining."

He kissed me, the electricity shooting down to my soul, and my chest expanded almost painfully from how much love I held for him.

I took a shaky breath, and he leaned back a little and asked, "Are you okay?"

"When we touch, it's—" I didn't know how to explain it.

Winking, he booped me on the nose. "It's because we completed the bond the best we can." He leaned down and sniffed my neck where he'd bitten me and growled, "And damn, I love that my scent is all over you." He brushed his lips against the spot, and a shiver ran through my body. Need building up once more.

When my hand inched downward to slip under his jeans and boxers, he gripped my wrist.

The rejection burned, and I jerked back. "I'm sorry. I just—"

"Oh, you thought right." He smiled at me tenderly, and

that spot in my chest warmed again. "But I need to talk with Keith, Adam, Josie, and Lucy for a minute."

I snorted bitterly. "Yeah, without the human. Got it." Not even ten minutes after having sex for the first time and bonding as mates, he was excluding me from his friends. And here I'd thought the secrecy thing was over.

"Hey," he said gently, turning my face back toward him. "It's not like that. They'll know something is different about me even without you biting me. My scent won't be the same since I bit you. It'll be clear that I'm taken and that nothing can come between us. That's how the fated-mate bond works, so believe me when I say I'm not trying to hide it. But Keith will get angry and potentially shift, which could put you in danger. I can't allow that to happen, so I need a chance to handle him before you join us."

My cheeks hurt, and I realized I had a huge smile on my face. Then understanding washed over me. "Wait. Your parents will also know immediately?" Though I didn't want us to be secret, I'd understood why he'd wanted to ease his parents into the knowledge of us being together.

"Yup, and don't worry. I understood what was at stake when we bonded. Like I told you earlier, I can't live without you, and I refuse to." His eyes glowed and he huffed. "I really don't want to go, but Keith and Adam are demanding that I join them. The four of them have been working on trying to hide what happened in the woods without involving the witches. They're finishing up, and he's about to head here, so I need to meet them outside. I'll text you when it's time for you to join us. I shouldn't be more than fifteen or twenty minutes."

That was enough time to shower and clean up so I didn't show up smelling like blood and sex. I suspected that would only add to the tension. "Okay." I stood, not bothering to grab my clothes, and winced slightly from the tenderness between my legs. There was no point in being shy around him now, especially since Lucy wasn't here. "Let me go get *feline Keith* so she doesn't attack you. Then I'll take a quick shower."

When Raffe's irises glowed, I suspected it had everything to do with me. He smirked. "You're going to get clean so I have to claim you all over again as soon as we get home?"

"Unless you want to go for another round now?" Even if I was sore, I could easily have sex with him again.

"Not a chance, even though I want to." He stood and fastened his jeans then kissed me gently. "I saw you wince when you stood up. You need time to heal, so no more sex tonight."

My jaw dropped. "But you just *said—*"

"That I would have to get my scent all over you again. We've done that plenty before tonight. There are other ways to orgasm, though nothing will ever beat doing it inside you." He slipped his shirt on. "Tonight, we'll have to make do. I refuse to hurt you."

Damn him for taking care of me. At least with this. I pouted, and he chuckled.

"Go get your cat so I can get out of here before wolf-shifter Keith comes in and makes things worse. If he insults you or threatens you, I could very likely kill him. That's part of why I need you not to be with us at first."

That spot in my chest tightened with rage, and I had no doubt Raffe meant every word even though it was directed at one of his best friends. "Fine. You would miss him, and I don't want that on my conscience." That, and I didn't want Raffe killing anyone over me. That didn't sit right, but damn if it didn't thrill me to know he would without hesitation. Something had to be wrong with me.

I opened my door to find Keith, the cat, in front of it. Her back was arched as if she'd been waiting for Raffe to leave so she could attack him. I wasn't sure if she was protecting me or herself, but either way, I admired her vigilance.

As soon as I picked her up and held her to my chest, she began to purr.

Raffe didn't hesitate, and within seconds, he was out the door to meet up with his friends.

I carried Keith into the bathroom and turned on the water in the shower then put the cat down and grabbed a towel. I looked at my reflection in the mirror ... and stared.

My cognac-brown eyes looked brighter, and my cheeks were rosy, giving me a happy glow. I'd never seen this version of me, but I sensed I'd found a piece of me.

Maybe there was something to this fated-mate bond, and Raffe and I truly were each other's missing link.

I couldn't help but worry about what was going on between him and wolf-shifter Keith. Lucy swore Keith was loyal, and I hoped that was the case. Our bond had been completed as much as it could be, so it wasn't like Keith could do anything about it.

The mirror fogged over from the steam, and I tried to force my worry away as I climbed into the shower. Keith huffed and plopped onto the counter, probably upset that she couldn't find a warm place to lie down.

The warmth of the shower eased some of the soreness between my legs. After I got clean, I quickly dried off and headed back to my room, Keith following me.

In the room, I noticed the bloodstain on my sheets, further proving what Raffe had claimed. My cheeks warmed at the memory, and I dressed in a sweater and jeans then changed my sheets.

The spot in my chest boiled hot with anger. I grabbed my phone from the nightstand and checked for Raffe's text, worry weighing on me.

Something was wrong.

I'd missed three messages, but one was from Slade and two were from Hecate. It was almost eight, and I was supposed to have met them five and a half hours ago.

Slade: Hey, are we still meeting at the student center? Sorry, I got tied up, but I'm on my way.

Thirty minutes later, I received a second message.

Hecate: Where are you? Slade and I are worried.

Shit. I'd forgotten that I'd told them I'd meet them there. I'd seen Josie leaving the men's apartments, and my blood had gone crazy.

Hecate: You aren't answering your door. Please respond.

I was a huge ass. I sent a message to both Slade and Hecate.

Me: I'm so sorry. My blood went crazy, and I passed out. Josie and Raffe helped me, and I'm just now functioning. I didn't mean to worry you.

Within seconds, my phone buzzed.

Slade: Thank goddess you're okay. We were gathering a search party for you. Did Raffe hurt you?

Of course Slade would think the worst of him.

Me: No, he didn't. I'm about to meet him in the woods, so can we meet in the morning?

I hated to brush them off, but I didn't want to spend another minute away from Raffe, and I hadn't heard from him. The spot in my chest got even hotter.

Things with Keith must not be going well. I needed to get to Raffe before he did something he regretted. Not waiting for a response, I shut my door and rushed outside.

Within seconds, I was heading in the direction of my meltdown. If they were near the spot where I'd almost imploded, then they weren't far inside the woods, and I would be fine. If something happened, Raffe would hear me.

I passed through the tree line. "Raffe?" I called out, wanting him to know I was coming. I didn't want to surprise them, though I doubted I could.

Silence was all that responded. I hadn't gone far in the woods, so they should be within range to hear me.

A tingle sprouted on my neck, but it wasn't the same sensation as when Raffe watched me.

Holy shit.

Please don't let it be a vampire.

My blood jolted as I glanced over my shoulder.

Something *was* wrong.

I needed to get the hell out of here.

"Raffe!" I shouted, needing him more than ever.

I heard a pop, like a rifle, and something stabbed me in the neck. A sharp, burning sensation overwhelmed me, and I grabbed on to something cold and cylindrical. As my vision grew fuzzy, I yanked it out and looked at what had to be a tranquilizer dart.

What the *hell?*

"Raffe!" I screamed, or I tried to, but my body felt like lead. I tried to head back out of the tree line, but Dave appeared, blocking my path.

Dave? Why would he do this to me? He'd genuinely seemed like a nice, caring guy.

I dropped to my knees, unable to stand anymore, and tried to crawl. My blood attempted to jolt, but not even that worked.

I was helpless.

Had Dave done something to Raffe?

Though I wanted to fight and find my love, I couldn't even win the small battle of keeping my eyes open.

"It's done. Come and get her," Dave rasped. "And remember, we're even. You can't ever tell Raffe it was me."

That sensation in my chest burned as I pulled up Raffe's image in my mind. I held it there as I succumbed to the darkness.

ABOUT THE AUTHOR

Jen L. Grey is a *USA Today* Bestselling Author who writes Paranormal Romance, Urban Fantasy, and Fantasy genres.

Jen lives in Tennessee with her husband, two daughters, and two miniature Australian Shepherds. Before she began writing, she was an avid reader and enjoyed being involved in the indie community. Her love for books eventually led her to writing. For more information, please visit her website and sign up for her newsletter.

Check out her future projects and book signing events at her website.
www.jenlgrey.com

ALSO BY JEN L. GREY

The Forbidden Mate Trilogy

Wolf Mate

Wolf Bitten

Wolf Touched

Standalone Romantasy

Of Shadows and Fae

Twisted Fate Trilogy

Destined Mate

Eclipsed Heart

Chosen Destiny

The Marked Dragon Prince Trilogy

Ruthless Mate

Marked Dragon

Hidden Fate

Shadow City: Silver Wolf Trilogy

Broken Mate

Rising Darkness

Silver Moon

Shadow City: Royal Vampire Trilogy

Cursed Mate

Shadow Bitten

Demon Blood

Shadow City: Demon Wolf Trilogy

Ruined Mate

Shattered Curse

Fated Souls

Shadow City: Dark Angel Trilogy

Fallen Mate

Demon Marked

Dark Prince

Fatal Secrets

Shadow City: Silver Mate

Shattered Wolf

Fated Hearts

Ruthless Moon

The Wolf Born Trilogy

Hidden Mate

Blood Secrets

Awakened Magic

The Hidden King Trilogy

Dragon Mate

Dragon Heir

Dragon Queen

The Marked Wolf Trilogy

Moon Kissed

Chosen Wolf

Broken Curse

Wolf Moon Academy Trilogy

Shadow Mate

Blood Legacy

Rising Fate

The Royal Heir Trilogy

Wolves' Queen

Wolf Unleashed

Wolf's Claim

Bloodshed Academy Trilogy

Year One

Year Two

Year Three

The Half-Breed Prison Duology (Same World As Bloodshed Academy)

Hunted

Cursed

The Artifact Reaper Series

Reaper: The Beginning

Reaper of Earth

Reaper of Wings

Reaper of Flames

Reaper of Water

Stones of Amaria (Shared World)

Kingdom of Storms

Kingdom of Shadows

Kingdom of Ruins

Kingdom of Fire

The Pearson Prophecy

Dawning Ascent

Enlightened Ascent

Reigning Ascent

Stand Alones

Death's Angel

Rising Alpha

Printed in Great Britain
by Amazon